WICKED FALLOUT

KELLY CHARRON

Dark Arts Publishing

This edition first published in Canada in 2017 by Dark Arts
Publishing.

Library and Archives Canada Cataloguing in Publication

Charron, Kelly, 1979-, author   Wicked fallout / Kelly
Charron.

(Pretty wicked series) Issued in print and electronic formats.
ISBN 978-0-9952765-3-6 (softcover).--ISBN 978-0-9952765-4-3
(Kindle).-- ISBN 978-0-9952765-5-0 (EPUB)

    I. Title.

    PS8605.H3727W53 2017   C813'.6   C2017-
902751-4

C2017-902752-2

For more information, visit www.kellycharron.com

DEDICATION

For my partners in writing crime.
You know who you are.

OTHER BOOKS BY KELLY CHARRON

Pretty Wicked

At his best, man is the noblest of all animals;
separated from law and justice he is the worst.

– Aristotle

CHAPTER ONE

Thursday, November 23

"Keith, why is this file five inches thick?"

Dr. Nancy Clafin hefted the mass of paper in her hands and gestured it toward him before placing it aside and grabbing the one beneath. It was nearly as robust. She stood. Her pulse thrummed in her ears. *Breathe.*

Keith, the practice's director and her longtime friend, kept his gaze steady but said nothing as he sat on the opposite side of her desk.

"When you said you had a new case for me, I wasn't expecting . . ." She knew instantly what a file that size meant, and she hadn't dealt with one in over three years. Keeping him in her periphery, Nancy slowly opened one of the four mammoth folders. Her lungs spasmed, as though she was trying to suck in air after being kicked in the stomach.

It was a close-up of a young girl's bashed-in skull. Gasping, she closed the file. She tried to center herself and quell the wave of nausea. Blood and brain matter, open blue eyes, and a discarded, bloody brick flickered in her mind's eye. She shook her head gently.

"Are you okay?" Keith rushed around the desk to her side.

She lowered herself back into her chair. "What the hell? I was expecting a police report or transcript, not . . . *this*."

"It's the case I told you about the other day." Keith made his way back to his seat. "The one I was hoping we'd get. I know it's a big one, but—"

"A big one?" She stopped for a second to compose herself. "Why is there a . . . *murder case* on my desk? We've talked about this." The blood rushed from her head and she was glad she'd had the foresight to sit.

"I'm already spread too thin, so I need you on this. It's a huge case, and you're the best I have."

Her arms and legs quivered. She fought the tremors. She didn't want Keith to see her looking so weak. "I'm not ready. Farthest thing from it, actually. We had an agreement."

Keith reached across the desktop and put his hand on top of hers. "It's time to move on, Nancy. There was nothing you could've done. No way for you to know."

Nancy exhaled a controlled breath. "My whole profession is based on my judgment, which—if you need a reminder—was faulty. When I came back to work, we had an understanding that I didn't have to handle any murder cases."

"And now you need to step up and get over whatever bullshit guilt you're still harbouring. You made a decision. That's the nature of our work. There's no way to know what's going to happen after an inmate is released or rejected for parole. You know that. We can't predict the fucking future." He took a breath, and his narrowed eyes steadied on her. "You aren't the only one to have recommended . . ."

She felt the bite on her tongue before she said the words.

"Falsely? I know. But those cases didn't have the same fucking outcome."

"So, here's your chance to redeem yourself."

She bit her lip and opened the cover of the file again. Her fingers spread the stack of photographs apart so she could see a few of them at the same time.

Blood-matted blonde hair. The small female body lay crumpled on her side.

Her trembling fingers traced the girl's face. "You could've warned me. I was expecting a witness statement or police report. Not that." She pointed to the girl's battered head.

His eyes moved to his feet. "It's difficult, but you've seen things like this before."

"And if I refuse?" She met his gaze and tried to read him but was left with no hint of his thoughts.

He straightened back in his chair. "I can't keep excusing you from things that everyone else in the practice has to do. No one wants these cases, but it comes with the territory. If you can't bring yourself to take this on, then perhaps you should retire this year instead of next." He stood.

His words washed over her. She couldn't take her eyes off of the picture. She knew that girl's face. "How many victims?" The words came out before she could stop them.

Keith swallowed hard, his eyes on his feet for a second before meeting her gaze. "Six."

It hit her. Fast. Harder than a punch in the stomach. Her fingers frantically flipped through the rest of the photographs: a darkened, rainy alleyway, the bloody brick on the cement. Nancy rifled to the middle of the file and pulled at a small, clipped stack of images. A teenage girl with red hair lay crumpled on the floor with fresh purple ligature marks around her neck.

Nancy knew this case. *Everyone* knew this case.

Her head shot up and she thrust the file toward him. "Ryann fucking Wilkanson? Are you serious?"

He looked as though she'd just slapped him. "This is a high-profile case. I need you to keep it together."

Nancy refused to speak, afraid of what she might say. She untied her sweater and waved each side back and forth, hoping some air would cool her down.

Keith stepped back tentatively, like he was evaluating *her*. "Ms. Wilkanson is our patient. We've been hired by her new legal team to evaluate her." His scrunched brows eased a bit, the frustration giving way to a fleck of empathy. "We've been friends a long time. I wouldn't ask if I didn't trust your judgment. You need to start trusting it again too." He opened her office door, one foot out.

She returned her attention to the crushing stack of information in front of her. "It'll be fine," she said through gritted teeth. "Who in their right mind is representing her? Who thinks getting her released is a good idea?"

"Wagner and Roche have taken her on. Pro bono."

She threw her head back and laughed. "Of course. Those media whores will do anything for the spotlight. No wonder they aren't charging. She's going to up their profile to an international level. It doesn't matter what she's done, only what notoriety those two will see." She shook her head.

"Everyone deserves a fair defense."

"She got that twelve years ago and was found guilty."

"A lack of adequate defense is one of the issues Wagner and Roche are re-examining." Keith cleared his throat softly. "I've got a session. Familiarize yourself with the case and we can talk in the morning, when you've had some time to digest it." He closed the door behind him.

Nancy didn't need to familiarize herself with the case. She knew it nearly as well as she did her own history. She'd been obsessed with it at the time, watching every news story, interview, victim profile, and documentary on the tragedy that unfolded in the summer of 2005. And she was equally knowledgeable about Ryann Wilkanson, the teenage girl who had murdered six people in cold blood, sending a town into a frenzy of panic and fear.

A shaky hand opened the bottom drawer of her desk. She fished around until her fingers felt the cool, smooth glass. Pulling out the bottle and then the glass, she poured herself two fingers, closed her eyes, and drank.

CHAPTER TWO

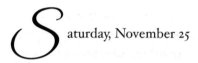

aturday, November 25

It takes me hours to get to sleep, when I sleep at all. The women housed in the Dungrave County Correctional Facility run on instant coffee, honeybuns, and the heroin and meth they smuggle inside. It's clever, really. The mastermind inmate-slash-dealer works in the laundry room and sews small pockets of drugs into the edges of the towels and sheets. I've seen women rip open their tampon boxes like it was fucking Christmas morning, only to yank out the cotton and pull out a small baggie of whatever junk they were being told was meth, coke, or heroin. The way these bitches act, I have to wonder if there's a little rat poison or bath salts mixed in.

They snort and smoke all night long, laughing, dancing, screaming, and carrying on like we're in the middle of Mardi Gras and not left to rot in freezing concrete and metal cells that smell like piss.

I lay on my bunk with a blanket over my head to block out the light. The main fluorescents are always on in this godforsaken place. Utter chaos reigns each night, and the guards don't bother to come out of their warm offices unless they see something on one of the monitors they absolutely can't ignore. It's rare, since most of the fights happen in the showers, where the inmates know there are no cameras.

I check my clock radio: 5:57 a.m. I've barely slept again. The only time quiet enough to catch an hour of sleep undisturbed by screaming, crying or fits of laughter is between five and six thirty, when most of the inmates are coming down from their highs and crashing.

"Hey, Wilks. You up?"

I don't take the blanket off my face. "Do I ever sleep?" I have two bunkmates, Jodi and Steph, who are decent enough. I recognize the high pitch of Steph's voice, especially the way her words go up at the end like everything she says is a question. It irritates me beyond belief, and if it were under other circumstances, and I didn't kind of like her, I might do something about it.

Stephanie grumbles faintly. "I'm fucking nervous. My insides are all jittery."

"What's so damn special about today?" I ask, though I don't give a fuck. The days blur together in here. There was a time when I marked them on a calendar, but that lost its charm around year three.

"Joshua's supposed to come for visiting day."

"So?" I groan through the thick, rough fabric.

"So, I ain't seen him in three years. What if it's weird, or he thinks I look like shit now?"

"Remind me who he is again." I should listen when she rambles on, but I usually have more important things on my mind, like getting the fuck out of here.

I hear her sigh. "We dated when I was seventeen. He started writing to me again a few months ago, and now he's coming to visit. I'm shitting myself. Haven't slept all night."

"It'll be fine. It's a bloody miracle he decided to look you up

and visit you in this hellhole. That should tell you he's interested."
The only person who ever visits me is my mother, who tries to make it every other Sunday.

"What are you two yammering on about? I'm trying to sleep, fuckers."

I throw the blanket off, and a rush of frigid air hits my face. "Excuse us."

Jodi turns in her bunk to face us. "The guy knows you've got two more years in here. He obviously likes you, or he's fucking nuts." The last part of her sentence trails off.

Of all the colorful inmates I've had to live with, these two are the most tolerable. It isn't like I'd be friends with them under any other circumstances, but spending thirteen hours in the same cell day in and out doesn't give me a choice. I've noticed Jodi's grown a touch pissier lately. Maybe my good fortune has her yellowed panties in a bunch.

Jodi is in her early thirties and in for manslaughter. Twenty-year sentence, and she's only done six so far. According to her, she killed her ex-boyfriend in self-defense 'cause he used to beat the shit out of her. One day he went after her four-year-old daughter. She acts all innocent and sweet, but I've been around her long enough to know that she enjoyed getting rid of his ass. Takes one to know one, I guess.

Steph, on the other hand, doesn't have a malicious bone in her hundred-pound body. At eighteen she was caught in her friend's meth house. She got five years for possession and trafficking. I believe her when she says she didn't make or sell the stuff, even though the cops and court didn't. She's no criminal mastermind. She just has horrible taste in friends.

"What a way to have a first date. At least he'll get frisked," I say, and Jodi laughs..

Steph glares at me with a hand on her hip. "Look at you, all cocky. You really think you're gonna get out of here, don't you?" She grabs her brush and pulls it through her brassy hair, the product of the prison salon and women who don't know what they're doing.

"And you don't?" I stare at her. She amuses me. She has no idea who I am. Sure, the inmates know *of* me. I've been on TV countless times over the years, my picture punctuating various accounts of my 'heinous and reprehensible' crimes. But it's clear by their ease around me that they don't fully understand what I'm capable of—what I could do to them. They have no clue that *not* strangling them with a bedsheet or stabbing them in the neck with a filed-down toothbrush is a conscious choice I make every day.

Time and distance from the murders, not to mention my good behavior inside, have softened my image. I'm almost nice. Which is fine, since it's going to help me get out of here once and for all.

Jodi keeps her eyes trained on me and says, "You killed six people, Ryann. Including a fucking cop. I can't see any board releasing you after that, no matter what your new fancy lawyers tell you."

I smile. I like that people underestimate me. It's one of my biggest assets and one of their worst mistakes.

The rest of the lights in the block turn on. A deep, male voice carries down the corridor. "Count!"

The three of us jump out of our beds and stand in front of the bars. We're counted like cattle four times a day. One officer walks the bottom tier and one walks the top, where our cell is.

There are about eighty cells in F Block with two or four inmates per cell, so it usually takes about twenty minutes to do the count. We're made to stand in the front of our cells until they're finished and everyone's accounted for.

The bell rings just before the cell doors roll open all at once, controlled electronically by the COs in the office. The thunderous steel clanging and rattling causes the ground beneath my feet to vibrate.

When roll call is finished, we're allowed to step out, form a line, and be escorted by guards to the showers, which are also housed in the block. They take us in sections, forty inmates at a time. We get twenty minutes to wash our bodies and hair, shave and moisturize if we bother, and brush our teeth. Some girls do makeup and blow-dry or curl their hair. I hate being in there, since it's a prime spot for someone to sneak up and attack you with a homemade shank.

It's one of the places I would do it.

As soon as we finish, we're walked to the mess hall for breakfast.

Most of the women have been convicted on drug-related charges. Nearly all of the armed robbery and assault convictions are connected to possessing drugs, trying to get drugs, or finding creative ways to get the money to buy drugs. There are quite a few murderers in here, just none quite at my level.

"What do you think it'll be today? Cold, runny eggs or cold, lumpy oatmeal?" Jodi says. Meals are the only real socializing we get aside from visiting day and a Christmas dance, which is only fun for the lesbian and gay-for-the-stay chicks—they get to slow dance and openly touch each other without getting in shit from the COs.

I cringe. "It doesn't matter since it's all disgusting. That's why I buy protein and chocolate bars. I could be three or four inches taller if I hadn't been malnourished as a teenager by eating this crap." Stephanie laughs behind me.

"What's the first thing you're gonna eat if you get out?" she asks. I want to take that inflection in her voice and throttle it out of her.

"I haven't given it much thought. I have more important things to consider, like where I'm going to live and how I'm going to support myself, since no one is going to hire me." I wish it wasn't true, but the fact remains that I'm sort of famous for my crimes, especially in Colorado. I can't imagine any sane person hiring a serial killer—however reformed—to do anything. "Maybe I'll be one of those people who works with the cops, helping them look at evidence and hunt down criminals."

Jodi belts out a "Ha!" and I don't blame her. It is pretty hysterical.

We keep walking, first down the stairs since our cell is on the top tier, then through the ground floor of F Block and out the first set of locked doors, where we have to stop again as a second set of metal doors is unlocked. We're shuffled by the guards along another two hallways before we make it to the mess hall.

We file in and go directly to the counter, grabbing gray plastic trays and waiting for our fellow inmates to dole out what constitutes breakfast. I slide my tray along the metal counter until I get to the first station. I can't help but visualize myself hoisting the rectangular plastic over my head and thrusting it down on Jodi, hammering it into her face, breaking her nose, and watching the blood spread down her mouth and chin. I can almost hear the screams and see the women around me scurry off as I try to whack her again, though the tray is slippery with her blood.

My fantasies help pass the time.

It's my turn next, and a haggard, brown-haired woman with four-inch white roots plops a large spoonful of eggs on the plate. "Oh yummy, thanks!" I smile wide.

She glares at me, and I wait to see if she'll say anything. I crave it. It's clear she's about to tell me off, but she stops short when she recognizes me. Word travels fast in a place like this, and it makes my time here a lot less fun, what with the element of surprise annihilated and all.

Three more inmates dispense the rest of my meal. Burnt toast, some sort of greasy meat—bacon?—and a fruit cup. D-E-L-I-C-I-O-U-S. I join Steph and Jodi at a table with a few other women we associate with.

"I can't wait until we can switch jobs. I swear if I have to fold one more pair of your skanky, gross-ass underwear, I'm gonna hurl." Jaylene's only been on laundry duty for eight months. It's a minimum of a year on any job before you can switch out. "I want something cushy like your little book gig."

She's talking to me. Instead of answering, I take another bite of toast and chase it with a sip of orange juice to soften the cardboard texture. I wait, knowing her sidekick, Rhonda, will put her two cents in any minute.

"Come on, Ryann. You've been in the library for years." Her nasal, whiny voice makes me clench my teeth.

"You can have it when I'm released. Besides, you need to know how to read to do the job, Jaylene." I smile before taking a bite of bacon.

Both Jaylene and Rhonda's eyes narrow on me, but as usual they don't offer any rebuttal.

We sit here like we do three times a day, every fucking day. They gossip about who's doing what, or who, and I picture one of the guards walking into the laundry room to find Jaylene's blubbery corpse in the dryer on the heavy load setting.

"So you're going to therapy or some shit?" Rhonda asks, and I detect bitterness in her voice.

"Good news travels fast in here. You guys truly are the queens of rumor," I say.

Rhonda and Jaylene edge in closer. Too bad there's a tabletop between us, or they'd be on my fucking lap. Jodi's ears appear to perk up too.

"So it's true?" Jaylene asks.

"I'm seeing a shrink, but it's not for therapy. My lawyers are getting me evaluated." I keep my chin up. I know I have an air of superiority about me, but I can't help it. I *am* better than them. There's no point in hiding it or playing down the facts. I made certain I became well educated in here, so much so that I could probably represent myself. It isn't as though these lawyers picked me out of the fucking blue. I made it happen. Half of these chicks couldn't pass a sixth-grade math test or read *Harry Potter* without a dictionary.

Rhonda clears her throat. "No offense, Ryann, but how are your lawyers going to get you out after you . . ." She stops to clear her throat again. ". . . Allegedly murdered those people in cold blood?"

My smile widens. I raise my glass of OJ to her before taking a long sip. "I like how you said *allegedly*, though I can assure you that I did it. Every. Last. One. The bacon is actually not that bad today."

I see Steph giggling in my periphery as the others let their jaws hang open. It's the I-can't-believe-she-just-said-that kinda look, which I adore.

Before I can continue my fun, I notice Officer King standing at the end of our table. "Come on, Wilkanson." He motions with his fingers for me to get up.

This is it. My first appointment.

I stand with my back to King and wave to the girls. "Wish me luck, ladies. Oh, you don't mind clearing my tray, do you, Jodi? Thanks, hon, you're a peach." I notice the fire in her eyes and blow her a kiss before walking off to meet the person Wagner and Roche think is qualified to figure me out. Butterflies caress the inside of my stomach.

Let the games begin.

CHAPTER THREE

*I*t was the day Nancy was finally going to meet *her*. The famous teenage killer. The girl who slaughtered six people when she was merely fifteen years old.

In less than two hours Nancy would sit across from her, close enough to touch, or be touched, by her. She shivered and shrugged off the thought as she wrapped the throw around her and sunk back into the familiarity of her sofa. She would be in a prison. Protected. There would be correctional officers watching—besides, she'd done this countless times before. But despite the murderers, rapists, and despicable criminals she'd encountered during her twenty-five years of forensic psychiatric work with convicted felons, she was always a tad jittery.

And she'd never met a serial killer. That was a new one.

She pressed her hand into the file. She wanted to feel the hardness of it. Every page inside documented horrendous things and did nothing to explain why a young girl with the whole world ahead of her would want to murder people for sport. It was her job to make that discovery: to find some way to assess if this girl—now a woman—would ever kill again.

Her stomach had been acidic and knotted since Keith dropped the bomb two days before. When he said they'd discuss it the next morning, he meant he'd give her a crappy pep talk and there was no way out of it. She could quit, but she had only one more year until retirement and couldn't live with herself if she took the coward's way out. That's what she'd been doing for the last three years, and Keith was right. It had to stop.

Lifting the weight of papers onto her lap, she swallowed hard. She'd gone through some of the police reports and crime scene photos. Twelve-year-old Olivia McMann's report was devastating. So much so that Nancy had closed the file Thursday evening and had not reopened it. But the images, as graphic and horrific as they were, would give her a window into Ryann.

Nancy resented her trembling hand as she lifted back the beige folder cover to reveal Olivia's face and those staring, vacant eyes. She flipped to the next clipped stack of photographs: Yvonne Borgdon was laid out on her bedroom floor with a dark purple line wrapped around the base of her throat. She closed her eyes for a moment to center herself. The image of the girl's tongue protruding slightly from her mouth sickened her. She'd seen similar photos before, but that was years ago. Regardless of how desensitized she'd become working murder cases in the past, it was as though she was gazing on her first crime-scene photo.

Inhaling a calming breath, she forced her eyes open. She could do this.

She shook her hands out before she inspected the next grouping of pictures, but it was no use.

There was no easing herself into the image of a pretty, blonde, fifteen-year-old Ryann with her soulless eyes and cheerleader-next-door appearance. It was reminiscent of the public's shock when they learned Ted Bundy was the serial killer the police had been hunting. People were stunned that a man so attractive and charismatic could be a ruthless, heartless killer. He was a wolf in sheep's clothing.

And that's exactly what Ryann was. Or used to be? How on earth would Nancy know which? She wasn't sure someone guilty of such brutal murders could ever *not* be a risk.

Flipping toward the middle of the file, Nancy stopped at a chunk of white papers clipped together: interview transcripts between Ryann and Detective Roberto Estevez, the officer who solved the case. She remembered her astonishment when it was reported that Ryann's father was a police officer and partner to Estevez at the time of the killings and arrest. Nancy couldn't fathom what it must be like for Detective Wilkanson. She'd had enough struggles and heartbreak with her daughter, Kim, but nothing of that magnitude.

The first transcript featured Estevez asking Ryann about Olivia's murder. Her eyes hurriedly scanned the pages for a shred of remorse or explanation.

Person Interviewed: Ryann Elizabeth Wilkanson
Date of Interview: June 29, 2005, at Mercy General Hospital
Time of Interview: 8:17 a.m.
Case Number: 07-001049
Interview Conducted By: Detective Roberto Estevez
Transcribed By: Larissa Carington
Page 5 of 48 pages

Det. Estevez (D.E.): So why did you pick Olivia?

Ryann Wilkanson (R.W.): Besides the fact that I knew she'd be easy? I hated her. She was a spoiled brat who always got her way and used to get me in trouble all the time with Brianna when I'd go with her to babysit the little bitch.

D.E.: Seems like a shoddy reason to kill a person. She was a brat—that's what you expect me to believe?

R.W.: Believe whatever you want. I wanted to get rid of igno-rant, useless, entitled assholes—wipe 'em from existence—and I had to start somewhere. She was physically small, and I knew I could gain her trust because she knew me. I didn't really want to risk going up to someone random on the playground where anyone could see me.

D.E.: So you planned it all ahead of time?

R.W.: Yup. And it went off without a hitch. If I hadn't fucked up with Eric, you'd still be scratching your balls wondering who Dungrave's killer was . . . (laughing).

D.E.: You stated earlier that you tapped on Olivia's bedroom window to get her attention. After she opened the window to speak to you, what did you say to get her to leave with you?

R.W.: Her ego was her downfall. At first she was all snotty, but I gave her some lame excuse about apologizing for how mean I'd been to her before and said I wanted to take her for frozen yogurt to make up for it. I helped her through her window onto the grass and we began walking. It was ridiculously easy. You'd think she'd at least question me a bit more considering how much we hated each other, but there was the ego I mentioned. It was more important to hear me grovel for her forgiveness than to listen to the nagging feeling I'm sure she had that something was up.

D.E.: Where did you go after you got her down on the grass?

R.W.: (Coughs.) We walked through her backyard and out the gate into the alleyway behind her house.

D.E.: And what time was that?

R.W.: I don't know exact times, but maybe around 9:30.

D.E.: So you're walking with her in the alley. What happened next?

R.W.: You saw the body. You know what happened next . . . (laughs) . . . or do you want to hear me say the words?

D.E.: It would be best if you could tell me exactly what happened.

R.W.: Okay, then. I led her to an area that I knew was secluded. I'd brought a knife with me, but decided at the last minute that I didn't want to stab her. I saw a stack of clay bricks at the edge of the path and used one to bash her head in. I lost count of the blows after a while.

Nancy shut the file. There was nothing in the girl's words to indicate remorse. Of course tone was impossible to read in a transcript, but the laughter . . . Ryann had thought her murder of a twelve-year-old girl was amusing. Nancy's heart pounded like she'd been on a jog. How was she going to do this?

She placed the folder on the coffee table and checked the time on the grandfather clock next to the fireplace. It was 8:02 a.m. She had about an hour before her first session with Ryann. She hadn't been able to eat, and with her upset stomach and already-racing heart, coffee was a horrible idea.

Nancy turned off the radio, preferring to make the trip in meditative silence.

Although she pulled up to the prison a few times a month, it was still a daunting, looming, gray sight. It was by no means one of the larger U.S. prisons, but still it held nearly seven hundred inmates. Male and female populations were segregated at opposite ends of the property with zero ability to make contact with one another. Of the nearly seven hundred incarcerated, just over two hundred were women. Ryann lived in F Block in the least populated women's zone, probably so they could keep a better eye on her.

Nancy drove up the winding road as the multiple buildings, watchtowers, thirty-foot electric fences, and fields of green came into view. Her chest tightened as it always did when she made the drive.

There was more to her nerves than the knowledge of what the inmates—patients—had done. It was about what Nancy had done. Or rather, failed to do.

The cold November air whipped against her as she made the short walk to the front of the intake building, briefcase in hand. But it was the burst of warm, filtered air behind the heavy glass doors that made her tremble. The familiar smell of the place flitted across her nostrils: stale dampness, with a hint of Clorox to mask the putrid odor of sweat and urine.

She showed her lanyard and badge, and the officer at the counter waved her forward. She placed her briefcase and coat in a bin on the counter and walked through the x-ray machine.

"Hello, Dr. Clafin. How are you today?" The officer—Josh, if she remembered correctly—returned her coat and bag.

"Thanks. I'm doing well." She took in a sharp breath. "Here to meet with a new patient." Just saying the words made her legs weaken.

He took a step back to let her pass and nodded his head slightly.

"Thanks." She waited at the next set of doors and was buzzed through. The ambience was totally different. The lighting was dimmer and the walls and floors were gray concrete, making it colder, especially in winter. Fluorescent lights that flickered and buzzed lined the hallway ceiling to her makeshift office. Warden Connelly had been nice enough to assign her the room, since she worked with inmates so often.

The tightness running through her neck and back loosened slightly when she saw Officer Han sitting in his cubicle in the adjoining room. "Good morning."

He smiled and slid off his stool to stand in the small doorway. "Hi, Dr. Clafin. I was asked to accompany you today. Must be talking to someone notable."

"I'll be assessing Ryann Wilkanson." At least she got the name out without choking.

Han's eyes grew large as his lips puckered and released a high whistling sound. He ran his fingers through his thick chestnut hair. "Did you lose a bet?"

Nancy gave a half smile. "Feels that way. Anyway, she should be here soon, so I'd better set up."

Han nodded. "Don't worry, I'll keep my eyes on her. Just say the word and I'll be there. You remember where the panic button is?"

"I can't see that I'll need it. Ms. Wilkanson is trying to get *out.*

Besides, as I understand it, she's never had a violent infraction since she's been incarcerated."

He jumped back up on his stool, looked down and said, "First time for everything."

CHAPTER FOUR

*A*h, my first therapy session. The beginning of a lengthy, methodical round of poking and prodding devised by my new lawyers to determine if I should be given a commuted sentence. Which basically means I'll keep my criminal record but be able to walk out of here a free woman. Hopefully the Executive Clemency Board agrees.

Not that I don't deserve to be prodded at. *Technically*. At least according to the laws of the great state of Colorado.

It isn't easy to sit across from someone who's there to determine if you should be kept locked up. Kept guilty. It's tough to plead your case with no real hope, because he or she knows every deplorable thing you've ever done and has probably already made their mind up—regardless of what my diligent lawyers and I hope for.

I walk through a maze of hallways to a part of the prison I've never been to before. Officer King unlocks a door and motions for me to go in ahead of him.

"Officer Han will bring you back when you're finished. Behave, Wilkanson. No funny business. There'll be an officer stationed in there watching everything on a monitor," he says in a stern, fatherly voice, which I find amusing since he's less than ten years older than me. "He can be in there in fifteen seconds." I want to say that I only need four to five to do any damage, but I bat my eyelashes instead. "Go through there. The doctor is waiting for you inside."

I narrow my gaze on him and smile. "Goody."

I hear the soft click of the door closing behind me and allow the temporary and false sensation of freedom to settle in. No cuffs or shackles, and no guard within reach. Only the doctor and me. I wasn't told who would be doing my assessment, and I'm not surprised to see a woman get up from her chair. There's no way Warden Connelly would sign off on putting a man alone in a room with me, on camera or not. She's afraid I'll seduce him—manipulate him to let me out somehow. She knows how weak the male species is, and she's not entirely wrong. She has no clue that a chunk of her principled COs are as crooked as Nixon.

"Hello." She bounds toward me with a gaping smile. She looks right at me, her hand out. "I'm Dr. Nancy Clafin. May I call you Ryann?"

I shake her hand firmly, returning the smile, fully aware that she's going to analyze everything from the way I sit to how I keep my nails. To shrinks, everything means something. "Sure, Ryann is fine."

Dr. Clafin appears to keep her guard up as she eyes me carefully, making sure there is at least three feet of space between us. She doesn't want the psycho to see into her soul, or lunge at her, which means she's done her homework on me. Good girl. "It's a nice change, since everyone inside calls me Wilks." I smile widely and gingerly tuck a piece of hair behind my ear.

"This room has a small kitchen, so I can make us tea or coffee if you like. Why don't we sit down and get to know each other a little better?" She points to the brown chairs and sofa just behind us.

What Nancy really means is that she wants to get to know *me* better. I highly doubt she'll tell me anything about herself, which is fine. I have my own ways to get information. I sit on the sofa, and she sits back in the opposite chair. There's a small table that's fashioned to be a desk behind her, and Nancy has her briefcase on it.

"Normally we'd have something called doctor-patient confidentiality, but because this evaluation will go to the board, it's important you know that anything, and everything, you say will be used toward my assessment of you and therefore by the clemency board. Do you understand?" I nod. "Your lawyers will also get transcripts of our sessions. Do you still wish to proceed?" she asks oh-so-politely. Her eyes are wide. She sits, her back ramrod straight, her ankles crossed, and her hands in her lap. She wants me to see her as a professional so I'm more willing to trust her.

"I wish to proceed, yes."

"We have an extremely tight deadline as it is, so if you don't mind, I'd like to get right to it." She pauses, and I assume she's waiting for me to respond.

"That's fine."

"Great. First, do you have any questions for me?"

Her face is stone. No hint of emotion, which is odd considering my reputation. Most people who meet me are visibly nervous, though they try to hide it. I can always tell by the way their cheeks flush, their voices quiver, or their knees bounce up and down.

"No questions, but I'd like to say something, if that's all right?"

"Of course."

"Thanks for agreeing to do this. I know it's a daunting task considering my crimes and history. It's comforting to know that I might have another chance, thanks to you."

Her eyebrows remain perfect, unmoving arches above her eyes. "Don't thank me just yet. I've been assigned to perform an honest evaluation of you, and that's what I intend to do. I'm not guaranteeing any sort of recommendation. Did Mr. Wagner or Ms. Roche say something to the contrary?"

I put my hands up. "Oh no, I didn't mean that I thought you were going to absolutely recommend release. I'm just thanking you for being open-minded enough to work with me and consider what I have to say. There are a lot of people that would keep me condemned and not consider the aspects of my case that my lawyers believe were unjust."

The doctor doesn't appear moved. "Shall we get started, then?" Dr. Clafin reaches behind her and pulls down a leather-bound pad of paper and a pen.

"I guess . . ."

"What did it feel like when you were killing them?"

My head jolts up. I burrow my shoulders into the cushion of the sofa, tilt my head, and take stock of her. Her bluntness is a tactic to catch me off guard. She's already testing me, and I *almost* respect her for it. I'm not sure what game she's playing, however, since my team hired her. Isn't she supposed to be on my side? I meet her gaze and decide to give her a little something. "That depends on who you're asking about."

Dr. Clafin glares at me. She obviously doesn't like it when her methods are used back on her.

"How about your first victim, twelve-year-old Olivia McMann?"

I resent that she throws in Olivia's age, like a subliminal scolding. "I remember how old she was." The room's muted palette matches the rest of Dungrave prison. You'd think the powers that be would put some effort into cozying up the crappy improvised office if they expect you to feel warm and fuzzy and spill your deepest, darkest secrets. Nope. Instead we get a worn-out couch, a barred window, beige walls, and a shrink sitting on her high horse, grinning at me over her coffee cup.

"It was a long time ago. I was a different person back then." Of course, the doctor is trying to hide her fascination, since that would be unprofessional, but this woman has an interest that goes beyond fact seeking. I can feel it in the twisting of my gut. "I'm assuming you've read the police reports, so you already know what I did to her."

Dr. Clafin nods. "Yes, and I read a transcript from the interview you gave to Detective Estevez while you were in the hospital after your arrest. You had some pretty blunt things to say about her murder."

I rub my hands along my thighs, trying to appear nervous and restless. "I don't remember what I said. I told you, it was a long time ago."

Dr. Clafin shifts in her seat, tugging on her too-short skirt. She's a bit matronly to pull off fitted and black. "The hope is to identify what was happening for you mentally and emotionally and help you discover why you did what you did. I want you to tell me about the murders as you remember them from your perspective at the time, even if it's not the way you feel now. You were . . ." She stops to peruse her file, though we both know she has everything about me memorized. "Fifteen at the time."

I do my best to appear unfazed. "And reliving it is supposed to help me?"

"A lot of patients in the penal system have found a sense of peace and redemption after going through the process. It allows you to take ownership and responsibility for your crimes. It can be very helpful." Her hands remain clasped tightly on her lap, covering her notepad and pen.

Her buttoned-up-to-the-collar blouse, tight French twist, and unmarred three-inch pumps tell me she's a perfectionist control freak who cares more about how others perceive her than about who she actually is.

"I'm game to try, I guess." I take a deep breath so she thinks I'm centering myself or whatever bullshit quacks like her expect. I've been working out my spiel in my head for weeks now. It's finally showtime. I continue to rub my palms along my thighs. The material could benefit from a bottle or two of fabric softener. "I don't like talking about it, but if you really believe it's going to help me heal, and maybe even get a second chance, I'm willing to try anything."

Dr. Clafin smiles—the kind of smile reserved for wedding proposal acceptances and winning the lotto. She's probably surprised I gave in that easily considering my history.

"I'm so happy to hear that, Ryann. We're going to make some real progress. I can already tell." She flips to a new page, fancy etched pen in hand. She leans forward. "Tell me about Olivia."

I release a sigh of 'distress.' "I don't remember everything."

Doctor Clafin crosses her legs and leans forward, keeping me in her sight. "Is that so. When did that begin?"

Keeping my gaze on her, I say, "I think a few weeks after I was arrested. It's such a long time ago now. It's difficult to recall everything. I can get confused when I think back to it."

"I see. Well, we'll go slowly and see if we can't make sense of it. Sometimes talking about your memories can help them surface. I'm assuming you do have some memories about the murders?"

She already thinks she can swoop in and save me. Find some repressed childhood trauma or abuse that will explain everything. "Of course. I don't have amnesia, though sometimes I wish I did."

Clafin purses her lips.

Maybe my appearing like a bundle of nerves will make her go easier on me. "What do we do? Are you going to ask me a bunch of questions or something?" She gives me a placating smile and I give her one back. She's trying to manage me.

"I'll ask you a series of questions, but I'll also ask you to describe what you remember. Don't worry. I'll take you through the process. You can start with what you remember about the murder of Olivia. Start with how you felt at the time, not how you feel about it presently."

"I'm so different now. What I felt then . . . It's wrong." I lean forward, squinting my eyes in concentration.

"I understand that, but in order to know who you are today, I need to know who you used to be. Does that make sense?" She adjusts herself in her chair, uncrossing one leg and then crossing the other.

I keep my gaze down. "I guess. As long as you promise not to hold my past against me."

"Ryann, I already know a fair bit about you and the things

you've done. I'm taking your case on with an open mind, I promise."

I study her face and body. Her shoulders are slightly tensed and hunched. Her jaw clenches every so often. There's no way she's on my side. That'll change soon enough. "All right. I'm ready, ask away."

"What did you feel when you killed Olivia?"

CHAPTER FIVE

*N*ancy wasn't normally so blunt, but it was crucial to jump right in before Ryann had time to finesse her answers. Ryann's big green eyes widened further, and her forehead creased slightly. Nancy remembered seeing her on television: rotating pictures of her as a child and pre-teen, each one with a sweet smile, soft eyes, and blonde hair framing her fair complexion. Seeing her now was surreal, creating a dreamlike state that Nancy wanted to wake up from. Ryann was still beautiful, but her eyes . . . they'd changed. She supposed that was a given with everything Ryann had been through. Everything she'd been responsible for. Remorseful or not, her eyes had been forever altered.

"Wow, so you're just going to go right there, huh?" Ryann wrapped her arms around herself and rocked forward slightly.

Nancy remained silent and fixed her gaze on the girl. Ryann was stalling. Looking to deflect.

"Okay. I guess I have a few memories from that night."

"Great. Start with the first thing you remember." She wasn't about to let Ryann off easy. She wrote Olivia's name and the date at the top of her notebook.

"The first thing I can clearly recall is walking from her backyard to the alley. I was irritated. She was whining about blaming me if she got caught for sneaking out. Olivia had always been a self-centered brat. Everything was always about her. I knew that, and used it to get her out of the house that night. I told her I wanted to apologize for being so mean to her."

"Did you babysit her often with your sister?"

"I don't know, maybe once or twice a month."

"If my math is correct, you were twelve when you started helping your sister watch her. Why did you go along, especially if you didn't care for Olivia?"

Ryann placed her hands flat on the cushion on either side of her. Her fingernails were short, bitten and torn where she'd picked at the cuticles and surrounding skin. Being in prison would be stressful for anyone, though Ryann's hands were a strong contrast to the rest of her. In such close proximity, Nancy noticed her freshly washed hair, neat and clean prison scrubs, dewy complexion, and the slightest scent of coconut.

"I didn't have a choice. My parents both worked shifts and I couldn't stay by myself, so I had to tag along with Bri." Her eyebrows shifted ever so slightly, as though she was withholding a frown. "My parents were overprotective. Came with the territory of being the youngest daughter of a cop."

"How did you feel about that?"

"Annoyed. I felt perfectly capable of taking care of myself. Of course, looking at it now, I realize they were right."

"And why is that?"

Ryann shifted on the couch. "Because I was just a kid and didn't know how to take care of myself the way I thought I could."

Nancy's steady gaze narrowed on Ryann.

Ryann's eyes remained focused on Nancy's face. Unflinching. No hint of recognition or emotion. "I see what you're doing. Yes, Olivia was twelve at the time of her death."

"Did you consider her a child back then?"

"No. She was only three years younger than me. It didn't seem like a big age gap. I saw her more as my peer than most people did, obviously."

"And now?"

"Now I understand that Olivia was an innocent child. I manipulated her into trusting me and then I betrayed her in the most horrific way possible." She looked down at the floor. Her body stilled.

"I read in one of the interview transcripts that you brought a knife with you that night, intending to stab her. The cause of death was determined to be blunt force trauma. A clay brick was found next to her body. It had brain matter on it." Nancy intensified her stare, interested to see if there'd be a shift in Ryann. "What happened in the alley to make you change your original plan?"

Ryann rocked in her seat for a moment. "I thought our meeting was going to be me talking about my parents and childhood and where my life went wrong. At least to start out." She leaned forward, her hands clasped between her knees with her shoulders hunched. She looked like the weight of the world was on top of her and she could barely keep herself upright.

Nancy jotted a note: *Ryann seems to be uneasy with my line of questioning about Olivia. Is attempting to change the subject.* "We'll discuss your childhood and parents, but right now I want to know about Olivia. Could you answer the question, please?"

Ryann inhaled a slow breath before she said, "Yes, I brought a knife with me. The very one I practiced with, but in the end . . . I don't know, I chickened out."

"If that were true, Olivia would still be alive. The truth is you didn't chicken out, you only killed her by a different method." She wasn't going to play a game of semantics with this woman, who clearly hadn't matured much beyond the fifteen-year-old Ryann in the transcripts.

"Stabbing her seemed scary. I was overwhelmed and I started to panic. I remember having the knife in my pocket, but I just couldn't bring myself to pull it out."

"Then what did you do?"

"I don't know."

Nancy's face grew hot. Her legs began to shake—a symptom of her unexpected raw anger. "What do you mean, you don't know?" She forced her voice to remain slow and steady, refusing to allow her rage to take control.

"The next thing I remember is kneeling on the concrete with Olivia's . . . body next to me. She was bloody. Her head had been smashed in." Ryann's voice trembled.

Nancy's pen moved along the smooth paper. *Convenient memory loss? Looked away when recounting the sight of Olivia's battered body.* "You have no memory of actually hitting Olivia?"

Ryann nodded, her forehead heavily creased. "I know that seems convenient, but I'm telling you the truth. I have no memory of the murder, only getting her out of the house, walking down the alley, and then seeing her lying there. I had the brick in my hand, though, so I know I did it. I mean, no one else was around. I went there intending to kill her, so it was obviously me."

A tornado slammed Nancy's insides. "In the interview transcript you recounted Olivia's murder in great detail, so how do you explain your lack of recall now?" It took all her strength to ignore the reeling in her gut. How was she expected to spend three weeks with this woman if this was how the first thirty minutes made her feel?

"I was told that I explained all the murders during the interrogations at the hospital. The only thing I can say is that I must've remembered at the time, but it slipped away somehow, because I promise you I don't remember it now. Haven't for almost the entire time I've been locked up. I remember wanting to kill my victims, planning some of them, even parts of the actual murders, but I don't recall everything. It's like chunks of time have gone missing, and no matter how hard I try to look for them, I can't find them again." Ryann sat up straight, her hands gripping the edge of the coffee table, and stared directly at Nancy. "I know this looks bad, but I also know my team hired you to help me. I'll do everything I can to give you what you need, but I can't do that if I feel like you already think I'm lying to you. Of course I want to get out of here, but I also own what I did. I know I killed all those people, and I don't need to have every gruesome memory intact to believe it. I'm not sure why some time is lost. I'm hoping you can help me figure that out. I'm not trying to hide anything, especially from you, the only person who may be able to help me. I only want a fair chance here."

Nancy dropped her pen onto her lap and clasped her hands neatly on top of her notebook. "I appreciate that, Ryann, and I want to assure you that I take my position very seriously. I've been doing this for over two decades. I value your trust, and I'm not insinuating that you're purposely keeping anything from me, but I want to convey to you one more time how crucial it is to tell me everything that you can. The more I know, the better able I am to make my recommendation. And yes, your lawyers did hire me, but I'm not working for them. I'm an independent consultant, and I promise you that I'm in no one's pocket. Ethics and profession-alism are incredibly important to me, and I'll not waver for anyone, including the impressive media darlings of Wagner and Roche." There. She'd said it. Her blood pressure began evening out and her legs settled.

Ryann's nostrils flared a second before she bolted up from her seat. Nancy gasped and pulled back—instinct, considering that her senses were already heightened in close proximity to the killer.

The door opened and Han sprinted inside. "Are you all right, Dr. Clafin?" His hand rested above his pistol as his eyes trained on Ryann.

Nancy looked to Ryann, who seemed upset but calm, and held her hand out. "It's fine."

Ryann had her palms up, as though she was actually being held at gunpoint. "I stood up, can we all calm down?"

"Everything's fine, Officer Han. You can go," Nancy said.

Han made a show of glaring at Ryann before he returned to his observation room just outside the door.

Ryann remained standing, arms crossed across her chest. "It's clear that you don't believe me. You think I'm lying about my memory lapses, and you know what? Yes, I did horrible things, but I need someone who can see who I am now—someone who won't suggest that I'm holding back information. What do I have to gain by doing that? This is my last chance, and I know it. I'd never jeopardize my freedom. So if it's all the same to you, I think I'll see if my social-media-darling lawyers can't find me a new shrink."

Before Nancy could say another word, Ryann was at the door and Han had escorted her out.

CHAPTER SIX

I wait until I'm away from the cameras outside the office to smile. Officer Han is behind me, so he can't see me gloat. It's a fantastic feeling to know I haven't lost my touch. Manipulating other inmates, even the guards, is fun but poses no real challenge. But the poised and arrogant Dr. Clafin . . . she is someone worthy of my talents.

Lucky for me, Roche told me Dr. Clafin's name and I was able to do a little research before this meeting, not that I got much in the fifteen minutes I could get to a computer. Seems the doctor isn't quite as boring as I'd anticipated. Thank God for Google. I manage to see what I think is a family photo. A younger, smiling Dr. Clafin under the arm of a tall man, cleanly shaven man with brown hair. In front of them sits two children. The boy looks to be about five and the girl's possibly around thirteen. Picture perfect family.

It only takes a handful of news clips and interviews to surmise that the perfection was all a show.

Not that Dr. Clafin having a secret or two is a surprise. All people hide things. Even the almighty professionals who "right-eously" cast judgment on everyone else. People like her, who prescribe advice to fix other people's poor decisions, usually have their own skeletons. But what did my perfect doctor do? Dr. Clafin regularly attends charitable functions, most of them supporting mental health, which is no surprise considering what she does for a living. And then I see Kim's name. It's a copy of a speech Nancy has given at some benefit. I skim it until I see what I've been waiting for: Kim ran away at sixteen, got into the drug scene, and has remained transient since. Nancy doesn't say it in so many words, but it's clear Kim is probably a prostitute to support her "lifestyle"—or at least Nancy's worried she is.

A child doesn't just run away for no good reason, does she? Maybe for a night at a friend's house after a fight at home, but not for years. Surely not for over a decade. Where is Kimmy now? Working some prestigious career somewhere, or hooking on some corner so she can keep shooting poison into her veins?

Why hadn't I thought of this before?

She's a do-gooder who loves to fight for the underdog. I'm sure she thought I was going to be sweet as pie, begging for mercy and apologizing up and down for my sins. What she didn't anticipate was me walking away, which—okay, it's risky, but I have faith that Nancy can't stand to lose. She won't want to quit something she's started, especially a challenge. Especially after she failed with her own daughter. I bet she swims in perpetual guilt. It's in her nature, clear in some of the interviews she's given. She's always blabbering on about justice and second chances, so renouncing her help and accusing her of unfair treatment is sure to get under that wrinkly skin of hers. I'll be back in there in no time, the difference being that she will actually have an open mind.

"You looked right pissed in there. Someone steal the prize out of your cereal?" Han says. He's walking so close I can practically feel his hot breath on the back of my neck. Ew.

"I don't appreciate being toyed with," I say haughtily, still playing my part. Han is one of the few guards with a thread of empathy left.

"I've known Dr. Clafin a long time, and I can't see her doing that. She's too professional."

We keep walking and I don't turn around. I'd probably get an elbow to the head if I did. "Great. You calling me a liar too?"

"No. All I'm saying is that you could've misunderstood, that's all. She's a fair woman. She's helped a lot of people. Helped quite a few inmates get released, so I would've been nicer if I were you."

We've maneuvered down the hallways and are outside the first set of double metal doors. The only reason I'm not handcuffed during transfer between sections of the prison is because I've been a perfect angel for all of my twelve years inside. The violent inmates are kept in the hole, where they're quarantined from the rest of us so they don't pose a threat to other inmates and the COs. If I have to spend my years locked up, I'm certainly not going to spend them in a five-by-five cement box for twenty-three hours a day.

Officer Han opens the doors and escorts me through. At the end of another concrete hallway the words *F Block* are bolted high up on the wall. Home sweet home. At least the hallways are a welcome reprieve from the migraine-inducing noise and the constant odor of shit and piss that I'll never get used to.

The jingling of Han's keys as he searches for the one to this door is like an ice pick in my brain. He has no idea how easy it would be for me to kick him in the knee and send him to the ground. I'd elbow him in the nose so hard his eyes would water, and he wouldn't see me take his baton, which I'd slam into his skull over and over again until his head caved in and bits of blood and bone were scattered around us. My chest is tight and my breathing is hastening. And that's only from daydreaming.

The final door opens to the common area, where we stay unless we're in the mess hall, the bathrooms, or our cells for the night. As anticipated, it's obnoxiously loud with the typical screaming and laughing. Grown woman of all ages run about, dancing and jumping like schoolchildren at recess.

The TV is always on in the common area, at least until lights-out at ten. The block boss is usually in charge of the remote. Block boss is whichever inmate dominates the herd. It rotates depending on who's around. It should be me, but the risk of going up against someone to earn my rights would only harm my potential to get out. Currently, block boss is a bitch named Jinx. I forget her real name and I don't care. All I know is she's a complete nut job, possibly bipolar, who will fight anyone.

"Like I said, Wilkanson, the doctor is all right. If she gives you another chance, I suggest you take it." I turn around, surprised Han would bother to say this a second time.

"Why do you even care?" I say it without attitude. It's a genuine inquiry. No one gives a fuck about any of us in here, especially lifers—which I am unless this commute goes through.

He squares his shoulders and peers down on me as though I've caught him off guard. "I don't." He turns around and leaves, slamming the door behind him. The echoing clang makes my head feel like it's going to explode any second. That's it. A room full of rage-filled, crazy criminals, some legitimately certifiable, and no guard in sight. Sure, there are cameras, but it usually takes the guards five to ten minutes to come in if anything goes down. By then it's usually too late for whoever had her ribs kicked in.

Pressing the button to the speaker at the side of the door, I wait for a response. I have to press it two more times before anyone answers. "What?" a woman half-yells at me. I'm probably interrupting whatever show she's watching.

"Sorry to bother you, but I've got a migraine. Can I please get my medication?"

I hear a distinct huffing on her end. Poor thing actually has to work. "Number?" she barks.

"It's 57629847. Thanks, I really appreciate it."

"Someone will be there soon." I hear the speaker click, which means she's already hung up. It will be a Christmas miracle if I get pills in the next eight hours, but I'm hopeful. What else do I have if not hope? Hope that this Clafin broad will eat up all the shit I'll be serving her and I'll finally get the fuck out of here. It's been

over a decade since I've been able to kill someone. My restraint
astonishes me. These bitches don't know how lucky they are.

"Hey Wilks, how was your first shrinking?"

It's Margot Acker. Word travels fast in hell. She eyes me with
her shit-eating grin. I smile. "Just great. Thanks for asking." Now I
have multiple sets of eyes on me—all staring and waiting to see my
reaction.

"You were gone awhile," Margot says. She's sitting at a table
across from me with three other women, all holding cards. They're
obviously not too enthralled with their game to stop and gawk.

"Were you watching the clock? You must have missed me."

Before she can answer, the door bursts open as COs in full riot
gear explode into the room, guns trained on us. "Get down on the
ground! Get down on the ground!"

I drop along with everyone around me. I put my hands on top
of my head and lay on the disgusting concrete floor. It's freezing
through my scrubs and sweatshirt, like I'm face down on a sheet
of ice.

Heavy, black-booted feet stomp around me. The vibrations
carry through my body, making my head thump and ache even
worse. I'm probably not getting my meds now. Fuck.

As the COs keep their rifles trained on us, a few other guards
sweep the room. It's referred to as a shakedown: the entire area
gets searched for contraband, including cellphones, drugs,
weapons, and anything else that we're not supposed to have. It's
amazing the things that get inside.

I keep my cheek to the ground. A few cups and food items are
knocked off the tables, hitting the floor and spraying some nasty
orange drink on me. My fists clench at my side as I see them flipping through magazines, books, and some of the women's journals
before throwing them carelessly back down, some falling to the
floor. Everything will be a complete mess when they're done, and
we'll have to clean the motherfucker up. I breathe slowly to
contain myself. There are twenty times in any given day when I
want to absolutely lose my shit, but then I envision being back on

the outside with a knife in my pocket, staring into the bedroom window of some poor, unsuspecting soul who has no idea what I'm about to do to them. It keeps me going. It's the only thing that does.

"Got something!" I can see a female officer out of the corner of my eye holding up a cell phone and a small baggie with white powder inside. Another guard seizes the items as she continues to feel behind the TV for something more. They don't even try to ask whose it is, because no one would snitch. Besides, I don't think they give two shits. It's not about our safety, as they like to claim, but about making our lives more miserable than they already are.

The cell and drugs belong to Roxie. I turn my head slowly, keeping it as close to the ground as possible. She's across the room by the bathroom doorway, and even from here it's obvious that she is fucking furious. I find it amusing. I will her to look my way. A minute later, she does. I don't gloat like I want to because it could start a fight, but I think she can tell I'm enjoying myself. That's satisfying enough.

About ten minutes later the dozen or so officers in riot gear leave the room. The remaining two stand in front of the door. One shouts out to us, his voice muffled through his mask. "Carry on." It's all he says after tearing our entire world up and locking the doors behind him.

Seconds later the moaning, yelling, cussing, and overall bitching commence as we look at the mess around us. We stand, dust ourselves off, and begin to clean. At least it prevents Margot and her cronies from badgering me about my session.

None of my stuff has been trashed. While everyone else is whining and picking up, I right a chair and take a seat in front of the television. The remote is on the table so I pick it up. "Hey, Jinx!" She looks over at me and I wave it in the air. "Okay?" She nods, so I start flipping through the channels. A wave of adrenaline hits me, and I turn it back a station with a shaky hand. I've been on TV a lot lately.

It's a video of me wearing an orange jumpsuit with my wrists shackled to a chain around my waist. I look so young. The court officer is walking me to my seat behind the defendant's table. My eyes narrow and my mouth dries as I see myself sit next to my lawyers, the three idiots responsible for me being locked away to rot. I always promised myself that if I ever got out of here I would hunt them down and slit their throats from ear to ear. How sad it was when one of them, a Mr. Drew Langford, died of a massive coronary four years ago. But his incompetent, bumbling partner Marc Bernese seems to be alive and well. When I checked six months ago, he was living in Pueblo, still happily married with three beautiful children. By my calculations, he's forty-four years old. If things go my way he won't make it to forty-five. If I am released by March, I'll have plenty of time to hunt him down in time for his birthday in April. *Yippee.* That leaves Heidi Jelinski. Living abroad won't help her if I get out. Sure, the men kicked her ass out of the firm a few weeks after my confessions, but that's not punishment enough for letting them happen.

What did I expect with court-appointed representation? God, I was stupid. Who confesses and brags after they're caught? Young and dumb. I thought I was done for, since I'd literally been caught with blood on my hands and a knife to my friend's throat. If I was going down for that, I wanted everyone to know I'd been responsible for all the killings in Dungrave over those six weeks. Stupid fucking glory hog.

"Is that you, Wilks?" Jinx pulls up a chair next to me.

"Yup."

"That's some crazy-ass shit."

I'd like to say, "You bet your ass!" but instead I nod solemnly.

Jinx, with her dyed red hair and broad shoulders, says, "We get bitches in here for holding a gun to some punk ass and never pulling that trigger. They can't seem to stay outta the hole for throwing down all the time, but you . . . you come in after murdering some five or six and ain't never had no beef." She shakes her head in disbelief. "If you so raged out to kill all them people, how the hell you sit up in here twenty-four-seven and ain't never go

crazy on one of these bitches? You got some self-control or what?"
Her eyes are wide as she assesses me. She seems authentically
interested in how I've managed to curb my murderous rage.

I suppress a smile. I like Jinx. She's a no-bullshit, you-get-what-
you-see kind of woman, which is a rare commodity in a place like
this. "Fair question." My answer must be careful. I can't say
anything that can be used against me. Fellow inmates flip on you if
you get reduced time or added benefits like a TV in your room. No
one in here is happy to see someone else get out. But I can't let
Jinx think my urges are completely gone. I'd become a target. The
only thing keeping me from getting my ass beat is that no one is
sure how crazy I really am. No one messes with the girl who could
sneak up on you in line at the food counter and stick a blade into
you a dozen times. "Let's just say no one has made me that mad." I
wink and she grins.

Maybe deep inside, Jinx can relate to wanting to carve someone
up like a Thanksgiving turkey. It's got to be a more common
impulse than people admit. When I was a kid, I believed I was
special. I relished that most people couldn't relate to me or bring
themselves to do the things I could. But last I researched, there
were 437,000 murders in the world every year, and fifty active
serial killers in the great USA at any given moment. Warms my
heart a little.

"I feel you. Still, that was some crazy-ass shit you did when you
was a kid," Jinx says. She laughs a little, like we're bonding over
embarrassing moments.

I'm sick of her voice. She's making me miss what they're saying
about me. I harden my eyes and feel my teeth gnash together
behind closed lips.

Jinx tenses, stands, and takes a step back. "I'll let you get back
to it, then," she says and points to the screen. The reporter, a slight
young woman with brown hair and a green down jacket, is saying
that a lot of people are in an uproar because I might get a new
trial, clemency, or—God forbid—a commuted sentence. A crowd
of people behind her have homemade signs that say things like,

Protect our children. Keep Ryann locked away and *Satan's sister! Ryann is pure evil!*

I can't help but notice the small gathering of inmates accumulating around me. I refuse to change the channel. They can deal with it.

I can't tell where the reporter is until the camera pans away to the front of the building.

"Holy fuck! Is this shit live?" a woman named Jasmine says in a far too excited tone.

"They could be out here right now," another voice says.

"Maybe they'll come in here and interview you, Ry." Steph walks up beside me, eyes glued to the TV.

Before I can answer, Jodi butts in. "There's no way they're going to let some reporter come in here to talk to Wilks."

My head snaps in Jodi's direction. "What the fuck do you know about it?" I glare at her and she puts her hands up, backing away behind a few other inmates. Big mouth, little backbone. I wish everyone would shut the fuck up so I can hear what's happening.

The camera moves to show someone at the reporter's side. My heart plummets in my chest and my whole body is overcome with instant heat as the olive-skinned man in the cheap suit looks into the camera. My fists clench at my sides.

"Detective Estevez, you were responsible for catching and arresting Ryann Wilkanson. Do you have any comment on the possibility that she could be walking our streets again?" The reporter shifts the end of the mic to face Estevez.

"It is a travesty for the families of her victims and the citizens of Colorado to be faced with the possibility of her release. I will continue fighting, as I know many others will, to keep her locked away for the rest of her life. I know from first-hand experience that she's a monster. She hasn't changed. She's as cunning, ruthless, and deadly as ever. I urge you all to sign petitions, write the governor, do anything you can to keep her behind bars where she belongs."

Before I realize it, I've shot up from my chair, thrown the

remote control, and captured the attention of fifty or so rubber-necking inmates who have no idea what to make of my sudden outburst. I attempt to compose myself, smoothing away the deep frown lines between my eyes and inhaling calming breaths, before I storm off to the bathrooms.

CHAPTER SEVEN

*M*onday, November 27

Nancy got to the office early to go over a few things. Ryann walking out on their session had made her strangely conflicted. It was the ideal opportunity to rid herself of the case. Keith couldn't contest it when it was Ryann's choice and not hers.

But she couldn't stop the uneasy feeling in her stomach that something was wrong. It was the same sensation she had when she thought of her oldest, Kim: a hybrid of guilt and resentment. As much as she was tempted to run away, let Ryann Wilkanson be someone else's problem, and never look back, she couldn't bring herself to sever the weak tie. She'd made a commitment to Keith and the practice, but more to herself. If she could do this, she would prove to everyone that she was still a relevant player in the game. It was a new revelation that surprised her.

Her part in the bid to get Ryann released would soon become public knowledge. How would she face the public scrutiny? People loathed this girl. There was a very large part of her that felt the same way, but she had a duty to put her personal opinions aside and do her job. She believed in the legal system. Her late husband, James, had been a very successful lawyer who would have encouraged her to face the challenge head-on.

Nancy spent twenty minutes on the phone with Wagner after he'd learned about his client storming out of the session. He begged Nancy to remain on the case. No wonder Wagner's retainer was exorbitant—the man was good. His ability to manipulate was incredible, and for the first time, she feared Ryann might actually go free, with or without her recommendation. Wagner said her original defense team didn't get her further psychological testing, not to mention that she'd only met with them on three occasions for an hour each—not nearly enough time to prepare her for what was in store at the trial. No one clearly advised her of her rights, and her lawyers didn't fight when she refused parental and legal counsel during her lengthy interrogations.

The Dungrave murders had made international news, which meant the whole world was waiting to hear what drove a sweet fifteen-year-old girl to become a crazed serial killer.

The intercom on her desk buzzed.

She pressed the speaker button. "Yes, Claire?"

"I have a Sergeant Estevez here to see you. He doesn't have an appointment. Should I let him through?"

Estevez? A flood of nerves ran the length of her arms and legs, and an unpleasant prickling sensation found its way into her stomach as she put the pieces together.

"Uh, yeah . . . Yes." She cleared her throat. "You can send him back." She hurried to organize the stacks upon stacks of files, old coffee cups, and takeout containers from her desk. It was no use. All she did was rearrange the mess.

A knock on her door made her heart leap into her throat. Smoothing down her skirt, she opened the door to the man she'd seen on television all those years ago. He was a little worse for wear, with a few more gray hairs and wrinkles around the eyes and mouth. "Sergeant Estevez, won't you please come in?" She stepped back with an arm extended toward the desk that made her look like she belonged on an episode of *Hoarders*.

"Thank you." He strode in wearing a heavy gray jacket peppered with rain. "I appreciate you seeing me." She couldn't quite read the mixture of trepidation and confidence on his face. His hand moved his jacket to the side, exposing a badge secured to his hip. She could tell he'd done it on purpose, probably to reassure her that he was who he claimed to be.

She closed the door behind him. "Would you like to sit down?" He nodded and pointed to the sofa to the right of the entrance. "That's fine. Could I get you some coffee?"

"No thanks, I'm okay." His brown eyes were framed under heavy dark brows. He didn't smile. He looked like he hadn't seen a good night's sleep in months, which wasn't unusual with cops. She'd worked with many. The long shifts, physical and mental exhaustion, and overall stress did a number on them. Not that she'd gotten off much easier.

Her knees quivered slightly as she made her way toward him. "What can I do for you, Sergeant Estevez?" He sat on the sofa, she in a wingback chair opposite.

He leaned forward with his hands clasped. "I was informed you were assigned the evaluation of an inmate who is attempting to gain clemency. I'm here, off the record, to beg you not to try to free this woman. She is a dangerous psychopath."

Nancy cradled her mouth in her elbow the way schoolchildren are taught to stifle a cough. When her lungs had calmed, she said, "This is very unorthodox, Sergeant, and could be construed as highly unethical."

"I've never made a visit like this before, but this is a critical circumstance. The inmate *will* reoffend. I witnessed the crimes firsthand for nearly two months. I personally conducted the interrogations and I know there is no remorse, no rehabilitation, no redemption."

"With all due respect, I haven't even had a chance to study Ms. Wilkanson's complete file, and I've only met with her once. I'm certainly not ready to make my assessment yet. I assume she is who you are referring to?"

He nodded, swallowing so hard it looked like his Adam's apple was going to pop out of his throat. His eyes never wavered from her face, and his intensity unsettled her. "She murdered six people. She stalked them, hunted them, plotted, and devised plans to end their lives in painful, torturous ways. She killed children." The sharpness in his voice made her draw back suddenly. He put a hand up. "I apologize for getting heated. This case is very personal to me."

"I imagine all of your cases are."

"Not like this. Ryann's father was my partner for eight years. I watched Ryann grow up. She destroyed that family along with all the victims."

Nancy worked to keep her face unresponsive and simply nodded. "I'm sorry to hear that. I'm very aware of her case. I watched the news coverage like everyone else."

"So then you know how malevolent she is. How terrifying."

"I assure you I'll conduct my assessment thoroughly, but I can't promise you what you are asking. It's unethical. I empathize with your circumstances, but I took an oath. I'm sure you understand." She began to stand. She was already tired of the conversation and wondered how many people would plead their case to her, pushing their opinions and theories, and demanding their own ruling. Not to mention judging and hating her for simply doing a job she didn't even want.

"Wait, please. There's one more thing."

Feeling the weight of his silent judgment, she lowered herself back down, barely prepared to argue further. "Quickly, please. I have a lot of work to do."

Estevez held out a plastic bag. She hadn't even noticed it when he'd come in. Great. If this was a sneak peek at her trained observational skills, maybe she should retire sooner.

She didn't take the bag. "What's that?"

His dark eyes implored her. "It's all the interrogation videos. She admits to every single kill in disgusting detail."

This time she stood. "You know that I'm not usually privy to *all* police evidence, especially interview footage. I'm assuming if I was sanctioned to, Ms. Wilkanson's lawyers would have provided me with copies."

"That may be so, but with all due respect, you need to see them."

Taking a step back, Nancy said, "You could get into a lot of trouble for this. I could as well if I look at them. Why would you bring these here?" She found herself whispering the last part even though no one else could hear it.

He stood toe to toe with her. Their noses mere inches apart. "Because that's how desperate I am. Ryann Wilkanson is manipulative and cunning, and you'll want to see the true monster before making the wrong decision. Please, just watch them. If you let her go, you'll never forgive yourself. She *will* kill again, Dr. Clafin." His face was drawn as he pleaded. He seemed truly afraid. "I'm risking my badge to do this. That's how dangerous she is. Promise me you'll do this."

"I'm not promising anything, but leave them with me."

He bolted up with slightly more energy. "Thank you." He reached out his hand and she shook it. His skin was rough and dry —the hands of a hardworking man. He strode toward the door but turned before leaving. "I trust this stays between us." He nodded before closing the door behind him.

Nancy ambled back to her desk, the discs in her hand. Her chest tightened and she forced herself to swallow past the lump in her throat. She wasn't prepared to watch one child discuss in callous detail how she'd lured and murdered another child. Yet she had to.

The image of Sergeant Estevez—desperate, tortured even— lingered in the room. The air around her remained heavy and difficult to breathe.

Nancy opened the package and removed the bundle of DVDs

held together by a few elastic bands. The top one read, *Interview 1–R. Wilkanson–06/05*.

June of 2005. What a rare opportunity to see the teenage Ryann recount her actions. Almost unheard of, since most criminals deny their crimes.

She gingerly slid the first disc out of its sleeve and inserted it into her computer. A grainy image came on but quickly cleared, showing Estevez seated next to Ryann, who was reclined in a hospital bed.

Nothing could've prepared her for what she was about to see.

CHAPTER EIGHT

*T*uesday, November 28

"Wilkanson!"

There is a man screaming my last name through the block. Since this is the woman's side of the prison, it's a CO.

A few of the girls stop to stare, first at me and then at him, attempting to reason what this is all about, since it's unusual for a guard to bother with any of us beyond meal times and checks. I make my way over to the door.

"Hurry your ass up, I ain't got all day," he bellows. We both know he has a good twelve hours here each shift, so he's got plenty of time.

I bat my eyelashes at him. "Hello, Officer Penn. What can I help you with?"

"You got a phone call." He waves impatiently for me to walk through the doorway ahead of him.

"But we're not allowed phone calls," I say innocently, though I suspect Dr. Nancy let them put her through.

"It's your lawyer."

I slink back, slightly disappointed it's not Clafin. He walks me to a neighboring room near the guard's office where there's nothing but a desk, computer, and phone.

"You have five minutes," he says and closes the door. It's a rare moment. I'm never alone, not even in the fucking shower. I close my eyes and inhale, taking in the silence. It's wonderful.

Four minutes and thirty seconds left. I pick up the plastic handset and bring it to my mouth. "Hello."

"Ryann. It's Don Wagner, how are you?"

"Fine, Don. You?"

"Good. I just got off the phone with Dr. Clafin, and she's agreed to see you again."

"Who says I want to talk to her?" I'm playing hard to get—it's more fun. I'm perpetually bored in here.

"We talked about this, Ryann. You don't have many options, especially not with a psychiatrist at Dr. Clafin's level. If you want to get out, you'd better play nice with her—so nice that she believes you would never hurt a fly. You remember what we talked about, right?"

I'm smiling, though he can't see me. I love thinking about how hard he must be right now, picturing the fame that's about to come his way for setting the infamous teenage serial killer free. "I remember." I sigh so he can hear. "Fine, but you have to promise me she'll be open-minded, because I can't work with someone who doesn't believe in me. There's no point in wasting my time or hers."

"She's on board, so much so that she's on her way over to see you this afternoon."

I sit back in the chair and put my feet on the desk. "Really?"

"Do me a favor and cooperate. She needs to believe you're reformed."

I twirl the phone cord between my fingers. "Like you do, Don?"

"Exactly. I believe in you, Ryann. We can do this."

"I hope so."

"Okay, I've got to run. Call me if you need anything."

"Thanks, I will."

I knew Dr. Nancy would be back. How could she stay away from the challenge of figuring me out? Never underestimate the human ego, especially in a shrink. It's the most arrogant profession there is. Sitting back, judging someone's life, all the while believing you can fix whatever's wrong with them. Bullshit.

Officer Penn opens the door. My brief but glorious moment of solitude is gone. At least he doesn't try anything with me in here. He'd never admit it, but he's probably scared shitless of me, afraid I might bite off his dick or something equally unpleasant. He waits at the door until I'm next to him, and his odor of stale sweat is much more noticeable now that I've been alone.

I'm not back in F Block more than a few hours when I'm called out again and led down those few corridors to the corner office. Officer Evans accompanies me this time.

"Busy day for you," she says in such a flat tone I can't tell if she's being sarcastic.

"Yup. It's nice to have a change of scenery, even for a little while."

She gives a sharp laugh. "Don't go getting used to it."

It's enough to tense all the muscles in my body. I clench my teeth so hard that my temples feel like they could explode.

We're at Clafin's office, and I'm happy to see Officer Han inside the booth.

"You can go right in, but remember: I'm watching you," she says, as though it's intimidating. She has a baton and some pepper spray—nothing I couldn't handle if I really wanted to.

I open the door and Dr. Clafin immediately jumps from her seat.

"Hello, Ryann. I'm pleased you decided to meet me again. I fear we got off on the wrong foot." She smiles the same polite and detached smile as last time. A fake one. The muscles around her eyes don't move.

"It's partially my fault. I suppose I'm pretty sensitive."

"I don't blame you. You are in a unique circumstance."

That's an understatement.

"Please come and sit. Can I get you a coffee or tea?" Nancy takes a few steps toward the kitchenette that's in front of me.

"The idea of having a coffee that's not from a plastic jar with wretched bathroom water sounds great. Thanks."

Dr. Clafin nods. "Sugar or cream?"

"Normally I drink it black, but I suppose a little cream would be nice."

She pours the black liquid into a ceramic mug, which kind of surprises me. She must have some faith in me to give me hot liquid and a weapon I could use to cut her face wide open.

I take my mug and we sit in the same spots we did the last time, her across from me. This time she's wearing a navy pencil skirt, pantyhose, and brown pumps. Really ugly ones, the kind a grandmother wears, though I suppose she could be one.

I blow on the creamy liquid before I take a small sip. She can make the first move.

"I'm glad you agreed to see me again. I apologize if I gave you the impression that I wouldn't be impartial or treat you fairly. My patients are very important to me, and I'll do everything in my power to ensure you get a fair process."

"Thanks, that means a lot."

I notice she hasn't moved her gaze from me since we sat. She gives me a brief smile. "I thought we'd begin by watching a video together." Clafin opens an old brown cupboard that houses a television. She slips a DVD into the attached player.

I regard her as she sits back down. The muscles on either side of my spine have tightened. *What video?* I want to believe that it's some sort of therapeutic self-help crap, but I'm all too aware of the queasiness in my stomach when the screen changes to a fuzzy image I recognize. "What's this?"

Her eyes don't leave the screen. "It's you in Mercy General Hospital being interviewed by Sergeant Estevez back in 2005."

The picture clears and I see myself—my fifteen-year-old self—sitting up in a hospital bed, Estevez perched on my left and one of my lawyers, Mrs. Jelinski, on the right. He has what looks like a tape recorder on the table in front of me. The bandages that cover the gunshot wound to my shoulder protrude past the material of my hospital gown. My stomach rolls as I get a flash of a memory.

Before I can stop myself, I burst up from my chair. "What are you doing with this?"

Dr. Clafin remains seated, calm, her palms on her thighs. "Since you have memory issues, I thought watching the interview you gave about your first victim, Olivia McMann, would help jog a few things for you. As you said, it has been a long time."

I'm not certain what fucking game she's playing, but I can handle this. I've come too far to freak out now. She's testing me. Seeing if she can rattle me.

Truth is she has. I know exactly what I'm about to see, and it scares the living shit out of me.

CHAPTER NINE

*I*t took everything in Nancy to appear cool and collected when Ryann jumped out of her chair. She fought back a hitched breath. "I'm going to ask that you sit back down, Ryann. There's nothing to be afraid of. All we're doing is watching your interview to refresh your memory and discuss Olivia." Could Ryann see how labored her own breathing was? The last thing she needed was for Ryann to gain the advantage by thinking Nancy was frightened of her.

Han was in the room now. Nancy put her hand up. "It's okay, Mike."

He motioned for Ryann to sit back down. "That's the second time. One more and you can have these meetings through Plexiglas. Got it?"

"Okay," she said before Han left again.

Ryann sat, allowing Nancy time to unclench from the arms on her chair. She tried to slow the beating of her heart.

"How do you have those?"

"It was given to me as part of the investigative files around your case."

The little color that remained in Ryann's face drained suddenly. Nancy saw her throat bounce as she swallowed hard. A clear sign of anxiety. Ryann's gaze fell for a moment before she drew her eyes back to meet Nancy's. "Have you watched them?"

"Some, but not all. I would like to hear things from you, for the most part."

Ryann crossed her arms tightly. "Then why watch any at all?"

"It's part of the process. I need to evaluate all available evidence pertaining to your case. But I base a large part of my assessment on these sessions. My advice is for you to be as honest and open as possible."

Regardless of what she'd said to Estevez about ethics, she'd watched the videos. How could she not? She was paralyzed, and anything that could shed light on who she was dealing with was essential.

She was only five minutes into the first one when she realized just how handy they'd be.

Sitting across from Ryann was a tad surreal. Nancy was still in some sort of shock. She needed to let go and trust her instincts like she used to, but all that went through her head was that her incompetence could cost other people their lives.

"I wasn't going to do anything when I got up, you know. I was just shocked. I haven't hurt anyone since."

"I know that." Nancy offered a reassuring smile. "I'm going to play it now. I ask you to remain quiet and seated for the duration. We can talk about anything you want afterwards. Okay?"

Ryann nodded.

Nancy pressed play. She had screened all the interview tapes— not that she was going to let Ryann know that.

The camera was set up in a way that showed Estevez on the left and Ryann, in her hospital bed, front and center. On the right side of the screen Nancy recognized defense attorney Jelinski. At the time she'd been a court-appointed public defender, and not a very good one. Nancy had heard rumors she had married an Italian man, given up law, and moved to Venice.

Nancy kept Ryann in her periphery as the DVD played. Ryann's shoulders were tensed, her eyes unblinking. Her breathing was louder than it had been before the announcement of the video.

Ryann's gaze was on the screen.

Estevez's demeanor is calm, as to be expected from a seasoned cop. "This is Sergeant Roberto Estevez. The date is June twenty-second, 2005. I'm sitting with Ryann Wilkanson at Mercy General Hospital at eleven forty-seven a.m. Miss Wilkanson's attorney, Mrs. Heidi Jelinski, joins us. Miss Wilkanson, you have been charged with the murders of Olivia McMann, Yvonne Borgdon, Omar Murphy, Stanley Hastings, Marvin Dodson, and police officer Eric Knox, and with the attempted murder of Bao-yu Ng." He stares at her, unflinching, intense. Yet she doesn't cower under his heavy gaze. "Why don't we begin with the events leading up to the Olivia McMann murder?"

Ryann smiles widely. She attempts to pull herself up higher on her pillows and winces. Mrs. Jelinski moves to help, but Ryann holds her palm out. "I'm fine, thank you." She narrows her focus on Estevez. "I bet you've been waiting for this moment. How much sleep have you lost over me?" She chuckles lowly.

Mrs. Jelinski puts her hand up. "Ryann, that is not appropr—"

"Relax. We're just having fun, aren't we, Roberto? I already told you I'm waiving my rights or whatever. Do you know how long I've been waiting to tell everyone my story?" Her face is bright and cheery. Her voice animated. Detached, like she has no idea of the severity of her crimes or the consequences she is about to face.

"You can't waive your rights, Ryann. You don't know what you're saying," Mrs. Jelinski pleads.

"I said I want to talk. That's my right. If you can't handle it, there's the door."

Estevez clears his throat and crosses his right leg over his left. "Actually, Ryann can waive her rights if she pleases."

"And I highly advise against it," Jelinski says. Her face is flushed and a small vein protrudes from her temple. Her dark hair is up, highlighting the crow's feet around her shadowy eyes.

Ryann pulls the blanket up higher across her chest with a faint smile. "Besides, my father wants me to talk all about it." Her gaze quickly sifts from Mrs. Jelinski to Estevez. "You must be happier than a pig in shit that you finally caught me."

"I am. You needed to be stopped. What I want to know is why, Ryann? What did any of your victims do to deserve to be murdered?" His hands are clasped on his knee. He reclines slightly, like he's having a beer on a patio somewhere. "Did you just wake up one day and think, 'Gee, maybe I'll kill someone today'?"

"Maybe." Her singsong voice becomes harsh in an instant. "Did you ever stop to consider that every one of them got what they deserved?"

"Why did they deserve it?"

"Because they were spoiled little brats who never appreciated what they had. They just took and took. Entitled, arrogant, and whiny, which happen to be qualities I can't tolerate. The world is better off without them. Surely even you can see that."

Estevez jots something down in a large black notebook. "What made you do it right then? Why not wait?"

Ryann laughs. "Do you want to psychoanalyze me? You may have put the proverbial cuffs on, but you don't have the qualifications to pick my brain."

"Did you decide one day that you wanted to do more than simply read about murders and watch them on television or in the movies?"

"Don't answer that," Mrs. Jelinski snaps.

Ryann's eyes narrow on the dark-haired woman. "You can leave now."

"But Ryann, I'm here to protect you. I have a job to—"

Ryann puts her hand up, silencing her. She refocuses on Estevez. "Can you kick her out or something? I mean, you are drooling for all the details, and I can't tell you with her piping in every two seconds."

Estevez's face doesn't change. "You heard your client."

Jelinski bursts up from her seat. "I'm calling your parents!"

Ryann gives her a smile and wave before fixing her gaze on the camera lens. "This is still taping, right?" Estevez nods and she smooths her hair. She looks into the camera as though she's making an audition tape for a reality show and not confessing to serial murder. "I started to have these urges to do things. Not-so-nice things. I wondered what it would be like to hurt people. I started to dream about it, and then I was thinking about it during the day. It wasn't until I watched a show about serial killers that I recognized myself in someone else. Kindred spirits, you could say."

"Did you ever talk to anyone about the dark thoughts you'd been having?"

"I considered it, but I knew no one would understand. I was special, you see. Gifted. Able to carry out actions others couldn't even daydream about. That's when I knew I was like them."

"Who were you like?"

"The Greats—serial killers. I wanted to learn everything I could about people like me and ready myself for my mission. But I wasn't going to half-ass it. I was going to be the best."

"And you decided to start with Olivia McMann?"

"When all was said and done, she was the perfect first. Olivia was young, small, and easy to overpower. She wasn't a risk the way a man or woman would be. She was the perfect practice run, so to speak."

Estevez's fingers are clenched around his pen. It is difficult to tell from the angle of the camera, but he appears wide-eyed, hanging on each word. "So you'd been having urges to hurt someone—to kill—for a few weeks before you murdered Olivia?"

"At least." *She rolls her eyes.* "Are you going to harp on me about her just being an innocent kid? Because I'm really in no mood to hear about poor, sweet Olivia." *Her arms cross over her chest.*

"She was an innocent kid who didn't deserve to be targeted and executed like an animal, alone in a dark alleyway."

"Oh please, you didn't know her the way I did. She had everyone fooled except me. I saw who she really was."

"So what did you do after you decided Olivia had to go?"

"Look who wants all the sordid details." *She chuckles.*

Nancy saw the glimmer in Ryann's eyes on the video and slowly glanced over, wondering if it was still there. Did the film rekindle old memories? Was she getting excited, reliving the details, as serial killers often did? But to her surprise, Ryann's countenance remained stoic. Not a flicker of her eyelid betrayed her. She knew it was difficult for a person to override natural physiological reactions, and Ryann had no obvious tells so far.

Nancy concentrated on the television and the cocky, teenaged Ryann full of bravado.

"Oh, I'll tell you everything. Keep your pants on." Ryann's gaze moves around the room for a minute. "Did my father hand-pick you to interrogate me, Sergeant? For old times' sake? I think you were the only one who suspected me. Good for you. Truth is, I didn't think you'd actually succeed." She shakes her head, both hands up as in prayer. "Well, I guess my dear old dad actually got me, but you were there first." She laughs as her hand covers the bandage.

An eerie giggle from the recording inspired goose bumps along Nancy's skin.

"It must've been hard for you to be on to me, all the while knowing your partner—my own father—would never believe you. Was it difficult to keep the details away from him while you hunted me down?"

Estevez readjusts himself in the chair, sitting up straighter, squaring his shoulders. "We're not playing this game, Ryann. You got sloppy, and you got yourself caught. You agreed to talk to me, so talk. How did you get Olivia out into the alley?"

Ryann grabs the cup on the table in front of her and takes a long sip through the straw. "All business? Fine. Olivia was easy . . ."

Nancy hit the stop button and froze the screen on Ryann's face. The room was silent. She refrained from speaking, to see if Ryann would jump in with justifications, objections, or commentary of any kind. She forced her gaze to remain on Ryann, observing her physical reactions to what they'd just watched. But Ryann's stare was fixed ahead, her hands clasped neatly in her lap, and both feet on the floor. Her back was straight, and there was no discernable expression on her face.

She had a hard time reconciling the girl on the tape with the pitiable, misunderstood, and 'rehabilitated' woman that her lawyers had manipulated the media into reconsidering. Forget dangerous predator. They were touting her as a troubled, mentally ill youth who'd been railroaded by a faulty system and Ryann's own father. Wagner and Roche had started the media frenzy weeks before, and as far as Nancy could see, it was gaining ground.

Nancy fought to keep still and not fidget in her seat the way her body wanted to. She craved to break the tension, but knew she shouldn't. Instead she'd wait to see what Ryann would do under the weight of it. How she'd react.

After nearly five minutes of nerve-racking silence, Nancy finally spoke. "What are your thoughts?"

Ryann adjusted herself in her chair, all the while keeping her head down. "I don't really know what to think."

"Do you remember what you were feeling when you gave your statement to Estevez?"

"I don't remember giving that statement at all. I see myself on the tape. I hear my voice saying those words, but I don't recall any of it." She paused for a moment and then added, "Well, not most of it. I do remember bits of being in the hospital. I was in pain. I think my parents both visited me, and my grandparents . . . I don't remember seeing Bri. I have a few memories of Estevez being in the room, but they're not coherent. He's there asking me questions, and then I see my mom, then there's a nurse and a doctor. Nothing is in order. Maybe it was the pain meds I was on?"

"It's possible some of the medication inhibited your recall, but you seemed quite alert and lucid in the video. I would imagine that if the meds affected you in the way you are suggesting, we would see glossy eyes, slurred speech, and you looking groggy or disoriented. But as we both witnessed, you were none of those things."

"Then how do you explain my memory gaps?" Ryann's shoulders were relaxed. Her forehead was smooth and unfurrowed. Her eyes were clear and sharp as she met Nancy's gaze.

"I can't yet. It's something we'll have to explore in our sessions. So if I understand correctly, you're now saying you have no memory of Olivia's murder?"

"I have no memory of giving that interview to Estevez, but . . ."

Nancy stopped writing, dropping her pen. Something in her stomach fluttered.

"I believe I've started remembering parts of Olivia's death. At least I think I do."

CHAPTER TEN

*D*r. Clafin takes a break from her coffee to gulp water so hard I can hear it five feet away. She's nervous, though she's putting on a brave face—like today is just another day on the job.

My father, the detective, should've helped me. He should've forbidden me from talking to Estevez, no matter what I'd done. Wasn't it his job to make sure I was protected? I was a kid unable to make the best decisions, but he just wanted it all to go away. He wanted me to go away. I was the tarnish on his shiny badge.

Dr. Clafin's hand must be cramping with the amount of notes she's jotting. She'd probably love to write a book about me. Too bad it's unethical.

She stops scribbling and tightens the belt on her sweater before readjusting herself in her chair. She clears her throat gently and pretends to look over the paper in front of her. I know she doesn't need to check anything. She knows what she wants to ask me, but she doesn't want to seem too eager.

"I have a few follow up questions, if you don't mind."

Of course, I'll make it easy on her. She helps determine if I'll ever see the light of day outside the prison yards again. "You're the expert. Ask away."

She gets her shiny pen and notepad ready. "How did you feel after you left the alley? You did say your memory came back after the murder." No hint of emotion in her voice. You'd have thought we were having a conversation about what to order for dinner, not about how I bludgeoned Olivia to death with a fucking brick until her brain came out of her skull. I found out later that I'd bashed her with it a dozen times, though I only remembered four. I must've blacked out.

I nod and act uncomfortable. She wants me to talk about the murders in the mindset I had at the time. To basically be a voyeur on my naughtiest exports. Perhaps she believes that my deepest, darkest memories and thoughts will give her a sense of what went fucking wrong with me and how she can fix it—that is, if she doesn't declare me fixed already.

This should be fun. A rare moment to be myself. "I remember feeling excited. I'd finally done it. I'd imagined how it would be, but now it was real."

"So is it fair to say the kill made you feel exhilarated?"

I nod. "I had achieved the first step in my mission. I was on a high—feeling more powerful than I ever had before."

"Why didn't you use the knife?"

"I really don't know. Maybe there was a part deep down inside of me that didn't want to go through with it."

"So then why did you? You could have walked away at any moment, yet you decided to simply change your weapon."

I sigh, leaning forward, clasping my 'shaky' hands together over my knees. "I'd convinced myself it was something that needed to be done. I thought I'd be weak if I walked away. I didn't want to fail like I did with everything else I tried in my life."

"I read through the evidence found in the alleyway. What do you know of a blue and green knit bracelet? It was found on the ground next to Olivia's body."

I know exactly what she's talking about. A rush of pin prickles covers my arms and chest. I try and squelch the adrenaline that wants to surface. Olivia had been wearing it, and I wanted the souvenir. "I think she had it on her wrist."

"Had you read about trophies? Is that why you felt tempted to take a memento of your first kill?" Her eyes are glued to me, studying me harder, if that's possible.

"Yes, I guess so. I was tempted, but there could be no evidence connecting me to Olivia. It would've been perfect too. Innocuous, common, small enough to hide, even. But in the end I dropped it on the ground. I couldn't take the risk."

I know it's time to ramp things up a bit. Honing my skills over the years has made me an even more proficient liar. I bend my neck and look down until I have produced a few tears. Looking up, I meet Dr. Clafin's gaze. "I'm embarrassed that I ever felt that way. I killed a girl, then wanted to take her bracelet? It's shameful to even say the words out loud, but you told me to be honest about what it was like for me back then. You have to know that I don't feel that way now."

Dr. Clafin nods and writes. I watch her hand twirl the pen around the yellow pages and try to imagine what she's recording.

"How do you feel now?"

"Horrible. Repulsed. Disgusted." My voice is tremulous and I grab my glass with a visibly shaky hand before taking a sip of water. "It's difficult for me to discuss. I hurt a lot of people. When I think back on the things I've done . . . it's like it wasn't really me. I have these disjointed memories, but it's like I'm disconnected from all of it. It's been over a decade of trying to get past it. Trying to prove I'm not that monster anymore. Not that I'm sure that even matters to anyone."

"Is that how you see yourself? Like a monster?"

"It's how everyone sees me. It's a fair assessment, don't you think? You've seen hundreds of criminals. I bet most of them haven't done anything remotely as horrific as I have."

"We're not here to discuss other people. We are here to talk about you. Ryann, can you tell me, in your opinion, why you think you were drawn to serial killers? How was it you used to refer to them?" Dr. Clafin grabs a beige file and begins riffling through the thick stack of papers within.

I tilt my head back and stare at the blank ceiling like I'm too horrified to say the words. "The Greats. I called them The Greats." As if she didn't already know that part.

She drops the file and its contents back on the desktop. "Right. Who fit into that category?"

Dr. Nancy already knows full fucking well *who*, but if she wants me to say the words, I will. "Prolific serial killers that I studied and admired."

She nods and jots something more down. "I see. Were there any in particular with whom you identified?"

I shrug. "I guess they each had the appeal of being free. They did what they wanted, when they wanted, without fear. Truth is, I don't know what made me that way, especially since I haven't had those feelings since shortly after I was released from the hospital."

She takes a long sip of her tea, draining it, before setting it back down in the exact same spot. She always places the mug on the same small square of space on her desk. It's curious. "And what do you think of them now?" She glares down her pointy, judging nose at me.

It's obvious what she wants me to say—that The Greats are reprehensible fiends who deserve to suffer for their crimes. "There's something mentally wrong with people like that." I let my voice catch a little when I say, " Like me. I've studied psychology while I've been in here, you know, to try and figure out what made me so different from almost every other person I encountered."

Dr. Clafin allows the smallest smile. I think it's meant to be empathetic. Probably to keep me at ease so I'll keep talking.

"My father owned these books about serial killers in our home office, which meant he must have read them. I remember wondering if there was a part of him that got pleasure from what he found inside. Why else have them? Part of me hoped that his urge to become a cop was him trying desperately to fight the darkest parts of himself." I look down and pick at my cuticles, 'unable' to meet her eyes at that moment. "I know now how wrong that assumption was. He had them so he could learn what to look out for. Who to take down in his quest to protect the innocent. And he never suspected me. Never connected his own daughter to all the horrific things he'd read or seen in his career. I don't think he was capable of seeing it. Maybe suspicions grew in his mind about me toward the end, but he never came right out and said anything. He was probably in denial. It is a pretty unfathomable thing to ask someone to see in their own child, though I'm sure Sergeant Estevez tried."

Dr. Clafin keeps a small metal kettle in the office. She stands, cup in hand, and walks to the counter, clicking the *on* button. A low humming sounds. "I need a refill. Do you want a cup?"

I nod. "Please." I can't take my gaze from the shiny, hard metal.

Reaching for her ceramic mug, she drops a single tea bag in. "Did you have a close relationship with your father?"

This is the hardest question she's asked so far. I don't quite know how to answer it, so I shrug. "Sometimes. I thought so."

"What do you mean?"

"He was hard to please, but we were pretty close."

"Would you say he was a perfectionist?"

"You could say that. He was a high achiever and had equally high expectations of the people in his life. He wanted the best for us."

"'Us' meaning you, your sister, and your mother?"

"Yes. He could be tough on people. Even the people he worked with. He meant well, it just didn't always come across that way."

"How did you feel when you discovered your affinity with serial killers?" Doctor Clafin walks toward me, each hand holding a steaming mug. The scent of peppermint flits across my nose as I take it from her.

"Happy. Relieved, I guess." I blow into the mouth of the mug. "I don't remember having as much as a second thought about murder or killing even six months before that summer. When the feelings hit me, I felt special. Call it immaturity or selfishness or mental illness—whatever works—but it felt extraordinary to be in such a tiny niche of people. It was like I had this epiphany and saw the world clearly for the first time. There I was: smarter than, and superior to, the masses. It was a game to me. The hunt, the stalking of my prey, and finally the catch and kill."

"When you think of the things you did to those people, what does it feel like now?"

I bring my elbow to my mouth and cough hard. I lower it, my eyes water on cue, and I meet her gaze. "I'm sick to my stomach. I try to never think about it, because I can't believe I did any of it. It feels like a movie I'm watching. That might seem strange to understand."

"It's not strange at all. It's called dissociation, and it often happens when someone has undergone traumatic experiences. The individual can emotionally and sometimes cognitively separate themselves from the incidents."

I crumple in on myself in apparent distress. "Yeah, but I chose to do those things. They weren't horrible things done to me. I did them! Willingly! Happily!" I can tell by her face that I look and sound as frantic as I hope.

Dr. Clafin puts her hand up as if to shush me, and I listen. "Ryann, the guilt you feel can be enough to dissociate the memories of your actions from the person you've become. Your brain is trying to reconcile the person you were, and the things she did, with who you are now."

I force my voice through the fake frog in my throat. "Maybe you're right. I feel like a totally different person than I was before, but it's not like people will believe that. I was convicted in an hour. The jury was sure I should spend my life locked up. Not to mention that I've lost appeal after appeal. The fact is I'm guilty . . . of all the things I was accused of. Maybe things I still don't remember. I know logically that I deserve to be locked up, but part of me believes that I deserve a second chance." Dr. Clafin hands me a box of tissues.

My hand reaches out to grab one, and I wipe my cheeks free of the tears.

Clafin gives me a minute to compose myself before saying, "Why don't you take a sip of tea?" I do, keeping my head down, but I feel her eyes on me.

"It's honorable that you're taking responsibility for your actions, and the only way to truly move on is to keep doing that." She tilts her head and I watch the edges of her mouth curve up ever so slightly—a kind smile, I think. But then she says, "Tell me about Hayden Cook."

I stop my head from jerking up. I don't want her to know she's got my attention. "Not sure what you want me to say."

She straightens her head. Her leg is crossed tightly over the other, her ankle rotating clockwise with a quiet clicking sound. "Did you frame him for the murder of Yvonne Borgdon?"

Perhaps I underestimated her grit. She's pulling out all the stops, trying to catch me off guard, see how much pressure I can take before the crazy in me comes bursting out. I remain unruffled. "No. I know that's hard to believe coming from me, but I didn't frame him. Yes, I knew he'd be a suspect, but it wasn't like I planted false evidence or orchestrated the cops in his direction. The fact that he was Yvonne's boyfriend automatically made him a suspect."

"When you found out he'd been arrested, what did you think?"

"I'm ashamed to admit it, but I was relieved. It was perfect. The cops had someone they liked for it. They even found a trace amount of his blood in her bedroom. His DNA was all over, and yeah it was because they were together and he was probably over there all the time, but it didn't rule him out. There were cheating rumors, and the timeline of her murder fit." I scrubbed my face with my hands and breathed deeply. "But that was after I had time to think about it. After my friends had brought him up and discussed it for the fiftieth time. When he was arrested, it didn't faze me at all. I wasn't thinking about him. He didn't factor into my mission. It was only after everyone at my school kept on talking about him being arrested and charged that I realized no one would connect *me* to Yvonne, which made me feel more powerful. Untouchable. I thought it was a sign from the universe that I was being protected to keep doing my work."

Dr. Clafin writes on her notepad for a minute while I sit there. What I wouldn't give to read her little assessments of me, her judgments and findings, even though our chats will never allow her to really understand me, fancy degrees or not. "Did you target Yvonne because she was dating Hayden?"

"It was more than that. Of course, I wasn't thrilled that he broke up with me and then started dating her so soon after, but honestly it was more about who Yvonne was as a person. At the time I thought she was horrible. She started rumors about me, bullied me at school, and got a bunch of her friends to make my life a living hell." None of which actually happened but I need the sympathy so I indulge in a little story telling.

"And how would they do that?"

"They'd come by my locker and laugh about how Hayden dumped me for Yvonne and how ugly I was. They made fun of my clothes and laughed that I was poor. A few of them even painted the word *loser* on my locker for everyone to see. I was humiliated." I stop as though I'm collecting myself. "It hurt at the time, but I understand that teenagers do that sort of thing. Back then it felt like the end of the world. I had my mission, and I thought Yvonne was the perfect candidate."

"You've mentioned your mission a few times now. I have yet to see any mention of it in the interview transcripts. Can you describe what it was?"

I was praying she'd ask me this. "I kept it a secret back then, even after I was caught. Like I mentioned, I thought I was starting this personal crusade against the arrogant, soulless, entitled few who stomped over the innocent. Yvonne thought she was superior to me, always throwing Hayden in my face. Her parents catered to her, not unlike Olivia. I suppose the fact that I had to work so hard for everything I had stung when I saw people like them parading around in their new clothes and shoes, riding their new bikes, going on countless holidays, and shopping sprees."

"Children often have trouble coming to terms with things they feel are unfair." Dr. Clafin looks at her watch. It feels like I've been blabbering on for hours now, and we haven't even gotten through half of my victims yet. How long am I going to have to suffer through this torture?

"Do you have to go?" *Please say yes.*

"I'm afraid so, but I'll be back tomorrow."

I can hardly contain an outburst of joyous relief that I'm done for the day. F Block sucks, but spewing my tragic history and repentant sorrow is exhausting. Lying on my steel cot actually sounds good right now.

"You're making some excellent progress, Ryann. I know this is challenging, but it's only going to help the healing process."

I nod and smile thoughtfully.

Dr. Clafin stands and I follow. We walk to the door, where Han dutifully leads me out.

"See you tomorrow." Dr. Clafin waves.

I'm led away, but I turn at the last minute. Her face is still visible through the glass. She glances up and our eyes meet. It is unexpected, and she's no longer looking at me with the same regard as a moment ago. There's a flash of contempt in her eyes before she startles out of it, realizing what she's done.

And I know I won't stop until I break her completely.

CHAPTER ELEVEN

*I*n regards to: Ryann E. Wilkanson
            DOC#57629847
9712 Sterling Way
Dungrave County Correctional Facility
Dungrave, Colorado 34764

November 16, 2016

Executive Clemency Advisory Board
    136 State Capitol
    Denver, Colorado 80203-1792

To Whom It May Concern:

I was asked to write a letter either for or against the release of

Ryann Wilkanson. I first met Ryann when we were in ninth grade at Cloverdale Secondary. We knew each other socially for about six months before we began dating. We were only together for a couple of months before we broke up. We remained friendly. I believed that Ryann was a really great person. That was until I was watching the news from jail after I'd been arrested for Yvonne Borgdon's death and saw that she was the one responsible for multiple murders of innocent people, including my girlfriend. It's so unsettling to think about how I could have easily been one of her victims. I think about how close I might have come all the time.

I spent a few weeks in prison and was not allowed to attend Yvonne's funeral because at the time I was the sole murder suspect. I believe that I would have been convicted of her murder and spent the rest of my life in prison if Ryann hadn't been caught.

While it is difficult to reconcile the girl I thought I knew so well with the cold, heartless killer I later discovered her to be, I must ask that you do not grant Ryann Wilkanson clemency. Not now and not ever. If she was able to seamlessly manipulate and hide her true self for so long while committing such atrocities, then I have no faith that she is not still that same conniving and dangerous person today.

It is not for me that I make this decision, but for Yvonne, her family, and for the life that she and the rest of Ryann's victims will never have the chance to live. I cannot in good conscience believe that Ryann is redeemed, and even if she is truly remorseful for all the terror and pain she caused, she does not deserve to live a good life when so many others cannot.

Sincerely,

Hayden Cook

Wednesday, November 29

After the last session with Ryann, Nancy contacted Dr. Maiser's office and booked an appointment for the next morning. Dr. Maiser was on rounds and asked that Nancy come to Mercy General instead.

Hopping on the elevator, Nancy traveled to the ninth floor—the psych unit. The doors opened into a small nurse's station where a bald, black man with a goatee, and broad shoulders typed away while on a phone call.

He hung up a moment later. "Name of the patient you're visiting?" he said without looking up.

"I'm here to see Dr. Maiser, actually."

The man glanced up. "Oh, sorry. It's kind of busy, and we're short two nurses. Do you have an appointment?" His voice was calm, but his eyes were rushing her along.

"Yes. She should be expecting me."

He stood. "Come with me, then." He brought her to the last office on the right and knocked on the door.

Nancy hated the smell of hospitals. They all used the same cleanser, iodoform, which was supposed to be milder than ammonia but nauseated her just as much.

"Come in."

The man positioned his body in front of Nancy so he was blocking her view as he cracked open the door and stuck his head in. "I have a Dr. Clafin here for you."

"Send her in."

Pushing the door open the remainder of the way, he stepped back to let her pass. She turned to thank him but he was already gone.

"Marissa? We spoke on the phone. Nice to finally meet you." They shook hands and Nancy sat across the desk from her. The office was dark, cluttered, and depressing. The window was small and the walls were beige, but they'd probably been white when the paint was fresh. The shelves were packed with books and a layer of dust, and patient files were piled high atop the filing cabinets.

"I have to say I was a little shocked to hear from you under these circumstances." Dr. Marissa Maiser leaned back in her chair, clasping her hands on her protruding stomach, and looked down her bifocals at Nancy.

Nancy internally sighed. The judgment. She knew what was coming. "Shocked in what way?" She'd make Marissa own it.

"That you're assisting Ryann Wilkanson's legal team in the hopes of getting her released."

"Where did you get that idea from?"

Marissa smoothed her gray hair behind her protruding ears, pronouncing her jowls further. "Isn't that why you're here? To garner support for her release?"

"I'm here to gather information and discuss your professional opinion based on your assessment of Ryann when you treated her back in 2005. This will inform my recommendation, which has certainly not been determined yet."

The lines around Dr. Maiser's eyes eased a touch, though it was difficult to tell since she was of a particular age. She picked up a pen, which she proceeded to fidget with. "I have to say that's a bit of a relief, Dr. Clafin. I was awfully concerned."

"As am I. Do you mind if I make a few notes?"

"Not at all. I took the liberty of gathering Ms. Wilkanson's file. My memory is a touch spotty. It was such a long time ago."

"Do you remember the state Ryann was in when she was first admitted? Physical and mental, if you don't mind."

Maiser rocked back and forth in her chair, and her eyes moved up and to the left, which indicated that she was thinking— recalling experiences and emotions. "I could never forget that. Some patients just stick with you. I'm sure you know all too well what that's like."

"I've had a few that are hard to shake."

"Ms. Wilkanson was recovering from a GSW to her shoulder, so by the time I saw her, she was a day out of surgery and still a bit groggy. She asked who I was, and when I told her, she told me to . . ." Maiser paused for a moment. "Eff off, but not in such nice terms. She said she didn't need a shrink because she was perfectly sane and knew exactly what she was doing."

"Was your first impression that she was sane?"

"I had no idea. Normally when we get someone in who's committed a violent crime, they either refuse to talk or go on incessantly about how the police have it all wrong and they are absolutely innocent. That, or the voices told them to do it. Not her. She proceeded to tell me . . . Wait. Let me find it in the file." Dr. Maiser opened the brown folder and flipped through a few pages. "Ah, here it is. *Patient has stated that she killed six people and is a serial killer. Patient is quoted as stating: 'I killed them all and I would do it again. They deserved it. I did the world a favour. Did you know that my own father—a detective—had no idea it was me?' Patient laughs and says, 'All that time I was right under his nose and he couldn't see me. He doesn't appreciate my talents. He only sees his failure, but what about everything that I've built? I am a Great. Finally, I did it.'"* She made a tsking sound with her tongue. "She was a right evil one."

It was interesting that Ryann had mentioned her father. Could the murders be extreme attention-seeking behavior? "Just hearing that . . . her words strike me as manic, definitely narcissistic, and possibly detached from reality. I assume you did a full eval?"

"Of course. Sure, she presented as narcissistic, but that didn't prevent her from being held accountable. It was my conclusion that Ms. Wilkanson had her full faculties in check and had a complete understanding that what she had done was morally and legally wrong. She outright boasted about murdering six people. Obviously I was right, because she was deemed fit to stand trial."

"It's rare to encounter a person so willing to admit their guilt without heavy interrogation or irrefutable evidence. Did she appear delusional at all?" She wanted to mention her concerns about Ryann's 'mission,' which presented as highly delusional, but since it had been revealed in session, she couldn't.

"No, though I'm sure you won't be surprised to hear that she scored extremely high on both the sociopath and psychopath scales."

"Did her demeanor change over the few days she was in here?"

Dr. Maiser's eyebrows knit together. "I only saw her once."

"I don't understand. My reports indicate that she was here for three days before she was transferred to Dungrave prison."

"That's correct."

"Well, why didn't you see her a few more times?"

"It was a pretty open-and-shut case."

"Who was your second opinion?"

Dr. Maiser pushed herself back from her desk. A pink hue warmed her cheeks. Nancy sensed it was anger rather than embarrassment. "I didn't get one. I didn't feel it was necessary. Ms. Wilkanson admitted to her crimes, I ran the standard tests, interviewed her, and made my conclusion. We both know that she was going to be reassessed pre-trial by multiple doctors." She leaned forward. "I did my due diligence, and I resent the implication otherwise."

"It was such a unique and public case. I just assumed you would want to confer with a colleague."

Maiser straightened. "I am confident in my ability to perform my job. If there's nothing else, I have patients to see."

Nancy knew when she was being dismissed. "I appreciate that, Dr. Maiser and I'll leave you to it." She stood but stopped. "I'm in a challenging position. Is there anything else you can think of from the time Ryann was in here that would lead you to believe that—"

Maiser was suddenly on her feet, causing Nancy to startle. "I know the Ryann Wilkanson that I spoke to, and I hope you'll see her for what she is.

I'm not sure what kind of stories she's spinning for you now, but God help us if you help that maniac get out." She stalked to the door, opened it, and extended her arm into the hallway. "As I stated, I have patients waiting."

Nancy stood, shell-shocked. "Thank you for your time, Dr. Maiser." Stopping before the doorway, she said, "Do you know if any of the nurses that treated Ryann are still employed here?"

"I couldn't say."

Nancy was certain Maiser knew. And Nancy would find out.

CHAPTER TWELVE

*D*r. Clafin finally looks up from my file. It's grown quite big since we started just over a week ago. "Last session we began to discuss Yvonne Borgdon. Would you like to describe the planning and execution of her murder?"

I notice the effort it takes her to sound nonchalant when she asks me. I want to say, 'Of course I do. It's a free pass to relive my kills out loud and to an audience. It's the closest thing to heaven besides actually hunting again.'

"I guess." I sit quietly, staring at my feet, while I 'gather my thoughts.'

"How long after you and Hayden broke up did he begin seeing Yvonne?"

"Days, I guess."

"And that angered you?"

I run my fingers through my hair and decided to give her a few small truths mixed in with the bullshit. "It made me feel like I hadn't meant anything to him. And then there was the fact that he chose her, of all people. I already didn't like her because of the bullying, and Hayden always said he hated her. He used to make fun of her, saying she was gross. He had these jokes about her red hair and freckles." That part was true. We totally made fun of her, and she was hideous compared to me, which obviously was a huge insult.

"So their relationship came as a shock?"

Why does she have to repeat and rephrase everything I say? It's getting beyond irritating. "I was blindsided. It made me feel like I couldn't trust him, like he'd lied to me. I wondered how many other things he'd said to me that were lies too."

"Why did you focus your anger on her and not Hayden?"

"Because she rubbed it in. Always throwing it in my face that they were together. She even started a rumor that he'd cheated on me with her and she was the reason we broke up. It was her smugness. She thought she was better than me." I realize I'm clenching my fists at my sides. I relax my palms. Funny how just thinking about that bitch all these years later can still rile me up. Then I remember my hands yanking the belt around her throat and her limp body collapsing under me, and my breathing eases again.

"And you wanted to prove to Yvonne and everyone else that she wasn't better than you, so you killed her?" Her pen is perched, waiting on the page.

"I thought she was trying to steal my life. I believed I needed to get rid of her before she replaced me in the eyes of everyone I cared about. I'd have no friends at all. I'd be all alone." Poor me.

Dr. Clafin grabs the remote control and my stomach lurches. My dumb teenage self is not helping my case. I know what she's trying to do. She thinks she's going to catch some reaction from me that will let her know I'm still the same psycho that I was on the recording. *Not gonna happen, Nancy.*

"I'm going to play the interview of you discussing with Sergeant Estevez the days leading up to Yvonne's murder, and then we can review it."

I want to scream, stamp my feet, throw something. I have no power. All I can do is sit like a good girl and watch the video. "Do we really have to?"

Dr. Clafin gives a small nod. "We do, Ryann."

The video starts, and I see Estevez pulled up in a chair next to my hospital bed. My wrist is cuffed to the rail at my side. I thought I was so badass having to be restrained in there, police officers stationed outside my room so I wouldn't escape. I wasn't going far considering the pain I was in. I couldn't use my arm for a week.

It's the same interview day as when I spoke to Estevez about Olivia. I was such an idiot for sending Jelinski away. These fucking tapes have haunted me. First at my trial—the judge ruled that they not be publically released, so the families didn't have to suffer—and now when I have my first real shot in twelve years to actually get out.

Estevez cocks his head and stares at the teenage me. "How did you get inside Yvonne's bedroom?"

I laugh. (God, why did I laugh?) *"It's pretty obvious I went through the window. Unless you and your cop buddies are so dumb that you didn't notice the cut screen?"*

"Was Yvonne already in her room?"

"I wanted to surprise her. I knew she was going to the movies with Hayden, so I snuck into her room and hid in her closet until she came in." I remember being really proud of myself; the risk of being caught at any moment in my hiding spot was a rush.

"Weren't you worried about being discovered?"

"Yeah. Almost was, too. Her fucking mom came in with laundry to put away. I thought she was going to open the fucking closet door and see me standing there."

He takes a swig of his paper-cup coffee. "What would you have done then?"

"What I would've had to. I would've killed her and then gotten the hell outta there. It would have fucking sucked, too, because there'd be no way I could've targeted Yvonne then. It would've been too risky."

I make sure I'm leaning forward now; my fingers laced together, me biting my bottom lip. I do whatever I can to look devastated instead of gleeful.

"What did you do when you heard the door open?"

"I half-popped out when her mom came in and almost ruined every-

thing, so that time I waited until I could see Yvonne. She turned on the lamp next to her bed. I watched her change into some other pants and took the opportunity to catch her when she was already off-balance. She never knew what hit her." My eyes narrow in a pissed-off stare. "That's my biggest fucking regret, too."

"What is?"

"That she never knew it was me. I got her from behind, put the belt around her throat, and squeezed the breath from her. She fought, kicking and flailing, but I was stronger. I wanted it more. But that slut never looked me in the eyes." I smile into the camera and nod slightly. "That, my friend, would've made it perfect. But there was always next time."

I want to cover my face with my hands. I forgot I said that. I close my eyes instead and hear Dr. Clafin's voice.

CHAPTER THIRTEEN

$\mathcal{N}$ ancy sat back in her chair. She waited eagerly to see if something would shake lose in Ryann. By the look on Ryann's face, Nancy was optimistic she was close.

Nancy wondered if Ryann had memory gaps around Yvonne's murder too. There was a strong possibility that it was an all-too-convenient excuse, though Nancy couldn't discount the possibility of partial amnesia.

She had watched every video Estevez had given her. It was police procedure to allow a suspect to talk for as long as they wanted, to give them enough space to get tangled in their lies. But Ryann was unique because she had essentially admitted to everything.

The video began with Ryann sitting up in bed, seemingly energetic. The pressure and rate of her speech when she spoke of Olivia and Yvonne made Nancy wonder if she'd been suffering from an acute manic phase. Her mannerisms were exaggerated, her gaze constantly shifted, and the cadence to her voice was high and fast. She definitely appeared excited, but was it because of the thrilling aftermath from the killings or something more?

In the video, Estevez asked Ryann about how killing Yvonne

made her feel. It was the perfect opportunity for Nancy to study her.

She looked away from the screen and set her gaze on Ryann. Ryann's breathing seemed calm and steady. Her hands were relaxed at her sides. But her face . . . She appeared as though she was in pain. Her shoulders were hunched in as she slouched forward, almost as though she wanted to take up as little space as possible, or possibly shrink like she could hide herself. People did when they were lying. They also did it when they were overwhelmed by something in their external environment.

Was it possible that Ryann found watching herself in that state too distressing?

Ryann answers Estevez. "Oh, Yvonne's death made me feel incredibly satisfied. Olivia had been a test of sorts, to see if I could do it, but she hadn't posed much of a challenge, which is half the fun. Yvonne, on the other hand, was bigger than me. The fact that I managed to subdue her and kill her with my hands was everything." Ryann sounds like she's talking about a fun party. She seems completely disconnected from the severity of what she's done.

No one could be so soulless, Nancy thought.

"Do we have to keep watching this? I think I may need a break, if that's okay."

Nancy startled at the contrast of Ryann's current voice as it broke through the audio of the recording. "There's one more part I want you to see. It's up next."

Ryann didn't respond. No nod, no okay. She simply turned her gaze back to the screen, sighing under her breath. Nancy couldn't help but notice the look on her face—her overall reaction was not unlike the ones victims have when they are forced to relive something traumatic. Even her leg was shaking.

Sergeant Estevez pulls his chair a foot closer to her hospital bed. "Do you think killing these people was wrong?"

"What do you mean?" she says.

"Do you think taking the lives of these people, all six of them, was wrong of you to do?"

"I understand the question. I'm not an idiot. What I'm asking is, do you mean wrong morally or legally?"

"Both, I guess."

"Depends on how you look at it."

"What the hell does that mean?" Estevez is furious but trying his hardest to hide it.

Ryann shrugs. *"What's wrong is subjective. What's wrong to me may be fine to you."*

"You know if something is right or wrong, legal or illegal, so stop playing games. I know your father—your whole goddamn family—and you damn well know right from wrong."

Nancy hit the pause button. The screen showed Ryann smiling with what Nancy interpreted as joyful defiance. "Can you understand why I wanted you to watch that?"

Ryann kept her head up but her eyes downcast. She twiddled her thumbs, which rested on her lap. "Not really, no."

"Sergeant Estevez asked you if you thought what you did was wrong, and you refused to answer him. Why was that?"

She swallowed hard. "I remember that part of the interrogation. I didn't want to give him the satisfaction of an answer, but the truth is, I didn't believe what I was doing was wrong. I thought I was doing the world a favor." She made a sweeping motion with her arm. "I knew what I'd done was illegal, but I didn't think it was morally wrong. You see, I'd developed my own sort of moral code."

"The one you used to judge other people. You said it was what helped you decide who your victims would be."

"That's right."

"You spoke extensively about your first two victims, Olivia and Yvonne. Would you bring me through the events of the murder of your third victim, Omar Murphy? Start wherever you like." It would be good for Ryann to feel like she had some control during the session, perhaps encourage her to open up and share more.

I really love how Dr. Nancy has to use their full names every fucking time she refers to them. She probably thinks it's going to stir up more remorse or guilt if I keep hearing it. "Why, don't you have a video for that one?"

"I do, but I would like to hear from you, if that's all right."

I roll my shoulders and inhale a sharp breath. "It had been weeks since I'd killed. My friend Lucas had finally agreed to take me to a school dance. I thought I might find someone who fit my profile there. High school was a breeding ground for my type of target. I'd stolen a handful of Ativan from Bao-yu's purse earlier. It never hurt to be prepared, and, because of my small size, subduing someone with pills was way easier than having to physically over-throw them.

"The pills were wrapped in a Kleenex like a used tissue. The chances were slim that the door monitor would open it to see what disgusting substance was inside. She was looking for obvious stuff, like a flask or some weed. I'd asked my friend, Lucas, for some drugs—I didn't care what. He always had some, especially at what-ever social function was happening. He gave me a packet. The drugs—likely OxyContin, plus the eight or so Ativan I had—would do some real damage. I was betting it would be strong enough to stop someone's heart.

"I remember seeing Omar on the dance floor, gyrating with a few girls. It infuriated me for some reason, like he thought he was some ladies' man. He was an athlete and always received special treatment from the teachers, which also didn't sit well with me. I don't know if it was because he looked so sleazy and conceited under the gym strobe lights, because he got A's he didn't earn or deserve, or the smug way he hit on every female, single or not, but I snapped. I wanted him gone." Dr. Clafin's face has softened marginally. The tiny, throbbing vein in her forehead is less notice-able, which I'm taking as a positive sign that she's starting to see me as a human being and not just a psycho killer.

Dr. Clafin writes a few lines before rubbing her forehead with her thumb and index finger. Her blue eyes are heavy with dark circles under them. She looks more exhausted than she did a week ago. I'm not sure if that's a good thing for me or not. "So you snuck the drugs into his drink and he collapsed at the dance? It says in the file that he was taken by ambulance to the ICU, where he remained in fair condition until he died the next afternoon."

I nod. She's got all her dirty little files and reports on me, so why can't she just read them, ask me a few questions, and write my fucking recommendation already?

"His doctor testified that Omar was in stable condition and looking to make a recovery when he died unexpectedly. Omar's father testified that he saw you leaving Omar's room shortly before he went into cardiac arrest. Want to tell me about that?"

Not really. "When I heard he was still on life support, I panicked. I couldn't risk him waking up and telling someone that I'd drugged him. I mean, I probably could've gotten away with it— it would be my word against his, and he was already drunk. It wouldn't be far-fetched for people to believe he'd taken some random mix of drugs. Kids OD all the time."

"Yes, but they usually don't use Ativan to party, considering it makes you extremely drowsy. It would've been found in his blood work."

"People take all sorts of things and are sold the wrong drugs. It's not like most drug dealers are honest. Everything is cut with something."

"So what did you do the day after the dance, when you realized he was still alive?"

I tuck my hair behind my ears, pull my legs up, and sit cross-legged on the sofa. "I took one of Brianna's syringes with me to the hospital, snuck into Omar's room, and injected an air bubble into his IV line."

"Why did you do that?"

"I'd seen on it television. The guy injected air into some woman's vein and she died of an embolism. I thought it would be a clever way to finish him off without leaving any evidence behind. My hope was that the doctors would think he took a turn, or that the embolism had been a tragic fluke resulting from all the injections he'd had while they were working on him."

"You really thought of everything, didn't you?"

The tone of utter pissyness is back in Dr. Nancy's voice. I feel like a ping-pong ball with all this back and forth—she's reserved and empathetic, and then her voice drips distain and disgust.

"Do you regret killing him?" There's a biting sound on the word "regret."

I make my eyes wide. "At the time I didn't, but now all I can think about is Omar convulsing on the grimy gym floor. The paramedics cutting his shirt open and jolting his heart with those electric pads. And his father . . ." I stop like it's all too much.

Dr. Clafin tilts her head. "What about his father?" she asks empathetically again. *Make your mind up already.*

"After Omar died, his father asked to speak with me, since he'd seen me coming out of his room. My dad made me meet him at the station to explain why I was there. I gave him some lame excuse, but his face . . . He looked so completely broken. Mr. Murphy sat in front of me and cried, and I was completely detached from it."

She makes a quick scribble in her notepad before leaning in and making her dreaded eye contact with me. "I'd like to move on now, to what you did after you drugged Omar and left the dance. I'd also like you to see the video of you discussing it with Sergeant Estevez."

I inhale a long, loud breath, making my eyes well up, but I don't say anything. Dr. Clafin gets up and changes the fucking DVD, ignoring my pending emotional meltdown.

"The clip is only a couple of minutes long. Bear with me. You're doing great. I really mean that, Ryann. I'm very proud of your willingness to go through this process. It's obvious you're putting a lot of effort in, and I appreciate that."

And now she's nice again. God, I can't keep up.

I ask for a bottle of water and she gets me one from the minifridge. We both know it's a stalling tactic, but she lets me have it.

She presses play, and the television screen goes from black to the grainy image of me and Estevez. It must be a different day, because my hair is up and I'm wearing a yellow shirt instead of the hospital gown I wore in the other videos.

Nancy skips ahead and I wonder how she knows when to stop. Maybe she has the timestamp memorized.

"Okay, are you ready?" she asks me.

"Whenever you are." I pull in my legs and wrap my arms around them, resting my head on my knees.

I'm bracing myself. I truly have no idea what the 'me' on tape is going to say. Each time it's about to play it feels like I have a small heart attack. I wonder if Dr. Clafin can see my reddening face or the small beads of sweat that spring up at my hairline.

Teenage me is sitting up in the hospital bed. I have a bit more color to my cheeks and my hair looks fresh, the embarrassing greasiness finally gone. It was difficult to concentrate on my interview about Yvonne when all I saw was how gross my hair looked. I remember my mom had come in and helped me shower. A female officer had to be in the bathroom just in case I attacked my mother or tried to escape.

"Listen, Sergeant, can we speed this up? Talking to you each day is boring me." In reality I loved talking to him about it. I loved watching him hang on my every word. I loved the repulsion in his eyes. But he didn't need to know that.

Estevez is leaning back in his chair, playing with a pen on the tabletop between us. (I wonder now if he wanted to stab me with it. At the time, I'd wondered how long it would take me to grab it from him and stick it into the side of his throat. Funny, the things you remember.) *"The faster you tell me about your crime spree, the sooner I leave and you can be locked up in prison for the rest of your life."*

Teen Ryann moves her hand like it's a mouth. "Blah, blah, blah."

"You were pretty careless at Stanley Hastings's house. Very sloppy leaving your bike on his front lawn." *He makes a tsk, tsk sound.* (I remember that really infuriated me.)

"It wasn't my finest moment, but it still wasn't enough to get you or your merry band of idiots to arrest me."

"Yeah, the 'my bike was stolen' excuse was real original."

I shrug. "Your point?"

"I know you didn't like your teacher, but why not leave a burning bag of shit on his front porch like other kids? Why did you have to burn him alive?"

"Hastings was a prick. Not unlike yourself, actually."

"I received some statements that Stanley Hastings used to pick on students in class and that not long before his murder, he singled you out. Is that why he fit your profile—because he embarrassed you?"

"He was more than rude. He was cruel. The school never did anything about it, and if I didn't step in, he would continue to bully and harass inno-cent kids. I couldn't have that. I had a responsibility to get rid of him."

"So now you're a hero? Judge and jury?"

"Something like that."

"How'd you do it?"

"I took a canister of gasoline to his house, poured it on his door, lit the match, and he burned. Simple as that."

"If it was so simple, why did you screw up and leave your bike behind?"

"I liked the flames. They were pretty. I guess I spent a little too long admiring my work. I heard the sirens, had no idea how close they were, and couldn't risk going back for my bike. The neighbors had already started coming out to watch the show."

"You took off before you were one-hundred-percent sure Hastings was dead. How did you know you weren't going to screw up and leave him alive —a witness to turn you in?"

Teenage me smiles a big old grin, edges a touch closer to Estevez, and says, "Because I watched him through the glass. I watched him burn."

CHAPTER FOURTEEN

*N*ancy paused the video. It seemed a good place to stop. Her patient was slack-jawed, with two startled green eyes, staring. "Are you all right, Ryann?"

Ryann swallowed a gulp of water from her plastic bottle. "I don't know."

"Why don't you start by telling me how you're feeling?"

"I'm completely freaked out. I'm . . . confused."

Nancy remained silent, hoping to encourage Ryann to keep speaking and exploring her emotions.

Twiddling the bottle cap between her thumb and index finger, Ryann stared at the paused image of her younger self. "You can't understand how weird this is. I'm watching myself. I know it's my face, my voice. I even have some memories of the things I'm saying, but I don't remember the interview with Estevez. I hated him. Why would I have sat there and told him all of that?" She kept her knees pulled up to her chest, hugging them. She looked like a scared child, not a crazed killer.

Nancy shook the thought away and remembered the callous glare in Ryann's eyes as she told Estevez—with glee—that she'd watched her teacher burn. A small pang clutched her insides. "Had you ever experienced memory loss before the summer of the murders?"

Ryann's eyes moved around in her head, first to the left, then to the right. "Not that I know of. But . . . I didn't even know I was having memory loss when it was happening."

"You never had gaps of time that were unaccounted for, or found yourself someplace you didn't remember going?"

"Maybe a few times, but doesn't that happen to everyone?"

"So you recall all the details that you told Sergeant Estevez?"

"I guess. I don't know. Look, I already told you I don't remember giving the stupid interview! Are you trying to trick me or something?"

Nancy shook her head. "No, I'm not trying to trick you. I'm asking if you told the events accurately in the taped interview, or if you embellished any of the details. Did you fill in any gaps because you didn't want to admit to Estevez that you didn't know something?"

Ryann was quiet for a moment. Head resting on her knees. After a few minutes, she said, "I guess it's possible. But some of the gaps could be because it's been so many years. What if I've rewritten history in my head since then? I'm not sure I'm the most reliable, considering my mental state all those years ago."

"That's you reasoning now as a twenty-seven-year-old woman. Think of a confused, teenage Ryann. Would she be so confident to admit she didn't know something? Perhaps you didn't want anyone to see that you weren't as fully in control as you appeared."

"Maybe." She bit her bottom lip, huffing aloud.

"Do you remember killing Hastings?"

"Most of it. I remember pouring the gas around his front door, lighting the match and throwing it down, igniting the flames. They were so hot and bright. The flames spread so quickly, I remember being shocked and stepping back before I ran off."

Nancy's heart skipped a beat. "Wait, what?"

"I said I ran off."

"You ran off after you set the fire in the front of his house?"

"Yes."

"Did you go into the back yard, Ryann?"

"No. I lit the front on fire and when I heard the sirens I ran down the side of the house into the neighbor's back yard, and then through to the street on the other side."

Nancy sat up straighter. "Are there any blackouts or gaps of time from when you set the fire to when you ran into his neighbor's yard?" Her voice possessed an urgency that she couldn't disguise.

"I don't think so. I remember that murder, I'm not sure why, since some of the others are so shaky. Why?"

Nancy didn't answer right away. "The forensic report on the fire showed that gasoline had been poured on the front *and the back* doors of the house. On the tape you said you watched him burn through the glass. His body was found at the back door. He'd been trying to escape, but didn't make it. The report corroborates that the fire started in the front, but gasoline had been poured all over the back entrance and set on fire there as well. That's what killed him."

Ryann sat staring with a blank, confused look on her face. "That . . . that can't be right. I was there, and I never went to the back. I could've sworn he died in the front. I saw him when I first got there. He was asleep in his recliner." Her voice rose higher with each word.

Nancy removed her glasses and rubbed the bridge of her nose. The way Ryann's eyes searched the room frantically as if searching for the memories—the answers to what really happened that night —nearly convinced Nancy that she wasn't lying.

Nancy had the gaping file on her lap, like a security blanket. The file was factual. It encompassed the things she knew for certain: names, dates, addresses, causes of deaths, evidence found that connected Ryann directly. Her decades of experience and research taught her that memory was a tricky and complex thing. Most people failed to recount specific instances with perfect accuracy. A huge majority of witnesses mistakenly identified perpetrators when presented with prison line-ups or collections of photographs to choose from. Had Ryann blacked out, or was she just misremembering?

"Do you think you remember everything about Hastings's house? This is important."

"I don't know," Ryann panted, her breath coming in short, panicked bursts. Her normally smooth forehead was wrinkled. "I was incredibly emotional back then. All I could focus on was completing my mission and getting as many kills as I could." Her hands covered her face. Nancy could hear her heavy breathing beneath. "That sounds so heartless." Ryann lifted her head and met Nancy's gaze. "It's like I was under some trance or something. I was obsessed with getting rid of people that deserved it and was sure I'd chosen wisely, but now I worry that I was using any excuse to justify what I was doing."

This was Nancy's moment. Ryann was vulnerable. She had to strike in the hope the girl's guard was down and she'd break and show her true colors. Nancy kept her voice stern. "And you still think some people deserve it?"

"No! I may not always like everyone or agree with them, but I don't want them to *die*. I don't want to hurt anyone. Not anymore. But how . . . how could you or anyone else trust that?" Ryann pulled herself against the back of the sofa, rubbing the tops of her thighs, something she often did under duress.

"Admit it, Ryann. You would kill someone now if you had the chance. If you knew you'd never be caught," Nancy snapped.

Looking up with pleading eyes, Ryann said, "No. It's not who I am anymore. The best way I can describe it is that it's like having an epiphany. You wake up one morning, and things that would've seemed crazy to you before suddenly seem completely reasonable. Necessary. But you don't see the line—the distinction between before and now. You're just different. I didn't notice it. Didn't question it. I can't tell you . . ." Ryann inhaled a ragged breath. She sounded on the verge of frantic tears.

"I need you to think back. Did you ever have moments when

you felt like you weren't quite you? Did anyone in your life ever tell you during that time—before, even—that you possessed a different personality?"

Ryann shook her head and gave a sharp laugh. "What, like multiple personalities? You can't be serious."

Nancy's back straightened. "It is a real psychiatric disorder and quite serious."

"No. I wish I could blame this horrific mess on an alternate personality." She laughed. "Yes, I've read about it. Watched reruns of *Oprah*—the women love that crap in here—but no. I did what I did. I may be missing some time, but I remember enough to know it was all me." She paused for a long moment. "Though it feels like it was a different version of me entirely."

Nancy relaxed. The tension behind her eyes eased slightly. It would have been easy to use that scapegoat. It wasn't the sole reason she'd proposed it, but she was curious to see how someone as desperate as Ryann would react. And yet there she sat, owning all the horrendous things she'd done. "What made you believe you were missing time?"

"I'd be somewhere and have no knowledge of how I'd gotten there or how long I'd been there. Sometimes even why I went there in the first place."

Ryann's thin arms poked out from her baggy sleeves. She usually wore a hoodie, so it startled Nancy to see just how frail she looked. That those slight arms gripped a belt around Yvonne Borgdon's throat and smashed a brick into a young girl's head. "And when was the first time you noticed you were somewhere or doing something you couldn't explain?"

"I'm not one hundred percent sure, but I think sometime in May. A month before Olivia."

"Can you explain what happened?"

"I woke up, got ready, and went to school. My first class was English, then all of a sudden it was third period and I was in history. I thought I was crazy. I checked my notes, and I'd written pages for all the classes in between. I must've attended, taken notes, and talked to my friends, but I didn't remember any of it. Two hours gone. It was really odd. I didn't say anything to anyone because I was too freaked out."

Nancy jotted some notes. *Traumatic brain injury? Silent seizures? Brain tumor? Drug or alcohol use?* "Did that happen regularly?"

"Several times that I know for sure, but I suppose if I had memory loss I might not remember all of them, right? The chunks of time started getting longer. Once, there was a two-day hole."

She underlined the words *retrograde amnesia* in her notebook. "Did your parents or sister notice anything odd going on with you?"

"Not that I know of. No one said a word to me. I thought I was hiding it well enough. Maybe I was. There was obviously a lot they didn't notice." Ryann picked at her fingernail. She hadn't answered Estevez. Maybe she'd tell Nancy, now all these years later.

"Did you know your actions were wrong if you were hiding your activities from everyone?"

"I remember thinking at the time that no one understood what I was trying to accomplish. No one could understand me because I was special. It was as though I was some sort of chosen one, and I had a job to do." She winced, pinching the bridge of her nose. "This sounds ridiculous, but kind of like Batman. Secret identity— normal by day, vigilante by night. It sounds insane, I know."

Nancy nodded, underlining *identity crisis* and *psychosis* on the yellow paper. Ryann still wouldn't say she knew it was wrong at the time.

Ryann's eyes were trained on her. "Do you think the time gaps had something to do with the murders?"

Nancy was careful to remain stone-faced. "In what way?"

"I don't know. It's just that the two kind of started around the same time. Like I said, I don't think I had any blackouts or whatever before spring of that year. And then my personality started to change. I didn't always fantasize and dream of murdering innocent people. It wasn't my childhood dream." Ryann looked down and picked at her cuticles.

"It's something to look into further." Placing her pen and book on the desktop, Nancy leaned closer to Ryann. Proximity aided in building rapport. "What do you remember of Yvonne Borgdon's murder—not what we viewed on the recording, but actual memories?"

Ryann leaned back, exhaling loudly. "Watching her the week before. Going to her house and looking through her bedroom window, sitting behind her in class, that kind of stuff. The next thing I remembered was standing over her body in her bedroom."

"So you don't recall the bike ride over, breaking into the house, hiding in her closet, or the strangulation?" *How could this be?* The kill was the most intense of all the activities. Normally such high emotion tied the individual to the experience. It was surprising that after all of Ryann's apparent excitement and planning she didn't remember the pinnacle event.

Her head jolted up. "No, I don't, and I don't understand why." Her voice was strained with what appeared to be anxiety and possibly grief. "We both watched me sitting there, practically giddy, explaining every detail. How can I have remembered it so clearly back then but not now? People have memories from years and years earlier. I remember Christmas from when I was six. I got a ballerina Barbie and a turquoise tricycle. It doesn't make sense, and it's so frustrating."

"Why is it frustrating?" It was risky, but Nancy needed to push her. "Is it that you worked hard to plan and plot the murder and it's as though you never actually accomplished it because you have no recollection? Does it upset you that you can't relive the kill in your head whenever you want?"

Her eyes widened, leaving the fine skin around her eyes to crease slightly. She was young to have the beginnings of crow's feet, but the stress of being locked up would wear on anyone. "I don't do that."

"Do what?"

"Relive the kills. You're asking me questions I can't answer, and if I can't answer you, I don't have any chance of getting out of here." Ryann crumpled in her seat.

Nancy rolled her chair closer to her. "I want you to try to do something for me. I know it's difficult, but try to stop thinking about what will or won't get you released. Concentrate on the process. Trust me and what we're doing here. If you continue to focus on the end result, it will be a much harder road to travel down. I have your best interest in mind, Ryann. I promise." She smiled and was surprised that she'd meant every word. Ryann nodded. "Tell me what happened after you left the Borgdon home."

"I rode home, put my clothes in the laundry, and showered. I dried off, changed and made a drink. My plan had succeeded, so I thought I deserved it."

"Was that part of your ritual?"

"Yes. I always drank after."

"Why?"

"I don't know. *The Greats*—God I hate saying it now—they seemed to do that, so I suppose I thought it was a sophisticated, celebratory thing to do after."

"Was there any other reason?"

She looked thoughtful for a minute and gave a small, shy grin. "Maybe. You hear me in the videos all cocky and proud, but I was shaky and freaked out after Yvonne. It could have been the amount of adrenaline going through me, but I'd been nervous. Drinking took the edge off."

"So what was your drink of choice?"

"Usually rum or vodka with a bit of Coke. But by the end I was able to down straight shots."

"Did you tend to drink often, or a lot at one time?"

"At times. I thought I was seasoned enough to handle it when I totally wasn't. I was even sick to my stomach a few times."

"Did you ever get drunk enough to black out?"

"Only once. And I'm not even sure that's what it was. I was drinking in my bedroom one night after a kill. I woke up the next morning with no memory of having fallen asleep. I suppose I could have just passed out. When I woke, I panicked and checked the activity on my cell and computer to make sure I hadn't revealed anything to anyone."

"And had you?"

Ryann's shoulders relaxed a touch, just enough for Nancy to notice. It was a gesture of relief. "No, thank God. But it scared me enough to cool it on the beverages. Wait, you don't think all my blackouts were from drinking, do you?"

"You tell me. Were all your memory gaps after you'd engaged in drinking?"

"No. Not at all. It was only that one time. The others were during school or on weekends hanging out at home. There was no way I could've drank at those times."

Nancy nodded and wrote *aware of consequences* in her notebook. "After you killed Yvonne, were sure you had gotten away with it? Was there any part of you that was worried or frightened about what you'd done?"

"No. None at all. Like I said, I thought the universe was taking care of me somehow. As long as I carried out my work, I'd be okay."

Nancy jotted down the words *God complex.*

The session was coming to the three-hour mark and Nancy's eyes burned.

She needed to address the nagging feeling in her gut that had crept up during the last two sessions. Serial killers relished the kill, but they also enjoyed reliving it, which meant talking about it, remembering the sensory details associated to it, and using trophies or any other means of connecting them back to the moment of death and the victims themselves. There were physiological responses, unable to be repressed by the person, which happened when they were excited. Ryann should have had at least a few of them when she spoke of the murders, but there'd been nothing.

Nancy had seen tears, heard Ryann speak of shame and even remorse, but was that for her benefit, or was it real?

She needed to go over her notes. Regroup. "Ryann, I think we covered a good amount. Let's call it a day. I'll be back tomorrow. Thank you for your candor and hard work. I know this isn't easy for you."

Ryann's shoulders rolled forward like she was releasing a burden she'd been carrying. "If you're sure you've had enough."

CHAPTER FIFTEEN

*J*bet Dr. Clafin would poke me with a stick for eight hours a day if I let her. It's obvious she's been playing nice with me, acting concerned about my well-being and health. It's all to build a 'connection' and get me to trust her. I should be angry that she's attempting to manipulate me, but it's sort of fun. It's been a long time since I've had a challenge.

The bell rings inside the block, signaling that it's chow time. We line up, single file, along the wall. A few COs, one in front, two in the middle, and one at the rear, usher us out to the cafeteria through the two sets of steel doors and down the hallway. We're cattle.

"That was a long one, huh?" Steph whispers in my ear from behind. She and Jodi have sidled up next to me.

I nod and keep walking, head up, eyes forward. We're not supposed to talk in line-up. I don't need any reprimands on my file when I'm so close. "The doctor has a lot of questions," I whisper when the guard closest to me looks away. I know Jodi wants to hear the answers too. Everyone in here does. I appreciate that they're all too terrified of me to ever ask. Valentina made that error once. Cornered me in the library and asked if everything everyone was saying about me was true. She pushed me into a shelf, pressing her giant chest into me. She towered over me by a good foot and a half, her hot, rancid breath blowing in my face. I have a standard answer: "Depends on what they're saying." But the threat was intensified that time. I straightened my back, squared my shoulders, pressed my nose against hers and said, "I stabbed a cop in his gut and turned the blade inside him as he looked up at me with terror in his eyes. He was a lot bigger than you." I glowered at her with a crazy 'test me' kind of look. She backed away, muttering.

It was a stupid thing to do, but I'd only been here a few weeks and needed to secure my rep. Everyone knows that you need to stand your ground or you'll be someone's bitch—or worse. I knew I'd be an instant target. But I hadn't been bluffing with Valentina. I would've clawed through her face if I had to. She might've had size on her side, but I had rage and nothing to lose.

Unlike now.

Most inmates would trade their own mothers for a reduced sentence, so I fully expect Valentina to suddenly remember our encounter twelve years ago and tell one of the COs.

At the lunch counter I hold out my gray plastic tray with the white plastic plate, deflating when I see meatloaf, some waxy green beans, and a cube of what I think is mashed potatoes. It's accompanied by a small container of milk and a half-melted chocolate cupcake that's sweating in a clear plastic bag.

I miss my mom's cooking, especially around the holidays. When she visits, she brings cookies or brownies. Every year I get a small chocolate birthday cake, but I really yearn for her turkey dinners with all the fixings. You can't bring a whole dinner to a prison, though I'm sure she's tried.

Visiting with her is nice, but it also kind of sucks. She asks me how I am over and over. We do the small-talk thing—she briefs me on my dad (not that I give a fuck), Brianna and her kids (also no fucks), the rest of the family, and even Bao-yu, though Mom's the only person who will still talk to me. I always thought I didn't need people. Maybe that was because I had so many to choose from and could take what I needed from them when I wanted it. Now I get to choose from the eighty ladies in here and my mother.

Dinner's over and we're herded back to F Block. At least Dr. Nancy's office gives me a break from this desolate scenery. Most of the women sit in front of the television or at the tables for a round of cards. I head to the TV in the hope that something else about my case will come up.

I'm not seated for more than five minutes when Jodi and Steph pull up chairs.

"So you've been seeing the shrink for what now, a week?" Jodi says.

I nod, but don't take my eyes off the screen.

"What kinds of things does she make you talk about?" Steph asks with an inflection at the end.

Jodi doesn't let me answer before saying, "Do you have to go over all the murders with her—like tell her all the ways you did it?"

Truthfully, I'm kind of shocked she has the guts to say this to me. Guts, or she's a complete idiot. "We discuss a lot of things. None that I'm allowed to talk about. It might hurt my case." Even if I could tell them, I wouldn't. "Hey, Steph, what ever happened with your visit from what's his name?"

"Oh, Joshua? Yeah, it was good." She gets a stupid love-struck look on her face that I suppose is sort of endearing. "He's adorable."

"Too bad you can't get a conjugal visit." Jodi elbows me and chuckles while sweet Stephanie blushes. Okay, I'm over this now.

I look at the clock. It's 7:00 p.m. I call my mom every Wednesday evening. She always blocks that one night off so she'll never miss my calls. I stand and stretch. "Catch you girls in a bit."

There are six payphones on the south wall. I dial and wait for the dreaded robotic voice that says, "There is a collect call from the Dungrave County Prison. Will you accept the charges?" A small part of me always clenches up. Shoulders and jaw tight. Fingers a death grip around the receiver, because maybe this time she won't accept the call. Maybe she's finally gotten sick of me and moved on. I get a strong though brief wave of sickness as I remember the first few times I called my father. He hung up every single time. I knew better than to try Bri. I have nothing to say to her anyway.

"Hello."

"Hi, Mom. How are you?" I breathe out and my body relaxes.

"I'm good, honey. How are the sessions with the psychiatrist going?" My mom always speaks to me with a smile in her voice. It transports me back to a time when I lived with her and she'd make me dinner, when we'd watch a movie and talk over half of it, or when she'd nag me to be home on time.

"They're intense, but going fine. It's so hard to read her, but she's really nice. I have a pretty good feeling about it."

"That's wonderful. Are you staying healthy in there? I worry you're going to get pneumonia. You'd think they'd allow you extra blankets. It's flu season and it's not like they sufficiently heat the place. I'm always freezing there on Sundays."

My sweet mother. Discussing the little things is her way of coping. We've never discussed the real possibility that I might die in here. Ever since I was arrested she's pumped into me the idea that I'll be free again one day. I don't think she's ever accepted the things I've done. How could she, and still look at me like I'm her little girl? That's the thing that really amazes me about her—she didn't look at me any differently after she found out what I did. Not like my father, and Bri, and everyone I've ever met. Like the friends and family who sat across from me in the courtroom over those three weeks, staring at me with white-hot hatred.

"I miss you, Mom."

"I miss you too, darling, but I'll see you in four more days. How are you holding up?"

"I'm used to it. A decade will do that to you."

"I know, but I can imagine it might be a bit harder knowing you could be so close to getting out."

My mother, the eternal optimist. "It's true. I'm getting a bit antsy. I have another week or two of seeing Dr. Clafin, and then I think Mr. Wagner and Ms. Roche are going to have a meeting with me and go over it all before they send the package in. They're aiming to get me a commuted sentence. I don't know what I'll do if this doesn't go through. I can't spend another year in here. I really will go crazy."

"Don't say that. You're so strong. The board will see how much you've changed. Chin up, my darling. We can do this."

"I appreciate the pep talk, but *we* have not been wasting away in a cement cell for half our lives." It comes out harsh, and I know she's only trying to help, but her silver-lining, bright-side-of-life attitude is hard to swallow today.

"I know, I'm sorry, I didn't mean to—"

"No, I'm sorry I bit your head off. Thanks for believing in me." The familiar static interrupts. The robotic voice is about to tell me I have a whopping twenty seconds left. "Ugh, you'd think they'd let me talk since they're not paying a fucking dime. It's all about control in here." My hand vise-grips the receiver. "Anyway, I'd better go. I love you."

"We'll get through this, honey. I love you too. See you Sunday."

CHAPTER SIXTEEN

ancy shuts the door to her bedroom. Her sanctuary. She'd remodeled it after James's death. It held too many memories, too many emotions of them together.

She traded her black dress pants, pink silk blouse, and high heels for flannel pyjamas and fuzzy socks. Exhausted, she made her way to the bathroom, washed her face, and brushed her teeth. Anything to get the day off her.

She barely managed dinner. After leaving the prison, she'd gone directly to the office. A moderately warm bowl of soup and four pre-packaged saltines was all she'd had the energy—or appetite— to make. The idea of snuggling into bed with a good book or losing herself in a movie sounded like heaven, but she couldn't get Ryann out of her thoughts. She needed to go to bed and shut it all out. At least for a few hours.

Turning on her bedside lamp, she wriggled under the covers, bringing them up to her chest. She placed her glasses on her chest and allowed her eyes to close for a minute, savouring the quiet. No heavy clang of metal doors or shouting women, no odors of sweat and bleach, and no harsh fluorescent lighting assaulting her eyes. How did Ryann do it day after day, year after year?

Her thoughts jolted back three years.

It was always in the back of her mind. Haunting her so fiercely she didn't think she'd ever escape it.

Keith referred to it as her 'mistake'—as if she'd simply put a red shirt in a load of whites. Three years before, Nancy had been assigned the case of a twenty-five-year-old woman accused of killing her husband. Everything seemed to line up perfectly. The wife looked good for it. Nancy was certain. Her evaluation was as close to perfect as possible. Evidence doesn't lie. So Nancy voted against parole and made such a compelling argument that the majority of the board were swayed. One even said he wasn't qualified to decide, because what did he know about the criminal mind? She was the doctor. The expert. She swelled with confidence and blind faith. She didn't want to feel superhuman, but she did.

Two weeks later the woman hanged herself in her cell.

A week after that, new DNA evidence was found that exonerated her.

Nancy had condemned her to a life behind bars. She was responsible for her death.

And here she was again, praying she'd get it right this time.

It was ten thirty, and her body wanted her to call it a night. Instead, Nancy reached across her bed to where she'd tossed her briefcase and took out Ryann's file. The weight of it bent her wrist back as she attempted to lift it from the tight leather pocket. She propped herself up on her pillows and set it against her knees before guiding her glasses back on.

"Who are you, Ryann Wilkanson?" She was a just over a week into the evaluation and she still didn't have an answer. Her opinion seemed to move on a continuum, sliding back and forth between her belief that Ryann was a calculated and cold-blooded killer and her conviction that she was a sweet young woman who may have been so mentally ill that she made irreparable choices with tragic consequences. What had been documented pre-trial about her mental capacity and her ability to stand trial? How could any doctors declare her fit with all the blackouts and symptoms Ryann appeared to have had? She was clearly delusional with all her mission talk.

Unless no one knew?

She was still waiting to get her hands on a copy of both the prosecution's and the defense's competency evaluations.

Keith had sent Mandy and another assistant, Gerry, to see if Nancy needed any help sorting through the endless files. But there was something about this case. Something that made Nancy want to keep it close and share it with no one—not even Keith. Speaking of, where had he been? She was sure he'd be checking up on her but it had been radio silence.

Sorting through the papers, Nancy stopped at something—a stack of letters for or against Ryann's release. On the top of the pile was a letter from Ryann's sister, Brianna.

Regarding: Ryann Wilkanson
    DOC#57629847
    9712 Sterling Way
    Dungrave County Prison
    Dungrave, Colorado 34764

November 8, 2016

Executive Clemency Advisory Board
    136 State Capitol
    Denver, Colorado 80203-1792

To the Distinguished Board,

I am writing in regard to my sister Ryann Wilkanson.

Ever since we were young, I knew there was something different about my sister. She seemed like your average kid, playing, singing, and dancing around the house, annoying me when I was with my friends or boyfriend. On paper, she appeared to be the poster child for a well-adjusted, middle-class kid. But something was off. It was subtle. Perhaps it was only a feeling—an instinct—I had about her.

It wasn't obvious and so I could never quite pinpoint it, but my sister was never frightened growing up. Creepy tales and horrifically graphic news reports didn't get to her—well, not until she noticed that I'd been observing her. It was only then that she claimed fear, notably shivering and taking shaky breaths.

But it was all for my benefit and for the benefit of every other person she was around. You see, there were glimpses of who my sister really is, even back then. A cold, ruthless killer. A psychopath. A sociopath. Call it whatever you want. Label it however you need, but know one thing: if my sister is released, she will do it all again, and this time she'll be smart enough not to get caught.

I ask the board that you keep my sister, Ryann Wilkanson, in prison for the remainder of her life, without ever giving her the opportunity to apply for parole again.

I have no love left for her. She is nothing to me. People ask me if I'm afraid of her, and the truth is that I am afraid of what evil lives inside her and what horror she is capable of. I ask you to consider this: if she killed six people with such brutal means at fifteen years old, what will she do now, as an adult?

I pray you never find out because you keep her locked away.

Thank you.

Sincerely,

Brianna Shrunk

Nancy found it intriguing that both Ryann's father and sister not only abandoned her, but condemned her. Most parents and siblings of child murderers stand by them. They love them unconditionally, and often make excuses for their horrid behaviors, but Brianna didn't seem to have an ounce of empathy for her sister. Had they ever been close?

Nancy needed to speak with Brianna, but the elusive sister had ignored four emails and two phone calls. Her home address seemed to be unlisted, though perhaps Sergeant Estevez could help with that.

Nancy's head was too heavy to lift off the pillow, so she pushed the files beside her, curled up, and went to sleep.

Nancy's alarm beeped. Her hand reached through the maze of blankets, fumbling for the cruel device. Her eyes were crusted shut with sleep. Grabbing her glasses from the bedside table, she slid them on and immediately checked her email. It was the first thing she did on weekdays, before she even put a foot on the floor. It helped wake her up.

Her inbox was overflowing, typical and dreadful, but her gaze froze on a familiar name. *Elizabeth Wilkanson.*

Intrigued, she clicked. Ryann's mother was on a list of people she wanted to speak to, though she hadn't gotten around to contacting her yet. As the mother, she knew the most about Ryann's childhood and upbringing, but she was also the only person who stayed in close touch with Ryann. Nancy understood that Elizabeth's take on things would be skewed. But then so would Brianna's, just in the opposite direction. Maybe between the two of them, Nancy would get some semblance of who Ryann had been all those years ago.

Elizabeth's email was short, a few sentences thanking Nancy for working with Ryann and asking to meet. She'd left a phone number. While Nancy normally wouldn't call when she could email, she had a cancellation in her schedule for the afternoon and hoped to fill it.

She dialed the number, though her eyes were still tired and could barely focus on the screen. It rang four times before she heard a woman's voice.

"Is this Elizabeth?"

"Yes."

"Hello, this is Dr. Nancy Clafin. How are you?"

"Oh, what a pleasant surprise. I wasn't expecting to hear from you so soon. Thank you for getting back to me." Elizabeth sounded perky and a touch erratic. Not unexpected for a mother who'd gone through the trauma she had.

"I know it's last minute, but I have an opening today. Would you be able to meet? I'd like to discuss some things pertinent to Ryann's evaluation."

"Today . . . Yes, of course. What time?"

"Could you come by my office around one?"

"Yes. What's the address? Wait, I need a pen . . ."

"I'll email you the details. See you then."

"Okay, great. Thank you again, Dr. Clafin."

The glee in Mrs. Wilkanson's voice made Nancy want to burrow back under the covers. Mothers were one of the most difficult subjects to interview. They were usually overly emotional, with attachment issues that prevented them from being unbiased. It was understandable but also frustrating. This meeting was meant to establish a baseline for Ryann, not provide an opportunity for Elizabeth to plead her daughter's case.

She arrived at the office around nine, giving her enough time to go over some evidence before Mrs. Wilkanson arrived. Because Nancy hadn't told her to come alone, she wondered briefly if David would be with her. Truthfully, Nancy didn't even know if they were still together. It wasn't unusual for couples to divorce after a huge family heartbreak, and this more than qualified.

From what she'd gathered, Officer Wilkanson was much less involved in his daughter's case than Elizabeth. Nancy wanted to get their impressions separately. They'd had the last twelve years to discuss it and had likely built a joint narrative around their daughter and her crimes. But perhaps not. Parents sometimes harbored drastically different views of a situation. It would be interesting to observe.

Settling in her desk, she propped her bagel in front of her and took a long sip of her coffee before pulling out a clear plastic bag full of eight-by-ten crime scene photos. She was looking for any clues that were atypical for a serial killer or psychopath.

Maybe the bagel could wait.

For some reason, she was drawn to the ones of Olivia. That poor girl. Maybe studying her little body would help Nancy see something in Ryann. She breathed slow and deep, causing slight light-headedness. No one wanted to see dead bodies, especially gruesome ones, but child victims were even more challenging. Her stomach clutched and tightened pre-emptively.

Olivia lay crumpled on her side on the gritty concrete of a darkened alleyway. A pool of blood had settled under her body, mostly at the head, where the worst bodily damage had taken place.

The little girl had been struck in the head and face with a clay brick approximately a dozen times. Small fragments of brick, along with tiny pebbles, were embedded in her pallid cheek and forehead. Olivia was blonde, though you couldn't tell with the volume of blood that her hair had absorbed. She was on her right side. Her arm hung limply on the ground. Her legs were splayed. But worst of all, her eyes were open.

They were a startling blue.

She was small, even for the tender age of twelve.

Nancy flipped to the next picture. It was a cropped shot of Olivia's face and head. The gashes were severe and jagged. Bits of brain matter speckled her face. Some was embedded in the brick that had been discarded beside her. Why had Ryann left the murder weapon at the scene? Maybe she didn't care about hiding it, or perhaps it thrilled her to think about leaving it for someone to find. Or maybe she didn't realize she needed to get rid of it, because she was so dissociated from the crime.

Nancy's mouth was dry. She reached for her coffee and swallowed, though her stomach was in no mood to accept it without a fight.

Her hands fumbled for the other picture. It was a school photo. Olivia sat straight, eyes bright, big silly grin, gorgeous blonde hair framing her petite face. It was nice to see her this way, but it only magnified the horror of what had become of her.

Nancy rifled through the binder until she found the ninth-grade photo of Ryann smiling widely, wearing a pretty green sweater that matched her eyes. The two could have been sisters.

Nancy went through a mental list of what she knew so far. Ryann had clearly remembered the events when Estevez questioned her in the hospital. She had seemed of sound mind, even ordering her lawyer out. She claimed she knew what she was doing and confessed to all of it, waiving all her legal rights. The Ryann in the tapes was brash, sharp, and maniacal. Her confessions were much more than informational. She was bragging. Yet she appeared almost equally detached. Perhaps it was something in her eyes. A near vacancy.

"What happened to you, Ryann?" Nancy collected the pile of photos and traded them for the next set. The first image was of a red-haired female splayed out on her bed, half undressed with her sweatpants down around her ankles. Her face was obscured. The room was pink with lavender shelves, and porcelain dolls and teddy bears crowded in a huddle on the bedspread. It was a sweet girl's room. Except for Yvonne Borgdon's strangled body in the center of it.

Nancy flipped through the remainder of the Borgdon pictures but stopped when she landed on one that showed the victim's face. A gasp tore from her throat. Her hand went to her mouth and she dropped the photo. Her body quivered as her stomach lurched. Examining the pictures was necessary to truly understand what her patient had been capable of. She reopened her eyes. A thick purple ligature mark encircled the girl's neck, and her eye was nearly out of its socket. The intense pressure required to do that . . . Ryann must have been in a rage, but even then . . . Could a hundred-pound girl have the strength to impose that kind of pressure?

As a doctor, Nancy understood what could happen to the body during strangulation, but this type of injury usually occurred from hanging, not manual choking—even with a belt. Perhaps a large, muscular man could have the strength, but Ryann? Nancy considered intoxication. Cocaine, meth, and some hallucinogens were known to elevate physical strength. But Ryann had insisted she only indulged in alcohol, which was a depressant.

The intercom on her desk rang. Nancy picked up her phone. "Yes."

"Your eleven o'clock is here. Liz Wilkanson."

"Thank you, Claire. You can send her back." Where had the time gone? She hadn't even eaten lunch yet. She hurriedly collected the photographs and tossed them into her top drawer. It wasn't a long walk from the reception area. There was no time to arrange them neatly in their plastic sleeve. She didn't want Mrs. Wilkanson to see her daughter's victims. She hoped fleetingly that Elizabeth had had the good sense to leave the courtroom when they were exhibited twelve years before.

There was a light rapping on the door. Nancy strode over and opened it, revealing a tall, thin, blonde woman with a reluctant smile. "Hello, Dr. Clafin. Thank you for seeing me."

"My pleasure. Please come in." Nancy took a step back and cleared the way. She was relieved to see that Detective Wilkanson hadn't accompanied her. "Why don't we sit? Can I offer you a coffee, tea, some water?" Nancy led Mrs. Wilkanson to the small seating area to the right of the room.

"Maybe tea, if it's no trouble. I can even make it myself, if you want."

"No need. Would you care for green or orange pekoe?"

"Orange pekoe please, if you have milk," Mrs. Wilkanson said.

Nancy held back a smile. The woman was already a pleasant surprise, since she'd been prepared for an overprotective mama bear in total denial. She thought there might be hope of a real dialogue. "I have milk. Sugar?"

Mrs. Wilkanson shook her head. "No thanks."

Nancy walked the steaming mug over and placed it on the glass coffee table in front of her. "I'll grab the coffee on my desk, and we can begin."

She settled across from Mrs. Wilkanson, who cradled her mug, blowing into it. She always made mental note of her first impressions. She was a good judge of character—well, she used to be. Elizabeth's blonde bob framed her face and hung just below her angular chin. Her eyes, a beautiful blue-green, were tired, with a touch of crow's feet and a slight purplish cast underneath. Just like Ryann's.

"I appreciate you coming in to speak with me about your daughter's case, Mrs. Wilkanson."

"Liz, please."

Nancy smiled. "Liz. Please call me Nancy. As you know, I've

been assessing Ryann. We've met a few times and have discussed quite a bit about the incidents. I know this must be very difficult for you, and I'll try and make this as quick and painless as possible. What I need is for you to answer some questions about Ryann's childhood, personality, and usual behaviors growing up, that sort of thing."

Liz nodded. "Anything that you think will help."

Here it was. "I won't be able to disclose anything that Ryann and I have discussed in session. This meeting is more for me to get to know what kind of child and adolescent Ryann was."

"You're trying to establish a baseline?"

Nancy felt her head bounce back. Maybe Liz was a tad more educated than she'd anticipated. "It's a little more complicated than that, but yes, essentially I want a complete background on Ryann."

Liz finally took a sip of her tea. "Okay. Ask away."

The energy in the room subtly intensified. Nancy could see Liz attempting to appear calm and collected, but the tension was practically tangible. She gathered her notebook and pen. "What was Ryann like as a toddler?"

Liz's eyes brightened as any mother's would at the thought of their baby, even one who would later turn out to be a killer. "Oh, she was beautiful. Blonde ringlets, rosy cheeks. And her laugh. She was always happy and giggling. A mischievous little thing." Her face changed as though catching herself saying the wrong thing. "In a cute way, not in a trouble-making kind of way."

Nancy smiled. "I understand. Were there ever issues with her behavior?"

"Nothing that I didn't go through with Brianna. There was the normal misbehaving and tantrums that all kids go through, but Ryann was really playful and content."

Nancy wasn't expecting to hear anything unusual at this point in the history. Most psychopaths didn't display antisocial behaviors until at least the ages of seven or eight. "When she had a tantrum, what did that look like?"

Liz's eyes moved up and to the side. "Ryann would shout, stamp her feet, cry, and whine. The same things all kids do."

"Did it take her a long time to calm down once it started?"

"Ten minutes to a half hour or so. Depending on what mood she was in."

"What sorts of moods did she generally have?"

"If she wasn't happy, which I assure you she usually was, she'd sometimes feel sick or tired. She wasn't always a great sleeper. Sometimes she'd get cranky, but she was too stubborn to sleep. I think she was always worried she'd miss out on something if she went to bed. Once in a while she'd get angry. Usually it was because she was not given something she wanted."

"Like what?"

"Extra sweets, staying up late, something she saw in a store—that sort of thing."

Nancy nodded, her pen in constant motion as she tried to keep up. "Did she ever ruin anything in the house or yard when she got upset?"

The brightness in Liz's eyes dulled. "I don't know if it was on purpose."

"That's okay. What happened?"

"Ryann was four or five. We were out in the backyard. I was gardening, and Dave was playing with the kids on one of those slippy slide things. He had the water going and he, Bri, and Ryann were taking turns running and belly flopping down it." Her face lit up. "It was so funny to watch them. Ryann insisted it was her turn again, but it was Brianna's, so Dave made her wait. She started to yell, arms flailing. I got up and went over. She tried to tell me it was her turn and it wasn't fair. I'd heard the whole thing and told her she had to listen to Daddy." The smile was gone. "She screamed and ran over to my flowers and started yanking them out. She was frantic, crying, and tearing at them. I remember she wouldn't calm down, so Dave had to pick her up and bring her in the house. I think it took a while before she stopped yelling and fighting."

"How long, if you had to estimate?"

"I think about forty-five minutes. She wasn't trying to wreck things the whole time, though. We got her to sit in the rocking chair with her blanket and listen to music." Liz inhaled the steam and took a small sip.

"How often would Ryann escalate to that point?"

She held the mug in her hands, a comforting action. Most people liked to fidget or share their focus when they were feeling stressed. "Maybe every two months or so, but that dwindled when she turned eight. She'd grown out of tantrums by then. I think she knew how to use her words more and wasn't so frustrated trying to express herself."

Or it could have been that Ryann was becoming more aware— of herself and how others perceived her. She may have realized she wasn't getting anywhere by acting out. "Tell me about what Ryann was like around ages ten to twelve."

Liz's shoulders rounded as she hunched forward slightly. "She was a good kid, helping me and her father with chores, playing with friends, great grades at school. She was in gymnastics and dance."

"No issues with her personality or behavior?"

"No, not that I'm aware of—not besides normal pre-teen drama like fighting

with her sister or complaining about doing the dishes. She seemed to get along fine with friends, a few arguments here or there, but nothing that stood out. Bri went through the same thing. Girls can be mean to each other. There were a few in her gymnastics class that picked on Ryann a bit."

"And why do you think that was?"

"Ryann is . . . *was* a perfectionist. Some of the kids thought she was a suck-up. I think they were jealous of her ambition. She had a lot of drive for someone her age."

"What about when Ryann entered high school? How was that experience for her?"

"She loved school. She had a great group of friends. It was an odd grouping, but they all got along really well."

"Why odd?"

"Well, typically kids hang out with others who have the same interests. Theirs was a sort of motley crew. A few of them were athletes, some hated academics while others excelled, some were video gamers. They had various hobbies, but it worked for them. They complemented one another." Liz smiled again. "They were good for her." The smile faded. Her eyes watered. "And she was bad for them." She wiped a rolling tear with the back of her hand. "Sorry."

Nancy passed a box of tissues over. "Don't apologize. This has all been extremely difficult for you and your family. It's a lot to ask you to dredge up, but you're helping your daughter."

"I hope so."

"What made you get so upset just then?"

"I was thinking of Ryann's best friend growing up, Bao-yu. I'm sure you've read about her, about what Ryann did to her. It was all over the news."

Nancy nodded. "Do you still have contact with Bao-yu or any of Ryann's former friends?"

"Not really. I'd like to, but I don't blame them for not reciprocating. I think they want to move on, away from that part of their lives. I spoke to Bao-yu after the sentencing. I wanted to apologize for what she'd been through. It's a small town though, so I see them all around. They seem to be doing well, thank God."

"And how did Bao-yu react to you when you spoke to her afterwards?"

"She spoke to me, we cried, hugged. It was nice."

"I'm sure that Bao-yu and everyone involved understand that you and your husband had nothing to do with the murders. There must have been a lot of guilt. As a parent, it's our default, but I hope you don't blame yourself now. Did Ryann ever have any memory issues or blackouts? Did she ever talk about having gaps of time missing at any point in her childhood?"

Liz's brow furrowed and she looked down at her lap. Another mannerism that Ryann shared. Genetics were a funny thing. "Not that I'm aware of. She became a lot more secretive that summer—which is a ridiculous thing for me to say, for obvious reasons—but she never said or did anything that led me to think so. Why, did she say she did?"

Nancy readjusted herself on the cushion. "I'm sorry, but I'm not at liberty to share anything from our sessions." She gave a weak smile, feeling terrible. As a mother, Nancy could imagine what Liz was feeling. At least to a small extent. They each had one normal child and one troubled one. Though Kim never resorted to murder, Nancy was certain she'd broken a number or laws to support her drug habit.

Liz gave a weak smile. "What were the signs I missed, Dr. Clafin? Was there something I should have seen?" Her eyes welled again.

Nancy had asked herself that very question thousands of times. She wasn't sure she'd be able to cope if Kim had done a fraction of the evil Ryann had. "There are signs, but they're general, and not every perpetrator has them. Sometimes they are too subtle to pick up on, and sometimes they are hidden. Some people who display psychopathic tendencies are intelligent enough to know the signs. Ryann may have not wanted you to see them."

"I've done my research. I know the typical traits people look for in a . . ." her voice quivered. "Psychopath. Or is she a sociopath? It's hard to tell." Liz's shaky hand held the tissue to the corner of her eye. Her mascara had smudged a bit underneath. "I never found dead animals, or disturbing pictures that she'd drawn. She was never abused. Ryann was loved. We paid attention to her, and she had everything she could've wanted. She never seemed unhappy or dark. There was nothing evil about her. I've read stories about parents whose children were serial killers." She took a breath. "Except . . ."

Moving to the edge of her seat, Nancy put the paper and pen

down. She wanted it to be two mothers talking, not Liz feeling like she was under a microscope. "What is it?"

"Ryann's grandfather, Dave's father, had schizophrenia. He could be violent at times. He was heavily medicated and hospitalized on numerous occasions. He had these delusions when he'd go off his medication. He'd feel better and think he didn't need the pills anymore. He committed suicide, about ten years ago now." A look of fear seemed to grip Liz. "Oh my God, do you think that has something to do with what happened to Ryann? I mean she's not schizophrenic—at least she didn't seem to be." Tears welled up in her eyes, but she quickly blotted them away with the tissue. "Did I miss those signs too?"

"Nothing has been concluded yet. I'm taking all of this into account, Liz. That's why we're here. Some parts of her case don't add up. I appreciate you trusting me to figure out the missing pieces. And yes, mental health can be hereditary, including psychosis. I'm going to keep investigating all the angles of your daughter's case. I promise." An alarm went off in her mind. The grandfather was nowhere in the files. "I didn't see mention of any mental illness in the family history in my research."

Liz blinked back a few tears. "That's because Dave refused to talk about it. He also forbade me to say anything. I'm sorry I didn't speak up." She scrubbed her face with her hands. "God, did I help put her away? Could knowing that at trial have helped her?"

Nancy spoke as gently as possible. "It's very hard to say, but probably not."

Liz nodded. "Thank you so much. You can't know what this means to me." Crumpling the tissue in a ball, she put her mug on the table. "Is there anything else I can do?"

"Not right now, but I will contact you if something comes up. Thanks again for coming in last minute like this." Nancy stood. Liz followed and she walked her to the door.

"There's so much I want to ask you, but I know I can't. Please take care of my little girl. She's not this monster everyone thinks. She did some horrible things, but she wasn't herself. Something happened to her back then, but I don't think she should have to pay with the rest of her life."

"I've got to be honest, Liz. It's almost unheard-of for people charged with first-degree murder to ever be released. And if they are, it's after thirty-five or forty years in prison. What Ryann has on her side is that she was a minor at the time, so life without the possibility of parole is now considered cruel and unusual punishment. Even if this clemency fails, she still has a shot at parole one day."

Inhaling a sharp breath, Liz steadied herself on the doorframe. "I don't know if she'll make it much longer. Prison's been very hard on her." She waved her hand and shook her head. "I know that people will say she deserves worse, but it's difficult to watch her. She's a shell of my little girl, you know? Anyway. Thanks again for your help, Dr. Clafin."

Liz turned and walked down the hallway, leaving Nancy with a gnawing emptiness in her own stomach. Both mothers who had lost their daughters.

CHAPTER SEVENTEEN

*N*ancy went over her notes again once she was comfortable on her own couch. Of course Liz would want to see the best in her daughter. Even still, she'd met some parents who had turned their children in for various crimes. Parents who were angry with their kids, blamed them, criticized them, so Nancy couldn't simply assume Liz was wearing rose-colored glasses when it came to Ryann. She had to consider that her account of her daughter was accurate. She would, of course, interview many other people about Ryann. It would be interesting to see how their accounts stacked up.

There was time for a quick bite, and then she had more work to do. The study of Ryann's case had monopolized Nancy's evenings, leaving little time for anything else in her life—not there was much of it to speak of, especially with Mr. Wagner checking in with her almost daily. She'd like to believe he and his partner were taking the case because there'd been a miscarriage of justice, but she doubted it.

Ryann had been denied her maximum appeals, so her only hope was for new evidence that exonerated her or proof that her original defense team shit the bed. Dave Wilkanson was asked specifically if he or any members of his family suffered from mental illness, and he'd answered no—knowing that the information could've helped his daughter. Was he so proud that he would risk her life instead of admit his father's condition? The man was schizophrenic. Despite what she'd told Liz, the admission of a familial mental illness might have given Ryann an insanity defense.

Unless Dave had no intention of helping her. But how could he do that to his little girl?

Nancy scoured the newly acquired psychiatric evaluations. The prosecution's seemed complete, but the defense's folder was a fraction of the size. She searched through it. Was this serious? Right away she saw a few glaring areas she would have flagged. Her stomach fluttered with sickness.

Ryann had been assigned a crappy public defender who only visited her a couple of times pre-trial. Perhaps Ryann hadn't been fully aware of her rights and the defense strategies available to her. Her dad sure didn't help. Estevez had clearly noted that Dave gave permission for Ryann—a minor—to be questioned without parental supervision. Nancy couldn't help but wonder if Ryann even understood what pleading guilty and waiving her rights to a lawyer in police questioning would actually do to her.

She ran her fingers roughly through her hair, staring at the page in front of her. Increasingly, the courts were looking at brain development in youth, but this hadn't even been considered at the time of her trial. Perhaps there was more to it than simply cold-blooded murder? The connection with Ryann's grandfather, her memory gaps, and her so-called mission to rid the world of useless, entitled people: they all pointed to the possibility of mental illness. But what kind of illness could've afflicted her so severely at the time yet not recurred once in the last twelve years?

"Are you in here?"

Nancy's eyes burst open and her heart hammered in her chest as she attempted to gain her bearings. She'd fallen asleep on the couch. "Hello? Who's that?" She was up and moving in seconds flat. Fast enough for her blood pressure to plummet, causing her to sway a bit on her feet. She heard footsteps. Her eyes scanned the living room for a weapon. She lurched forward and grabbed the fireplace poker. Surely that could do some damage.

The footsteps were getting closer. She lifted the iron behind her head like a baseball bat, ready to strike.

"Hey, Mom— Ah, what are you doing?"

She went to swing but saw that it was only Ray. "Holy shit! Sorry." She let the poker fall to her side, her other hand clutching her chest.

"What the hell?" His creased forehead smoothed and he chuckled. "Too much caffeine? What's gotten you so jumpy?"

Nancy sat back on the couch, her pulse evening out. Ray sat next to her. "Nothing. I fell asleep, and the sound . . . I forgot where I was for a second. I'm getting old, you know." She smiled.

"Oh, I know." She swung playfully at him and he laughed. She loved his laugh. It hadn't changed since he was a little boy.

"Yeah, but you're not usually this jumpy." He stared at her as if trying to see into her mind. She resented that—the way he analyzed her. It got worse after James died. Ray had taken over the protector role from his father, and she hated it. It was sweet, but she could take care of herself. She'd been doing it a long time. He snapped his fingers at her in a way that made her jump again. "I know it's that case. Being so immersed in those murders must be giving you nightmares."

"It's not that at all, and would you stop it? I'm fine. No nightmares, and stop trying to figure me out."

"What? You can do it to everyone, but no one can do it to you?"

"Oh, people can, only you're not qualified."

Ray laughed, leaned in, and put his arms around her. "It's nice to see you, Mom."

Nancy patted his shoulder. "You too, sweetie." She pulled back and sat to face him. "What's new?"

"Nothing much. School is crazy busy, Josh is complaining that I don't spend enough time with him, and I'm overdue for a haircut and one of your homemade dinners—but I can see that will have to wait for another time. No offense, Mom, but you look exhausted. Are you sure you've been sleeping okay?" He tilted his head and gave her that look. The one that said he could see the truth and she couldn't get around it the way she did when he was ten.

"I'm a little tired. I've been working late a lot."

"I still can't believe you took her case. I know you're not supposed to talk about it, but can you tell me one thing? What's she like? I mean, I've seen her on TV, but they edit that shit. What's she *really* like?" He perched himself on the edge of the cushion, gaping at her.

Nancy rolled her eyes. Her son had the gift of bluntness. "I'd rather not get into it."

Ray's fingers burrowed into her leg. "Come on! What good is it having a mother who is a top forensic shrink to a famous serial killer if you can't get the inside scoop? She's horrible and nasty and terrifying, isn't she? You're not alone in a room with her, are you?"

"One question at a time." She patted his knee. "I've only met with her a couple of times and she seems nice. Normal. I'm still assessing her. I'm at the preliminary stages. It's hard to say. And yes, I'm alone in a room with her, but a CO watches us from an adjoining room. I assure you I'm perfectly safe."

"Normal and nice. That's ludicrous. She buttered a half-dozen people in, what, like six weeks?"

"Come on, Ray."

"It's hard to think that someone with her history sits across from you drinking tea and discussing the weather. Or does she blame it all on her dysfunctional childhood? What—was she not hugged enough?"

Nancy shook her head as his poor attempt at humor. "Her crimes were many years ago. She was practically a child. A lot has changed since then, and it's not out of the realm of possibility that Ryann has changed too. Obviously enough people believe she has been rehabilitated and that certain aspects of the original case were flawed, or I wouldn't be evaluating her, would I?"

"Yeah, and she's somehow got a chunk of pseudo-celebrities on her side. The media is eating this case up. I saw a press conference with her lawyers or whatever, and there were even a few actors there, wearing shirts with her picture on it."

"Yes, but there's just as many people who think she should stay locked up forever. Her team is doing a great job stirring up attention for their cause, but they still have to convince the powers that be that she's reformed."

"Don't tell me you believe it."

"I have no opinion yet." Nancy stood and brushed her thighs with her hands. "Now, are you hungry? I have lasagna in the fridge."

He stood up to follow her. "But she admitted to all of those murders. I don't understand how she could ever be let out. Other people have done far less and spent their lives in jail." Ray was a full head taller than Nancy now. With his hands on her shoulders, he said, "You can't let her out, Mom. I just feel it. Don't let her out."

Thursday, November 30

It was a day Nancy wasn't particularly looking forward to. Any minute she was going to be in front of the Borgdon's house, about to go in and discuss the most traumatic day of their lives.

She pulled her sedan in front of the address she'd been given and turned off the ignition. It was already getting dark. She hated that about winter. That and the cold, snow, ice, and freezing rain. They'd told her seven o'clock. The dashboard read 6:54. Should she wait the six minutes in the car? What if they were still eating dinner? Would they even have an appetite, knowing they would be discussing how they discovered their daughter's strangled body?

After three minutes of sitting, Nancy got out and made her way up the driveway. It was a nice house, a Tudor, probably built in the 1950s, finished with black shutters and a red door. Small snow-covered shrubs filled the space under the front windows. She forced herself up the steps, actively quelling the urge to turn around.

She knocked on the door and counted to five in her head before it opened, revealing a large woman with bright red hair that was swept off her shoulders. She was tall and round, and would have been intimidating if not for the smile that transformed her face.

"You must be Dr. Clafin. Please, come in."

Nancy smiled back and stepped into the tiny foyer. "Nice to meet you, Mrs. Borgdon." It was always odd when she entered someone's home. Should she offer to take her shoes off, hang her own coat?

"Call me Joelle. Let me take your coat."

Nancy slipped it off and handed it to her before bending to unzip her boots.

"No, no, leave them on. I have to vacuum later anyways." Nancy followed her into the adjoining living room. "Please make yourself comfortable, and I'll go grab Rick."

She practically bounded from the room. Nervous energy, perhaps? Nancy sat on the sofa seat nearest the door. It felt more comfortable to be closer to the exit, which made no logical sense since she was in the home of the victims. Why was she ill at ease here when she regularly sat across from convicts and killers?

Her gaze swept the room. A large portrait of a teenage girl

hung prominently over the fireplace mantel. Yvonne. It was a relief to see her smiling, looking pretty in her bright blue sweater, her red hair half up in a clip, and . . . *alive*. Nancy stared at it, hoping it would replace the horrific crime scene photo that was burned into her brain.

If Nancy thought Mrs. Borgdon was tall, she should've been prepared for her husband, who must have been six-six. He walked straight for her, hand outstretched. "Hello, I'm Rick."

His huge palm consumed her hand. "You can call me Nancy." She lowered herself back to her seat while they sat together on the loveseat across from her.

"Thank you for agreeing to speak with me." Leaning beside her, she rifled in her briefcase for a pen and pad. "I'll be jotting down some notes, if you don't mind."

"Not at all. We're happy to talk with you. Anything to prevent that monster from being released," Joelle said. She sat tall, cross-legged, reaching across to hold Rick's hand.

"Did you know of Ryann Wilkanson before the night of the murder?"

Rick was stone-faced, but Joelle's eyebrows rose before she answered. "No. Yvonne and her friends had never mentioned her."

"Even though Ryann had been Hayden's girlfriend before he and Yvonne began dating?"

"Yvonne wasn't the type of girl to be jealous or insecure, so there was absolutely no reason for her to talk about an ex-girl-friend. Hayden was with her, not that thing." Joelle's foot tapped roughly against the carpeted floor.

She'd expected protective parents, but the vibe she was getting was closer to defensive. "A lot of teenagers don't tell their parents everything that's going on. Is it reasonable to assume that the two girls knew each other? I have a document from Cloverdale Secondary that states they sat next to each other in English class."

Joelle pushed her fluffy hair out of her face. It seemed to be growing since Nancy had arrived. "Maybe they did, but they certainly weren't friends. My daughter wouldn't have associated with someone so deranged."

Nancy hated asking, but any little bit of information helped. "Do either of you have any clue why Yvonne was targeted?" It wasn't as though she could simply go by Ryann's word.

Joelle's eyes welled up. She began to cry so hard and so suddenly that she was nearly hyperventilating. Rick put his arm around her and guided her toward his chest. "She gets very upset talking about it." He cleared his throat. "We racked our brains. The only thing the police could come up with was that Wilkanson was jealous of Yvonne and her relationship with Hayden. If it wasn't for that boy, our daughter might still be here."

Grabbing a handful of tissues from the box on the table, Joelle wiped her eyes and cheeks. "That's not true, Rick. Hayden was devastated to lose her. It wasn't his fault his crazy ex targeted our girl." Her downcast eyes moved up to meet Nancy again. "It's been twelve years, but it doesn't get any easier. Not ever. We miss her every single day." She buried her face in the tissue again.

Nancy wondered if coming here had been one of the worst ideas she'd had besides taking the case in the first place. "I truly am sorry for your loss. I'm know it never gets easier, especially when your loved one is taken in such a violent way."

"You're not going to help her get out, right? I mean . . . you can't. She's an evil monster." Joelle's tears had been replaced with a fire in her eyes. Nancy had seen it before. Ferocious rage.

"It's not up to me. I'm assisting with the overall evaluation, but there are many factors and stages ahead."

Joelle jumped up, and before Nancy could blink, the fluffy red haired woman was kneeling at her feet, holding her hands. "Please, please, you've got to tell them they can't release her. She'll do it again. Didn't you see the television specials—the interviews? That girl has no heart. She enjoyed it! She's crazy! There's no redemption for someone like her."

Rick was on his feet. He reached his arms around her and directed her back to her seat. "We have had a hard time through this whole thing. When she was convicted, she was given multiple life sentences. How is it that there's even a discussion of her being released?"

This was the question she was dreading, because she had to speak the truth and the truth was ugly. Taking a slow, deep breath she said, "There are many things that go into it. The crimes were committed when she was a juvenile, and even though she was charged as an adult, there's new research suggesting that children's brains aren't fully formed and therefore a juvenile perpetrator may not be as responsible for their actions as an adult. Her defense team is also looking at her mental state at the time of the murders. Her pre-trial psychological examination may not have been adequate, and therefore there are questions as to her criminal responsibility at the time of the crimes. In addition, Ms. Wilkanson has completed her high school and college education, acted as a tutor, and helped many other inmates graduate. Since her arrest, she's never been violent or had any additional offenses. All these things are being considered, as well as statements from people just like yourself. I assume you are writing a letter of recommendation against her release?"

"Of course," Joelle cried. "I'll do everything I can. Her lawyers think they're so clever getting public sympathy and celebrity support, but I can do that too. What about the victims? How can the media rally around someone like her?"

"I'm sorry to have upset you. I should probably be going." Nancy stood. It seemed a mistake to come. The Borgdons were still drowning in grief and not ready for the conversation. If anything, she'd only made the situation worse for them.

Joelle put her hand up. "Wait. I know I get emotional, but it's hard not to. So much was stolen from us. Yvonne will never get the chance to grow up, live her life, make her mark on this world. She wanted to be an artist. She painted and sculpted. Our daughter was thoughtful, sensitive, talented, and sweet. She cared about people, and a lot of people loved her. Rick will never walk his daughter down the aisle. We'll never hold a grandbaby. There is a hole in our life that can't be closed again. What world do we live in where the person who broke into my baby's room and strangled her with her own belt gets another chance?" Her voice was soft and broken.

A little piece of Nancy's heart withered.

Why was she continually dissociating the woman in her prison office from the one who did all those things?

CHAPTER EIGHTEEN

*S*unday, December 3

I'm led out of F Block, through the hallway and down another corridor to the visitor's 'lounge.' It's basically a big, gray room with a bunch of round tables and benches bolted to the floor, a few vending machines, and a guard station. At least there are windows. They wouldn't want the visitors to think we're trapped animals.

Officer Penn opens the door. "Best behavior, or I pull your ass back out in five seconds."

"Have I ever gotten into any trouble?" I smile, flip my hair, and head over to where my mother is sitting. She looks thinner than usual. She was never good with change, even the good kind like the possibility of my release. Her partially blonde, partially graying hair is swept off her face in a clip, which only highlights her protruding cheekbones and darkened eyes. My chest feels heavy, like I can't take a deep breath.

And people think I'm incapable of guilt or remorse.

My mom looks over and stands. "There she is! Hello, my beautiful girl." Her arms are extended, and I reluctantly walk into them and embrace her back. I've never particularly liked being touched, and it's especially strange since it almost never happens now except for these hugs a few times a month.

I pat her back, my subtle cue that it's time to pull away. "It's good to see you, Mom. Thanks for coming."

"You never have to thank me. I'd do anything for you."

The guilt grows, because I've never felt that way about anyone. Though if I did, it likely would be about her. "How are you?"

"Oh, fine. What about you? Are you sleeping enough? You look tired." She reaches out and brushes my hair off my face.

Once a mother, always a mother. "I'm okay. Hopefully I'll sleep better in a few months once this is all over. Don't get me wrong, I'm thrilled I have the chance to apply for clemency. It's just an arduous process."

My mother straightens, placing one hand on top of the other. She looks like a teenager about to plead their case to stay out past curfew. "I should tell you that Dr. Clafin and I met a few days ago. She wanted to ask me a few questions." Her eyes perk up as though she's just stuck her foot in her mouth. "Nothing bad. Just standard stuff, I think."

My eyes can't help but wander. I see a few women from my block in here with family members, some with their young children. I read a statistic that female inmates get far fewer visitors than men. Woman are more loyal to the men in their lives and will keep visiting, whereas most men will leave their partner in favor of a woman who isn't incarcerated. Pigs.

I refocus on my mother, who is staring and waiting for a response. "It's all right, Mom. I suspect she'll be talking to a lot of people who know me . . . knew me. Let me guess: 'What was Ryann like as a child? Did she have anger issues or seem different than most kids? What about in comparison to Brianna?' Am I close?" I try not to sound as bitter as I feel, if only so Mom won't stress out more.

"You always were sharp, kid." She gives me a thin smile. "She was quite nice. I think she likes you, Ry. I got a good sense about her."

I allow a small laugh. "I wouldn't go that far."

Mom waves me off. "No, no, listen. She seemed very open and positive. I think she really is seeing the wonderful woman you've become."

"I hope so, because if she's not, I have zero shot. I know Dr. Clafin's recommendation is only part of it, but it's a big fucking part. If a mental health expert said, 'Hey don't release her, because I think if you do she'll go and kill a bunch more people,' how many people would then say, 'Gee, I think we should release her anyway.' Her opinion is everything. I want to be positive, but I'm not as convinced as you are that she's seeing the *new* me."

"Why, honey? What makes you think that?" My mom does the head-tilt thing and stares at me with the sad eyes I've seen far too much in the last twelve years.

"I've seen the way she looks at me. She's judging me, thinking about how evil and malicious I am. Probably wondering if I'm going to lunge at her and attack every five minutes." What I don't say is that Dr. Nancy is right. I have my fantasies about killing her. What self-respecting Great wouldn't? Too bad it has to remain a fantasy—not that I don't like her. Nancy puts up a good front. I respect that at least.

"Oh, Ryann, I'm sure that's your worst fears and your wild imagination at play. I don't think she's afraid of you. If she were, she'd have a guard in the room." My mother reaches over the tabletop and puts her hand on mine.

I shrug. "I hope you're right. Have you been watching much TV?"

She inhales a long, slow breath, which means she's feeling overwhelmed. "I have. You've been on there a lot. Have you been watching?"

"A little, though it's difficult in here because no one wants to see me get all this attention after what I've done, especially from celebrities who are, by some fucking miracle, pleading my case in public."

"Try not to swear so much, dear."

I pull my hand back. Seriously? That's what she's worried about?

We talk for a little while longer and then the buzzer goes off. It's time to say goodbye. Mom stands and pulls me in for another hug. Her hair smells like coconut, just like when I was young, and I close my eyes for a minute to soak it in. "I love you. Be strong. I'll call you tomorrow," she says.

I walk over to the doorway where Penn is waiting. Ugh, the next part is not pleasant, but worth it to get out of the block and see Mom. Penn accompanies me through the door and into a small room where a female officer is waiting.

"You know the drill, Wilkanson. Come on."

It never gets any easier. I take off my long-sleeved shirt, followed by my T-shirt. Next I remove my pants, then my socks. I wish that was it, but it's not over yet. I face the wall, because who wants to look at some dumb CO's face while I take my underwear and bra off?

Without warning I feel her gloved fingers move through my hair, yanking a few of the strands before moving around my ears. "Face me." I spin around with my arms up. "Turn." I do as instructed and control my breathing so my fury doesn't show, though my veins are on fire and I want to put my fingers around the hair at *her* scalp and twist and pull. "Lift your feet." As if I'm hiding anything on the soles of my fucking bare feet. "Spread your cheeks, squat, and cough." It practically guts me every time I have to do this. If I was going to hide something, it wouldn't be in either of those places, though a lot of the inmates do.

The CO throws my scrubs at me. "Get dressed." It's all I can do to not jump on her from behind and put my pant leg around her fat double chin.

It's okay, though, because I've made mental notes in here. Everything from the COs' full names and badge numbers to the names of their children and spouses. The COs are idiots, never considering the fact that some of us will get out. If we wanted to do something about the way they treat us, we know more than enough about them to make it happen.

And I want to make it happen.

CHAPTER NINETEEN

*M*onday, December 4

Nancy waited in her office. Both the coffee and hot water were ready, depending on what Ryann wanted. It had become part of their little ritual. A way to ease into the conversation.

"Are you ready for me?"

Nancy turned to face Ryann, who was poking her head through the door. She'd told the officer it was fine to let her through without buzzing, in the hopes Ryann would trust her more. It wasn't like the officer was gone. She was safe. "Sure am. Come in."

Ryann let the glass door close behind her. She usually beelined for the couch, but that day she walked over to Nancy, who was getting a few cookies out on a plate.

Her shoulders and back remained lax, her stomach stayed settled. The initial trepidation of being in a small room with a serial killer had eased in the time they'd been meeting, though Nancy wasn't sure that was wise. "What do you feel like today, tea or coffee?"

"Coffee, please. It's so much better than anything I can get inside." Ryann smiled. "One sugar and a little cream, please. Actually, can I help with anything?"

"Sure. Will you grab the cream in the fridge?"

Ryann placed the carton on the counter. Nancy was aware of her eyes tracking her as she filled the cups. "I love the smell, don't you?"

"Yeah, but the only time I get that pleasure is in here when you're making it," Ryann said. "Are you putting cookies out?" She eyed the plate with big, wanting eyes.

"I hope you like chocolate chip. I figured it would be a nice treat."

"I love them, thanks."

They fixed their cups, and Nancy led them to their respective seats. Ryann sat upright, her legs crossed, wearing her usual baggy prison garb. Her hair was down, cascading over her shoulders in waves. "Your hair looks pretty. Did you do that yourself?"

"Thanks, I braided it last night." Ryann's gaze moved away from Nancy. Her foot bounced up and down. "What do you have planned for me today?"

"What do you mean?" Nancy asked, sensing a touch of nervousness in her.

"Are we going to watch another interview?" She swallowed loudly, rubbing her fingers over her bare arm in an odd repetitive manner.

"Did you want to?"

"Not really." Her bouncing foot picked up speed.

Nancy reached for her notebook and pen on the desk. "Well, I was thinking we could talk today. No video. How does that sound?"

Ryann nodded spiritedly. "Okay. About what?"

"I was hoping we could discuss your family and what it was like growing up in Dungrave."

"Okay."

"Why don't you begin with Ryann at age five. What were you like?"

"I don't know. A regular kid, I guess. I was in kindergarten, I played with friends, played make-believe, was harassed by Bri." The corners of her mouth turned up slightly.

"What kind of things did you fantasize about when you played make-believe?"

"I started out pretending to be a princess, but that soon changed to me becoming a prince saving one of my dolls from an evil queen. I didn't think it was fair that only the boys got to save the day. I really liked TV shows and movies with lots of action—I'd always re-enact the scenes later. One of my favorites was Power Rangers. That's so embarrassing now."

Nancy wrote, *liked to be in control, resisted feelings of helplessness, sense of good and evil.*

"So you distinctly remember fighting the bad guys?"

Ryann nodded. "I didn't grow up picturing ways to hurt people, if that's what you're wondering. I was a normal kid. I had friends, I felt safe, I belonged. I don't know what changed. You could say it was as quick as someone flicking on a switch."

"You never derived pleasure when thinking about bad things happening to anyone before the spring prior to the murders?"

Ryann continued to rub her arm. The area was red and irritated. It was a sign of anxiety. Perhaps she was touching a nerve after all. Getting closer to something that would help explain what had happened. "Typical stuff, like if I was fighting with friends, I wished they'd get in trouble at school or trip and embarrass themselves in front of a group of boys. Nothing like picturing them dead and bloody. That wasn't my idea of an entertaining pastime."

"Did you encounter any bullying in elementary or high school?"

"You mean, like, was I bullied?" Nancy nodded and Ryann continued. "A little, but nothing too serious."

"What happened?" Nancy asked, genuinely curious. All Ryann's past events had helped shape her.

"In sixth grade there was a group of girls I was friends with. It was kind of cliquey. This one girl was kind of the leader of the five of us. Whatever she said went. If she said she was mad at someone, then the group had to follow suit."

"And if you didn't?"

"Then she'd turn her wrath on you. You'd be completely shut out with no friends. And it wasn't like they just ignored you. They knew all your secrets, like who you had a crush on, or if you ever said anything bad about anyone. They'd threaten to expose you and make a fool of you. It was torture."

"Did the group ever bully you?"

"Everyone got a turn—well, except for the fearless leader. Usually whoever was on the outs would apologize and bargain with whatever we could until she decided to 'forgive us' and let us come back. You were never at ease. And the worst part was, we all took part in it. Even though we knew there was no reason to be mad at the target, we were too scared to stand up to her. So we joined in."

"What do you feel about what you did during that time?"

"Shitty. But we were equally responsible. We all let it happen. I don't think if I stood up and tried to point out how we were being manipulated and controlled it would've helped. The fear was too great. I was happy when it was over."

"What made it end?"

"High school. We all went to different ones. Besides, we grew out of that crap. Well, maybe not completely, but it was never as bad as that. High school has its own politics, but I'd learned to stay away. I could see it a mile away."

"Is that why you had the mismatched group of friends at Cloverdale?"

Ryann smiled wide. "I think we were perfectly matched. We got each other. Complemented one other. I loved my friends."

"Was Bao-yu in that sixth-grade group?"

"B? Yeah, she was. Thank God I had her, too. She was the only one of us with brains. She kept me sane. Even if she 'wasn't allowed' to talk to me, she'd call me that night. Sometimes we'd bicker like an old married couple, but we never let each other down. Until . . ." Ryann's voice dropped off. She bit into her bottom lip, her head shaking. "Until I did what I did to her. She didn't deserve that, but I was so afraid of being locked up . . ."

Nancy ignored the writer's cramp in her hand. *Seems to understand healthy friendships, had a good connection with a 'best friend,' didn't isolate herself, apparent normal socialization.*

Ryann slapped her thighs with her palms energetically, as if trying to shake off her sorrow. "I tried to reach out to her. Did you know that? I tried calling, writing letters, email, going through other people. She won't talk to me. I don't blame her or anything, but it hurts, which is insane, because why would she want to speak to me? I don't deserve it. Of course she'd be terrified of me. She thinks I tried to kill her. I loved her and put a knife to her throat." Ryann paused. Her eyebrows stitched together. "I still don't understand how those two things can exist in the same space. How can I love her but then do that?"

"What were you thinking when you were holding the knife to Bao-yu's neck?"

Ryann's eyelids fluttered, releasing tears that rolled down her cheeks. "I don't know."

"What do you mean? Are you too emotional—"

"No, I mean I don't know. I don't remember all of it. The rest I know because my dad told me what I did. I didn't believe it at first, but Estevez's story matched my dad's. I remember being at the library with her, and Eric showing up, but not . . . what happened just before I was arrested."

Maybe that explained why there was no interview from Estevez in which Ryann admitted to almost killing her best friend. If she didn't recall it, she'd have no version of events to recount.

"I know this is difficult for you," Nancy said, "but I need you to think about what I'm about to ask and give me the most truthful answer you can. Did you automatically believe your dad, or did you doubt that you would have hurt your best friend like that?"

A few more tears trickled down. Ryann wiped them away with the back of her arm. "My father told me I did it. He was honorable, he used to love me, he wouldn't have lied. Besides, there was another person who confirmed that I'd attacked her." Ryann's gaze shifted from the ground and met Nancy's eyes. "B told me."

Nancy's stomach grew heavy. *How was she unaware of this?* "I thought Bao-yu had decided not to see you." She made notes to confirm the exchange between the two girls. Had someone neglected to give her that part of the file?

"She didn't want to see me. She promised she'd never be alone with me again, and she kept that promise." Ryann took a slow, steadying breath. "She wrote me a letter, about three months after I was in here. A long letter where she told me everything I'd done to her—not just at the library, but what I'd done to her mentally and emotionally. She told me that I killed her best friend and that she didn't know who I was. She said she wished I was dead and would spend the rest of my days locked up like . . . the animal I was." Her voice was shaky and she gasped back a tearful breath. "She hates me. Ten years of friendship. We were closer than sisters, and it's just gone. For both of us, but I did it. To her, of all people."

Nancy reached across and put a hand on her quaking knee. "Just relax, Ryann. Take a few deep breaths."

Ryann nodded and slowly inhaled, keeping eye contact with her.

"Better?" Nancy asked. A jabbing in her gut yelled at her for being legitimately concerned.

Taking a tissue, Ryann blew her nose. "Sorry. I know you're not here to make me feel better about what I've done. I wasn't expecting to get worked up like that. I thought I'd gotten pretty good at compartmentalizing my shit, but I guess a little snuck out."

"It's perfectly normal to have an emotional reaction. It's healthy. You should allow yourself to feel your emotions. It's the only way to heal."

"What if I don't deserve to heal? It's easier to keep it all locked away. It's not like I can make amends. No one wants to hear what I have to say." She reached for her coffee for the first time since they'd sat down, but she didn't drink. She just cradled the mug in her hands. Nancy thought of Liz.

Ryann bit her lip again. "I finally stopped trying to contact B three years ago. I was advised that it was considered harassment, since the letters were unwelcome. I suppose five years is a bit over-board." She gave a weak smile. Nancy noticed a touch of blood where her tooth had been on her lip.

"What would you have said if you'd had the chance?"

"How sorry I was. I wanted her to know that I still loved her and that I didn't mean to hurt her. I wanted to beg for her forgive-ness." Ryann's face was flushed. Her nose dripped.

Nancy gained her bearings. How was it she could so easily forget who was sitting across from her? She couldn't help but wonder if Ryann was sincere. Physiological reactions for that level of remorse were extremely difficult to simulate. At the same time, Ryann's guilt and angst were perhaps stronger for Bao-yu than for someone with whom she'd had no emotional connection. Maybe that was why, amid the boasting in her interviews, Ryann had no memory of Bao-yu. She wasn't exhilarated to have attacked her friend as she'd been with her other victims. The police report had stated that she grabbed Bao-yu as a hostage to get away. She was never an intended target.

"Ready to keep going?" Ryann nodded. "Did you get along with your parents?" Nancy asked.

"Mostly. We had arguments like any family, but most of the time it was good."

"What's your mother like?"

"She's sweet and kind, sort of innocent and naïve. She's really nice and kind of funny, though she doesn't know she is."

"What else?"

"My mom's a pushover. She used to let my dad and Bri run all over her. She'd always give in and had a hard time standing up for herself."

"And what did you think about that?"

Ryann shrugged. "I don't know. She was always a people

pleaser. It was annoying to watch everyone take advantage of her, but it was worse that she let them."

"Do you find those characteristics to be a weakness?"

"I used to, but now I see that she was trying to keep the peace and make everyone else happy. But she suffered for it."

"How?"

"Because she'd give and give, and the more she gave, the more people would take. It left her empty."

"Is that a fear of yours—to be empty inside?"

"No. I won't let that happen."

Nancy could tell she was getting somewhere. Ryann's guard was down. It was the first time she appeared completely at ease. "What about your father? What was he like to grow up with?"

A snide laugh escaped her. "Exhausting."

"Why do you say that?"

"Because he never left you alone. He was always watching, judging, seeing how you could be better."

"That must have been very difficult."

"Nothing was ever good enough for him." Ryann's forehead scrunched up and the muscles in her jaw flexed as she spoke. "I'd come home with an A and he'd ask why didn't I get an A+. I was on the cheerleading team and he'd push me to try out for captain. Bri was captain, he'd say. Didn't I want to be the best?" Her breathing got heavier. "He always did that—compared me to Bri—and it wasn't fair. I was a different person, but he couldn't see me for who I was. He wanted me to be perfect, but do you know how hard that is to do every day?" She was crying, nearly sobbing, though she tried to contain it with deep inhalations.

"It sounds like it was rough. I noticed earlier that you spoke of your dad loving and supporting you in the past tense. Do you believe he no longer loves you?"

Ryann's expression sobered as she gazed stoically at Nancy. "I know he doesn't."

That was something Nancy would get into a bit later. "Did you ever confront him about his unrealistic expectations?"

Ryann rolled her eyes. "You could say that. Well, I'd try, but he'd shut me down, tell me that I was being negative and that I'd 'never be a winner with an attitude like that.' He never heard me. And when I busted my ass and succeeded, Bri would come home with bigger, better achievements, and I'd be invisible again."

"How did you cope with that?"

Ryann let out a loud, brazen laugh. "I guess not very well." Her gaze flicked across the office. "When he seemed disappointed in me when I was little, my mother comforted me and smoothed things over with my dad. As I got older, I didn't want to be like her. I loved her, but she was fragile. I saw the way my father looked at her—like she was a delicate flower—and I refused to be coddled. I wanted to earn my father's respect, so I tried harder, no matter what it was: school, sports, a game of fucking Scrabble. Anything to prove . . ."

"To prove what, Ryann?"

"That I was worthy," she said, choking back tears.

"Do you feel you succeeded?"

"Seriously? I'm locked up for killing a bunch of people and terrorizing my town—the town my dad spent his life serving and protecting. No, I don't think I succeeded. My father will hardly speak to me, let alone visit me. But I get it. How would that look for him? God, he convinced me to plead guilty. He just wanted to get rid of me as soon as possible, so he could move on and pretend I never existed."

Nancy swallowed her shock, though she felt her face warm and hoped it wasn't reddening. He encouraged her to plead guilty? Was that why she went and told Estevez—his bloody partner—everything? "It still hurts. You're still a human being with feelings, regardless of what you've done. You're allowed to feel grief, anger, and resentment. Is it possible the things you did were connected to your home life?"

"I don't see how, and I'm not going to pass the blame to other people. Are you saying that what I did was my parents' fault?" Her mouth gaped as her eyes narrowed.

"Not at all. Everything in our life is a product of our experiences. Our experiences inform our perceptions and actions. Perhaps you were crying out for attention?"

Ryann's hand flew up. "Hold on. I did not kill those people because of daddy issues." She smoothed her hair and straightened up. "I'm tired. Are we finished for the day? I'd like to go back to my cell."

Nancy felt like the wind was knocked out of her. What had just happened? They were getting on so well, and Ryann was making real progress. "Just one more thing before you go. I want you to think about why you chose the victims you did."

"I already told you why, but you seem to have a theory, so let's have it."

"Consider the character flaws you cited in your victims. Do you think it's possible that you were, on some level, killing pieces of yourself? The fragments of yourself that you didn't like, the parts that your father pointed out as flaws? Perhaps you sought out people who you believed had those negative qualities in order to exorcize your self-hatred." Closing her notebook, she waved for the CO to open the door. "Something to think about. Get some rest, Ryann. I'll see you tomorrow."

CHAPTER TWENTY

*I*t's almost lunchtime by the time I get out of Clafin's office. Good thing I didn't miss out on whatever exquisite meal we'll be dining on this afternoon. There's a dull aching behind my right eye, shooting into my temple. I would kill for a rum and Coke right now. I'm so not the woman who lives to emote every private thing about them.

I leave the line with my clam chowder, packet of saltines, and green Jell-O cup and find my roomies. They are sitting next to Georgina, one of the loudest, biggest pains in the ass in this place, and I'm in no mood, but I go anyway. I need to get something for my head. We share things in here. For a price. Even if Steph is dry, someone might have something stronger than a fucking Tylenol.

My tray clatters as it hits the tabletop, making my head spin. I started getting migraines about seven years ago. The stupid doctors won't give me much of anything for them, because they say I don't get them frequently enough. Maybe they'd like to know what it feels like to have a bashing, squeezing, stabbing sensation in their heads. I could arrange it. My own version of a lobotomy.

"What the fuck, Wilks? Ease up on the tray," Margot says.

"Sorry. Hey, do any of you have any benzos?" I whisper.

Georgina snorts. "Is the soul shredding getting to you, princess?"

My face heats in an instant. "Fuck off. At least I have a chance of getting out. How much more time you got—twenty-five more?" I snap.

"Come on, ladies, let's be pleasant," Steph says, so I smile.

"If you need to know, yes, the shrink is making me crazy if I wasn't already. She's asking me all about my childhood and what kind of parents I had. My head is throbbing, and I just need a little something to take the edge off."

"That's so fucked up. I'd never want to know what people like that think of me. They think they're all better than us with their fancy degrees. Let them stay on their side of the fence and I'll stay on mine. Some things are best left alone." Steph takes a spoonful of the chowder. "I have a few pills left. I'll give you one when we get back to cells."

"Thanks, you're a life saver." The smell of the soup in combination with the pain in my head is nauseating. I open the crackers instead and shove one square in my mouth. I'm finally starting to cool off from Georgina's princess comment when I hear a clatter and then a crashing sound behind us. I spin around and see two women rolling on the ground, hair flying. Fights are a pretty rare occurrence, but when they happen it's nasty. I once read that men fight to injure, but women fight to kill.

Sounds accurate.

The women roll closer to our table, and we all jerk out of the way in case some of the action heads toward us. I can hardly see who it is, but Georgina is quick to say it's Roxie and Jinx. And they are going at each other: hands whacking, hair pulling, face slapping, and rib kicking. The whole nine. But it doesn't go on for too long. Two guards descend on them, yanking the women apart. Some damage is already done. Jinx has a bloody nose and a swelling eye, and Roxie's lip is split open.

"Fuck, man. Did you see that? Roxie almost killed the bitch! Bam!" Margot slams her hand on the table and my head rings. Jodi laughs. Must be nice for her to sit back and chuckle, since she's never actually fought in here.

"Enough, Margot, or the guards are gonna be over here next." Steph eyes her and Margot settles down.

The cafeteria is returning to normal so we sit again, and I try to force a spoonful of my cold, lumpy lunch down. It takes all my concentration to swallow the disgusting mouthful. My stomach clenches, so I drop my spoon.

"No offense, princess, but you look like shit," Georgina says in between shovels. She's a fat pig. No matter how disgusting the food is in here, don't take your eyes off your plate or it'll be in her goddamn mouth before you know what's happening.

I lock my gaze on her. "Thanks. Just giving you a chance to feel a bit better about your ugly ass."

She shoots me the finger.

"Seriously, you look pale, like even more than normal," Stephanie chimes in, sounding far too motherly for my liking.

I smile. "Thanks, ladies. You sure are the fucking cheer committee today."

"This shrink is really taking the piss outta you, huh? I ain't never seen you so frazzled before," Jodi says.

"I'm just tired. Been sleeping like shit, the food is inedible, and yes, talking in circles about your feelings is agony. So I'm taking donations—any booze, pills, or weed is welcome." Most of what I say is bravado. Keeping up appearances is key to survival in this hellhole. I can't afford to get caught with any contraband in case a miracle happens and I have a chance of getting out. What a kick in the tit that would be, if I got approved only to have a stupid joint found in my bunk.

"We're all suffering in here, princess, so buck up." Georgina braces her gigantic noggin on top of her propped arms.

It takes all my strength to stay calm. Sometimes people in here forget what I'm capable of. Maybe some of them don't believe in my history and are willing to take a chance by coming at me.

Too bad I'm on my best behavior.

Margot puts a hand in Georgina's face. "Lay off her, Gina. Ain't none of us know what being examined under a microscope like that feels like. I know I'd be stressed to fucking shit if my whole future relied on talking to one damn bitch for a couple of weeks."

"Thanks, Margot, but you don't have to defend me."

"Yeah, princess is a big girl. She can take care of herself, or so she wants us to think."

I glower at her and swallow the scream that threatens to explode out of me. I'm afraid if I release it, I'll never stop. "You got something to say?" I sit on my hands. Just in case I'm a little too tempted to gouge her eyes out.

Georgina stands up from her spot at the table across from me and walks around to my side. "Actually, yeah. I think you're a fucking weak-ass bitch who ain't no one afraid of in here, especially not me. You walk around all high and mighty, thinking you're better than us, smarter and prettier than us, but guess what—you in here just like the fucking rest of us, and I ain't scared by your supposed past." She makes finger quotations an inch from my face.

I stand. We're eye to eye. I can feel her hot, stinky breath on my face. Her finger jabs me in the chest. My blood fills my ears and I can't hear much past the intense rushing. I clench my fists at my sides. Ready. I want her to come at me so badly. "Is that so? You gonna do something about it then?" I say, smacking her finger away from me. My eyes narrow on her acne-scarred face.

Before I can register what's happening, I feel her two bony hands dig into my chest. The air is pushed out and I gasp. My legs tremble. Teeth clench.

It only takes me a second to leap onto her. Her fingers are entwined in my hair and I can feel the pressure as she yanks. I elbow her, and she lets go. The top of my hand swings across her cheek and I hear a loud slapping sound. Her head flies back, her arms wave wildly as she tries to grab a hold of me, but my adrenaline is pumping so hard that I don't feel anything. My hands find their way to her neck. I squeeze and squeeze. Teeth gritting.

The power of my fingers pressing into the flesh of her neck

makes me shiver with excitement. It feels like I can breathe for the first time since that day in the library all those years ago.

I have tunnel vision. I only see her eyes rolling back and her mouth attempting to suck in air. My heartbeat increases in my ears. Thump. Thump. Thump. My hands and wrists must be aching, but I don't feel them.

Her arms keep flailing. Her fingers attempt to dig at my face. I don't feel that either, I just keep pressing my hands into her. Squeezing. I wonder how much longer until she dies. I'm tingling all over.

And then I feel hands on me—pulling and yanking me off her. I fight harder, and then so do the hands.

My grasp is broken. I'm being lifted into the air. I'm screaming and swearing. I'm shaking, ferocious with rage. It's a sensation from a time very long ago, yet it's so familiar to me.

A man's gruff voice breaks into my trance. My arms are twisted behind my back where I'm cuffed. Tightly. "That's enough, Wilkanson! You're done! You're done!"

Now that I'm off her, I realize in a sobering moment that he might not be talking about just the fight. A hurtling wave of nausea makes my stomach twist and my mouth water.

I may have just ruined any chance I ever had to get out of here.

I'm whisked away by two guards who throw me into solitary.

They aren't gentle with me as they literally launch me inside the room. I've never been in here before, but I've heard enough horror stories to know I never wanted to see it. I land on the ground with a thud. My bones vibrate from the motion. My arms are sore and bruised above my elbows where I was manhandled.

"I got to say, I'm surprised to see you in here, Wilkanson. There goes your perfect record. Was it worth it?" The guard, Han, shakes his head. He looks like a disappointed daddy and not some guy who's getting underpaid to deal with us lowlifes.

I remain quiet, as is my right. It's about the only thing I can control in here.

The other guard that has kindly accompanied me to the hole is Rickers. Unlike Han, has a smug smile on his face, like he's been waiting for this moment with a lousy fifty bucks riding on it.

Han spins me around and unlocks the handcuffs. My wrists are sore from being forced into the cold, hard metal. I rub them, trying to get the circulation back into my hands. My brain finally registers where I am as I look around the closet-sized room. There's nothing in here but a sweat-stained pad on the floor and a disgusting dirty blanket that I wouldn't touch for fear of contracting scabies or countless other contagious diseases.

"Someone will be in later to bring you to your hearing. Do you want anyone else there with you?" Rickers asks.

"What do you mean? I don't understand what's happening," I say, and it's the truth. I've never committed an offense before. My anger has dwindled, and I'm left in a state of confusion and shock. My body trembles. I can even feel my ribs shaking. What did I fucking do?

Han stands tall, shoulders squared, with his hand on his baton. He looks like he's ready to take down a linebacker and not some hundred-and-ten-pound chick. "You'll be taken in to see an adjudicator. You can bring in witnesses if you think it'll help your case. You'll tell them what happened and plead guilty or not guilty of the offense—in this case, assaulting a fellow inmate."

"But Georgina started it. She hit me first!" Ugh. I hear the pitiful whine in my voice and I wonder how I suddenly became a petulant child. I need to get my shit together before the hearing if I have any hope in hell of being taken seriously. "Can you ask Stephanie Harvey and Jodi Brown to come? They were there."

"We'll see what we can do," Han says.

"So what, I have to stay in here until then? How long does this hearing take to set up?" I ask. My palms are slick, and I wipe them on the thighs of my pants.

"It could be a few hours."

"Oh, great," I exhale, relieved.

"Or it could be tomorrow," Rickers adds.

My eyes and mouth widen. "What? You mean to tell me that I could be stuck in this hell hole overnight?" My mind reels. My bunk is shitty, but it's the Westin compared to this hovel.

"That's right." Rickers smiles. "Shoulda thought about that before you tried to kill someone in here." He walks out with Han right behind him.

My hand goes up and I wave for them to stop. "No, wait. You can't leave me."

Han takes another step away. "I'm afraid we can, and just in case we're not back today, sleep tight." The hefty steel door slams shut. The sound reverberates, echoing painfully in my ears. I'm dizzy. The walls look like they're getting closer. The air is cold and stale. My stomach turns over.

Think, Ryann. Lunch was served at one o'clock. The fight happened just after, which puts it around two. There's got to be enough time to get a judge or adjudicator to see me. What if the warden won't let Steph and Jodi out to testify for me?

I need water. My mouth is so dry.

Surely someone will come soon. In twelve years at this prison, I've never so much as hid a candy bar I wasn't supposed to have. I don't deserve this.

Fighting is a major infraction. Georgina wanted this. This was probably her fucking plan the entire time.

What the fuck did I do?

CHAPTER TWENTY-ONE

I have no means to tell the time. There isn't even a window. It's not set up like this for sheer punishment— that's a bonus. It's suicide proofed. Considering all four walls and my side of the door are padded, the only way I'd be able to end it all is to choke myself on the filthy blanket.

It could have been an hour since the door slammed me inside. Or six.

Pacing, crouching, and standing are no longer options, as my feet are killing me. Begrudgingly, I make my way to a seated position on the hazardous mat. It reeks of sweat and piss.

At least it's soft.

I'm fairly certain it's late in the evening. I have no idea how late adjudicators work, but maybe there's still time . . .

I hear something. The clanging of keys and steel. This is it. The door slides open with such violent noise compared to the steady silence that it shakes me. I'm up in one fierce motion before I even see who my visitor is.

Standing before me is Han. Good. He's still on duty.

"Thank God. Are you here to take me to the hearing?"

He reaches out into the hall and turns back to me, holding a plastic food tray with a wrapped sandwich, an apple, a bag of chips, and a bottle of water. "Nope, got your dinner. Sorry it's a little late. You must be pretty hungry."

I am, but that's the least of my fucking worries. "Why, what time is it?"

"Just after nine." He pushes the tray toward me and I grab it. I crouch, placing it on the pad. "What?" I shrink back down but my eyes remain on him. "What the hell happened?"

"I guess it was too busy to get your case in today."

"So what, I'm fucking stuck in here all night?"

"Afraid so." He hands me a paper. "This is a copy of the incident report for you to look over. So you can prepare for tomorrow and everything." He turns to leave again.

"What about the girls? Are Jodi and Stephanie going to be allowed to come and testify on my behalf?" Please, please, please. At least give me that.

He averts his eyes and purses his lips. If I didn't know any better, I'd say he feels bad for me. "Don't know yet. Just eat your food and try to get some sleep. You might be up first thing at eight tomorrow morning, and you want to be sharp."

I say nothing more and watch helplessly as he slams the door behind him. The imposing crash of steel echoes in my ears, and I flinch.

The light in the hole is harsh, and I wish they would dim it or turn it off completely. The low hum and flickering of the fluorescent bulbs are driving me mad, not to mention making my headache worse. I lower my gaze to inspect my dinner. My hands feel stiff and a bit sore, but I manage to open the plastic wrap and take a bite of the sandwich. Tuna, I think. It's even more repulsive than the cafeteria food. My lip is swelling, making it harder to eat. I suppose that bitch snuck one to my face after all.

Chewing, I resist the urge to spit it out. Perhaps they save the really repugnant cuisine for those of us unlucky enough to find ourselves in lock.

I eat just enough to quell the pit in my gut and drink the water.

My cell and the rest of F Block are usually cold, but in here is far worse. I can't stop shaking, which is quickly making the rest of my body hurt from tensing up.

I do the one thing I promised myself I wouldn't do.

I lie down on the stupid, disgusting pad, yank the gray, reeking blanket over me, and try to get some sleep.

Tuesday, December 5

The clanging of metal rips me from darkness. My eyes open into small slits. The light assaults me, and my arm instinctively covers my face as I adjust.

"Get up, Wilkanson. Your hearing is in forty-five minutes. You can change and grab some grub first if you move your ass." I look up. Rickers and Han must be off shift now. To my dismay I see officer Owens. She's not my favourite guard, but this isn't really my day, so I'm not fucking surprised.

Owens is a head taller than me—not such an accomplishment considering I'm all of five feet three. If it wasn't for her perma-scowl she might even be pretty. She snaps her fingers. "Move it, will ya?"

I bound up and smooth my hair with my hands. I don't want anyone to see me a mess. I'm not exactly vain, but it feels somehow violating to be seen with a greasy face, dirty bedhead, and sleep still in my eyes. "Can I have a quick shower?"

"No time." She motions for me to turn around. Before I do, I notice another guard just outside the door. She's one I've never seen before. Must be new. Lucky her, though why anyone would choose to spend twelve hours a day in this place of their own viola-tion is mind boggling. The lifers always say that the COs are doing half their time. I turn as instructed, hands together behind my back, and Owens snaps the cuffs on me. Not as tightly as yesterday, so I'm grateful.

She grabs me by the upper arm and leads me out. I suppose word of my little altercation yesterday is cause for a pair of guards instead of the one I usually have. That, and I'm not usually handcuffed. Anytime you go into or come out of lock you're cuffed. The guards don't know if you'll be super pissed and lash out again.

"You're going to meet your council now, to prepare your statement and that stuff," Owens says.

"I get a lawyer?"

"Something like that." She smiles and brings me to a room with a glass door. Inside is a small, balding man with a graying moustache flipping through his briefcase. Owens opens the door for me and leads me to a chair opposite him.

He takes me in—the infamous Ryann Wilkanson—and looks underwhelmed. It's almost comical. "Hello, I'm Mr. Lespool." He extends his hand and then laughs manically. "I guess you can't shake with the, the cuffs."

"No, I can't." I give him an awkward smile.

He takes out a chunk of paper. "These are the rest of the forms we need to fill out for today." His gaze moves from the paperwork to Owens, and he motions for her to remove the handcuffs. "She'll need to write."

She comes over to me. "Be a good girl or you'll be back in lock."

I shake my hands out at my sides. "What do I have to do, Mr. Lespool?" My eyelashes flutter and I smile at him. He's nerdy and old. I may be a murderous criminal, but he's still a man, and I could use him on my side.

"Uh." He pushes the stack in front of me. "Write your full and detailed account of what happened in the Dungrave County Prison cafeteria on Monday, December fourth, with fellow inmate Georgina Manzerolli. What you were doing, what she was doing, who said and did what, and who witnessed the said incident."

Reaching into his case, he removes a thin ballpoint pen. His hand hovers over the table, stalling.

"I'm not going to stab you with it or anything." I smile wide. I know it's not the best thing to say, but I can't help myself. I attack when I feel insulted.

His face pales and he drops the pen in front of me.

"Thanks," I say. My eyes adjust to the small print and I begin filling it out, though truthfully I'm still half-asleep. It's hard to be rested when you're sleeping on the floor with a rag as a blanket under the brightest fucking light with screaming nut jobs on either side of you.

Mr. Lespool shakes his hand near the page. "Let me know when you need me to explain something."

"Oh, I don't think that will be necessary, but thanks," I say cheerily.

"Yeah, our little miss sunshine has gotten herself quite the education on the county's dime." Owens stands directly behind me, so close I can smell her drugstore-bargain perfume. Not sure why she bothers in here, unless she's aiming for another of the not-so-hot officers.

I write my account of things. I have nothing to hide, after all. Georgina jumped *me*. *I* was the victim. It wasn't my fault that I had to defend myself.

From what I've heard, Georgina Bitchface Manzerolli is in here for second-degree murder and drug offenses, and while that's bad, it's certainly not as bad as my rap sheet. That will surely be considered when they decide whether or not to charge me with this additional offense. A hot, tingling sensation sweeps over my body. In an instant, a fine sweat breaks out all over my skin. I push myself to finish, satisfied with my account of things. Hopefully Stephanie and Jodi back me up, that is if they're allowed to be here.

I sign at the bottom where the *X* is. "Finished. Is there anything else?"

Moustache looks impressed. "That was fast. Did you want a

chance to look it over, maybe confirm that you included all the pertinent information?"

I shake my head. "I'm sure. So what's your plan?"

"My plan? I'm not sure I know what you mean, Ms. Wilkanson." I could tell him to call me Ryann, but I like the formality. It makes me feel important, and it's a nice change from 'Wilks' and 'inmate.'

"Do you have a plan to defend me?" God, I hope I don't have to spell out everything for Moustache.

"It doesn't really work like that. I'm appointed by the prison to make sure you comprehend the process and complete the paperwork. I'll read your statement and then assist you in explaining the events to the room. I'll also explain any legal wordings you may not understand and then confer privately with you if a plea is offered."

I push my statement back over to his side of the table. "Then you'd better get started."

He's sure to reach across to grab the ballpoint. He meets my gaze and his eyes widen slightly. "In case I want to add any notes."

I grin and give him a wink. "Of course."

Owens produces the cuffs again. My shoulders and wrists are still aching. "Can't we use the fact that I haven't attacked anyone— that was self-defense—and have had zero infractions as a sign of good faith and skip the hardware?"

But Officer Owens is already placing them on me. "It's protocol, Wilkanson. As much as I'd like to ensure your comfort, I have to cuff you. But I'm also supposed to offer you a quick bite to eat before you go in for your meeting. What do you want—oatmeal, cereal, toast, what?"

My empty stomach gurgles and begs for food, but it's also churning with worry and I don't want to risk barfing in front of whoever's going to be at the hearing. If Jodi and Steph show up and see that, I'll never live it down. Not that I even trust Jodi to do this for me. But Steph will show up. We're friends. Besides, she's so goddamn sweet, I can't see her wanting to disappoint me.

"Hey, do either of you know who's going to be at my hearing? I asked for a few witnesses to testify on my behalf."

I'm answered with a blank stare and a shoulder shrug.

God, I hope they show up.

I'm cuffed and shuffled down a maze of gray, concrete-bricked hallways—unfamiliar this time. The guards lead me to a room where a woman and the warden sit behind a long, boardroom-style table. I feel each pair of eyes scrutinizing me as I walk the ten steps to the lonely seat front and center, which is clearly mine. I'm kept handcuffed as I sit and face them, helpless.

There's no need to look around. Jodi and Steph aren't here. My shoulders are really starting to ache. I keep my gaze down. I know I should look up at them all and smile, since this woman is about to determine my future, but I can't manage it. I'm too fucking nervous.

I concentrate on my breathing so I don't hyperventilate and pass out. It feels like a mini parole hearing, which doesn't work in my favor.

"Ms. Wilkanson, my name is Susan Darby. I'm the adjudicator for this hearing. I assume you know the reason you're here."

My head lifts at the mention of my name. A woman in a dark gray pantsuit and silver-rimmed glasses focuses intently on me. I wonder what she sees? Hopefully a sweet, misunderstood young woman who was attacked and doesn't deserve to be in here. I nod. Best to keep quiet until I have to speak.

"To my left is Hailey Marcel, who will be transcribing this hearing. You know Warden Connelly, and you've met Mr. Mark Lespool." She turns her attention to Moustache. "Do you have her forms and signed statement?"

He bolts up and fumbles with his briefcase before finally passing her the papers. *My champion.*

I finally meet the warden's eyes with the saddest puppy-dog

expression I can manage, complete with droopy lip. She's got a medium build, but sturdy. A few gray hairs speckle through her short dark curls. She always takes walks through the prison to show us inmates she's here for us. *Barf.* I haven't spoken to her before, but her reputation definitely precedes her. Hard ass. She could end me right here and now, and she knows it. Her opinion carries a ton of sway at these things, and I have no fucking clue what she thinks of me.

Ms. Darby gets right to business. "Mr. Lespool, would you read the prison report recounting the events surrounding the infraction?"

Moustache does, and the report doesn't completely blame me, which is encouraging.

It's Darby's turn again. Her gaze pins me down in my seat. "Would you prefer to read from your written statement or simply recall to us what happened in the cafeteria yesterday, Monday, December fourth, at twelve twenty-six p.m.?" Her hands are neatly placed atop the table. She reclines slightly, with a look on her face reminiscent of medieval times, when the queen would demand to be entertained by the court jester.

"I'll speak freely."

"Very well. How do you plead?" Ms. Darby asks.

"Not guilty," I say, head high, shoulders back. The eyes of someone with nothing to hide.

"In your words, please explain the events leading up to and including the incident."

I tell the room about how we were having what I thought was a light-hearted conversation when Georgina insulted me, so I insulted her back, and then she attacked me and I defended myself.

"I have been informed that you have requested witness testi- mony—a Stephanie Harvey and a Jodi Lynn Brown?"

My heart flutters and threatens to break out of my chest, I'm so excited. "Really? I mean, yes I have, thank you."

The door opens to Stephanie. She's straight-faced. Very professional, though when she doesn't smile my brain spins. What if it's because she's testifying against me? It's the first time I let myself consider the fact that just because I called for them doesn't mean they'll actually help me. My lungs seize, and I take a few breaths in between coughs.

Steph is directed to stand behind a podium next to me. I know her well enough to discern the unsettled look on her face. She wrings her hands together, cracking her knuckles.

"Ms. Harvey, you were witness to the altercation that happened yesterday, is that correct?" Ms. Darby's hands haven't moved from their neat little spot in front of her on the table.

My eyes move to Steph, though I can't see her whole face. She's staring straight ahead. Would it kill her to give me a side wink, a nod, something? "I was in the vicinity."

In the vicinity? She was right next to me, for God's sake.

"Ms. Harvey, could you please explain what you saw transpire between Ms. Wilkanson and Ms. Manzerolli?"

My neck is twisted so far to see Steph's expression that I'm afraid it might pop off.

"I was eating my lunch and talking to Margot and Jodi when I heard yelling. I turned to see what the commotion was all about, and that's when I saw the two of them on each other, fighting."

Darby clears her throat and writes something down. Is that all everyone does in here—jot fucking notes? "Did you see which inmate made physical contact first?"

Come on, Steph. I know you saw. Please, don't do this to me.

Steph flips her hair behind her shoulder. I can hear her swallow. "No, I didn't see."

My stomach bunches up and makes it way up my throat, yet I manage to find my voice. "What are you taking about, Steph? You saw the whole thing! Come on—"

Ms. Darby stands. "That's enough, Ms. Wilkanson. I will not have outbursts here. This is *your* witness, after all."

I leer at Stephanie, willing her to look at me.

"Thank you, Ms. Harvey. Dismissed." Ms. Darby checks her papers again. "Send in the next witness."

And just like that, Stephanie's gone. She lied, and there's nothing I can say. Looking at the door, I watch for Jodi. I know before she's even near me that she's going to do the same fucking thing to me. I'm not disappointed when she replicates Stephanie's cold shoulder and icy stare as she approaches. Fucking bitch. But am I really all that surprised? Jodi and I were never close, but Steph . . .

I don't bother to protest this time. Or try to get Jodi to look at me. I know she won't. They've clearly made some sort of pact to fuck me royally. And I won't forget it.

It's over in less than five minutes.

"Any last words, Ms. Wilkanson?" Ms. Darby asks in her nasally voice that now grates on my nerves.

I compose myself, relaxing my body and face so I appear extremely calm and rational, though inside my heart rate has to be near one hundred fifty. My neck and chest are hot and sweating. I just hope my face doesn't appear too flush. "It's difficult in here. People don't want to be known as snitches. Even though I know Jodi and Stephanie witnessed the assault on me, they're afraid to admit it and possibly have Georgina retaliate. I suppose on some level I understand why they turned their backs on me, but it doesn't alter my previous statement. I did not start the fight. I was merely defending myself." I lower my gaze in the hopes she'll take it as a gesture of genuine respect.

"As you know, violence of any kind is not tolerated. If such an offense is committed, there are many repercussions. Fighting is a very serious infraction, Ms. Wilkanson, however I have viewed the videotape from the mess hall, which corroborates that you were assaulted first. You did retaliate, however, and so it is my recommendation that you lose phone and visitation privileges for two weeks and work in the kitchen, helping to prepare dinners each afternoon for the next month. Dismissed." Ms. Darby stands, does up the button on her suit coat, and walks out the door behind her, leaving me with my mouth open.

The muscles around my ribs relax, and I take my first real breath since yesterday morning. I can't believe what I've heard. It's not over. I still have a chance. In fact, I'm going to use this to my benefit.

This could be the best thing that's happened in my entire case so far. When I'm finished, Dr. Nancy will feel compelled to get me out of here. She just doesn't know it yet.

CHAPTER TWENTY-TWO

*N*ancy was at the prison wrapping up a previous case with a male inmate when she received the call from Warden Connelly.

"I thought you'd want to hear it from me, Nancy. So what do you think?"

Ryann had never been in any trouble inside the prison. Besides, the surveillance video looked quite clear. "It seems that Ryann didn't instigate the altercation. A case can be made that she was defending herself."

Nancy heard the warden inhale a sharp breath. "It's the vicious-ness of the attack that concerns me. She didn't start the fight, but did you see the way she lunged at the other inmate, and the way her hands flew around Manzerolli's throat? It took two large male COs to get her off."

Nancy had noticed that, of course, and she'd be lying of she said it didn't concern her, but there were a multitude of reasons why Ryann could've reacted that way. "Ryann has been locked up almost half her life. We both know the stress the inmates go through daily *besides* being in cells, not seeing their families, and losing sleep. I'm talking about the threat from other inmates.

These women are on constant guard, which would make any person hyper-defensive. It's not at all surprising that Ryann reacted the way she did. We've seen enough altercations in here, and many of the inmates have presented similarly, if not identically. Ryann felt threatened, in danger. We don't know how many emotions she has repressed and supressed over the years. It's my conclusion that she reacted typically for someone in her situation."

Nancy had no idea what she was doing. She could've easily said that Ryann was a danger, that this fight was indicative of future behaviors, and that she was far from rehabilitated. She could have even talked the warden into tacking some time onto her sentence. But there was something about Ryann that kept her holding on. Some hint that there was far more to the story. If Nancy gave in now, she'd never get the answer to the puzzle.

The truth was, Nancy had no idea if Ryann's violent behavior was indicative of anything. It could be exactly as she'd said to Connelly, or the complete opposite. She needed more time with Ryann to know for sure. She could always recommend against commutation in the end.

"Warden, do you mind if I ask a few questions to the COs who have worked closely with Ryann?"

Connelly steepled her fingers under her chin and looked pensively at Nancy. "You're actually considering recommending for her release, aren't you?"

"I haven't made my mind up, which is partially why I need to talk to some of your staff. I'm trying to get a variety of opinions here. Besides, you have a say as well, Beverly. Do you already know what you'll recommend?" Nancy tried to read her, but she was a tough one. Too many years in the game. Hopefully Beverly was thinking the same thing about her, and Nancy wasn't wearing her utter confusion like a fricking neon sign.

"I think I'll keep that one close to the chest right now. I'm sure you understand." The women exchanged a few more pleasantries, and Nancy left with two new names on her list.

Nancy made her way to the main CO office situated in the middle of the women's blocks. Mike Han usually worked in that area on a set schedule.

She saw him through the glass door, sitting behind the desk, and she knocked before she popped her head in. "Hey, Mike, you got a second? I'd like to ask you a few questions, if you're up for it."

Mike glanced away from the cell-area surveillance cameras. "Oh, hey there. What can I do for you?"

She closed the door behind her and noticed they weren't alone. There was a female CO inside with whom she wasn't too familiar. The woman turned and smiled.

"Hello, I'm Nancy Clafin. I'm a psychiatrist—"

Before she could finish introducing herself, Mike cut in. "Yeah, she's been working with Wilkanson. You know, doing the evaluation to see if Ryann's sentence gets commuted."

The woman's eyes widened instantly, like she'd accidentally gotten a shock she wasn't expecting. "I see."

It suddenly felt like the room had shrunk to half its size and the air was running out. Nancy smiled, albeit awkwardly. It was the only thing she could think to do.

"Oh, how rude of me. Sorry, I'm Officer Owens—Abby." She put her hand out and Nancy shook it. "It looks like you guys might want some privacy. I can find somewhere else to be." Abby grabbed her coffee off the desk and stood.

Nancy took a step toward her, her hand out. "Actually, have you worked much with Ryann Wilkanson?"

Abby's eyes shifted to Mike before finding her again. "A bit." She cradled her cup in her hands. "More lately. I spent the better part of the morning with her today."

"You took her to her hearing, then?"

"Yup. I've been working in F Block a lot this past year, so I guess I have a few insights on most of the inmates. Just my opinions. I don't have the degrees you do."

Nancy smiled. "Maybe you could stay, if you have a few minutes to spare?" Abby nodded and sat back down. "I was hoping to get some of those insights from the two of you about Ryann."

Han crossed his arms and tilted his head. "Such as?"

"How long have you been overseeing Ryann?"

"Maybe three or four years," he said. "At least."

Nancy didn't have her pen and paper this time. It was an informal questioning for her own benefit. She wanted a better sense of how the COs viewed her patient. "Did either of you ever witness Ryann having any altercations with inmates before—physical or verbal?"

Both Abby and Mike shook their heads. "Nothing physical is on her record, and I'd know, since she's high priority," Mike said.

"I did hear a few rumors when I started in F Block about her threatening inmates," Abby said.

This got Nancy's full attention. Her stomach tightened. "Can you elaborate? What sort of threats?"

"I don't know how reliable it is, since a few of the other officers only told me what a couple of inmates told them. In any case, I heard that she likes to intimidate the other woman by reminding them about what she did back then . . . how she killed those people and how she's not to be screwed with in here. Might be a tactic to keep from getting jumped, but it could be more."

"I see. Do you know when these threats transpired?"

Abby looked up, her lips pursed. "Um, I think the last one was over a year ago. The others were two years before that."

"But she's never actually put hands on anyone?" Nancy asked.

"Not to my knowledge," Mike said. "She's always seemed quiet, like she keeps to herself. A lot of the other inmates get pretty wired up and rowdy, but not Wilks. She's always off in some corner reading or maybe watching the TV. Doesn't even seem to play cards much with the others."

Perhaps Ryann was simply keeping up appearances. Attempting

to protect herself from becoming a target. It could be all bravado. "From your knowledge of the other inmates, the ones who reported Ryann's threats, is it possible they lied?"

Abby's thin lips transformed into a gaping smile. "Every inmate in this place is a liar, so yeah, it's highly possible. Didn't you hear? They're also all innocent." Abby broke out into laughter. Mike joined in.

Something about their cavalier attitude made her feel hollow and cold. "Yes, these inmates have made terrible decisions, but I highly doubt that prevents all of them from telling the truth."

Their grins and snickers stilled. Mike put his hand up. "We didn't mean to be cruel. You get a little jaded doing this job year after year. We got to keep a sense of humor, you know?"

"In all seriousness, one of the inmates who said Ryann made threats shares a cell with Wilkanson. Not sure if her claims are true or if she has some agenda for saying it. Most inmates keep their mouths shut, so we were a bit shocked to hear anything. We figured it was because the inmates were legitimately scared."

"Was anything done?"

Abby pursed her lips again. "Nothing we can do. It's all hearsay, and nothing's actually happened."

Nancy's stomach dropped again, and she asked herself why she cared so much. "Does Ryann really have a perfectly clean record for the entire twelve years she's been here?"

"She did until her fight in the cafeteria yesterday," Mike said. He almost looked disappointed.

"Is that going to impact her case?" Abby asked.

"I can't discuss that right now, not while I'm still mid-process. Do you think Ryann should be released?" This was *the* question. The rest meant a lot less if they both had unequivocal no's.

Abby inhaled and blinked in quick succession. "It's hard to say. Off the top of my head I'd have to say no. Not after everything she's done. She seems like a nice woman, doesn't cause any problems, but that doesn't mean I trust her to sit beside my sister at the movies or shop in a store with my nephew."

"Mike?"

"I know you've been working really hard with Wilks, and I know there's probably a lot we don't know, especially since she is getting this chance. To have someone commit the crimes she has and only serve twelve years of multiple life sentences tells me there must be something pretty big that's come up—new evidence or something. So I don't think I can fully answer."

Nancy crossed her arms and suppressed her smile. She'd always liked Mike. He was a lot more thoughtful than most of the COs she'd worked with. "I can appreciate that. How about based on your own experience with her over the years? Do you feel on guard around her? Threatened?" she asked.

"Not one bit," he said. "If either of you repeat this, I'll deny it to my grave. I like Ryann. She's a nice kid. Never been a problem, always respectful, keeps outta trouble, always does as she's told. She helps the other inmates with their schooling. Worked in the library all those years. She even runs a fucking book club. It's difficult to put that girl and the one that did those murders together."

"Speaking of Ryann, she should be finished with the rest of her paperwork. I better go get her before Lespool falls in love with her." Abby rolled her eyes. "Guy is a bit of a weirdo."

Mike batted her away. "He's harmless."

"Thanks for your time. You've been a great help." But Nancy was no closer to knowing who Ryann really was. Master manipulator, or changed woman?

CHAPTER TWENTY-THREE

fficer Owens walks me back to my cell, where I'm finally uncuffed. "You sure lucked out, Wilkanson," she says. Truthfully, I'm stunned. "I guess."

Owens looks just as dumbfounded as I feel. "I've seen far worse punishments for less. It all depends on the inmate, the infraction, and the adjudicator. I've always heard that Darby's a hard-ass." Hearing her say *hard-ass* is comical, and I snicker. "I was sure you'd get a few months added to your sentence, and you sure as shit weren't going to get out."

I remain quiet for the rest of the short walk except to ask if I've also missed lunch.

Owens checks her bulky army-style watch. "Lunch'll start soon. Why don't you go to the showers first, then the cafeteria." It sounds like a question, but it's a polite order.

I nod. I'm not sure what I'll do or say when I see Steph and Jodi. The fact that I have to live in a fucking cell with those traitorous bitches is going to be the ultimate test of my self-control.

Twenty minutes later I'm showered and in the mess hall. It's bustling with inmates eating and gossiping. Looks like egg salad sandwiches next to a small pile of roots and leaves covered in a thick layer of ranch dressing. I'm not too late for lineup, so I grab a tray and head over.

Walking toward the crowded tables, my mind races. My eyes immediately drift to where Steph and Jodi sit with everyone. It's where I usually sit. And that's not going to change today. I want those two to have to look me in the face.

"Is she sitting at our table?" I hear someone say, and know the 'she' is me. I turn and glare at each of my so-called friends before I set my tray down and sit. It's as though the air around me stills. Everyone stops eating and talking in favor of simply staring at me.

"Can I just explain?"

"Explain what? How you hung me out to dry? Made me look like a complete asshole? Save it. It's clear where we stand. You do your thing and I'll do mine. Same goes for you, Brown." My blood thrums in my ears, something that always happens when I get angry. I want to punch something. Maybe someone, but I take another gulp of water instead. My glass trembles ever so slightly in my hand.

"Seriously, Ryann?" Jodi says. I don't respond. "Fine, well you can listen," she continues. She leans in and starts talking to me in a whisper. "Georgina put a few of her goons on us. Said if we went against her she'd make us pay. We don't want trouble. We wanna get out too, you know. I already got to watch my back, and that's without the Italian army out for me."

"Whatever," I say.

Stephanie slides down the bench until she's across from me. "I'm sorry, Ry. It's not like I said you started it or nothing. I just said I didn't see it. I had to or they were gonna kick the shit out of me, maybe kill me."

"Oh my God, you two," I breathe and lower my voice. "No one is going to kill you, except maybe me, but I'm too close to getting the fuck out of here and I'm not going to mess it up on you two fuckers." They stare, eyes wide and mouths slack. I forget what I'm in here for sometimes. "I'm not serious about wanting to kill you. I'm just pissed. You guys are lucky you didn't completely fuck me."

Steph's shoulders leave her ears. "Why, what happened?"

"I got a slap on the wrist. Phone time suspended and kitchen duty for a few weeks." I get multiple pats on the back, which make me wince, followed by a few whoops and hollers. I can't help but smile. For someone with my criminal history, committing a violent offense could've been it for me.

"You have a guardian angel or something?" Jodi asks, laughing.

"I must. And no thanks to you."

Jodi rolls her eyes before Margot jumps in. "Come on, Wilks. You know what it's like in here. Snitches get a beatdown. You can't tell me that if you was in the same spot, you'd have gone all savior in there. Bullshit."

She's right, but I don't tell her that.

"Well, you earned it. You got a perfect record in lockup all this time. That had to count for something," Jodi says again.

"Maybe. Anyway, I got the shrink again tomorrow. I'm sure she'll rip into me for it." I finish my salad and push the tray away from me. "So how brutal is the kitchen?"

After dinner I finish in the kitchen with enough time left to watch some TV. The common area is loud, as usual, and smells. Not all inmates make personal hygiene a top priority. But I find a spot in the back and close my eyes, listening. It's an episode of *Law and Order*. I've always found it comical how many legal shows people watch in here. Maybe it gives the poor saps hope that they'll get justice one day. Hilarious, since they're all as guilty as I am.

My head is throbbing. Again. Seems like it is more and more lately. I know I shouldn't get my hopes up, but Dr. Clafin seems to be softening, like she's eating all the bullshit I'm feeding her from a silver spoon. It's not like it's much of a challenge, considering how much baggage the woman has.

Yesterday's little altercation with Georgina couldn't have worked out better for me. I can't wait to see Nancy's face when she realizes I was attacked. I should almost thank Georgina. I'll likely find my own way of letting her know how I feel about her before I leave. Just considering all the possibilities makes me giddy. Thinking about the various ways of killing someone is the only thing that gets me through each day. The fact that I've had to *nearly* stop for over a decade astonishes me. But there was Lana. Sweet, stupid, crazy Lana.

It was my fifth year locked up and I was practically coming out of my skin. I needed something to play with, and like a mercy sent from the heavens, in walked Lana. She was young, maybe nineteen or twenty, with pretty strawberry-blonde hair, and a cherub face. At first I couldn't understand why she was here. She looked the picture of innocence and virtue. Then I got closer.

Lana had the telltale signs of what I like to refer to as a fucking hot mess. She had homemade tattoos on her shoulders and arms to cover the track marks that peppered her fair skin. I also couldn't help but notice scars all over her, the kind you get from cutting.

It didn't take me long to claim her. Nobody would challenge me, at least not back then, since I was still too new and unpredictable to be seriously fucked with. Who knew, I could've found a creative way to stab someone with a plastic knife.

Lana was a deer in headlights. Head down, hunched in a corner, crying all the bloody time. After the first few days I introduced myself, and wouldn't you know it? We became fast friends. We were the same age, liked the same things, and really bonded. Turns out Lana, who was in for—surprise, surprise—drugs, had been living on the streets, having escaped from an abusive household. The poor thing was beside herself. So depressed. Well, after three months of listening to her whine and cry, it was time to have a little fun.

I remember it like it was yesterday. We were sitting in one of the corners in the block, all huddled and chatting away. I made sure I was her only friend. If anyone else tried to talk to her, I'd give the look that told them to back off and mind their place.

I touched her knee and looked into her eyes. "Lana, you've

been so brave, but think about it. What do we have to look forward to? I mean, I'm going to die in here, and you . . . What's waiting for you when you get out? Life on the street, getting scammed and beaten up, falling back into drugs and doing all sorts of things you don't want to do just so you can escape the pain by getting high again. Is that the way you want to live?"

Tears welled her eyes. "No."

"What are you willing to do about it?"

"I dunno. I'm not good at anything. I dropped outta school, and I can't go back home."

I tilted my head and gave her a gentle and understanding smile. "We only have one option."

Her blue eyes perked up and a jolt of electricity coursed through me. Her eyes . . . I'd always loved looking in them because they reminded me of Olivia's. "What option?"

I took a deep breath, as though what I was about to say was difficult but necessary. "We have to end it so no one can ever hurt us again. It's the only way we can really be free."

Lana gasped. Her hands went to her mouth. I reached out to her and immediately shook my head, knowing full well I already had her. "Never mind. I'm so sorry, I thought you were ready. Forget I said anything."

Her expression changed from shocked to thoughtful, and her hands found mine. "Do you mean kill ourselves?" she whispered, leaning in.

"It's too much in here. I can't take it any longer, especially when I know I won't ever be free. That's all I've ever wanted. No one has ever understood me or loved me, and I'm tired." I pushed my voice to crack, like I was so choked up I could barely speak. "I just want to go." She ate up every word. I could see it in her eyes.

Her hands tightened around my wrists, gripping me. "That's exactly how I feel. You're not alone. What do we do?"

I bit the inside of my cheek to suppress my smile, but my stomach and chest warmed. My heart beat faster until I was almost dizzy. I had her.

We each planned to do it that night in our cells after lights-out, though I had no intention of doing anything but try and sleep despite the excitement of knowing it could be happening at any moment.

The next morning I woke to a shrill scream and stamping feet down the corridor. I heard a few guards approach the cell, and one of them spoke into their radio. "We have a section 33."

Lana had one cellmate, and I was sure that's who was screaming bloody murder. I craned my neck to see as far down the hall through the bars as possible. Lana's cell was only five down from mine, so I wasn't too far from the action. I watched the guards open the cell, escort the other inmate out, and then I heard banging right before two guards pulled Lana's lifeless body onto the walkway so they could work on her. One began chest compressions while they waited for the medics.

Lana's cellmate could be heard yelling through the whole floor. "I didn't hear anything! I was asleep! I woke up and saw her like that. I didn't do anything."

I could see the graying, ratty, prison-issued sheet still wrapped loosely around Lana's neck.

The thought still gives me goose bumps. It didn't have the same thrill as my real kills—the ones where my hands actually did the deed—but it had to suffice, since there were cameras and inmates everywhere, and there was no way I could risk getting another sentence on top of the ones I was already serving.

It was the only time I did something like that in here. I came to my senses. What if the next one chickened out and told a CO about it, or worse, left a detailed farewell note exposing our suicide pact? I couldn't risk the smallest thing.

In the meantime, I started getting more and more support mail from people who believed I was sick and deserved another chance. I realized if these total strangers could feel that way about me, maybe I had an actual shot.

Tomorrow is a new day with Dr. Clafin, and I'm not going to

waste it. I stand and shimmy past a few of the women who are still glued to the show and make my way to the bathroom.

Since on the surveillance cameras the guards can only see the main room and not the bathroom, I figure it's the perfect place to take this to the next level. I see a full bottle of soda on one of the tables nearest the doorway and it's unattended. I swipe it, praying no one sees me, and go inside.

Two stall doors are closed, but no one is at the sinks. I enter the last stall and lock the door. What I'm about to do will suck, especially with the pounding in my head, but it's worth it.

Taking a deep breath, I grit my teeth and smash the full one-liter bottle into my already scabbed mouth as hard as I can manage. Despite it only being plastic, I feel pulsating, white-hot heat radiate through me from the weight of the blow. My lip has gnashed against my teeth and I can already taste blood. I try and focus, but my vision blurs. It takes a second to steady myself. I close my eyes and brace myself against the stall before sending the bottle down on me again. The pain in my head explodes, causing my stomach to flip over. I bend down as fast as the ringing will allow and empty my stomach into the toilet.

I flush, kneeling on the grimy, cold ground, waiting for my brain to stop rattling. Something wet runs down my chin and falls onto the white plastic seat, leaving splashes of red behind. I wad up some toilet paper and hold it to my mouth. Two strikes will have to be enough.

Standing back up takes a second. The pressure in my head threatens to make me vomit again, but I swallow hard and picture the cold water of the sink in my mouth, removing the sour residue.

I stumble but make it over and run the water until it's cold, which doesn't take long since everything in this place is always fucking freezing. My hand is shaky, but I remove the tissue and see that I've broken open the small cut that Georgina gave me, which now looks pretty bad. I should probably get stitches, but a place like this doesn't tend to you unless you're one foot in the grave. I run my tongue across my teeth to make sure I didn't loosen any. They feel secure, though sore.

I clean myself up, and after a few minutes of pressure, the bleeding stops. This better work, because it's going to fuck with the image I've carefully crafted for myself in here. When everyone sees my face, they're going to assume I got beat up and that I'm not nearly as tough as I claim. It doesn't matter that I choked Georgina out yesterday and it took two male guards to get me off her. I look like a punk, and more inmates will try to fight me.

It's going to be especially tough to explain since no one witnessed or heard any struggle, and everyone saw me ten minutes ago with a small cut—not a gaping hole—in my lip.

Holding my head high, I square my shoulders and walk back out into the main area. A few women look up from their card games and conversations, some with confused expressions and a few with a distinct look of satisfaction. I make a mental note for future reference.

"What the fuck happened to you, Wilks?"

Margot and Jinx step in front of me, mouths equally agape and brows furrowed.

"It's nothing," I say. Speaking pulls at the cut and I wince.

"Who did that to you?" Jinx's head might as well be on a swivel with the way she glances around the place. Like someone is going to wave her over, screaming, "Me!"

I pull away from Margot, whose hands are grasping my upper arms. "Seriously, I'm fine. I slipped in the bathroom. Someone left water all over the fucking floor."

Jinx snorts and rolls her eyes. "Did you break the fall with your face? Try again."

"That's what happened, and I don't give a shit if you believe me." I walk off, back to my seat in front of the TV.

The only person that matters is Nancy. She has to believe that I'll be in danger if I stay cooped up in here. I run my tongue along my lower lip, which has begun to swell nicely.

And this is only the beginning.

CHAPTER TWENTY-FOUR

ednesday, December 6

Nancy decided to get to Dungrave prison early. She wanted more time to look over everything again. She truly hadn't believed her patient would be violent again.

Was Nancy delusional? Maybe her judgment was worse than she'd initially feared.

Her chest was tight. She tried a few deep, relaxing breaths but only managed to make herself feel more lightheaded on top of her low-grade anxiety. *Why'd you do it, Ryann? Was it really self-defense?*

It was an herbal tea kind of day. Caffeine would only make her more skittish. The last thing she needed was Ryann picking up on her unease. Letting the fragrant steam hit her face, she breathed in, this time slowly. Her heart began to pump a tad less ferociously.

There was no point in trying to figure out anything more until she spoke to Ryann.

She felt a vibration in her pocket. She pulled out her cell from her suit coat and saw it was Ray. "Hi, honey. How are you?"

"That depends."

His voice sounded ominous. Her now steady pulse raced again. "What is it?"

"I was out with the guys downtown last night, and I swear I saw her, Ma." She could hear his rapid breaths coming in short bursts.

She clenched the phone tighter. "Are you sure? Where?"

"We were down on Second and Main, about to go into Roosters. There were a few people sitting on the sidewalk across the street—you know how I always check them out. Well, I did, and I think she was sitting there. She . . . she didn't look good, Ma."

"Are you sure it was her?" Her blood pressure rose, making it sound like she was listening to him underwater.

"Pretty sure."

"Then why didn't you go over to her, talk to her—"

"I tried! I called out her name, she looked up, I went to cross, but the traffic was so heavy." He paused, sniffling. "By the time I made it over she was gone."

It sounded like her. Every time Nancy, James, or Ray had tried to approach Kim, she'd bolted. She didn't want to come back to them. "I'm sorry, Ray."

"Why are you sorry? I'm the one who lost her."

"She doesn't want to be found, darling. Don't beat yourself up." Easing into her chair didn't soothe her back pain. She was so tense, her ribs felt like they were cracking with every small breath. Before she could stop herself from saying the very thing she never believed she would, the words were out and she couldn't take them back. "Maybe it's time we stopped looking, Ray."

"You want us to give up on her? How can you say that?"

The pain in her son's voice echoed through every inch of her. She carried the same grief. The same ache in her bones. As Kim's mother, hers was worse. There was a piece of her walking around the earth that wanted nothing to do with her. It left an indelible scar on her heart that would never heal. "We'll never give up on her. I will never give up on her, and if she ever chooses to reach out or come back, we'll both be there for her. But I can't help but think that after fifteen years we should let her be in peace. If she wanted us in her life, she wouldn't have left. She wouldn't run like she has every time." Her heart crumbled and slowly slid into her stomach. She muffled a sob in her elbow.

"Mom, you don't mean that. Besides, she's back in Dungrave after what—five years? Maybe that means something. Maybe she wants to be closer to us now."

Nancy sucked in a breath, hoping it would take the sting from her throat. "That's sweet thinking, but I'm not sure it's true." Nancy's attention was pulled to the doorway where Han was patting Ryann down behind the glass door. She couldn't let Ryann see her like that. "My patient is here. We can discuss this later tonight. I love you."

"Me too."

She remained in her seat, unsure if she could stand just yet. She heard the door open and then footsteps. She twisted her body so her back was to the entrance and wiped the tears from her cheeks. Allowing herself another few seconds, she stood up and faced Ryann. "Hello. How are you today?" She discerned a minute tremor in her voice and swallowed hard, hoping to discard the lump that had formed in her throat. Ray's desperate and disappointed voice played on a loop in her head.

Ryann looked almost happy, and Nancy wondered when Kim had last felt joy. How could someone like *her* waltz around like a normal person, when Kim was so tortured?

Ryann eyed her and walked toward her regular seat on the couch. "I'm okay, I guess."

Nancy grabbed her cup and found her place across from Ryann, though as soon as she'd sat, she got right back up. "Sorry, I forgot my notebook. Give me a second." She turned and shuffled through the briefcase on her desk behind her and marched herself right back.

"Peppermint tea, huh? Rough day?"

Nancy's shoulders rose. Her gaze met Ryann's. "Why do you say that?"

"You only drink peppermint tea when you're stressed," Ryann said casually.

Her palms slicked. "And what made you come to that conclusion?" She tried an easy smile.

"Because the first two times we met you drank it, though it's been coffee every session since, no matter the time of day. I can't imagine anyone not being uptight before meeting me, since my reputation is what it is. Also, peppermint naturally calms the stomach."

"Oh, I see. Very attentive of you, Ryann." It was a little thing, but it was enough to send gooseflesh up her back. What else had she picked up on?

"Is it because of me? I mean, what I did?" Ryann sunk into the couch. She hadn't appeared that withdrawn since the first few sessions.

"I wasn't pleased to get an email yesterday explaining that you were missing our session because you got thrown in solitary for a fighting infraction." Nancy's back tightened as she absorbed the damage to Ryann's face. Her lip was swollen to twice its normal size, with a substantial gash down the center.

Ryann's head titled to the right and her hair swung across her eye. "I'm not pleased, either, so . . ." She played with her fingernails, picking at the edges.

"Do you want to tell me what happened?"

She didn't look at Nancy. "Thought you knew everything from your email."

"I want to hear your side of things. That email is a general report of the incident. I want to hear what actually happened."

She looked up then. "You trust me to tell you? Aren't you worried I'll spin the whole thing so it doesn't interfere with my chance of getting out?"

"Not at all. I trust you'll tell me. You haven't had one iota of trouble until now, so I'm inclined to listen to what changed that."

Nancy grasped her silver pen from inside the notebook. "Whenever you're ready."

Ryann's eyebrows unfurrowed. "I was in the cafeteria eating with my cellmates and a few other women, including Georgina. She's the one who did this." Ryann pointed to her lip. "We weren't friends, but we got along fine, or I thought we did. We were all joking around, and then Georgina made some snide remark about me being a princess who no one was afraid of. We exchanged words, and she jumped me."

"I see. Do you remember what she said exactly?"

"She called me weak and said I thought I was better than everyone else. She called me a baby killer." Her eyes widened and her nostrils flared.

Nancy couldn't imagine someone with Ryann's history taking kindly to being told she was a weak princess and a baby killer. "And how did that make you feel?" Nancy had the sense she already knew.

"Pissed, confused . . . scared."

"Care to explain?"

Ryann sighed and crossed her legs under her. "Pissed because she was calling me out on bullshit she knew nothing about, confused because I had no idea why she was suddenly targeting me after four years in here together, and scared because I was forced to defend myself, and it could cost me my freedom."

"Forced?"

"If someone comes at you, you fight back. If you don't, it shows weakness, and then you're everyone's target. I couldn't let that happen. Besides, I wasn't going to sit there and let her beat the hell out of me."

"I understand that you had to defend yourself, but you choked her. Do you think that was a bit overboard?"

"If you saw her, you wouldn't ask me that. Georgina is twice my size. She also has a bit of a reputation. I saw an opportunity and took it. Her throat was the only chance I had against her. If I hadn't, I would've been really hurt."

Nancy used her pen as a pointer. "I can see your lip is swollen and your eye is bruised. Are you sore?"

Ryann squirmed in her chair. She touched a finger over her puffy lip. "I'm all right. I know it looks bad, considering I'm trying to get released, but you have to believe that I wasn't out to start a fight or cause any trouble, especially now."

"Why do you think Georgina picked a fight with you when you've known each other for years?"

"I don't know." Ryann ran her hand through her hair. "The only thing I can think is that she's mad I have a chance to get released. She wants to make sure that doesn't happen."

"Why wouldn't she be happy for you?"

Ryann laughed. "There's not a lot of goodwill in this place, even among friends. Jealousy is stronger than goodwill. Georgina has a life sentence with no chance of parole. Unlike me, she wasn't a minor when she killed someone."

"I see." Nancy looked down at her page. She'd barely written a thing. She closed it and put it behind her on the desk.

Ryann's stare was fixed on her. "I hope you don't mind me saying so, but I think there's something more going on here." Her foot tapped rhythmically on the ground. Tap. Tap. Tap. "The peppermint tea is for something other than me this time. I'm not sure what's wrong, but you're a really nice woman, and I hope it all works out for you, whatever it is."

"It's my daughter. She ran away a long time ago, when she was a teenager. My son thought he saw her, but she ran off. She doesn't want to come home."

Her tongue barely finished forming the last word when her stomach dropped. What was she doing? A wave of embarrassment crashed into her, leaving her whole body hot and prickly.

"I'm so sorry. That must be just awful for you. No wonder you're on edge today. I knew it was more than the fight I had."

Nancy waved her off. "No. No need to apologize. Let's get back to you. I shouldn't have said anything."

"It must be hard to keep something like that bottled up. I can't imagine not knowing where my mom or sister was. How old was she when she left?" Within seconds, she covered her mouth with her hand. When she removed it a moment later she said, "I'm sorry, it's none of my business. Besides, I'm probably the last person you would want to talk to about this. Please forgive my intrusion." Her gaze found its way back to the floor.

"It's not that, Ryann. Yes, it is painful. But it's been a long time. We all have things we need to deal with and move through, and we use the hurt and the mistakes we've made to learn and become better people going forward, which is what I hope for you." She smiled, hoping it would be enough to remove herself as the subject of discussion without her having to put her foot down. They'd done a great job building a rapport, maybe even some trust. Nancy didn't want to ruin their progress by reaffirming the strict boundary between them.

"So, is the fight going to jeopardize my possibility of release?" Ryann was fixated on her fingernails. Nancy could hear the clicking as she picked roughly away at them.

"I don't see why it should."

The clicking ceased. Tired, blue eyes searched hers. "Really?"

"One misstep shouldn't penalize you." Before Ryann could get too excited, Nancy raised her hand. "You are being considered in the same way you always were. No determinations have been finalized yet. This is still an ongoing assessment."

Ryann clasped her hands on her lap and bounded up in her seat slightly. "Oh, thank you, Dr. Clafin. You don't know what that means to have someone see you for something other than the last mistake you made."

Nancy knew a little about that.

———

Nancy banged on the door and barely waited a second before she turned the knob and busted through. Keith was sitting at his desk, on his computer, like always. It looked like he'd recently had a haircut and shave. Sometimes he let his beard stubble grow for a week. It was peppered with more white than brown and made him look about five years older than he was. She much preferred this look—not that she had any reason to prefer anything on him.

"Well, this is a surprise . . . and by the looks of you, I'd say it's not a social visit."

She made her way to the empty chair on the other side of his desk and plopped down. "No, it's not. What did you get me into? I told you over and over that I didn't want a case like this."

He opened his top drawer and pulled out two tumblers and a bottle of scotch. "And I told you I needed you because you are the best—well, next to me. What's going on?"

"Right now I need to debrief, check in, be reprimanded . . . something. And maybe have a small glass of that."

Keith always kept a bottle and cigars on hand.

He smiled and poured two fingers into each glass, pushing one toward her. "Now why would you of all people need to be reprimanded? A debrief, sure. Anytime. What happened?"

"I fucked up." She took a swig and tried to hold back her cringe as the burning crawled down her throat. She choked back a coughing fit.

His eyebrow rose.

"Ryann knows about Kimberly. Not everything, but she knows she ran away, has been missing for years, and doesn't want to come back."

"How did she find that out?"

"That's the worst part." She covered her eyes with one hand, still holding the scotch with the other. "*I* told her."

He took a sizeable gulp of his drink. "What do you mean, you told her?"

"I didn't know what I was saying. Before I knew it, it was out of my mouth. I was all frazzled from Ray calling."

"Why, what did Ray tell you? Did something happen to Kim?"

"No. Not that I know of. He called me minutes before Ryann's session to tell me he saw her. She ran like always. I guess it was still on my mind, because I blurted it out. Ryann asked me why I was drinking mint tea of all things. She claimed I drink it when I'm stressed—like she knows me."

"And how did Ryann react when you told her about Kim?"

"That's just it. She was empathetic, sympathetic, seemed genuinely sorry that I was suffering."

"And?"

"Don't you see? It compromises our professional relationship."

"Nancy, we all make judgment calls in session. Sometimes we self-disclose bits here and there if we think it will help the client or further the rapport. You didn't go into detail. It didn't cross professional boundaries. Relax."

Nancy glanced up and groaned. "You don't get it. I don't like her knowing anything about my personal life. Not after everything she did. Not until I'm sure I know who she really is."

"You'll never know for sure. You have to let that notion go. There are no certainties. No absolutes. You've got your instincts. What's your gut saying about her? Is she reformed?"

Nancy's breath caught in her chest and her lungs burned. "I don't know if I'm the person who should get to decide."

CHAPTER TWENTY-FIVE

hursday, December 7

My fingers itch with excitement as I type Dr. Nancy's name into the search engine. My insides purr. It's a wonderful feeling to do something useful. Sitting here, as the victim, has been as pleasant as getting impaled with fifty rusty nails.

She thinks she's got me. I bet there's a whole lot more to her than just her pathetic daughter that gives her that broken look deep in her eyes. And I'm going to find it.

I am not a fucking sheep.

The internet is so fucking slow here that it takes minutes to click between links.

A guard is pestering me about my five more minutes when I see something exceedingly attention grabbing. I click again, tapping my foot and mentally urging the browser to get to it. I'm in a hurry.

An article pops up on the screen: Inmate Declined Parole Commits Suicide. Hmm. I skim until I find Nancy's name. At the bottom of the piece, I read the bit of information I've been looking for—the bit I knew was out there, waiting for me to find it.

My insides flutter with sweet abandon. I have all I need on Nancy.

CHAPTER TWENTY-SIX

riday, December 8

Nancy had barely taken off her jacket when she heard the buzz of the door. Continuing to unpack her briefcase, she didn't look at Ryann. Didn't say hello or acknowledge her presence in the room. Her notebook and pen were pulled out and set in their usual place.

She was being a petty child.

"Hello, Ryann. How are you?" This time she glanced up and forced the corners of her mouth into a semblance of a smile.

"Good, I guess. You?" Ryann looked wearily at her. Perhaps her face betrayed her after all.

Nancy followed her to the couches. "A bit tired, but quite well, thanks," she lied. They sat simultaneously. "Your lip looks a bit better."

Ryann's hand went to her mouth. "Yeah, it's easier to eat today. I hate walking around like that. It's like I'm a poster child for the weak and punchable."

Ryann's eyes darkened as her fingers worked away on her thumb, picking at the skin. Some people enjoyed small bouts of pain—self-harm—in order to avoid something worse. "Of course it makes me vulnerable, but I've been lucky, and no one else has tried anything. Yet," Ryann said.

"Are you concerned this could lead to another attack on you?"

"It's possible. Apparently a lot of people are pissed about all the attention I'm getting. I don't know if you've noticed, but my case has been on television lately. My legal team is not exactly . . ." Ryann paused with a slight simper. "Subtle. I appreciate their willingness to help me, especially for free, but the public exposure is a little much." Her expression changed to panic. "Not that I'm not incredibly grateful, because I am. It just makes me feel a little exposed."

"And vulnerable?" Nancy's foot bobbed up and down. Soon she would have to get up and pace. "How's your anxiety?"

"Not great. I was going to ask you about that. Would you be able to prescribe something to help me sleep and calm down?"

"What's the problem?" She scribbled, though her pen felt like a foreign object, clumsy in between her fingers.

"I'm having a hard time falling asleep. Sometimes it takes me two to three hours, and then when I finally do, I can't stay asleep. It's not nightmares as much as waking up in a panic. I jump up, sweating, a jolt of adrenaline running through me. Is that normal when you're stressed?"

"There's no normal. Every person reacts differently to stress. The body copes in any way it can, and when it can't, meds can help. What about when you're awake?"

"I'm okay most of the time, but sometimes I get a panic attack out of nowhere."

"And what makes you think that's what you're experiencing?"

She sat up taller and pressed her shoulders back. "Bao-yu used to get them all the time. She told me what they felt like. I even saw her have a few. I wasn't as sympathetic as I should've been. I thought she was too sensitive and overly dramatic, and that she could calm herself down if she tried. Now I understand it doesn't work that way."

"No, it often doesn't for people. How long have you had these attacks?"

"About six months."

Nancy noted it. "When you get one, how long does it last?"

"I don't know, it varies, but usually about two to three hours. I'm not really sure why they've started. I feel fine otherwise."

"That's a long time for a single attack. I'm sorry to hear that. I'll write you a script and send it in. It should ease some of your anxiety."

"Thanks." Ryann inhaled, like she could feel air in her lungs for the first time in a while, and smiled widely.

Ryann's mood seemed improved since their previous session, and Nancy almost hated to get down to business. "There are a few things about Mr. Hastings's murder that I'd like to go over with you."

Ryann's eyes tightened in a squint, revealing her faint crow's feet again. "We already talked about him."

"I realize that, but I need a bit more."

She sighed loudly. "You're the expert."

"You killed Hastings on the same night as Omar, is that correct?" Ryann nodded. "Why did you decide on two victims in one night?"

"It was risky and stupid and horrible and a bunch of other things. I can't remember exactly, but I know there was a night— no, wait, it was the night of Yvonne's memorial at the school—"

Ryann remains confused regarding her memories around the time of the murders. Nancy wrote the quick note before gazing back up. It was important to watch her closely so she could see if any mannerisms were off.

Ryann continued, "I had this plan to go after this girl named Melanie. She was on cheer with me and I didn't like her. B and I were standing in the middle of the memorial when I saw her. I'd been so pumped, thinking it was the perfect place to sneak in an extra kill. I watched her walk off to the dressing room, and there was so much happening that night I was certain no one would notice either of us missing for ten minutes. I followed her."

Nancy had never heard this. It wasn't in any of the files. Was there another victim that no one knew about? "What happened when you went inside after her?"

"I didn't kill her, if that's what you're worried about. I was going to, but I was interrupted before I could do anything."

"Did you plan to go after her later?" Nancy's heart had sped up tremendously. There was still so much she didn't know about this woman—things she might never know. How could she possibly write a fair assessment?

"No, Melanie was a kill of opportunity, not someone I had really pinned down. Hastings was actually an impulsive decision. I figured that after Omar overdosed at the dance, people would be too preoccupied with the drama to pay attention to much else. It was the perfect opportunity to go after someone else—sort of make up for the lost chance with Melanie. And I thought, who deserved it more than Hastings?"

Nancy had the spot in her file ready and opened it up to the readied page. "So you went home for a bit after the dance then to Hastings's home, killed him, and met up with friends at the café after?"

"I think so, yes."

"You said earlier that you watched him burn." Nancy's cheeks grew warm. Her fingers tightened around her pen. She was supposed to be gaining clarity, not the sensation that she was drowning.

"I did for a minute, and then I ran."

It took Nancy a second to find her voice. She cleared her throat, trying to make it seem like she had allergies and not like she was forcing back revulsion. "Yes, you heard sirens, or else you probably would've stayed to watch longer. Tell me, Ryann, what were you feeling when you watched him, frantic and panicked, trapped inside the burning house?"

"We both froze, separated only by a pane of glass. I swiped a match and threw the flame onto the accelerant. He banged on the door, calling out my name for help. He was frantic. I think I considered it—helping him after the flames began spreading so quickly—but I remembered the man who taunted and ridiculed me. He kept fumbling with the locked doorknob, but he couldn't get it open. He screamed at me to help him. He rattled the door handle, clearly in too much shock to realize he simply had to unlock it and step through." Ryann swallowed hard, an audible gulp that sounded like it was coming through a microphone.

"I remember his thrashing, fire-swarmed body. The way he hollered and burned."

Acid swished inside Nancy's stomach at the vivid picture Ryann painted. It had come to life in her imagination, and she prayed she wouldn't continue to carry it with her. "Was there anything in you that wanted to stop what you were doing? Wanted to rush in and help him? Regretted throwing the match? Anything at all?" Nancy's tensed body perched forward in the seat. Spittle speckled her chin.

Ryann's eyes widened under furrowed brows. Her mouth opened as if to speak, but no sound escaped. She appeared to try again. A soft, tentative squeak grew more discernable. "I . . . I have re-regrets. So many. I thought that was clear. You told me to talk about it the way it was for me back then. It's not how I feel now," she cried.

As if Nancy was taken by the shoulders and shaken, she snapped out of her trance. Before her sat her patient, frightened, shamed, and stunned. Blinking hard, she refocused. She needed to contain this. "What do you regret most, Ryann?" The hardened edge to her voice had been replaced by softness.

Their eyes met. "That I ever took pleasure from the suffering of others. That I ever hurt anyone. That I deserve the way you're looking at me right now." She slumped back into the sofa, her shoulders folding in on themselves as though she were trying to disappear. She did that often. "You told me to talk about everything, except now you're even more disgusted with me. And it's not like you shouldn't be, but it hurts. I'm not her anymore."

They were both quiet for a moment, Nancy unsure of how she felt or what to say.

"I don't know how to sit here and pour my heart out, how to tell you all the reprehensible things I've done—that made me feel powerful and alive, that I chose to do time and again for God-knows-what reason—and then convince you to spin it for my defense team to get me out." Ryann gestured wildly around her. "What's the point of all of this? Is it to watch me react? See if I squirm at just the right moments? Show enough guilt that you deem me repentant enough?"

"This is a process, Ryann, and I already told you it was going to be an arduous one. This is difficult, all of it, but no more than what you did to those people and their families. This is a cakewalk in comparison. You ruined countless lives, tore a town apart, caused utter panic, and you want to sit here and feel sorry for yourself about how hard I'm being on you?" She stopped to gather herself. "If you can't do this process justice, than we can call it. You can go back to the confines of your cell, and I'll send my assessment in with the information I have gathered up to this point. It's your choice." She was shaking, causing her notebook to bounce gently on her lap. This time she didn't care if Ryann noticed, because this time it wasn't the result of nervousness or fear. It was outrage.

"No, I want to continue. But I also want to feel like I have a chance."

"You do. Now make it count."

"All I can say is that at the time I was so fueled by adrenaline and my insane mission, I never stopped to think about what would happen after. Everything was this intense, moment-to-moment, thrill-seeking adventure. The best way I can describe it is like playing a video game or watching a movie. I was there, doing it, but it wasn't really me. I don't know if that makes any sense."

Ryann's shoulders rose up under her ears. "After I left his house, I remember thinking I needed to get to B's so she could be my alibi, but I still don't have any memories of how I got there or what we did. I do remember that the next day, B referred to something from the night before and I had no idea what she was talking about. She gave me this look and asked what was wrong with me. I tried to laugh it off, but I could tell she was worried. Those moments were happening more and more, and it was increasingly difficult to explain away to my friends."

"Did you worry that those lapses put you at higher risk of getting caught, because you might have made a mistake?"

"I suppose I should've been, but as I stated, I wasn't thinking rationally. There was a part of me that believed I'd never get caught." Ryann tucked a chunk of pale hair behind her ear and gazed at the coffee table.

"I want to play a part of the tape for you." Nancy pressed a button and an image of Ryann sitting in her hospital bed appeared on the screen. Estevez sat in his usual spot to her left, the tape recorder placed on the table in between them.

Ryann shot forward. Her eyebrows lowered over glaring eyes. "I thought we were finished with this. I cooperated with everything you've asked."

"I think it's important for you to see, especially with all the memory gaps."

Nancy listened to teenage Ryann's assured voice on the video as she simultaneously watched the young woman in the room with her.

"It was the first time one of my victims knew I was the person responsible for ending their lives. It was a high all on its own, separate from the hunting and kill. It was a recognition of what I was capable of, and it filled me up so completely that I didn't feel like anything was missing anymore."

Nancy stopped the tape. "Do you remember saying that?"

"No, but it sounds like me. What I mean is, I don't remember saying that specific thing, but I remember believing that I'd finally found my higher calling." Ryann shoved a fingernail into her mouth.

"What did you mean by *recognition of what you were capable of?*"

Speaking past the finger, she said, "Bri was great at everything, and everybody noticed. I wanted to be great at something. Do something that even she wasn't capable of. In my madness, I believed that ridding the world of these people was a service." She paused as if to reconcile what to say next. "I suppose most teenagers try harder at sports or school, maybe put some mix tapes of themselves singing on YouTube or something, but not me. For some bizarre reason I thought, 'Hey, why don't I murder people and see if I can get away with it?' Being smarter than everyone else appealed to me just as much as the rest of my ludicrous reasoning."

"Maybe you need to think about if any of your actions were meant to prove something to your father. Maybe even to Brianna. It can be your homework." Nancy grabbed the bulky file behind her and rested it on her lap.

"What are those?" Ryann asked.

"Your case files."

"Oh. They're really . . . big."

Nancy exhaled loud enough for Ryann to hear. "You've done a lot." Rifling through, she plucked out a single sheet and slapped it down on the coffee table between them.

Ryann's gaze rested on the paper. It was a photograph. "What is that?" she asked warily.

"That is the charred and burnt body of Stanley Hastings. That is what happened to him after you doused his home in gasoline and threw the match. That is what you did to him when he screamed and screamed for help and you just watched him catch on fire and burn."

Ryann gasped. Her hands grappled onto the cushion beneath her as if she were desperately trying to grab a hold of something tangible. It wasn't the reaction of someone enjoying the moment. Perhaps there was still hope.

"What are you thinking?" Nancy pleaded. Ryann shook her

head; her eyes darted away from the image. "Why can't you look at it? It's the result of what *you* did. This is what you wanted to happen. Look," she cried. It was as though she'd lost her last crumb of control.

Ryann rocked back and forth, shaking her head. "I don't want to. Please . . . don't make me."

"Look, Ryann. Tell me what you feel when you look at it. At him."

Ryann forced her gaze onto the photograph on the table between them before blurting, "Like I'm going to be sick to my stomach." Her hands still gripped the cushion, her knuckles white under her body's pressure. "I never thought of what he'd look like after. I just wanted to teach him a lesson."

Nancy threw down another photograph. "Look," she said flatly.

Ryann closed her eyes and bit into her lip.

"Open your eyes and look."

She did, slowly, her grimace easing. "Who is that?"

"This is a picture of Stanley Hastings's children and grandchildren." Nancy pointed to each person as she spoke. "This is his son-in-law, Peter. This is his daughter, Alana, and these are his four grandchildren. This is who he left behind. These are the people you stole from. You took a father and grandfather from them."

Ryann hid her face in her hands.

"Look up at me. You don't get to hide from this."

She peeled her fingers away, revealing a grief-stricken face. "I'm sorry."

Nancy kept her finger on the photo of the smiling group. "I can't hear you."

"I said I'm sorry," she cried out.

"Why?"

"Because I didn't have the right to take him away."

"Murder, Ryann. You murdered him in cold blood." Nancy settled her voice back down to a gentle whisper. "These people have to live with your actions every day for the rest of their lives.

Every birthday, Christmas, and special occasion, they're reminded of what they are missing."

"I . . . understand."

"Do you?"

"I think I really do."

CHAPTER TWENTY-SEVEN

*D*r. Nancy seems satisfied that I'm fully shamed for the day. I cower in my seat and give her glimpses of a distraught and somber woman devastated by her horrid actions and disgusted with who she used to be. *Ugh.* Give me a fucking break. Putting on these little shows are zapping my energy. Normally, it's almost fun for me. I mean, who doesn't like the challenge of shrewd manipulation? And on a fancy doctor no less. But today I leave her office shaking, white-knuckled, clenched-jaw, flared-nostrils, and pissed.

Who the hell does she think she is? I didn't sign up to be humbled and treated like a piece of shit, and I certainly don't need my nose perpetually rubbed in it like a dog who pissed on the floor by some failure of a mother whose daughter hated her so much she'd rather give blowjobs on the streets than be under the same roof as her.

I haven't experienced this sort of blatant chastising since I was a kid being told how I should be more like *Brianna* because *Brianna* would never get only ninety-two percent on an algebra test and *Brianna* would obviously make every team she tried out for *and* be voted class valedictorian. I replay an old mantra in my head. One I haven't had to use in so many years that it almost makes me sick to think the words. *No one has the power to make me feel any way I don't allow. I am in control.*

Officer Han leads me down the bleak hallway. "Must've been a doozy."

I cock my head slightly in his direction. "Huh?"

"You seem upset is all. Normally you leave Dr. Clafin's office in a relatively good mood—at least it looks that way. But today, I dunno, you look pissed off or something."

"Gee, Han, I didn't know you cared."

He straightens up. A faint blush tints his cheeks. He says nothing else the rest of the way back.

The jittering in my arms and legs eases, though my head is still pulsating. Probably from clenching my jaw. I hate that she caught me off-guard.

And those pictures? Dr. Clafin probably thought they'd make me crumble. I wonder how she'd react if she knew that they made me quiver with excitement inside. That I had to hold back whoops and hollers of blissful satisfaction because I, after all these years, finally got to realize the result of my hard work and see that motherfucking prick Hastings charred down to an oozing mess. I could've eaten a hamburger with extra grease while browsing through those images. And the clear attempt at manipulation with the pics of the oh-so-sad family left behind. Please. They probably hated the old prick just as much as I did.

Was that seriously the best she has? I bet I could find a picture of sweet Kimmy, put it in front of her, and watch Dr. Nancy weep for her daughter's stupid ass.

The better question is where the fuck all that came from, anyway. She'd been cordial, almost understanding, until today. I thought the good doctor and I were on the same side. I wonder what my lawyers will think about this.

I hear the jangling of keys and realize that we're here. Home sweet home. Han opens the doors and steps to the side. I'm in no mood to wish him a great day as usual. I simply walk in and hear the slamming of the heavy steel behind me.

Most of the women don't bother to look up from what they're doing, but a few still do. Nosy bitches. I meet their stares with cold, hard eyes. And then I see one face that makes me grow hot, and the pulsating in my head spreads into my ears until I can no longer hear anything but my own quickening heartbeat. Georgina sets her gaze on me, nods her head, and smiles. She has a toothpick protruding from between her teeth, and I immediately wonder if it would kill her to make her swallow it?

I smile and blow her a kiss. She does not seem pleased with my affection, and I wonder if she's going to come at me. God, I wish she would. It would give me a reason to take all the rage bubbling inside my chest out on her.

When it's clear she's not moving, I continue past her and sit on a chair at the other end of the room. The clock says it's nearly two, which means it's almost time to go to the library for my shift. It's only for three hours, but it's heaven to me, and I'll take every minute I can get away from this den of hellfire. I can use the computer to continue my research on dear, sweet Kimmy too.

The familiar scent of mildew and musty paper comforts me as I step inside the library doors. A few tables are occupied with a handful of inmates here for study groups. It's mostly high school academics, but occasionally it's someone with a university-level course, because the library's the only place quiet enough to concentrate. Tamara, a thirty-something inmate doing time for forgery, shares library duty with me, and neither of us puts up with any nonsense.

I walk over to her at the desk. She's hunched over the computer with a glazed-over countenance. "Hey, Tamara."

She lifts her head out of whatever trance she's under. "Oh, hey, Ryann. I'm trying to input these new books into the system. It's a right pain in the ass." Her braids are tied back at the nape of her neck, accentuating her high cheekbones and pouty lips. Lips I'd pay good money to have. And I just might when I get out of here.

I'm sure I can find some poor schlep with a few dollars who doesn't mind offering me the finer things, like expensive handbags and reconstructive facial surgery.

It's not like I'm not recognizable, and the last thing I need is to be gawked at everywhere I go for the rest of my life. I won't hide out like some fragile, wilting flower, or else what's the point of getting out of here?

I pick up the book on the top of the stack and inspect it. It's smooth and unblemished. I can't recall the last time I held something so new and perfect. "Brand new books? Like, actually new? How the hell did that happen?" In twelve years in Dungrave County, I've only seen one box of used-but-new-to-us books come in, and that was ten years ago.

"Remember Goldie? Well, she kept her promise and sent these in. Five boxes in all." I can hear the excitement in Tamara's voice. If I'm honest, I share it. The only books in here that I haven't read cover-to-cover twice are the tech manuals. "And good ones too. Look, there's some Jodi Picoult and Nicholas Sparks," she says in a singsong voice. She rifles through the pile on her desk to produce a shiny, fuchsia book that I can only surmise is the most gag-worthy of all romance novels and waves it in my face. "Nora Roberts!" Her voice has a dreamy quality that makes me smile.

"Lucky you."

"Oh, and there might be a few up your alley." Tamara bends to pick up something from the bottom shelf. She places six books down with a thud.

My eyes scan the spines: Stephen King, Gillian Flynn, Thomas Harris, Patricia Highsmith, Anne Rice, and Jeffery Deaver are staring back up at me. A rush of near-giddy joy fills me and before I can think better of it, I'm hugging Tamara.

"Whoa, Ry. I've never seen you get so emotional before." I pull away, a gaping smile still on my face. "In fact, I've never seen any emotion out of you at all, well, except utter frustration when people don't use the return carts."

I feel as safe around Tamara as possible in here. "It's just so nice of you to save these for me."

"I'm glad you feel that way, 'cause I was worried you'd be offended."

"Offended?" I say, taken aback. "Why?" I run my fingers against the glossy, blood-spattered cover of *Mr. Mercedes*. I've been dying to read it. Half is told from the point of view of a serial killer. I mean, *hello*.

"If you haven't noticed, those books have murder in . . . I think all of them." Tamara bites her lip and scrunches up her nose at me. "I'm not insinuating anything, I just know you like reading crime stuff."

I like her, so it's no fun to put a scare into her. I wink and say, "I'm thrilled you've paid attention. You really are the best."

Tamara gathers the remainder of the loose books together in two piles. "These are the ones that still need to be put in the system. If you have trouble, just leave it, and I'll try to figure it out again tomorrow."

I may have a prison education, but I'm leaps and bounds ahead of her—ahead of everyone in here, including the COs. All you need is a GED to get a paycheck in here. "I'll do my best, unless Mr. King has other plans for me."

After Tamara leaves, I put the books to the side and head straight for the computer. I type in *Kimberly Clafin*, but nothing comes up. If she's living on the streets, there likely isn't a digital footprint. It's almost like she doesn't exist at all.

All I manage to find is an obituary for Dr. Clafin's husband, James, dated June 16, 2012. Prostate cancer. He was only fifty-seven. Nancy must be a bit younger than he was. Or she's got one hell of a skin care regime.

Fifteen minutes in I decide this is hopeless endeavour. There has got to be another way to get the information I need. And then, like a fucking lightning strike in the dark, Han walks in.

I refrain from bolting up and running at him like I want to, waltzing over casually instead. "How's your afternoon going?"

He makes a confused face and glances around him like he doesn't realize I'm speaking to him. "Me? Fine. Seems you're in a better state than you were."

I shrug. Best not to appear too peppy and eager. He can smell that shit a mile away. "Being in here always makes me feel better. Not only that, but I got to thinking, and I may understand things a bit more." The little white lies I'm about to tell are risky since Han and the doctor are a bit chummy, but they're the only lead I've got.

"Understand what sort of things?"

I widen my eyes, big and round, and flutter my lashes a touch. "What Dr. Clafin is going through." I narrow my gaze and curl my lip as though I know we're both already in on the secret.

He takes a step closer and leans in just enough so I can hear his whisper, but not so close that the other inmates will think something inappropriate is going on. "What do you think she's going through?" His eyes attempt to read me, to see if I'm lying, but he doesn't know who he's dealing with, and his small-town intellect isn't quite up to the task.

"I just get why she's been a bit short-tempered lately. Her son saw her daughter the other day, but apparently she wouldn't talk to him and ran off. Dr. Clafin's pretty upset about it, but I mean, wouldn't you be?" I can tell by his scrunched eyebrows and pursed lips that he's comparing what I've said against what he already knows—which I hope is something.

"How do you know about Kim?" he says, and I know I've got him.

I give him another wide-eyed stare. "She told me. I feel so bad. It must be hard to be away from your child for so long."

He nods, one hand on his belt near the baton. "It would crush any parent."

"I just think Dr. Clafin should have tried a little harder, especially after her husband died."

"Now, wait a second," he says far too loudly before stepping in closer still and whispering, "Nancy tried for over ten years to find

Kim and get her help, but that girl just didn't want it. There's only so much you can do for someone if they don't want the help."

The way he defends her makes my stomach squeeze with excitement. It's another risk to put my educated guesses out there, but I need to know. "I get that, it's just that street kids get messed up in some pretty rough things. It's hard to imagine Dr. Clafin leaving her out on the streets to get worse each day. I know she's a doctor, but maybe she couldn't help her own daughter because they were too close, you know? I never listened to my mom, and it wouldn't have mattered if she were a psychiatrist or not. In fact, it would probably have made it worse. I would've resented the fact that she thought she knew better and rebelled twice as hard. Do you think Dr. Clafin blames herself?" I shake my head, the picture of empathetic commiseration.

I watch Han's gaze move from the floor to the ceiling and then straight ahead. He pulls himself back up. "This is a highly inappropriate conversation to be having, Ms. Wilkanson."

Shit. My chance is up. "Sorry. I was worried about her. I thought I could get some advice from you. She just seems so sad, and we've gotten to know each other over our sessions, and I've come to care about her. But I suppose you're right. I'm just an inmate." I try my best to look wounded and can tell it's working.

Han exhales, and his puffed-out chest settles a bit. "It's nice that you care. I've known Nancy—I mean Dr. Clafin—for a long time, and that family has been through hell, but she's a strong lady and can handle whatever comes. You don't need to worry about that." He seems so sure, but I witnessed a distinctive pain in her eyes that day in her office. One that tells me she is not as strong as she wants everyone to think. She *is* vulnerable.

We aren't so different after all.

CHAPTER TWENTY-EIGHT

*N*ancy wasn't expecting anyone when there was a knock on her front door. Her eyes moved to the clock. It was just after eight. A rush of nerves moved from her neck to her toes, complete with goose bumps and shivers. She peeked through the curtain on the nearby window to see Ray on her front step blowing into his hands. Giant snowflakes whirled around him.

She opened the door, thrilled to see him. "Ray—"

"I saw Kim again. She's still here."

"Where?" He came in and she closed the door, her arms wrapping around herself from the burst of icy wind that swept in with him.

"She was camped outside Blackburn Restaurant." Tears brimmed. "I talked to her, Mom," he said with a catch in his voice.

She put a hand on his cheek. He didn't look like a twenty-two-year-old man. He looked like her ten-year-old son with a broken heart. "Tell me everything." Her heart skipped from the surge of adrenaline.

Ray walked toward the living room. She followed, shaking and nearly breathless. "How did it happen?"

They sat next to each other on the couch. It was difficult to tell by his face if the conversation had gone well, though past experience made her stomach clench. He leaned forward, taking her hands in his and meeting her gaze. "It was about an hour ago. I pulled up in front—I was going to meet Derek for dinner when I saw a group of people huddled on the side of the restaurant. They were drinking and smoking, and jumping around all crazy. I walked a bit closer hoping to get a better look, and there she was."

Nancy kept her excitement buried, not wanting to feel the slap of disappointment if Ray said she'd run away again. With an even tone she asked, "You spoke to her?" She held her breath. Something in Ray's eyes told her this time was different.

His hands squeezed hers. It was soft and warm. Reassuring. "Yes, I did."

The squeeze of her palm mirrored the one around her heart. "What . . . what did she say?"

Ray pulled back and took a deep breath. His brows furrowed as his eyes welled. "She misses us." A tear escaped, and he brushed it away with the back of his hand. "She wants to see us."

The thumping of her heart vibrated through her chest and into her palm, quickening with each passing second. She shook her head gently, as though she had heard him wrong, but the swell in her chest told her she'd understood correctly. "She wants to see *me?*"

Ray nodded and in a swift motion, pulled her into him. She rested her chin on his broad shoulder allowing her own tears to trace her cheeks. After a minute she drew away, inspecting Ray's shirt. "Look what I've done. Your shoulder's wet."

He let out a belly laugh. "I don't care about that. She's coming home. We're getting her back."

Nancy's chest constricted, her breath pinched. She couldn't register the rush of feelings. Was it excitement? Anxiety? Fear? Joy? Maybe all of them colliding.

She was afraid for Kimberly. Afraid for herself. She'd failed to be the kind of mother Kim needed before. What if she couldn't help her now?

Ray's voice broke through her fractured deliberations. "Mom, you look like you're not breathing." He clasped her shoulders and gazed into her eyes. "Say something."

She wanted to, but her throat felt achy and strained. She forced herself to swallow the swell of emotion and managed to squeak out the words, "When?"

Her son's brow unfurrowed and the corners of his lips turned up slightly. "Tonight, if we want." He was practically bubbling over. His eyes were alight, his cheeks glowing. "So do you want to come with me?"

Nancy was on her feet and rushing for her jacket. Like a chicken with no head, she raced from one end of the room to the other. "Where's my purse? And my keys? Where's the—"

"Mom. Stop. You don't need anything but your coat. I'll take us."

Nancy was so grateful for her son. If there was ever a moment she needed to be taken care of, this was it.

The drive to the Blackburn Restaurant from her house took about fifteen minutes. It could have been hours.

All that time apart and Kim's illness had built a brick wall between them. Every small issue and fight was a brick in the wall, until it was so colossal that it blocked Nancy from her daughter completely.

Ray drove, slower than she could almost stand, but the weather had made the roads icy and slick. She watched the streets as they whizzed by and wondered what Kim would look like, what she'd say, how she'd act, and if her baby could love her again.

Chunky snowflakes swirled. The rhythmic rubber of the windshield wipers against the glass both lulled her mind and aggravated her. Nothing was simple. Everything suddenly had multiple meanings and could be interpreted for the better or worse. It felt like a cruel trick, and she worried they'd get there and find nothing but an empty street. No sign of her daughter.

The anticipation made her palms slick and her mouth dry.

Her eyes caught every person walking along the sidewalk, every bulb on every decorated tree, and every footprint that disrupted the falling snow. Yet she didn't recall any of it as they pulled over in front of the tall, brick building.

Stomach lurching, she gasped for a breath. Her sweaty hand gripped the handle, though she couldn't seem to make the car door open. A wave of dizziness filled her head, but she pushed and stepped out onto the white, glistening sidewalk. Her eyes scanned the street. Where was her Kimberly?

Ray moved beside her and grabbed a hold of her arm. She was grateful for his steadying presence. "Kim should be down here." He steered her toward a small, huddled group of people crouched together against the wall of the restaurant about ten feet away. Was she somewhere in that cluster? The people appeared dirty and disheveled. Some were wearing light summer jackets and had holes in their pants, their hair soaked from the snow. Cold and hungry.

She'd pictured Kim like this countless times, convincing herself that her daughter had made her way to California or Florida when one of their grueling winters hit. She'd been unable to cope with the reality of what her daughter was likely going through.

And then she made herself recognize that Kim had chosen that life. And every day she didn't call or show up at Nancy's or Ray's doorstep was her choosing it all over again. It was how Nancy got through, but deep down she knew someone as fragile as Kim couldn't make that choice. Not really.

She knew from her years of work that you couldn't help someone who didn't want it, or worse, didn't even see a problem. Didn't recognize their illness or the detriment they were doing to themselves.

She and Ray stopped in front of the group. Despite the frigid temperature, she could smell the stale, sour body odor every time the breeze flitted over her. Her eyes searched the crowd for Kim's familiar face. But she recognized no one.

Even up close it was difficult to say for certain who was male or female in the mishmash of grimy clothing, grimy faces, and damp hair. She saw a pair of kind, blue eyes above a beard. A head of long red hair. Kim was a brunette. Her mind quickly processed the others, and when she was about to call out, frantic, for Kim, a small face turned toward them. It was one she knew. One she'd know anywhere.

"Kimmy!" She pitched forward but was yanked back by strong hands.

"Mom, relax. Give her a minute," Ray said gently.

Nancy watched her daughter hide her face, letting her long, stringy hair mask her eyes. She shouldn't have called out like that. She knew how sheepish Kim could be. She breathed slowly. "Kim, it's us. Ray and Mom. We just thought we'd come over to say hello." It killed her to stay back on her side of the pavement when every motherly instinct screamed for her to jump into the middle of the lot and yank her baby out, holding on to her and never letting her go again. But she knew Kim. Anything except slow, calm, and steady might cause her to bolt, and they might never get this chance again. It was a near miracle that she allowed herself to be found at all.

Ray took a step closer. "Remember I said I was going to come back with Mom to see you? Well, we're here."

Nancy held her breath. It was the only thing she could do. Her eyes never moved from the mess of Kim's brown hair.

And then the hair was swept to the side by a small, gloved hand, revealing beautiful green eyes. Slowly, she seemed to register her visitors. "Hi."

Nancy covered her mouth with the crook of her arm, tears brimming. She tried to steady her breathing and finally managed to choke out a word. "Hello." The icy air stung her cheeks and made her eyes burn, but she couldn't blink. She didn't want to miss one second of seeing her daughter's face.

What should she say next? What should she do? Every word
and action had the power to alienate Kim again. Thankfully, Ray
reached his hand out, and to Nancy's amazement, Kim took it. He
pulled her forward, away from the rest of the bodies huddling for
warmth.

It was the first time Nancy had seen her in nearly a decade.
Her gaze progressed up and down Kim, and back again. "You're so
thin." She wanted to choke the words back down. "I mean, you
look lovely. How are you?" Forcing her arms to remain hanging at
her sides was painful. How long had it been since she'd hugged her
daughter? Kim hadn't let Nancy touch her for months before she
finally left. But Ray, he was still holding her hand. Maybe she
would let Nancy, too.

Kim smiled. "I'm okay, Mom."

The well inside Nancy burst, and she wept as silently as she
could manage. When she finally composed herself seconds later,
she said, "I haven't heard that from you in a long time."

"How does it feel?" Kim asked.

"Wonderful." She extended her hand. Her arms and legs
tingled. Kim reached out. Her skin was cold and dry.

"I'm sorry I was gone for so long."

"That's okay, honey. You're here now." Using the back of her
gloved hand, Nancy wiped the moisture on her cheeks away. "Can
I hug you? If not, that's okay—"

Kim's eyes glistened with tears. "I'd like that."

Nancy bounded toward her, wrapping her daughter in her arms.
She squeezed and cried. They both did. Kim was so thin. Her
cheekbones left shadowed hollows where her cherub cheeks had
once been. Blackened eyes replaced the former sparkle and curiosity. "Are you hungry? Do you want us to take you for something?"

"No."

Nancy hid her rejection the best she could, offering a smile.
"That's okay. Is there anything you want to do?"

In a tentative voice, Kim said, "Go home with you?" She
wrapped her arms around herself. "If that's okay?"

Ray put an arm around Nancy. None of it seemed real. "Of course." She nearly shouted it, she was so thrilled. She and Ray ushered her over to the car, sitting her in the passenger seat. It took willpower to not actually buckle her in so she couldn't run from them again.

Why now? Nancy wondered, though she was beyond grateful for this chance.

She decided to sit behind Ray. That way she could still see Kim's profile. She didn't dare let her out of her sight.

They drove slowly, carefully, through the snow-blanketed roads. Her mind played with her, taunting her with images of their car sliding along the slick streets and crashing—losing her daughter before she ever really got her back.

She pushed the waking nightmare from her thoughts and tried to take in the moment. Right there, in the warm car, she heard her son and daughter talking, laughing. They were all together again.

Almost all of them.

Was James watching them now from his perch? Smiling down on them?

James's passing was not a conversation she wanted to have with her daughter, especially after all the years of grief and pain between them.

The heater was on high, distributing Kim's stale, acrid body odor throughout the car. How often had she been able to clean herself up, eat, or sleep in a safe and warm place?

The car pulled into her driveway and Ray turned off the ignition. It was quiet, with only the sound of the wind sweeping against the metal of the car.

"We're here," Ray announced with a pep to his voice Nancy hadn't heard in a long while.

"I can't believe it," Kim said.

Nancy watched what looked like awe wash over her daughter. "What is it?"

"You still live here? I can't believe it. It looks the same." Kim pushed open the door and got out. Nancy quickly followed, as if not staying right behind her would give her the opportunity to bolt. She studied her daughter: every movement, facial expression, and cadence of voice. There was nothing to indicate that Kim was under the influence. But how could that be?

"It's freezing. Let's go in." She put her hand on Kim's back and guided her forward. Ray opened the door—had she even locked it before they tore out of there?

The warm air was a welcome sensation as it thawed her nose and cheeks. "You must be freezing, Kim. Do you want some tea or coffee? Some soup? A hot bath?"

"All of the above, actually." Kim laughed, looking every picture of radiance that Nancy saw in her dreams.

"Do you want me to take your jacket?" Ray asked.

Kim nodded, removing her thin, cotton, army green coat and handing it over. The smell filled the space between the three of them. "Sorry. I guess I need a shower more than I realized. You don't smell yourself when you're with a group of people who also reek."

"I have some clothes you can change into after if you want. We can wash yours, or we can go shopping and get you new ones tomorrow. Whatever you like." She wanted to offer for Kim to move in with her and let her take care of every need and want. She reined herself in. "What would you like first, shower or dinner?"

"Actually, I was hoping to see Dad. Is he home?" Her smile widened, and Nancy's heart shattered.

Ray cleared his throat. He was looking for a place to hang the jacket.

Nancy forced down the lump in her throat. "Maybe we should sit. There's something you need to know."

The smile disappeared from Kim's face. "Why, what happened? Did you guys get a divorce or something?"

"Let's sit, like Mom said. You've missed a lot." Ray gestured for them to make their way into the living room. She followed, clearly uneasy. Her shoulders rose to her ears. Her hands were clenched at her sides.

Nancy sat next to her on the sofa, Ray opposite on the loveseat. Normally, she would reach over and take Kim's hand in hers. Comfort her with motherly gestures. Instead her gaze focused on the tiny freckles across Kim's nose.

"Just tell me what happened." Kim reached out and grabbed her hand.

Nancy squeezed, feeling Kim's bony hands and paper skin in hers. "I'm so sorry, darling, but Daddy died four years ago. He had prostate cancer. We tried to find you . . ."

Kim yelped. "Oh my God." Her hands flew to her mouth and she muffled another cry.

Putting an arm around her, Nancy tried to comfort her. "I'm so sorry, honey. He loved you very much. Don't ever forget that."

She lowered her hands and inhaled slowly. "Did he suffer?"

"Not much. It was fairly quick," Nancy said, though it was a lie. She watched her daughter's eyes move around the living room, glancing on all the pictures of James and a few family photos from before Kim had run away. She was sixteen in the last one.

Kim buried her face in her hands and crumpled forward. "He died without me. I never got to tell him I loved him."

Ray stood and crossed the room, crouching in front of her. He took her hands in his. "He knew. We all knew you loved us, and we never stopped loving you."

Kim glanced up as tears ran down her cheeks. She was shaking. Nancy couldn't decipher if it was nerves or withdrawal.

Stroking Kim's hair, she said, "Why don't you have that hot shower now? It'll warm you up and make you feel better."

Kim nodded. Nancy walked her toward the guest bathroom, started the shower, and went to get her some dry clothes. Both her babies were home. For the moment, she had almost everything.

CHAPTER TWENTY-NINE

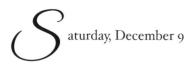aturday, December 9

I look at my watch. It's only 5:26 a.m. Some nights it's hard for me to fall or stay asleep. Tonight is one of them.

My mind wanders to Nancy.

Kim turning out the way she did explains a lot, and it couldn't have worked out any more fucking perfect for me. Dr. Nancy's eyes when she saw my face after I'd been attacked told me all I need to know. She was picturing sweet Kimmy alone on the streets, being roughed up by horrible men. Being vulnerable and taken advantage of. I have to make sure that when she looks at me she sees a helpless, lost, fragile girl—a girl just like her daughter—if there's any chance she'll get me out of here.

After a lukewarm shower and cold bowl of oatmeal, I'm waiting around to be called in for my morning session. I wonder what today will be. If we're working chronologically, which it seems we are, I haven't been shamed for Martin's murder yet. I bet he's on today's agenda.

I can hardly wait.

Ray had insisted on spending the night on the living room couch. Kim took the guest bedroom, and Nancy tried not to cry when she told her it had been nearly six months since she'd slept in a bed. If she wasn't on the streets, she was usually on a rickety cot in a shelter somewhere with nothing but a sheer blanket and a balled-up sweatshirt for a pillow.

A bathroom separated Nancy's bedroom from the guest room Kim was staying in. Living alone over the last few years had made her especially sensitive to noise. Her motherly instinct was switched back on with Kim there, and her eyes wrenched open at the sounds coming from next door.

Jumping from her bed, she went to see what it was. As she walked nearer, it almost sounded like someone was retching. The door was closed, so she knocked lightly. "Kimmy, are you all right?" Putting her ear up against the door, she waited for a response but only heard the horrible sound again, followed by coughing. "I'm coming in, darling."

"No, please don't," Kim said, but it was too late.

Her daughter was sitting on the floor, her head resting on the toilet seat. Her skin was a shade of white that petrified Nancy, especially in contrast to the vividness of her bloodshot eyes. Nancy steadied herself, careful to approach Kim slowly. She knelt beside her, using one hand to tuck a sweat-soaked chunk of hair behind her ear. "What can I do?"

Kim was trembling fiercely. Beads of sweat dripped down her face and neck. "Nothing. I'll be okay. It's not like it hasn't happened before."

Nancy took her wrist in her hand. Kim's pulse was quicker than it should have been. "Maybe we should take you to the hospital. They can prescribe you something to ease the withdrawal."

Kim yanked her arm away. "No! No hospitals. I'll be fine. You don't know what they do in there. It's so bad."

"Why suffer when we can—"

Kim's eyes changed from unfocused to wild in a heartbeat. "I won't go." She bent over the toilet rim then, coughing, but nothing more came out.

Nancy fetched a facecloth from the linen closet, soaked it with cold water, and placed it on the back of Kim's neck. "You should drink something so you don't get dehydrated."

Kim gave a chuckle. "Have any vodka?"

"If it will help."

"Well, I wasn't expecting that answer." She removed the cloth and wiped down her face. "I've come this far. I'm not going to give in now. That's what they'd want me to do. But thanks anyway."

Nancy had no idea who 'they' were, but Kim was in no condition to be questioned. They stayed there, quiet for another ten minutes.

"I think it's over." Kim pulled herself up with Nancy's help and they walked, arm in arm, back to the bed.

Kim got under the covers, still shaking violently. "Thank you."

Nancy pulled the comforter up to her neck. "For what?"

"Not judging me. Well, out loud anyway." She gave a small smile.

Kissing Kim on the forehead, Nancy pulled back and stroked her cheek with the back of her hand. "I love you."

"And for letting me come back after everything."

"You are always welcome. Now try and get some sleep. I'll be right next door, unless you want me to stay in here with you?" She knew it was a long shot, but she couldn't help herself.

"I haven't had anyone take care of me in a long time. It might be nice to have you so close. Just in case."

Nancy's heart leapt in her chest. "All right then. Scoot over." The sheets were warm from Kim's body. She likely had a fever. Lying next to her, Nancy was immediately sent back in time to when one of her kids had the flu and they'd sleep in bed together so she could keep an eye on them. Just like she had then, Nancy woke at the slightest sound or movement to ensure her child's safety.

The heat radiated off Kim, causing Nancy to lower the blanket. Getting back to sleep was never easy for her. Early menopause didn't help. Her eyes had adjusted to the dark and she glanced around the room. She never spent any time in here. Why would she? It was nice, not huge, but cozy with soft green walls and white furniture. She'd even hung up some paintings she'd done a few years ago. Nature scenes, mountains, streams, and forests.

Within a few minutes Kim's breathing evened out, and she closed her own eyes, drifting into a restless sleep.

A surge of adrenaline propelled Nancy's eyes open. What time was it? Her chest tightened. She looked next to her for Kim, but her side of the bed was empty. A wave of dread compressed her. Where was she? Had she left?

She was up on her feet. "Kim? Kimmy!" The panic in her voice was evident. She bolted straight for the bathroom. Maybe Kim was sick again. The door was cracked. She pushed it open, but it was vacant. Her stomach knotted. Downstairs?

Nearly tripping on her cat, Felix, she took the stairs two at a time. "Are you down here?" She stopped in her tracks when she hit the kitchen. Kim and Ray sat at the breakfast table together eating waffles. It was too late to compose herself.

"You okay, Mom?" Ray looked embarrassed for her.

"Yeah, fine. Just wondered where my kids were." She sauntered over to the table and peered down on their plates. Blueberry, my favorite." She forced a smile, but was certain they could see the vein pulsing in her neck. "It's nice to see you eating, honey. How are you feeling this morning?"

"Freaking out that I left, huh? Don't worry, still here." Her plate was heaping. Nancy noticed the hand tremor as she held the fork.

"What time is it, anyway?" Nancy looked at the stove clock. It was twenty after seven. Thank God she wasn't late yet. In all the excitement, she'd nearly forgotten about her session with Ryann at nine thirty. Maybe she could reschedule.

Ray took a sip of orange juice. "You're not going into work today, are you?" He glared at her. It was his disapproving stare.

"I have one session. This case is under such a tight timeline." What was she saying? There was no way she was going to pass up time with Kim for Ryann. "You know what? I'll reschedule it."

Kim squared her shoulders and met Nancy's eyes. "I'm fine. You guys shouldn't drop everything for me. I've been taking care of myself for a long time—I can handle being holed up in this beautiful house for the day. Go." Her tone was stern.

It went against her instinct, but Nancy worried that if she didn't give Kim space and show she trusted her, it would only alienate her daughter further. God, she hoped Kim meant it this time. Against her will, she pictured herself coming home to a ransacked house. Did her lack of absolute faith make her a horrible mother? "Help yourself to food and clothes. There are a stack of movies and CDs in the den if you want. I'll be back in a few hours."

Kim pushed a piece of waffle around on her plate. "Do you work, Ray?"

"Yup. I have a part-time job as a line cook, but I can call in sick." He fixed his stare on her.

Kim waved him off. "Go. I'm fine here. I promise."

"You'll be here later when I come back tonight, right?" he asked.

"Yes."

Nancy pitied Kim for the third degree they were giving her. She must be feeling so much pressure. Besides, they were virtual strangers to each other now. Sure, they were family, but they didn't know each other as adults. Kim was twenty-nine. More than a grown woman, and after everything, Nancy didn't blame her for wanting some alone time to process and regroup. It was a lot to take in, and Kim had already procured some good faith by not only coming with them in the first place, but staying there all night.

"I'm going to hop in the shower quick. We can meet back here for supper." Before Kim could argue, Nancy fled upstairs to get ready.

How would she concentrate on Ryann, today of all days?

CHAPTER THIRTY

My heart flutters in my chest. Dr. Nancy is never late. Maybe she decided I'm a lost cause after all and jumped ship. Since I'm not allowed to sit in her office without the great and powerful Dr. Clafin present, I'm stuck sitting in a crappy plastic chair in the hallway just outside. Fear not, though. I have the intriguing company of none other than Officer Han. How do I continue to get so lucky?

"Did you lose a bet?"

He glances up from whatever he's doing in his tiny cupboard. "Huh?"

"It's just that you're here again. Usually my guards rotate, but you seem to be at each one of my sessions. Curious." I smile a friendly smile.

"Dr. Clafin requested me."

"How nice. The two of you really are friends."

He looks as though he has no idea how to respond, but quickly turns his attention back to whatever he's been doing.

"So how are the wife and kids, Han?" He stares ahead as though he can't hear me. "Oh, she's annoyed with you today, huh? That's rough. What did you do?" I *tsk tsk* at him with my finger and he lets the tiniest of grins slip out. He likes me. Not in a pervy way, but kind of like a dad way, if that dad was resigned to the fact that his daughter was a famous killer with a heart of gold. "Come on, Han. What's new?"

"You know I'm not gonna talk to you about my life. Not sure why you ask day in and out, Wilkanson." He stands tall, his broad shoulders back. He looks like those burly men in the army or navy recruitment commercials. I'm very aware that he doesn't carry a gun, though I can imagine how much the pepper spray hurts from watching Dodson. The pistols were removed about ten years ago after an inmate in a male prison overpowered the guard and used his own weapon against him. That's not to say there are no guns. The guards that work over-watch detail on the catwalks and towers carry rifles and shotguns, and every guard carried their piece when they escorted me to and from court.

Regardless, we can't step out of line. No guard is beyond bludgeoning an inmate with a baton or even the butt end of their flashlight. Whatever works. But not Han. At least not that I've seen so far. I know people. I can read 'em like a fucking book, and Mike Han doesn't have it in him.

There are two types of guard in here: the kind that want to help us and keep prison a place for rehabilitation, and the kind that get off on caging us like the animals they think we are. Han is not the punishing kind. Poor sap.

He taps his pen on the desktop. "Your doc is late. I hope she's all right," he says, still not looking at me.

"Maybe she had a better offer." And just then there is the click-clack of her high heels against the linoleum. She scurries toward us, hair half-falling out of a clip, and she can barely manage her purse and briefcase. I'd offer to help her, but sudden movements and all that.

"I'm sorry I'm late," she shouts down the hallway.

I allow myself a soft chuckle. It's nice to see someone as put-together as Dr. Nancy look like a hot mess once in a while. "Better late than never, right?"

She stops abruptly in front of me, drops her bags to the ground, and lets out a loud exhale, her shoulders dropping dramatically. "I guess so. You might as well come in with me."

I look up at Han to make sure he hears this and doesn't accost me for following her. He gives me the nod and I move behind her. She turns on the awful, migraine-inducing fluorescent lights before beelining for her desk, where she dumps her stuff.

"You can sit. I'll only be a minute." She takes off her coat and hangs it on the rack by the door. She's practically buzzing around the room with an energy I've never seen before. It looks good on her. "Coffee or tea today, Ryann?"

"Um, coffee, please."

Filling the coffeemaker, she is humming a song I don't know. Did she get lucky or something? I know I'd be singing a different tune too. "You seem in a good mood."

She puts spoonful after spoonful of grinds in the top of the machine, but doesn't answer.

"Anything you can share?" It's a long shot, but why not?

"I think we should stay on topic."

"Meaning me and all the murdery things I did as a screwed-up kid?" I give a wry smile, but she appears shocked, not seeing the slightest humor in my wit. Her loss.

"Cream and sugar today?"

"Why not? Hit me."

"You seem in a playful mood. Anything *you* want to share?" she says over the hum of the coffee maker.

"I guess I realize how lucky I am to have this chance, especially after the unfortunate cafeteria incident and all. That could have been the nail in the coffin, yet here I am."

There's a little small talk before it's ready. Something is definitely up. She is different than I've ever seen her. Lighter. Dare I say . . . happy? She stirs the coffee and heads over to me, steaming mugs in both hands.

Sitting across from me, she crosses one black pant leg over the other. "How are things going . . . in here?"

"It's never easy, but the hope of being let out makes it bearable. I'm not a fan of kitchen duty, that's for sure, especially when half of Georgina's little buddies work in there with me."

"Really? I'm surprised to hear that. I was certain the COs would try to keep you separated." She fumbles with her glasses case for a second before and putting her glasses on.

I sigh lowly. "You'd think. So far nothing much has happened except for a few 'accidental' shoves and the occasional death glare."

"Do you want me to see if I can get you moved? I'm sure Warden Connelly will be fine with you being mandated to another area. Maybe laundry?"

I allow my eyes to widen like she's the savior I've been waiting for. "Really? You could do that? Th-thank you, Dr. Clafin." I lower my 'awestruck' head at her benevolence. Whatever the fuck has happened couldn't have come at a better time for me. "At least I still have the library. It's the only place I feel happy and safe." I chew on my bottom lip. Hopefully I look as nervous and delicate as I think I do.

"You seem drawn to libraries. I know from your files that you spent much of your free time in the Dungrave Public Library, and now you volunteer to work in the prison one. What's the appeal?"

I wind a chunk of my hair around my index finger, simulating deep thought. "I'm not sure. Maybe because they're always quiet and peaceful. I'm an introvert, but I could never be myself. I was always 'on,' funny and talkative, and being social was exhausting. At the library I could hunker down in a corner with a stack of magazines or books and be left completely alone. I didn't need to be anything to anyone, and it was great. And now, well I guess it's the closest thing I have in here to my old life. There may not be complete peace and quiet, but I get to suggest new worlds to these women who may never have experienced literature before." I let my hair unwind and drop from around my finger. "That makes me sound like a pretentious asshole, doesn't it?" I laugh, lean forward, and cradle my face in my hands. "Ugh, tell me to shut up."

It's the first time we've talked like people and not like a shrink interrogating a serial killer. Nancy smiles, clearly taken with me. "No, it's nice that you want to share something with others. There's not a lot to do in here, I imagine, and you give them a way to escape.

"You murdered Eric Knox in your favorite place—the Dungrave Library—though from what I can tell in your files, that murder wasn't planned." Reaching behind her, she grabs her trusty notepad and pen.

I knew it was too good to last. "Time to get down to business, huh?" I lean back and cross my legs, and my arms rest at my sides. I'm not sure if it's best to look surprised or wounded at the sudden shift.

Nancy holds up the pad and pen. "What, this?" She gives a small chuckle. "I suppose it's my tell."

"And here I thought we'd be discussing Marvin, but if you want to probe for the gritty details of one Eric Knox, be my guest." It's clear I've thrown her off-kilter with my candor, and I like that I can still do that.

Securing her pen between her fingers on top of the notebook, she says, "Where did you want to start?"

"Out of all the people I killed, he's the only one who deserved it."

"That's quite the statement, Ryann. Care to clarify?"

"I don't mean it like I'd do it again. He was a manipulative prick who took advantage of the vulnerable, and if he hadn't died that day I don't know how many other people he would have hurt. So, in a sense I actually protected society by . . ." I clear my throat. "Stopping him." Come on, Nancy. Make the connections.

Her eyes stare at me over steepled fingers. "I see. Would you mind expanding on why you believe he was a dangerous person?"

"I'm sure you know all about it. It might not be in my file, but I'm sure the cops gave you what they had on him. Or you could have seen it on any variety of news shows."

"If you're referring to Officer Knox being asked to resign from his previous posting for harassment, I am aware of it."

Very clever, Dr. Nancy. I'll play. "Are you also aware that he kept meticulous files in his apartment on the poor woman that he *stalked* for over a year? He did the same to me. He had pictures of me all over his walls, and detailed plans of crimes he wanted us to commit together. Murders, mostly."

"Officer Knox was quite unwell. I have to ask, Ryann, what makes you any different. Eric never actually killed anyone, and here you sit, having taken the lives of six people."

I push away my smile. "Yes, I did some crazy, monstrous things, but I don't believe I was in control. He was a police officer who suspected I was hurting people. Instead of stopping me, he begged to join me, like we were some kind of murderous Bonnie and Clyde."

"In one of the journals recovered at his residence, he had written that the two of you had a relationship. Is that correct?"

You couldn't shatter her gaze with a hammer. She had me in her sights, waiting patiently for me to say the wrong thing, blink the wrong way, breathe suspiciously. "Not in the way you think. He was charming and helpful. I thought I could use him to tell me things my dad wouldn't. He confused me. He made me think that he was a normal guy, and I was stupid enough to believe it. That's the problem with young girls—we think we're smarter than everyone else."

"But you had a sexual relationship?"

"Only once. Like I said—stupid. I had no idea who I was dealing with, and when he followed me to the library that day I saw how crazy he actually was." I sigh and wring my hands out at my sides. The memory of his arrogant face and wild stare still nauseates me.

"I'm not surprised you reached out to him considering the strained relationship you had with your father. He may have served as a surrogate for you in some way."

"Ew. Are you saying I wanted to screw my father?" My stomach twists.

"No, not at all. He could have been a substitute in other ways.

Perhaps he gave you the attention or approval you never felt you had at home."

I calm down. "Maybe. I never intended to kill Eric, but when he followed me to the library that day, proclaimed his love for me, and demanded that we kill together . . . it was obvious he was crazy. It's funny how I couldn't see the same thing in myself. I thought I was doing this righteous thing for the world, and he just wanted to play some sick, perverse game. I thought I could get rid of him, but he told me he knew Bao-yu was downstairs." I stop, swallowing hard as though I'm collecting the courage to say the next, painful thing. "I told him he was crazy and that I would never touch her. That's when he threw my bag on the ground—the one with my bloody clothes and the knife I'd used to murder Marvin Dodson. He said if I didn't kill her, he was going to do it himself and turn me in for all the murders. He said no one would ever believe me."

"What happened next, Ryann? It's okay. This is a safe place."

"I knew I had to kill him first."

CHAPTER THIRTY-ONE

*D*r. Clafin's heart was beating so frantically she feared Ryann could hear it. "This isn't in any file. Did you ever tell anyone that Eric threatened Bao-yu?"

Ryann lifted her head slightly. She tucked the falling strands of blonde hair out of her face. Only then did Nancy realize she was crying. "Come now, Dr. Clafin. Do you really think anyone would've believed me? You tell me how it would've looked." Her voice rose, almost strained. "The police come into the library and find Eric dying on the floor with a knife that I'm holding. You really think the cops are going to buy that I killed him in self-defense when I knew Estevez was getting closer? It was only a matter of time before they put it all together—my bike on Hastings' lawn, the bag of evidence at my feet from Marvin's house. As far as they were concerned, he was another victim, and I was lying to cover my ass. I had no proof of his threats."

By this point Nancy knew all the case files by heart, and she knew about the bag of evidence recovered from the library. She examined Ryann for the telltale signs of lying—flared nostrils, rapid blinking, looking up or to the side, long pauses, even changes to her voice—but nothing appeared off. It was nearly impossible to hide micro-expressions, which were physiological and mostly involuntary, but there was not even a blush to her cheeks to indicate the anxiety that comes with lying.

Nancy had to remind herself that if Ryann was a psychopath, she might not exhibit any signs of anxiety because she wouldn't have any anxiety. But that wasn't what she'd seen with Ryann. Nancy had decades of experience. She'd worked with sociopaths and psychopaths before, and there was always a detached coolness about them. No matter how hard they tried to come across as empathetic or emotional, it seemed hollow. Ryann appeared in all of their sessions to be experiencing genuine feelings and reactions.

"You're not saying anything, Dr. Clafin. This is partly why I never told you. It makes me appear like I'm looking for excuses, but I'm not. I take full responsibility for the horrid things I did. I'm not blaming Eric."

"You were a child, Ryann, possibly a very ill child. Eric was a man—a trusted officer who attempted to use your illness for his own sick thrills." And Nancy believed this. It made more sense than anything else.

But something was still off. If Ryann had told Eric that she refused to hurt Bao-yu, why did she hold her at knifepoint only moments later, when Sergeant Estevez arrived?

"Would you like to take a walk with me?"

Ryann's eyes widened, and an expression of confused shock replaced the anxious frown lines from seconds before. "Where?"

"Around the grounds. Some fresh air might do us both some good. What do you say?"

"Sure. But I didn't think people like you were allowed to go around the prison like that. You sure this is all right?"

"I have clearance to be on site. Besides, there are guards everywhere. Are you worried about my safety?"

"Well, yeah. There are some crazy chicks in here. Have you ever gone for a stroll on the grounds before?"

"Not exactly, but there's a first time for everything, and I like trying new things." She grabbed her coat. "We should stop by your cell to get yours. It's cold outside."

CHAPTER THIRTY-TWO

I watch as Dr. Clafin casually tells Han that we're going for a little walk.

"I can't allow that, Nancy. You know the rules," he says, blocking our exit.

I see her smile and tilt her head as though contemplating which way to shut him down. This I like. "It's all right, Mike. I have an arrangement with Warden Connelly." He gives her a look of disbelief. "Call her if you like. I'll wait." She crosses her arms and taps her foot.

He does as instructed and calls into his little walkie-talkie thing. He's wearing an earpiece and makes a show of putting his finger over it like he can't hear over all the ruckus our silence is clearly not making. "Over." Backing up, he extends his arm and gestures for us to pass.

I didn't realize Dr. Nancy had that kind of power around here.

"I hope you know that I'm going to follow you around the grounds to make sure you're safe," he says.

Pointing to myself, I say, "From me? I'm no threat to her."

"It's really not necessary," Dr. Nancy says in a polite voice that I don't fully believe.

His gaze is on me now. "I know you're not a threat, Wilks. It's the other inmates I'm worried about. Don't get worked up. I'll stay back far enough that I won't be able to hear what you're discussing."

"Very well, then. Thank you." Dr. Clafin leads the way out. We take a quick trip to my cell, where I grab my lovely brown prison-regulated jacket, and we're on our way, but not before I catch Steph gawking at us. It delights me in a weird way, like I'm getting special treatment. It'll probably come back to haunt me later. Just one more reason to be harassed.

I wish this special walkabout went outside the prison. I could use a little day trip. But alas, she brings me to the courtyard where I'm allowed to go every day. Woo-fucking-hoo.

"Is there a reason you wanted to go on a little stroll, especially when it's so cold?" I'm freezing, but don't want to spoil whatever therapeutic reasoning she's performing right now.

"I know it's chilly, but the fresh air feels nice, doesn't it? I imagine you don't get much of it during this time of year."

She's right. Colorado gets frigid, and I'm not a fan of shivering, frozen toes, and runny noses. As we walk, I'm hyper-aware that Officer Han is trailing behind us. You'd think the yard would be bare, but there are hordes of smokers out here during free time. I'm not one. I don't want premature wrinkles or yellow fingers and teeth, especially since I'm about to get out. The media will be stalking me, searching for unflattering images of the teenage serial killer, and I'm sure as fuck not going to help them out.

"Yeah, it feels good. Sometimes it gets so stuffy inside. Claustrophobic, even. Not that there's a lack of bodies out here. It's weird. When I'm out with the general population, all I want is to be alone and away from the noise and business. But when I'm in my cell, I want to feel the bustle of life going on around me." Which is bullshit. We walk along the fence line, hands in our pockets, plumes of white hanging over our mouths and noses as we speak. It's overcast today, making it feel ten degrees colder than it is. Figures.

"How do you like your two cellmates?" I can sense her eyes on my face, though I refuse to turn to see for sure. She's always trying to analyze me.

"That depends. I used to, but then after the fight . . . well, it changed things." Like in the cafeteria, the inmates outside segregate themselves into groups. I feel all sorts of eyes following us around. Everyone is wondering who the fancy woman is and why she's walking with me.

I can see Dr. Clafin nod in my periphery. "Your cellmates wouldn't testify on your behalf, I remember. It must be tough to feel so betrayed yet have to share your most intimate time and space together."

"It could be worse. They're harmless, just trying to survive in here like the rest of us."

"Is that how it feels—like surviving?"

I stop. My head is down and I kick a rock at my feet. "Every day. You never know what will happen. The women in here aren't in jail for social hour. Many of them are dangerous. You have to watch your back twenty-four seven, and you never really know anyone."

"That's a desolate way to view life, Ryann. You had good friends and a family that loved you."

"Maybe, but it doesn't make it any less true." My toes are going numb. My boots aren't well insulated, probably to add even more levels of punishment. The scrubs are rough and scratchy, the boots give you blisters and make your feet sweat, and the underwear can best be described as granny panties. Even the blankets have the lovely texture of a potato sack.

"The comment you made about not really knowing anyone— does that refer to anyone besides your cellmates?"

I shrug.

"Can I venture a guess?"

"Be my guest."

"You could be referring to Eric, who showed you a very different person than the one you thought you knew. It might be uncomfortable to admit it, but I think you might have had real feelings for him. And then he betrayed you, which only made you feel more isolated," she said, wondering if she should push a bit more. "It seems to me that you spend a lot of time and effort building and keeping walls up around you. Perhaps you should consider why. Maybe there is someone who thinks you're special enough to climb over and see what is on the other side."

I take a deep breath and start walking again so she thinks she's on to something. "You're pretty good at this stuff."

"I hope so. It's a big part of my job." She smiles, and it's kind. I almost believe her.

We keep pace, and I realize for the first time since this all began that I don't actually mind spending time with her. It's kind of nice to talk to her when she's not judging me. And as much as I hate to admit it, she might have a point about the walls.

I see movement to my right and turn my gaze. Three inmates are heading our way in matching brown jackets and navy beanies. I clench my teeth as they approach. Georgina is in the center.

I freeze, and Dr. Clafin stops. "Is something wrong, Ryann?"

"We've got company."

Georgina and two of her cronies stop in the middle of our path. My fists ball as my body remembers her hands on me.

"What do we have here?" Georgina takes a step closer to me. I move a step closer too, refusing to be intimidated by this piece of shit. "Take a wrong turn or something?" She spits the words. Her shoulders are back and she holds her head high, almost looking down on us.

I put my arm out in front of Dr. Clafin. "Stay behind me."

Han rushes up. "What's going on here?" His hand rests on his pepper spray.

Georgina smiles her ugly-ass smile, showcasing her yellowed teeth. She's a real looker. "Nothing. I just wanted to see who our friend is, that's all."

Nancy clears her throat and reaches a hand out. "Hello, I'm Dr. Nancy Clafin."

Georgina seems completely taken aback. Her eyes widen, and seconds later she's cackling. "Oh really. A doctor, huh?" And then she appears to register *who* Dr. Clafin actually is. "What, like a fucking shrink?"

Dr. Clafin tenses up. I want to get her out of here and away from Georgina. "Come on, let's go," I say.

She waves me away. "It's all right. Yes, I'm a psychiatrist. Why do you ask?"

Georgina slaps her knee and snorts laughter. "Fuck me. You're the crazy bitch doctor who thinks you're going to let this fucking cunt killer out of here? Well, if you can do that, sign my ass up next."

Officer Han steps forward with his hand up. "That's enough, Georgina. Keep walking or you'll find yourself back in the hole." His voice is stern and rough. I don't think I've ever heard it like that before.

My heart quickens. I recognize the look in Georgina's eyes, and before I can do anything she's lunging forward. I gasp and jump back. Georgina's hands are wrapped around Dr. Clafin's throat. She's screaming something I can't make out. The two women with Georgina are yelling and hollering for her to "get the bitch."

There's no time to think. I'm grabbing Georgina by the shoulders and yanking on her. It must only be a few seconds before I hear Han yelling at me to let go. I do as I'm told, and he throws Georgina off. She hits the ground with a loud thud and he sprays her in the face. She wails and thrashes like a wild animal, snot runs down her face, and her eyes are red and teary. In an instant I'm back in Marvin's living room, watching him writhe on the cat-hair-covered carpet as he begs me to spare him. But my knife slices into his pink, flabby neck from one ear to the other, a crimson line appearing in the blade's place.

Three other officers run over, shaking me from my memory.

Georgina is face-down on the ground with a knee in her back. She is promptly cuffed and led away by two guards, while another escorts her friends back inside. Han is crouched next to me, tending to Dr. Clafin.

"Are you okay, Nancy?" he asks. She is sitting on the ground, her hands around her throat. She's gasping for air and coughing. "Slow, deep breaths. You're okay. I'm going to get you help." He walkies for more backup.

I'm left standing here. My heart batters my ribcage as shivers embrace my neck and back. Familiar feelings . . . The tingling adrenaline and pure exhilaration . . .

. . . of watching someone be nearly killed.

CHAPTER THIRTY-THREE

𝒩 ancy sat in the prison infirmary, Han by her side and Ryann probably back in F Block. She was far too aware of her eclectic audience of sick inmates, guards, and medical staff.

"Are you sure you're okay?"

She couldn't stand the way Han looked at her, like she was a frail bird. "I'm all right. My throat is a little sore, but I'll live."

"That must've been terrifying. Sorry I didn't get in there sooner, but can you believe Wilkanson? Never thought I'd see a killer of her caliber actually help someone."

Nancy didn't know how to respond. "I was lucky you were both there. It could've been far worse." She took a sip of ice water—the chill relieved the ache in her throat. "Where's Ryann?"

"Back inside."

"And the woman who attacked me, Georgina?"

"In solitary."

"What's her story, anyway?"

Han wheeled his stool around so they were face to face. "She's in here for life without the possibility of parole, so I guess she thought she had nothing to lose by going after you. I gotta say I'm shocked as hell that she did it in broad daylight with me standing right there." He shook his head. "I should've been ready. I just didn't think . . ." He kept shaking his head.

"You and me both. Glad you were there. You might have just saved my life."

"Doc said you were okay. Gonna be a bit bruised and sore for a few days, so you should probably take it easy. Is there anyone I can call to come pick you up? You probably shouldn't drive."

"No thanks. I'm fine." Strangely, she felt okay. Ryann had actually helped her. And without hesitation. Ryann could play tough, but Nancy could sense that she was scared of Georgina. Yet she swooped in to protect Nancy anyway. That was not the behavior of a psychopath. Not at all.

Sure, she was a little rattled, but not nearly as traumatized as she'd expect. Standing, she smoothed her shirt and searched for her coat. Han held it out for her and she slipped inside it, exhaling as the warmth enveloped her. The shaking hadn't totally subsided. Her nerves were ruffled. Dying now would be the worst timing of all. She'd had Kim back less than a day. "I can drive." She paused, unsure if she should ask, but her apprehension won out. "Would you mind walking me back?"

"Of course not." He put his hand on her back and led her out.

It wasn't until she got into her car and locked the door that she broke down. Head-in-her-hands sobbing. The whole nine yards. She'd obviously kept it together because of all the gawking passers-by in the infirmary. Officer Han hadn't stopped tending to her. The poor guy looked absolutely wracked with guilt.

After five minutes, she glanced up into the last of the afternoon sun. "Get yourself together, Nancy. You're fine." A few deep breaths and she started the ignition.

Seeing Kim would make this hell of a day better.

Ray's car wasn't in her driveway. He was likely still at work at the restaurant. Nancy was going to visit with her daughter and try and reconnect. Hopefully her detox symptoms weren't as harsh today.

She opened the front door and called out in a shaky voice for Kim. When no answer came, Nancy's stomach muscles tensed. Not even taking the time to remove her coat, she flew through the main floor. There was no sight of her. "Kim! Are you here?" Taking the stairs two at a time, she continued to call out. The guest bathroom was empty, which only left the guest room. The door was closed. She didn't want to scare Kim in case she was in there, so she gently turned the handle and nudged the door open. It squeaked, something she'd never noticed before. Popping her head in the crack, she saw a lump under the comforter. She made her way inside and crept toward the bed. Kim's back was to her, but a cascade of brown hair covered the pillow.

The lead ball in her gut softened. She was okay. Still here, safe in bed. Nancy tiptoed around so she could see Kim's face. She needed to make certain Kim was still breathing and hadn't suffered a stroke, heart attack, or seizure, all of which could easily happen during withdrawal, especially for a long-term abuser like Kim. It was shocking that her daughter seemed as healthy as she did.

Kim's face was pale but serene. She put her hand under her nose to feel for exhalations. Thank God.

What was that smell? Bending down, she inhaled, instantly recognizing the distinctive scent of whisky.

"Oh, Kimmy," she whispered. Her hand brushed aside a piece of fallen hair on Kim's cheek. She turned and tiptoed out, although her daughter was unlikely to wake from her drunken state.

A swell of disappointment filled her. What had she expected— that her junkie daughter would come home after half her life on the streets and be the poster child for abstinence?

Nancy found her way downstairs to the kitchen and turned on the light. It was her fault, in a way. Why the hell hadn't she emptied or at least hidden the damn bottles? There was an empty container in the recycling bin, but the liquor cabinet in the dining room was still stocked. Grabbing a bottle of something brown, she went to her cupboard, pulled out a small glass, and poured herself a little. At least Kim hadn't finished them all off.

After the day, week, month she'd had, she deserved this. She downed the shot. It burned, and she coughed. Dropping the glass in the sink, her hand slapped the countertop. It was a bad idea considering how raw her throat was. But after a few deep breaths, the blackness of her vision began to clear again.

Her fingers found their way to her neck. The skin was sore and swollen. She walked to the main floor bathroom and looked in the mirror. There were purplish, fingerprint-sized bruises on either side of her neck. Georgina had squeezed with such force that Nancy was lucky there was no lasting damage.

She stared at her reflection, not recognizing herself. It was more than the gray roots of her hair or the dark circles under her eyes. It was who she was becoming. For the first time she was actually starting to believe that Ryann could be rehabilitated. But this was bigger than her—this was about the families of her victims. Nancy had been attacked, not killed, but still she wanted to lock Georgina up for life. So why was she working to release someone who had, admittedly and repeatedly, killed for fun?

The best thing she could do was get back to work and prove to herself once and for all that Ryann was still a danger. But how?

A few hours later, Nancy woke up on the sofa.

"You were snoring—you must have been tired," a voice said.

Startled, she calmed after seeing Kim on the loveseat. "Hi, honey. Sorry, how long was I sleeping?"

"I'm not sure. I came down about an hour ago and you were asleep, though I don't know how you could shut your eyes and drift off to la-la land reading that shit." She pointed to the open case file that was now on the coffee table.

Her cheeks flushed with heat. "You read my file?" Her voice betrayed her. She hadn't wanted to sound so accusatory.

Kim crossed her arms. "Well . . . sorry. I didn't know they were private."

Nancy allowed a small sigh. "The information inside is sensitive." She could see Kim was confused. "It's confidential. There are police files and legal documents. Never mind. It's all right, just promise never to discuss what you read with anyone."

"My lips are sealed." Kim made a gesture over her mouth of locking and throwing away the key. Her daughter was almost thirty, yet parts of her were so like the sixteen-year-old who ran away. It pained Nancy to think of what she could have been. The life she'd never have.

How much damage was too much to come back from? The drugs, alcohol, and lack of education had all taken their nasty toll. And who knew if she was really serious about turning her life around this time?

"Did you eat? God, what time is it anyway?" Self-conscious, she smoothed her hair out.

"It's just after seven. I'm not really that hungry. Are you, though? Maybe I can make you something, since you've been taking care of me."

She couldn't help but smile. "Maybe a little, though I still have a lot of work to get through. Unless . . . did you want to do something?" The balance between fawning over Kim and behaving with some sense of normalcy was delicate.

"Like what?"

"We could go out to eat, go shopping and get you a few things, go see a movie, anything you want."

Kim's eyebrows pinched together. "But you just said you had a lot of work to do."

"I can do it later."

"You don't have to drop everything because I'm here. I know I'm crashing into your life out of nowhere, after what feels like a lifetime. I don't expect you to wait on me."

"Darling, it's been so long since I've had you in my life . . . I've missed you, ached for you, for so many years." She took a shaky breath. "I don't want to waste any more time. Can I tell you a secret?" Kim nodded. "I'm desperately trying not to smother you."

Kim stood and crossed the room to sit beside her. A frail arm cradled her; her head rested on Nancy's shoulder. "I know, Mom. It's okay."

That was all the permission Nancy needed. Her dam burst, and she wept in her daughter's arms. "Please tell me if I'm doing anything wrong. I don't want to do anything to drive you away. Please don't leave."

"Shh, it's okay. I'm not going anywhere," Kim said.

A minute later, wiping her runny mascara from her cheeks with a tissue, Nancy said, "Can I ask you something?" A look of trepidation came into Kim's eyes and she immediately regretted it. "Never mind, it's not important—"

"No, please, ask me. I'm just embarrassed about what my answer will probably be."

Nancy fixated on her hands. They were old now, rough and full of lines. "If I ask something wrong or push too far, please tell me." Kim nodded. "I know that you were using out there, and that you had some detox symptoms last night, but why aren't you sicker? I assume you were using some really heavy stuff."

Kim bit her lip and kept her eyes down. Nancy wished she wasn't so ashamed. It broke her heart. "I was. And a lot of it, for a long time. I was in the hospital a few weeks ago. I overdosed, someone called it in. I woke up attached to an IV. While I was there, I was detoxed with the medications they give to make it easier. They released me a week later. I managed to stay clean for five days before I relapsed, but only with some coke and alcohol. Nothing hard. So that's what you're seeing. It's the alcohol. Mostly."

"That can also be dangerous. Maybe we should get you checked out tomorrow. I can call my doctor, get you in for blood work and maybe some—"

Kim rolled her eyes. "Mom, I'm fine. It'll pass."

Nancy knew to tread lightly. "Do you *want* to stop drinking?"

"Ideally, but to be honest, I'm still getting used to not using." She gestured around the room. "This is all new to me. I don't even know how to function. I don't even really know you." She winced, closing her eyes. "I didn't mean that."

"No, it's okay. You're right. We don't really know each other, but you'll always be my baby. And I'd love to get to know you now, if that's all right."

Kim smiled weakly. "That would be nice, but I might disappoint you. I don't know if I can do it."

"What, stay clean?" She nodded. "You'll have me and your brother to help you as long as you need it."

"Are you sure you know what you're signing up for?"

A tear rolled down Nancy's cheek. She whisked it away with a sweep of her fingers. "I always wanted to be there for you. Will you let me?"

"I'll try."

<hr>

Nancy's bed felt softer and cozier than usual after the hardness of the day. Swallowing still felt odd, like there was pressure around her throat. There might have been internal bruising. She was relieved she'd put the turtleneck on before she fell asleep. There was no need for Kim to know what had happened with the stress she was under. She'd have to wear one for the next week until her bruises healed. Time to go shopping. Or wear scarves. Thank God it was winter.

Lying there, she wondered if she should've confronted Kim about the empty bottle. It wasn't as though she'd really hidden it. Maybe Kim didn't care if it was seen.

Her mind raced with a scramble of visions: Kim clinging to life in the hospital, sleeping on the streets, prostituting herself, the attack in the prison yard, and Ryann's sweet face—the face of a killer.

CHAPTER THIRTY-FOUR

*S*unday, December 10

The blaring of the guards' voices breaks rudely into my slumber. I was having a brilliant dream. I was sitting on a white, wraparound porch in the middle of summer, eating ice cream and watching little kids playing across the street. The warm breeze caressed my cheeks and blew the scent of a nearby lilac tree through my hair. Now all I hear is a brute voice complimented by a baton banging against metal as the guard smacks each door he passes.

Before I even open my eyes I can feel the grit in them. My neck is stiff as I lift it off the pillow. It takes all my motivation to sit up, knowing there is nothing to look forward to. No visit from Mom today. She's sick, and the prison won't let you in if you're ill. I'll have to think of some other way to entertain myself today.

I won't do this for the rest of my life. I can't. If I don't get out of here, I'll make sure I'm free one way or another.

"You look like shit," Steph says.

I ignore her until I realize she's referring to me. "Thanks."

"All she means is, you look exhausted. Did you even sleep?" Jodi asks.

"I thought so, but maybe not as well as I thought."

Stephanie sits up, hugging her knees to her chest. "Are you still worked up about yesterday?"

My gaze narrows on her. What's she talking about? I never said a word to anyone about Georgina jumping Dr. Clafin.

She lets out a huff. "Oh come on, everyone knows by now. This place isn't exactly great at keeping secrets."

Georgina's buddies must have blabbed since she's in lock. The guards also have big mouths, and they like to gossip just as much, maybe more, than the inmates. It gives them something to do when they're supposed to be watching us. We're like their personal soap opera. "Nothing much went down." I know it's a lame thing to say, but I want to diffuse it, not sensationalize it.

"Did you really jump in and rescue your shrink? Heard you tackled Georgina and ripped the hair outta her head," Jodi says, bounding up from her bed.

I can't understand why they're approaching me with this now, when I heard nothing from either of them last night. "Georgina went after Dr. Clafin, and I pulled her off."

Jodi laughs, catching my eye. "Has our little killer lost her edge?"

I'm surprised when Steph joins in. "Yeah, weren't you the one doing the strangling? And now you're saving people. How the mighty have fallen." They both laugh like this is the funniest thing they've heard in years, and I resist elbowing their throats to remind them.

Instead it's a cold, hard glare. "What's the old adage, girls? Don't mistake my kindness for weakness." I stand up and walk so close to Stephanie that I can hear her breath quicken. "I'm still capable of putting my hands around someone's throat and squeezing until their flailing body ceases to move. I've watched the life go out of people's eyes. I've been the reason. I've pressed a blade into the soft, pliable flesh of more than one person and watched them bleed out on the floor at my feet while I smiled." The beauty of making such statements in here is that it's my word against other criminals'.

It takes me two steps to be in front of Jodi next. My shoulders back and my fists clenched, I say through gritted teeth, "Yeah, I pulled Georgina off Dr. Clafin, and I'd do it again. That woman's my shot to get the fuck out of here, and if I hear one more of you cunts trying to get in the way of that, I'll slice your fucking throat."

The looks on their faces are priceless. I half-expect one of them to piss themselves. Neither of them has ever seen me angry. A little annoyed and pissed, sure. Never like this. But scaring them is necessary for multiple reasons. One, they can't think they have any power in this relationship. Stephanie already tried that when she bailed on me in the hearing. Two, they are going to pass word of this little event to every other inmate in here, letting them know I am not to be fucked with.

After a shower and a glorious breakfast of burnt toast and cold eggs, I'm unexpectedly escorted to Dr. Clafin's office. We've yet to meet on a Sunday. Day of rest and all. I hardly know what to expect. Part of me is shocked that she's even shown up today, though I'm relieved she has.

The guard—not Han—alerts her that I'm here, and she motions for me to be buzzed in. I get a brief pat-down. Guess we're back to the safety precautions full force. I walk slowly and quietly inside, my hands in my pockets. I don't want her to feel threatened in any way. I suppose any normal person might feel jittery.

"You okay?" I linger by the doorway. It's probably better to wait for her to invite me in.

"I'm okay, thanks." She's dressed in a black pantsuit and an eggplant turtleneck. Her hair is down. It's the only time I've ever seen her wear it that way. That must be some serious bruising she's trying to hide. I wonder if she's embarrassed that she got jumped. More than that, I wonder if she's going to do anything about it.

"I was worried about you. I'm surprised you came in. We didn't have an appointment."

She's getting her coffee ready, business as usual. "There's no real damage done. We still have a lot to cover without a lot of time. Drink?" Her bubbly voice catches me off-guard. I eye her closely to see what she's attempting to conceal, but she looks *normal*. It's almost a disappointment.

"The usual, please."

We sit in our regular spots, each with a coffee in hand. Her cup is steady, not even a trace of a tremble. "You seemed shaken last night, but today you seem . . . fine. Like nothing ever happened."

Her gaze meets mine as she takes a sip. "It was a tense situation, but I'm no longer in any danger. I want to thank you for stepping in." She lifts her cup as though she's saluting me.

Lifting mine back, I say, "Of course. I'm sorry it happened in the first place. That was about me, not you. Georgina probably thought getting rid of you would keep me in here, too."

We're silent for a minute. I'm not sure what to say next. Technically this is her show, so I wait for her to take the lead.

"I can't imagine word of you helping me against a fellow inmate will bode well for you. Are you afraid of repercussions?"

After my little speech this morning to Steph and Jodi, I feel fairly confident my reputation has been cemented. "Hopefully everything is fine." I cross my arms over my chest and give myself a brief hug.

"If that changes, please let me know. There are safety measures I can put in place for you if needed."

"If you're talking about locking me up in solitary for my own protection, I'd rather take my chances."

Dr. Clafin nods. "Regardless, the guards are aware of the situation and will keep extra eyes on you, though I don't expect Georgina or her friends will be back in the general population anytime soon."

That's a relief. One thing about yesterday still bothers me. It's a touchy subject and I run the risk of her taking it wrong, but I have to know. "Can I ask you something?"

She looks taken back, tilting her head, her hair sweeping across her shoulder in a lovely, gentle way that makes what I'm about to ask her all the more odd. "You can ask. I'm not sure I'll have the answer, though."

"What did it feel like to be choked?"

Nancy nearly gasped. Did Ryann just blatantly ask what it was like to be strangled? Was this some sort of freakish, vicarious fantasy of hers—or a way to relive her kills through Nancy?

Her mind raced as she readjusted herself in her chair. Ryann sat across from her, wide-eyed and beautiful. Cupid's-bow lips and long, full lashes. The face of someone waiting to hear about a restaurant's specials, not manual strangulation.

Ryann pulled herself to the edge of her seat. "I just realized the way that came out. God, I'm such a moron." She light-heartedly cuffed herself in the forehead. "No, I'm not looking to re-experience any sick crime. I'm asking for a very different reason."

Nancy's back straightened. She clasped her hands tightly in her lap, unsure of what else to do with them. "I'm listening."

"I've tried to think of what it must have been like for my victims. It was part of a therapy I read about years ago. It's supposed to help me empathize and sympathize with what others have gone through. I put myself in my victim's position."

Nancy's pulse raced. Could Ryann see her veins throbbing from where she was sitting? "So you want me to explain it to you? I'm not sure that would be—"

"Of course. I'm sorry, you're right. I should never have asked, especially when it's so fresh. And because . . . it's me."

It *was* an opportunity Nancy shouldn't give up. "I suppose if you think it would help you understand the gravity of what you put your victims through, I'll tell you."

Ryann inhaled a measured breath. She leaned forward as though she was about to be let in on a juicy secret, not listen to an account of assault.

Nancy took a quick sip of coffee, placed her cup on the desktop, then fingered the top of her turtleneck and yanked the purple fabric down and away from her skin. She knew what the bruises looked like, purple joined by hints of dark blue that had appeared that morning. Refusing to blink, she watched Ryann gape at her battered skin.

Was she fighting to keep her composure?

"You want to know what it was like?" Her voice was gruff, but she didn't care. "I was terrified and wondered if I'd ever see my children again. Her fingers were cold and hard against my throat. Her nails ripped into my skin. I could feel them gashing into me. I couldn't breathe, the force of her hands was so intense, the unyielding pressure . . . It felt like my eyes were going to pop out of my skull. I tried desperately to swipe her hands away, but I couldn't. She was so strong. The force blurred my vision with small flickers of light before everything began to darken. It was horrific." Her throat tightened as she relived it, but she refused to cry.

She focused on Ryann's face. Did she see a glimmer of pleasure in her eyes?

Her own face must have betrayed her, because a second later Ryann's slight smile dropped into a frown. Shaking her head with apparent disbelief, she said, "Oh my God, Dr. Clafin, that sounds horrendous. I'm so sorry you had to go through that." She hung her head in what Nancy could only assume was a show of shame for her own deeds, though she wasn't sure how sincere it was.

Nancy cleared her throat. "Enough about me. We have important business to get on with. Why don't we delve into the murder of Marvin Dodson?" It was the perfect time to play one of her trusty videos. Ryann was primed by Nancy's tale of near death. What true colors would she reveal going over the dreadfully salacious details of her own crime?

She only needed to press play. "Are you ready?"

Ryann clapped her hands on her thighs. "I never am, but that's not going to change anything. You're still going to make me suffer through it, so hit it."

Here they were again. It was all about Ryann's suffering. Nancy could add *narcissist* to the long list of possible diagnoses. But narcissist didn't equal psychopath. Not necessarily. Nancy gave her a scolding glare and pressed the button.

This video was different.

Instead of the hospital room, Ryann was being interrogated in an office inside the Dungrave prison, on Ryann's first day there. For six days she had been on a concoction of antipsychotic meds prescribed for her by a psychiatrist when she was still in the hospital recovering from the gunshot wound. Medication usually took weeks to have any therapeutic benefits, so she was confident the Ryann in the interview was the same Ryann who's been arrested. Whether or not that girl was still sitting across from her was the mystery.

It tortured Nancy. She should've known by now. Should've been able to see something definitive in her, made some semblance of progress in her determination. But she was more conflicted than ever.

The video began. Estevez once again asked Ryann if she wanted any counsel present, and once again she scoffed at the prospect with an air of manic indignation. Because she couldn't wait to brag about it, especially to Estevez. Her revulsion for him radiated from the screen.

Ryann sits at a small circular table across from him. Her hair has been washed and is back in a low ponytail. She wears no makeup and is quite pale. The baggy gray sweatshirt she wears only makes her look more sickly.

Estevez says his name and the date and asks Ryann to identify herself. Sitting forward, hands clasped on the table, he says, "What happened on the night of June twenty-first?"

Clasping her hands in front of her and grinning hugely, she says, "Oh, that was a good one. That was the night I offed that old guy. Messy." She bursts out laughing.

It looks as though it takes every ounce of Estevez's professional restraint not to end her right there. "Walk me through the events of the night."

Ryann looks up at the camera and smiles. "With pleasure.

"About two weeks after the night of Omar and Mr. Hastings, I was at the diner, visiting my mom and scoping out possibilities. I was beginning to think I had hit a run of bad luck with no worthy prospects when this man opened his big mouth to my mother. Huge mistake. She was working her ass off doing her job, waiting on that lazy, fat fuck, and he was sitting at the bar barking orders at her and treating her like she was a piece of shit he'd stepped in."

Estevez fiddles with his pen. "Then what did you do?" he asks in his monotone interview voice.

Nancy remembered a different tone entirely when he had pleaded with her in her office.

"I followed him home. His light blue Subaru was like a beacon in the night. He only lived a few blocks from the diner, and he did that drive slow because he was wasted, which made keeping up with him on my bike easy as shit."

"When did you decide to return to his home?"

"I'm so glad you asked, Roberto. Can I call you Roberto?" She doesn't wait for an answer. "Four days later, I decided our time had come. The moments before were always special—knowing it was about to happen and picturing all the possibilities.

"When the coast was clear I snuck up the pathway to the front door, turned around, and did one more sweep of the area. The street was abandoned except for a few parked cars and a stray cat. I knocked on the door and waited. I heard the release of a deadbolt and held my breath as the door creaked open, revealing his face." Ryann smiles at Estevez. It's a self-aggrandizing grin. She laughs like she's having the most fun toying with him. "Let's cut to the chase, shall we? We both know you don't actually care about the details leading up to it. You're here for the money shot, so listen up, cause here it is."

Estevez leans forward with his full attention.

"After I pepper-sprayed him and tied him, I let him cry, beg, bargain, and try to bribe me, but we both know how that ended up, don't we? I

pulled out my knife and squatted down so I could be closer to him. I wanted him to feel my body so near and fixate on what I might do next. I traced the blade lightly against the moist skin of his cheek. He begged some more and I snickered, letting the tip of the blade pierce the underside of his jaw. I slowly trailed the edge of his chin. He cried out again, which made my heartbeat pick up.

"*I sliced through his grubby, stained undershirt before wadding it up in a ball and ramming it into his mouth, which I can tell you only made him flail harder.*" Ryann laughs again.

The callous cackle sent icy shivers down Nancy's spine.

"*I held onto the knife with one hand and grasped his sweaty, greasy hair in the other before I pulled his head back, exposing his neck. Staring him in the eyes, I smiled. I imagine that he saw me, though I can't be sure. I've never been pepper-sprayed before.*"

The matter-of-fact, excited way Ryann spoke was so far removed from the woman Nancy had come to know. She took her eyes from the screen and saw that Ryann was shaking, her hands balled in her lap and tears in her eyes.

She was not the same person. Not anymore. It couldn't be.

The video continued.

"*I closed my eyes and let the warm tingling of what was about to happen course through me. In one quick motion I swiped my blade across his throat. I blew him a kiss and dropped his head back on floor.*"

Nancy again attempted to glimpse Ryann through her periphery. Ryann's head was lowered. Her shoulders dipped and rose quickly with her breathing. "Are you okay?"

"I . . . I don't feel very good, Dr. Cla—" A moment later Ryann buckled, falling off the sofa and collapsing onto the floor.

CHAPTER THIRTY-FIVE

I sit at a table with a few women, playing cards. I'm winning, which means I get three dollars from each one's commissary for a grand total of twelve dollars. Might not seem like a shitload of cash, but it can buy enough. It's not like I have access to large sums of money. I was a teen when I was arrested. I have about four hundred bucks in accumulated birthday money to my name. All from my mom, of course. She adds some money here and there for my monthly expenses, or else I'd have nothing.

I 'fainted' and remained unconscious for a whole thirty or forty seconds before I came to, with Dr. Nancy and the guard standing over me. Dr. Nancy's a bit stronger than I anticipated, because she pulled me out from between the sofa and table and laid me on my side, feeling for my pulse. It would've been so easy to grab her right then. Pull her down, get on top of her, and finish what Georgina started. But I'm too close. And I've become quite fond of her, in my own way.

They sat me up, gave me some water, and I insisted I was fine, just shaken up. Dr. Nancy appeared unconvinced, but I assured her for five more minutes until she believed me, and here I am. Twelve dollars up. And there she is, telling herself, with any luck, that anyone so wracked with guilt must certainly be redeemed.

"You got a visitor, Wilks!" The voice echoes through the pod.

I look over from my winning hand. "Me?" I can't imagine Nancy has decided to visit me again so soon, especially not after what just happened.

The guard, a fat dude with a shiny bald head and black moustache, motions for me to get up and meet him over at the door. I don't want to leave—I'm about to clean up and could really use the cash—but he doesn't seem to want to be kept waiting. "I'll be back, wait for me. Actually, I'm taking my hand." I grab the cards and shove them into my shirt pocket, eliciting groans and moans and a few choice words.

Baldy opens the door. "Follow me."

"I'm not expecting anyone."

"Then I guess you'll have to fucking wait and see," he says in his nasally voice.

He opens the door and lets me walk ahead. I'm a little excited to discover who my mystery visitor is.

And then I see.

That slimy, greasy sonofabitch.

Sergeant Roberto fucking Estevez.

I stop in my tracks. He hasn't seen me yet. He's too busy checking his phone. Probably harassing a few new kids since I'm no longer a viable option. Ugh, the sheer look of him, even from twenty feet away, evokes all sorts of things: racing heart, heavy breathing, burning cheeks.

"Move it, Wilks. What the hell you waiting for, a fucking invitation?" Baldy pushes me forward. I catch my arm before it flies up to swat him. I hate when they touch me. It's like they can sense it, because they do it all the time.

Estevez is in his idea of a uniform, which I know from experience consists of a navy or black suit (cheap), a white dress shirt (yellowed), and beat-up brown shoes (that don't match the rest of his outfit).

Looking at the guard for a reprieve is pointless. I'm at his table now. The odor of his musky cologne is already making me light-headed. "This is an unexpected and unpleasant surprise." I spit the words.

"Nice to see you too, Ryann." He motions a limp hand in front of him. Probably like his dick. "Please sit."

"Do I have a choice?" He looks so much older than the last time I saw him. Deep crow's feet and graying hair. A little pot belly, even. I cheer on the inside.

"Nope." He smiles, and I want to smack it off his face.

I sit, arms crossed, death glare. "To what do I owe this displeasure?"

"Just thought I'd check in, see how you're liking your home here. Wanted to make sure you didn't have any hope of getting out. Not while I'm alive."

Telling him that I can arrange for him to be put down like a dog would only add charges for threatening an officer to my name. No one would believe that I didn't say it, so I'm careful. He's probably here to provoke me. Could be taping our little meeting, looking for ammo. Maybe I'm close to being released after all, and he's scared I'll get out. My heart warms a little. "Are you here just to threaten me?"

"What threat?"

"You making it known that you'll do anything to keep me locked away counts as one. You must have something else to do. Aren't there innocent people you can harass?"

He chuckles. "Innocent, huh? Like you were?"

"I admitted what I did. I'm paying my penance."

"And you believe twelve years is your debt to society? What about the families and your victims? You took their futures. Are their lives, and all the others you destroyed, worth only twelve fucking years? You got nerve, little girl." Saliva builds in the corners of his mouth.

My hands are crossed neatly on top of the table and I lean in a little. It's a tad reminiscent of the good old days, when we'd have our little chats. He thinks he can come in here—on my turf—and push me around. I will not be rattled. He will not take this away from me. "What are you talking about? I'm doing my time and minding my business, getting therapy, and doing everything I can to better myself and help the other inmates. I was a kid, and I was sick. Should I be punished for the rest of my life for something that was out of my control?"

"If you think I'm going to buy this bullshit, you're gravely mistaken. Maybe you've fooled some fucking celebrities and ridiculous advocacy groups, but the board will see right through this publicity stunt. I won't deny you're sick in the head, but you're not cured. You're as twisted as ever, and with all the families that you ruined, it's my mission to keep you locked away until you die in here."

"I don't need to do this." I stand up. There's no fucking way I'm going to sit here and allow this prick to berate me.

"Take care, Ryann. Be seeing you soon."

I'm back in the block. I wonder if I look like a beet because my blood pressure is so fricking high. It irks me that Estevez can still crawl so far under my skin.

Jodi approaches me cautiously. She's probably still thinking about my little speech from earlier. "What was that about?" she whispers.

"I had an unwelcome visitor." My body is so hot that I'm sweating.

Her eyes widen with that look of curiosity she gets, and I don't mind telling her. It might be good to get it off my chest. "Who was it?" she whispers more intently.

"That asshole detective who got me locked up in here in the first place."

"*Really?*" She drags out the word. "What was he doing here?"

"Oh, he wanted to make sure I knew he would die before he

ever saw me released. He's making it his solitary mission to make sure I rot in here." I grimace, jaw clenching, nostrils flaring. I'd prefer to act cool and nonchalant, but I'm too full of rage to pull it off.

"That's horrible."

She looks devastated for me, but is it real? Before I can reply, Jinx yells something that catches my ear.

"Hey, Wilks, looks like you're on TV again!" Roxie cranks the volume up. Now everyone is looking between the screen and me.

The television shows a crowd of people outside of a building. The ticker on the bottom of the screen says they're outside the Wagner and Roche offices. I can make out one of the signs with its thick black lettering: *Free Ryann!* There are actually quite a few of them. My breath rushes out of me. Part of me feels relieved, but it only paints an even bigger target on my back.

Feeling dozens of eyes on me intensifies my adrenaline. I manage to block them out and zero in on the screen. A man in his sixties with a gray beard and thick glasses pushes himself in front of the camera. He doesn't look happy. He grabs the mic from one of my supporters and yells into it.

"Ryann Wilkanson is a despicable human being who should never be set free! We have to protect our children and the people of this community from that crazy psychopath. You people who think she should be let out should suffer by her murderous hands so you know how wrong you are!"

The reporter, a dark-haired man in his thirties, looks like he's having the time of his life. I'm sure his boss will be happy he's getting some juicy coverage.

A second later the camera shifts, and Wagner comes into view.

The reporter chases him down. "Do you have any comment on the Wilkanson case?"

My lawyer, the cool, calm, five-thousand-dollar-suit-and-Rolex-watch-wearing egomaniac, stops dead in his tracks.

"My client has spent a dozen years locked away without the benefit of any psychiatric care. She was a minor at the time and severely mentally ill. Her case was mishandled by an unprofessional and weak defense team. Her attorneys prejudiced the outcome of the case and made a host of other grievous mistakes that prevented my client from receiving a fair trial. She has endured tremendous suffering, and we hope to rectify that so that she doesn't have to spend one more day unjustly behind bars."

For the first time I notice how eerily quiet the room is. They're already wound up and ready to pounce.

"So, Ryann, you think it's as easy as that, huh?" It's an inmate named Carla this time. She stands up and struts toward me. I plant my feet firmly on the ground. I can't budge or it'll be seen as a sign of weakness.

"I don't think it's easy at all. If it was, I wouldn't still be in here with three failed appeals under my belt." I say it as calmly as I can muster. I want to de-escalate the situation, not cause a fucking brawl in here. How would that look for me?

"So is that it? You were cuckoo-crazy, and slaughtering those people wasn't your fault? The voices make you do it or something?" She spreads her arms out wide. "Hey girls, did you hear that? She didn't mean to do it. Ha! I didn't mean to shoot my rapist father." She turns her attention to a young, heavyset woman with stringy brown hair. "Hey, Kallie, did you mean to sell drugs to all those people?"

Straight-faced, Kallie says, "Hell no. I never meant to do it at all. It was an accident."

Everyone laughs. I've never been the butt of a joke before. They expect me to retaliate, but I can't risk it.

"Look, the psycho killer is shaking," Kallie shouts. "Are you upset? Do you want to punch me?" She steps closer to me. My fists are clenched just in case. "Are you going to hit me? Maybe strangle me?" She makes a loud choking sound and puts her hands around her own throat. Everyone bursts out laughing.

I can't contain it any longer. "Fuck you, Carla. You stand here with an audience egging you on. You wouldn't be this tough if it were just you and me in a dark alley somewhere." I realize what I've said too late.

"Interesting choice of scenery. That's where you killed that poor kid, you sick freak. God, I hope you don't get out of here." She's so close to me I can smell her rank breath. The tip of her finger pushes into my chest. "We'd miss you too much."

Jodi and Steph rush toward me. It's as though they can see what I'm about to do.

I feel arms around me, pulling me away. "Come on, Ryann. Let's walk. You're too close. Just ignore them." It's Jodi. I'm grateful, because what I was about to do would have ended all hope for me.

Kallie's voice follows me. "Walk away, pussy!"

And I do walk away, because I have no other choice.

CHAPTER THIRTY-SIX

$\mathcal{M}$onday, December 11

I look at the clock that hangs on the wall in the center of the pod. It's 10:34 a.m. I'll be walked over to the other side of the prison soon to see Dr. Clafin. Using my excellent deductive reasoning skills, I'd say today's topic of conversation will be B.

I know I'm getting to Dr. Nancy. I can see it in her eyes. I almost lost her last session when I asked her about being strangled, but I just couldn't help myself. No matter, all she'll remember is the fainting, and my anxiety, and my trouble sleeping. I'll just have to appeal to the mother in her.

"Wilkanson!" a guard bellows through the pod.

Some of the women roll their eyes, others ignore me, and one of them flips me off. My fan base is dwindling. All the more motivation. I smile and wave, strutting toward the door. I know I shouldn't engage, but preserving my no-bullshit rep is crucial for my safety.

The booming voice belongs to Officer Rickers, whom I haven't seen in a while. He doesn't say much as we walk until we get closer. "So you thinking you gonna get out? You've been seeing this counselor a lot. Must mean something."

"I hope so."

"There new evidence or something?"

I'm caught off-guard. Does he know something I don't? "Not that I'm aware of, but if you've got some news I'd really appreciate hearing it." I bat my eyelashes at him but know Rickers isn't affected. I wouldn't be surprised if he was gay. Apparently he's got a wife, but come on. I'm hot, beige uniform and all, and he barely looks at me. A girl knows when a man looks at her that way, and I've never seen Rickers bat an eye at anyone in here. Granted, most of my fellow inmates are greasy, fat, acne-prone, and generally gross, but I still take pride in my appearance. A lot of the girls let themselves go. Just give up in here. That's the difference between them and me.

We get to the hallway before the office door. I know this route well by now. I'm surprised there aren't tracks worn in the floors.

He pushes open the door and lets me through first. Han is back, and it's kind of good to see him.

"Good luck in there," Rickers says, like he actually means it.

I smile and go in. Dr. Nancy is waiting for me and looking rather nice in a striped black and gray dress with a black scarf wrapped around her neck. "Morning, Ryann. Have a seat and we'll get started. We've a lot to cover in little time."

Fuck. Not even the normal offer of a hot beverage. She must be in business mode. And we were getting along so well. But whining inside my head isn't going to help anything, so I sit in my usual spot, cross my legs, clap my hands, and wait. I hope it's over soon.

Dr. Clafin lowers herself in her chair and grabs my file and a pen. "I want to go over something again with you. I'd like you to tell me exactly what led to you killing Eric Knox that day in the library."

"Whoa, right to it, huh? No 'Hi, Ryann. It's nice to see you today.'"

She gives me a thin-lipped smile. "My apologies. Hello, Ryann. It's nice to see you today. Now answer the question, please."

I don't want her to see how startled I am. She's obviously trying to fuck with me. "I thought we already discussed that. Eric threatened B and me. I had to defend us." I pull my knees to my chest.

"How, exactly? I know what the file says, but as you stated, you lied, and the file is inaccurate." Dr. Nancy doesn't move an inch. Just eyes me down her nose through her glasses, her pen at the ready, desperate to—what? Catch me in a lie?

"I already told you that he followed me there and explained his plan for us to kill B together. I refused. We argued. I got a hold of the evidence bag that he was going to blackmail me with and fished out the knife. He got angrier and more erratic. I knew he was completely off the rails, so I held out the knife and told him to leave. He rushed me, and I stabbed him in the stomach."

"And then what happened?"

Obviously Dr. Nancy wants the grisly and delicious picture painted for her. "I heard a distant, muffled sound, like a radio or someone talking. Then Eric dropped to his knees and started screaming that he needed help and that he was with me at the library. He'd managed to hit the speed dial for dispatch on his cell. It must have been only seconds later when B walked in. Eric was still on the ground, and I had no time to explain what had happened. She freaked out, screaming. I knew the cops were already on their way."

"What did Bao-yu do then?"

"She backed away. Her eyes were fixed on me, her mouth wide open, and her body was shaking. She'd expected to find me sitting on a chair waiting for her, and instead she finds me with a knife, ready to plunge into Eric for the second time. It wasn't anything I'd ever wanted her to see. I'd wanted to keep this side of me away from her. I tried to tell her that he'd attacked me, but she was too petrified.

"I realized I was still holding the knife, so I told her I'd put it down and that she didn't have to be afraid of me. My arm lowered, but her face didn't relax. She looked panicked. I think I could have talked her down, but then Eric yelled out for help again."

I remember it like it was yesterday . . .

"B, we've been friends our whole lives. You know me! You know I'm not capable of attacking anyone. Please . . ." I whimpered. She had to believe me.

B's eyes darted from me to Eric and back. "I . . . I don't . . . you said . . ." She shook her head, looking like she was about to run.

And I couldn't have that.

As B turned to run, I lunged forward. I grasped wildly at the first thing I could reach. My fingers sank into her hair. I squeezed, desperate to keep my hold on her. She yelped as I felt her body snap back under the tension being put on her scalp.

The knife was safe in my other hand. She fought me, flailing. Frantic. My hand kept its grasp on her as she pulled and thrashed.

"Stop moving, B. I'm not going to hurt you, but you need to calm down before you hurt yourself," I said as steadily as I could. I never wanted this.

She kept wriggling, her arms swinging and legs kicking, but her hair was wound around my fingers. She wasn't going anywhere. Her crying and begging, her pleading my name burrowed a hole in my gut. "Shh, you don't need to be afraid of me. I only need you to quiet down, then I'll let you go. I'll explain everything, B. I only grabbed you because I was worried you were going to tell someone I'd done something bad. But it was him. He's the bad one." I looked over at Eric, who was either unconscious or dead. I loosened my grip on her a tad so maybe she'd trust me. "I'm going to let go. Just take a deep breath. It's going to be okay."

B stopped moving. She took slow but shaky breaths.

"Good girl. One more," I said gently. She did as she was told. "Okay, I'm going to let go of you now, but you have to promise me that you're not going to scream or run. I need my best friend. Do you promise?" Her head shook below my fist.

"Just when I was ready to let her go, I heard the sound of a door opening. My fist tightened, and B screamed again. I looked past Eric's body toward the stairwell and wasn't prepared for what

I saw. Estevez was staring back at me, his gun drawn. My gaze moved from the barrel of the gun to the look in his eyes that dared me to move. And . . . you know the rest."

Nancy was well aware that minutes after Sergeant Estevez showed up, so did Ryann's father. "And that's when you were shot?" Her full attention was on Ryann, whose hands were shaking ever so lightly in her lap. Her eyes were red and watery, a stark contrast to her ashen complexion.

Nodding, Ryann pulled her knees into her chest and rested her forehead on top so her eyes were no longer visible.

Nancy didn't want to give her a minute. She needed to push to see what she'd get from her, now while Ryann was vulnerable "Who shot you, Ryann?"

Her head jerked up and her gaze met Nancy's. Was it a look of anger or annoyance? "You know damn well who." She didn't blink. It was as though she were challenging Nancy for dominance, seeing through Nancy's attempts to expose her weaknesses.

Nancy played dumb. She wanted to hear Ryann explain it. "It was never clear in the file I received. It only said you suffered a single gunshot wound to your right shoulder. You said on the video that both Sergeant Estevez and your father were at the scene. I can't imagine it was your father, so it must have been Estevez. Maybe that explains why you hate him so much."

She let out a brisk laugh. "Part of me wishes you were right. But the truth is my dear father pumped that bullet into me, and he didn't hesitate." Her shoulders stiffened as she squeezed her knees harder. "I hate Estevez for a whole slew of other reasons." She stopped for a beat. "I didn't even see my father reach for his gun."

"It wasn't in his hand when he was talking to you?"

"No. It wasn't. What he did wasn't an instinct. Shooting me was a choice."

Nancy's heart ached at what that moment must have felt like.

Of course, Ryann had just killed someone and had a knife to Bao-yu's neck, but having your own father shoot you was still a trauma. "How did the fact that your father pulled the trigger make you feel back then?"

"Devastated. A father is supposed to protect his daughter. Put his life on the line for her, not shoot her."

"Do you think he had another choice? You murdered six innocent people and were holding your best friend at knifepoint. He couldn't let you hurt her. Somewhere deep down, you have to understand that."

"Of course a part of me understands that!" The heels of her hands cleared away the tears from her cheeks. "But another part of me is still hurt that he turned on me. I guess I hoped he would see how sick I was and talk me down. Didn't he know something was horribly wrong with me? I never would have hurt B. I just needed her to get out of there. She was nothing more than a temporary hostage."

Nancy pushed her glasses up the bridge of her nose. "With the state you were in that day, do you really mean to tell me that he could've talked you down? Do you actually believe that? Because I don't. I think that the Ryann in the library was cornered, and terrified, and would've gone to any lengths necessary to protect herself. Even if that meant murdering her lifelong friend in cold blood."

Ryann sighed, sniffled, and finally reached for a tissue, dabbing her nose. "And there's nothing I can do about that now!"

Nancy flinched in her chair, not expecting the extent of the outburst. This was true emotion. Unfiltered. Raw and passionate. She needed to keep probing. See what other truths would breach the surface. "Are you more upset that you got caught, or that your father helped bring you in?"

Ryann practically squealed. "I know I was crazy and dangerous and my dad was doing his job, but I still *feel* betrayed. Do you know that he won't visit me? I haven't seen him in over eleven years. He gave up on me. I've never needed him more, and he abandoned me." She buried her face in her hands and cried.

Deep, shoulder-shaking sobs. Nothing comparable to her previous tears.

Nancy hadn't known that. She was aware that he wasn't in the visitor logs for the past year, but she hadn't realized he had *never* visited her. Liz hadn't mentioned that, and Nancy hadn't thought to ask. "Do you speak to him on the phone?"

Ryann lifted her head. "No, he won't talk to me. My mother makes excuses for him, but it's clear he wants to pretend I was never born. He and Bri have their special bond, and once again I'm not good enough. I only have my mother," she chortled, pointing at Nancy, "and you. I have you, which is completely fucked up because you're paid to be here. And my mother . . . my poor mother is barely hanging on. Pulled between her love for them and me. It's tearing her apart. I told her to stop coming, you know. I didn't want to come between her and them. I'm stuck in here. There's no reason she should be in her own prison, but she won't listen. A few times I refused to come to the visitor area, hoping she'd be hurt enough to never come back, but she always did. She's faithful and sweet. I used to think it was a weakness, but now I'm so grateful for it. Somebody else might have given up on me, but she shows up here almost every weekend."

"Sounds like you've learned quite a bit from her. I'm sorry your relationship with your father and sister is strained."

Ryann put her hand out as if to stop Nancy in her tracks. "No. Our relationship isn't strained. It's broken. Shattered into hundreds of pieces. Even if you tried to sweep them up and put them back together, there would still be gaps where fragments wouldn't quite fit. That's what my life feels like now. I have all these parts that no longer fit together."

"What do you mean?"

"I've lost family and friends, I'm segregated from the rest of the world, stuck in here slowly suffocating and suffering—the way I deserve to. I've done reprehensible things for reasons I either can't remember or can no longer relate to and there's nothing I can do to make up for what I've done to the victims and their families.

I embarrassed my family, caused them to hide and apologize for me. Did you know that Bri changed her last name so she wouldn't have to be associated with me anymore? She's never visited me either."

"It sounds like you're harboring a lot of resentment for many people, your sister especially. Are you angry with her, or is it more about your own feelings of insecurity? I believe that you compared yourself to Brianna your entire life, and *you* thought you never measured up."

Ryann sat quietly, not moving an inch, her face stone. After nearly a minute she said, "With all due respect, you didn't grow up in my house. You didn't know my sister. Sure, we had sibling rivalry like all siblings do, but it was more than that. She hated me. She believed she was the superior version of me." Ryann snickered. "And she was right."

Nancy saw her cellphone screen flash from the desk. "If you'll excuse me, I need to send something quickly. It's urgent."

"Don't mind me."

Nancy detected the snark in her voice and was certain Ryann wanted it that way.

She typed a quick text and pressed send, put the phone back, and turned her attention back to Ryann. "Tell me about Bao-yu. What was she like?" Nancy smiled, hoping to ease Ryann. She seemed to be opening up more and more, nearly making herself vulnerable. Getting insight on her friendship with Bao-yu was key.

Ryann slowly stretched out on the sofa until she was reclining and put her hands over her face. "Do I have to?" she muttered through her fingers.

"I'd really like it if you would."

She huffed and raked her fingers over her eyes. "Yes, she was my best friend. She was perky, sweet, and friendly. I remember being a shy kid. Always kept to myself, nervous about doing the wrong thing, but then B swept into my life, like a small but powerful force." She giggled, surprising Nancy. Ryann rarely laughed, and certainly not with such ease and lightness. "She was new at school, came right up to me, took me by the hand and said, "Let's play." She pulled me over and sat down next to me. I was astonished. She was so confident, and I was immediately drawn to her. That's how B was. Sassy and sweet. A tough cookie."

"And the two of you remained close until the night you were apprehended?"

"We did everything together—almost everything. B lost a little of that bravado as the years went by. She became a bit of a nervous wreck, actually: panic attacks, anxiety, insecurity. But she was still sweet, caring, do-anything-for-you B. Still feisty and snarky and put-you-in-your-place awesome when it was needed. It was mostly just our small group that hung out: me, B, Lucas, Asad, Mackenzie, and Katie. She had the craziest crush on Asad, but was always too chicken to tell him." She stopped talking, her smile reappearing. "I wonder if she ever got the courage. I picture them dating for years, going to the prom together, and maybe lasting through college. I hope they're all happy."

"Have you spoken to any of your other friends since the murders?"

Ryann shook her head. "Lucas came to see me in the hospital, but my mom refused to let him in. I'm grateful for that. I think about it now and cringe. The thought of chatting over hot chocolates or soda and trying to explain the nightmare my life had become . . . It was too much. He probably would've questioned every time I'd got in the passenger side of his ugly yellow Beetle or met him for a burger." She sighed loudly. "He tried to see me in here once. It was two years after the murders. I declined to see him then, too. I was too ashamed. What would I have said? There was no way to explain what had happened to me—or what I'd done."

"I understand that, but did you ever consider that you were being selfish in denying him that visit? That perhaps he had things he wanted to say to you? Maybe he needed closure. You had the power to give him that, and yet you refused. Was that your way of staying in control?"

"No. I never even thought about it like that. I guess I was protecting myself. I didn't want to face him. I wasn't the person he thought, and I couldn't watch him look at me differently." She bowed her head.

"And yet you stated that you attempted to contact Bao-yu more than once. Why were you willing to speak to her and not Lucas?"

"I didn't attack Lucas. I owed her more. She and I shared so much. Countless sleepovers, tagging along with each other on family trips, school year after school year in the same classes, sharing our deepest secrets."

"But you didn't share your darkest secrets, did you?"

Nancy heard her swallow. "No, I guess I didn't."

"Because you were having dark fantasies and urges for a long time and never told Bao-yu. You never shared with her your thoughts, or plans, or details of the murders, did you?"

"No."

"And why was that?"

"Because she wouldn't have understood what I was going through. We were close, but there was no way she could get the kind of intense emotions I was feeling. At the time it was like I needed to act out those fantasies. I didn't feel like I had control over myself."

"Do you think it was because some part of you knew what you were doing was wrong, and you didn't want to be stopped?"

"Maybe, but I also think I didn't want to get B wrapped up in the chaos."

"I don't believe that for a second. You didn't want your killing party to end, so you couldn't involve anyone, especially not someone as morally sound as Bao-yu. You knew she'd stop you and turn you in, best friend or not."

At that Ryann's eyes closed. Her breathing slowed to that of a brief meditation. "Fine. That's probably true, but I was also protecting her. Whatever madness was overcoming me, I knew enough to keep her as far away from it as I could."

"Until you couldn't." Nancy's tone was sharp. Raw. She was sick of the excuses.

The cell on the desk vibrated. Nancy picked it up, excited. Her hand trembled as she swiped the screen. She cleared her throat and stood. "I have a surprise for you, Ryann."

Ryann's hand went to her chest. "For me? What are you talking about?"

Nancy was already up and walking toward the door. "Someone is here to see you, and I think this visit is far overdue."

With narrowed eyes, Ryann craned her neck to see who was there.

The door opened. "Thank you so much for agreeing to do this. I think it's going to be a tremendous help."

"It's time I did. I have a lot to say."

Ryann stood at the sound of the voice. Nancy moved to the side to allow the two an unobstructed view of one another. As Ryann set her eyes on Bao-yu for the first time in over twelve years, her legs buckled beneath her as she fell back down on the sofa.

CHAPTER THIRTY-SEVEN

*T*here's an instantaneous film of moisture all over my body. My skin is on fire. Prickling. Somehow, I manage to bring myself back to my feet, but barely.

Dr. Clafin steps to the side and my eyes land on my friend. The last time I saw her in person was at my sentencing hearing. And now here she is, though her jet-black hair that used to sit in the middle of her back is now cut to her chin. Her black-rimmed glasses are missing. Maybe she's wearing contacts or got that Lasik surgery. She always hated the idea of putting her finger in her eye, but a lot can change in a decade. Her body is still slim and strong. She wears a gray T-shirt that shows off the definition in her arms. Despite the small changes, she looks remarkably similar to the way I remember her.

My head swells with wooziness, and I wonder if I'm about to pass out right here in Dr. Nancy's office, for real this time, with them staring down at me.

Maybe B will take a shot. A good kick in the ribs.

I never expected to have this moment. Not in my wildest dreams. And now that it's real, I'm not sure what the fuck to do.

My mouth opens, yet nothing comes out but a gurgle. I cough into my fist, clear my throat, and try again. "Hey, B." It comes out nonchalant, like we're catching up over coffee and our last encounter didn't involve my hand knuckles-deep in her scalp.

I'm not sure what I expect, but she barely acknowledges me. Her gaze sweeps past me. Her arms are crossed.

Dr. Clafin points to her chair. "Why don't you sit there, Bao-yu?"

She nods and sits in the black leather swivel chair, clutching her pale blue purse on her lap as though any barrier, no matter how slight, is better than nothing. There's a pang in my stomach. She's afraid of me, not that I blame her.

God, I must look revolting. She hasn't seen me in years and here I am, unflattering, beige scrubs, no makeup, hair dull and limp. But as my best friend, she's seen me look worse. Hungover, puking, with mono, and the chicken pox.

I catch myself. She *was* my best friend. I'm not sure what she is now.

Instead of the excitement I always imagined I'd feel, my mouth is dry and my body shakes. I knew she was judging me in her little corner of Dungrave, but now she's sitting across from me, and the tense hatred wafting off her is paralyzing.

I know I'm staring at her. I want to memorize every inch of her before she leaves and I never see her again.

Dr. Clafin clears her throat. "Can I get you anything to drink, Bao-yu? Coffee, tea, water?"

"No thanks." B keeps her eyes on Nancy.

She's probably nervous that Dr. Clafin is more than a few feet away. Is she that afraid of me? She must not have read any of my letters or emails.

"All right, then, let's get started. I've asked Bao-yu here today because I think it's important for the both of you to discuss what happened and hopefully start the journey to healing. You are both holding on to a lot of fear, pain, and confusion."

I find my voice, willing it to come up from my diaphragm. "Thank you for agreeing to do this, B."

"You can call me Bao-yu."

My heart breaks a little. A kick in the stomach. "Come on, B. We've known each other our whole lives—"

Her almond eyes shift and she glares at me. It's the first time she's really looked at me. "Do not call me B." Her voice is stern. My stomach clenches. "And we are nothing. We were never friends. I was friends with the girl I thought you were."

I say nothing and look to Dr. Clafin for direction. I'm floundering, and she knows it. Was it part of her plan to watch me suffer? See the pain in my eyes as B rejects me?

"If this is some sort of ambush, then I'll go back to my cell." I make like I'm getting up.

Dr. Clafin raises her hand. "No ambush, Ryann. Please stay seated."

I do. I am, after all, very cooperative. The model inmate, even when Dr. Nancy pushes her luck. "I'd love nothing more than to talk about things and see if I can help sort out what happened all that time ago." My gaze moves from Dr. Clafin to B. "Did you even read one of my letters? I tried to contact you so many times, but you never responded—well, only once to tell me never to contact you again, but I'm fairly certain that doesn't count."

"I received them for a while. I asked my parents to throw them in the trash right away. They were more than delighted to comply, seeing as what you did to me." Her tone is biting.

Dr. Clafin doesn't have B quite under control. Ha. That's my B, always sassy with a mind of her own.

"Bao-yu, would you like to begin? You said you had a few things you wanted to say to Ryann."

B reaches into her purse and pulls out a folded piece of paper. She starts to open it but stops, refolds it, and stuffs it back into the blue leather. "I thought I'd be too nervous to remember everything I wanted to say to you, but sitting here, seeing you . . . well, I have plenty to say, and I don't need any help."

My knees knock together. "I'm listening, and believe it or not, I want to hear it—everything—no matter how painful or difficult." I'm trying to be supportive.

She laughs. Snickers, to be precise. "Painful? Difficult? You have some nerve. What's painful is having your best friend since childhood, one of the people you most trust in the world, threaten to slice your throat. What's painful is having a chunk of your hair nearly ripped from your head. Being dragged around while two police officers have their guns drawn. Not knowing if you'll be stabbed in the neck or accidently shot. What's difficult is having post-traumatic stress disorder and needing years of therapy and medications. Not sleeping through the night because of horrific nightmares. Taking a leave from school and holing up in your room because it's the only place you feel safe. Difficult is when, every time you feel the pieces of your life coming back together, another email or letter or phone call forces you to relive it all again. So don't talk to me about pain and difficulty, because you won't win."

"I'm sorry," I say in my softest voice. "But don't think I haven't suffered too. At least you have a life—friends, family, school, a room of your own with your own things, an identity, and a future. I've lived like a rat in a cage for half of my life. Everything I do is monitored. I can't take a shit without an audience. I am known as inmate number 57629847. I'm told when to sleep, eat, shower, and breathe in here. I've been dosed with more medications than I can count and abandoned by almost every single person who ever knew me except for my mother. My own sister and father want nothing to do with me. I've barely slept, plagued with nightmares, and if I do sleep, I'm woken up by screaming women in the cells next to me. I'm constantly a target in here, attacked and berated for something that happened when I was a very sick child. I will pay for what I've done forever, and I know I deserve it, but don't tell me I don't know what it's like to endure pain. I'm in pain every minute of every day for what I did to those people and to you. Don't think for one fucking second that I don't think about it constantly, because I do, and I will until I die."

Her face remains blank. Not even a flicker of an eyelash. "And you deserve all of it. Probably more. You're still alive to experience things. So what if you find them hard or not? I'm sure Yvonne and Omar and poor Olivia would love to have experiences in this world, but you took those. You nearly took them from me, but I refuse to let you win."

"Hurting you is not winning for me! I loved you like a sister, more even. Hurting you was the last thing I ever wanted or intended, but you walked in when you shouldn't have, B, and I panicked. I never would've hurt you. You've got to believe me. You saw me and Eric and you freaked. I couldn't have you running to get help. I needed to calm you down and explain, but you wouldn't listen—"

"So you held a knife to my throat? The same knife you'd just used to kill Officer Knox? It was covered in his blood! 'There was no other way'—you're absolutely sure?" Her voice rises at the end, full of hatred and rage. Years of pent-up emotions are finally spilling out, faster than her voice allows. Her eyes brim with tears, a constant trickle down her cheeks. Do tears mean she still cares?

"I was young, and something was wrong with me. I didn't know what I was doing. All I knew was not to get caught. I would've taken you out the back stairs with me. We would've gotten outside, I would've explained it to you, and we would've been fine."

"You're still delusional. Do you hear yourself? Actually . . ." She stopped herself mid-sentence with a twisted grin. "How would you have explained killing Officer Knox to me? Knowing that you planned, stalked, and murdered five other people, how would you have explained stabbing him in the stomach? You had a relationship with him!"

"You're acting like he was innocent! He was crazy." I close my eyes, knowing how a remark like that sounds coming from me. "Eric cornered me. He followed me, had been for weeks. He knew exactly what I'd been doing and started threatening me. He told me he wanted us to kill you together. I refused. So yes, I stabbed him, but it wasn't like the others. It was to protect you."

"So you're what? A hero? A martyr? Should I thank you?" Her eyes narrow on me and her jaw clenches. Through gritted teeth, she says, "You make me sick." B wipes her cheeks with her fingertips. Her voice is nasally from crying so hard. "I watched the news and saw all the creepy and sick things he did. But that doesn't negate who you are and what you did. The fact is, you didn't want to share the gruesome spotlight. You wanted all the twisted glory for yourself."

I guess B knows me better than I give her credit for. "Yes, I did want the spotlight. I didn't want to share it with anyone, especially not a half-cocked psychotic who wanted me to kill my best friend. But that was then. I'm not that person anymore." I look at Dr. Clafin pleadingly. "Tell her, please. Explain how it wasn't all my fault."

B's eyes lock on Dr. Clafin's. "Is that why I'm here? Are you going to try and sell me some ridiculous spin on how poor Ryann didn't know what she was doing?"

Dr. Clafin leans forward, her hands resting on her knees. "Not at all, but there is evidence to suggest that Ryann may have experienced a psychotic episode at the time of the murders."

B shakes her head vehemently. "Wait. Evidence? What kind of evidence?" She doesn't look at me.

"Ryann, I have a theory about what might have influenced your behaviors, but I'll only speak about it with your permission."

My breath hitches. A theory? I nod eagerly. It's what I've been waiting for. I knew she was good. I gave her just enough to come to the conclusion herself, and here it is.

Dr. Nancy shifts to the edge of her seat and leans toward B. "I believe Ryann may have suffered from something called schizophreniform disorder. It's a psychotic disorder that can affect mood and cause delusions, hallucinations, confused thinking, and strange, possibly dangerous behavior. Sufferers can display a cold, detached manner, and lack the ability to express emotion. There can be mood swings. It can also mirror some aspects of bipolar disorder, with bouts of depression and mania."

I want to jump into the air and whoop and holler. Yes! Good girl, Nancy.

B's eyebrows knit together. "So what, Ryann wasn't responsible for what she did? Say I buy this theory." She spits the words. "How do you explain her killing multiple people over, what, six weeks?"

I stay silent, though it's tough not to defend myself with absolute indignation.

"The condition can last anywhere from one to six months. After Ryann was arrested she was hospitalized and put on a regime of antipsychotic medications, which she has stayed on. Gradually her intense and hostile behaviors dissipated, until there were no more traces of the mania to menace her thought processes. During a psychotic state, the sufferer can endure delusions and hallucinations that push them to act in ways they never would otherwise. It can also cause blackouts, from which Ryann suffered at that time."

Bao-yu is silent, as am I. I know what they mean when they say, *you could hear a pin drop*. After about a minute she squares her shoulders. "And you believe her? There's no evidence to prove her blackouts." She makes air quotations with her fingers. "She's clearly lying. She doesn't want to own up to the horrendous things she's done."

I can't bite my tongue any longer. "I am owning it! I admit that I planned to kill Olivia, Yvonne, Omar, Mr. Hastings, and Marvin, and that I followed through. I didn't plan on Eric, but I still did it. I'm not denying my culpability, or how cruel and despicable I was. All I'm asking is that you open your mind to the possibility that I wasn't in my right mind. Please, B." My voice cracks. I'm short of breath, which feels surprisingly real.

B groans and shakes her head.

I keep going. This might be my only chance to ever be in the same room with her again. "Think back to all of our time together. Can you tell me that my behavior, personality, moods, and actions were ever suspicious before that summer? Because I can't remember everything. All I know is that sometime in April I began to feel weird. Moody and obsessive. I was on edge and had gaps in my memory. It got worse, and I started having all these crazy, dark thoughts. If you think about who I was all the years before that, can you really say you noticed no difference?"

Dr. Clafin scribbles some notes and then stares at B, who continues to sit like a fucking statue.

After what feels like an hour, B finally says, "Maybe."

It's a victory. Small yet momentous at the same time. She's beginning to believe me. And if B of all people can believe it, so can the rest of the world. I can see the headlines now: *Teen Serial Killer Was Temporarily Insane—Poses No Threat.*

B huffs loudly. "I guess you *were* different during the time of the murders. You were moodier, jumpier, snappier, and a bit more anxious, which wasn't like you. I chalked it up to everything that was happening. We were all out of sorts with the murders. We thought there was a serial killer." She laughs harshly. "And there was: you. But how do I know if you were acting weird because of psychosis or because of the stress of killing people and trying not to get caught? Your own father was chasing you! And our friends . . . You went after people we knew. You went after children, Ryann. How do I accept that, let alone forgive it?"

I hunch, ball-like in my seat. She needs to believe I'm ashamed. "You always had a gift for calling me out. No bullshit, and I'm returning the favor by telling you the truth. There was something wrong with me back then. After I'd been on the medication for about six weeks, my thoughts and feelings started going back to normal. Whether it was the medication or the illness running its course I have no idea, but my head began to clear. I did everything I could to get better, attending every doctor's appointment that was set up for me in here. I tried countless concoctions of medications. Some made me feel like a zombie, others made me fucking drool, some made me want to die, but I took whatever the doctors said would make me better because I didn't want to be a killer, B. I didn't want to terrify everyone—not after I started to get better.

"I finished classes, I helped other patients and inmates with their studies, I volunteer at the prison library, I wrote apologies to all my victims' families, and I've never gotten into a moment of trouble again. If I were still sick, don't you think something would have reared its ugly head in the last twelve years? There's not been one reprimand or infraction, because whatever possessed me to do all those things is finally gone."

B stands abruptly. "I don't know! I don't know what to believe. There's a part of me that's praying you're telling the truth, but I can't trust you."

"Please, sit back down," Dr. Clafin says gently.

B does, clasping her purse again. "There's a sick part in me too, you know." My ears perk up at this. "That horrible part that I'm ashamed of can almost accept what you did to everyone, but not to me." She turns to face me. We are eye to eye, separated by a mere three feet. "We were best friends—sisters, like *you* said—and yet you yanked me to my knees by my hair and held a bloody knife to my throat. *Me!* You didn't care about me—you only cared about yourself. There was a time when I would've done anything for you, and you made me your victim."

Standing, I slowly make my way to her. She tenses. Out of the corner of my eye I can see Dr. Clafin twitch. I get on my knees, kneel in front of B, and take her hand in mine. Resting my cheek against it, I weep. It's for both their benefits, though I guess I am a tad sorry for ruining a chunk of B's life. "I'm so sorry, B. Please believe me. I'm so sorry." I expect her to yank her hand free or push me away, but she doesn't, which is an unexpected surprise.

I lift my head and meet her gaze. Her previously strained expression eases.

"I'll have to think about it." Her hand slowly pulls out of mine. "I'd like to leave now." She stands and moves behind the desk. I want to go with her, tell her again how sorry I am for hurting her, but I stay crumpled on the floor. It looks more desperate. B always liked a good show.

Dr. Clafin rises. "Very well, Bao-yu. Thank you for coming. I hope you've found some closure. Let me walk you out."

They walk out, leaving me on my knees with tears in my eyes.

I'd like to say I've given the performance of a lifetime, but it wasn't all acting.

CHAPTER THIRTY-EIGHT

"You should've seen her, Keith. On her knees and bawling like a little girl. I couldn't believe it." Nancy sipped her merlot. This restaurant was one of her favorites. Angelo's had the best chicken and veal Parmesan in town.

"I wouldn't have expected her to be so vulnerable, though she might be putting on a show for you. She *is* trying to get out, don't forget." Keith took a bite of his rare steak. The sight of the bloody meat turned her stomach. It reminded her too much of the grisly crime photos, of Marvin Dodson especially. She shuddered.

"I know. Believe me, I'm not ruling anything out yet, but I've spent so much time with Ryann, and I've never seen her so raw. Sure, she's cried and shown emotion, but she *wept* at Bao-yu's feet. Regardless of the authenticity of her tears for her victims, she appears to be legitimately sorry for the pain she caused her old friend." She took a mouthful of chicken and tried to enjoy the taste. She was on her second glass of wine, though, which helped her relax, a near impossible feat lately. She was a week away from making her formal recommendation. She couldn't extricate her fear of making another mistake from the back of her mind.

"What are you stewing about now?" Keith asked teasingly.

"I hate how you always know."

He chuckled. "It's written all over your face. Besides, you drifted away for a second."

She put her fork down, taking in a slow breath. "Same old neuroses, I'm afraid."

He matched her by placing his fork and knife down. "I thought we'd worked through that. When are you going to trust yourself again?"

"Maybe never. Even after this, I'll probably never know if I made the right call. Unless I recommend her for release and more people turn up dead." Her glass was at her lips in seconds. She made a loud gulping sound as she drank. Embarrassed, she pretended to get a text message.

"Is everything okay?" Keith asked as she fumbled in her purse.

"Yeah, I'm sure everything is fine."

"How's Kim doing?"

She was grateful for the change of subject. "Great. She's clean, getting healthier every day."

"That's fantastic. I'm so happy for you."

She left her phone at the bottom of her purse.

"You glow when you talk about her." Keith smiled and raised his glass. "To Kim."

She matched his gesture. "To Kim." They clinked and sipped.

"So you really think Ryann could have been suffering from schizophreniform disorder? It's rare."

"I know, but all the evidence speaks to it: the drastic change in personality, the mood swings, the obsession and fixation, the black-outs. If she were schizophrenic, her symptoms would have likely continued in a similar fashion. We both know how difficult it is to treat most psychotic disorders. They just aren't managed like this. Ryann was so manic when she was arrested and brought in, spouting off about the murders, proud of her deeds, bragging about her kills. It's not usual to have such a quick turnaround in a patient without something more going on."

"Those episodes can last months. She's on meds for a few weeks, and *bam*, she's in recovery?"

"I thought about that, too, but there's evidence to suggest that her symptoms had begun two months prior to the first murder. It's likely that the psychosis peaked during the murders and was already in gradual decline. The meds could've hastened it along. I also considered why she appeared to remember every detail during her initial interviews with Estevez after the murders. My guess is that Ryann was bluffing to him about some of the particulars. I fully suspect that she didn't actually remember everything she told him. She was so cocky, there was no way she was going to let Estevez know she had a weakness." Nancy noted her colleague's expression. "I know what you're thinking. I haven't made up my mind yet. But think about it. She hasn't screwed up once. Do you really think she could keep her moods and behavior controlled for over a decade if she were still mentally ill?"

"That depends."

Ugh. She knew Keith was setting her up, but for what she didn't know. "On what?"

"On how great a criminal mastermind she is."

She rolled her eyes. "I've racked my brain over this time and again. Say we go with your theory. Could Ryann pull off that level of manipulation for twelve years? That's quite the commitment. When she was taken into custody, she had no impulse control, no sense of self-preservation. She was in full mania, denying all parental and legal counsel—not that her father was any help there. She went on camera and admitted every murder to Sergeant Estevez in horrific detail. The girl was out of her mind. So to think that she suddenly got herself together and kept a perfectly clean record in prison for more than the decade following is exceedingly improbable."

Keith sighed and twisted his lips before biting his top one. "I hear you. You might have something after all." He pushed his half-eaten steak away and clasped his hands on the edge of the table. "What if there were a way to be more certain?"

"I'm listening."

"How would you feel if I crashed one of your sessions?"

She knew where this was going, and she was willing to try anything.

Tuesday, December 12

The next day, Nancy swiped her badge and entered the prison as usual, but instead of heading toward the office or the chamber rooms, she went to F Block. Nancy wanted to see Ryann in her regular environment for a change.

She entered the main lobby area, if you could call it that, and walked up to the long brown counter to ask to speak to Ryann. The prison hadn't been updated since the seventies and still had a retro feel: all beige, gold, and brown details. It was hideous. But there was certainly no money in the budget for a facelift, not that it mattered to the state how its prisoners lived. As one correctional officer had so eloquently put it, "It ain't the Ritz."

"Fill this out." The stocky woman with the curly black hair shoved a paper and pen at Nancy before turning her back. She couldn't help but notice the activity around her. There were new inmates coming in and others being released. She'd never been to this part of the jail before. It was cold, drafty, and loud as all hell, with guards yelling for men and women to "stand on this line" or "put their hands over there." People were getting fingerprinted, mug shots were being taken, and inmates lined up to get changed, either putting on scrubs or getting their street clothes back after God knows how long.

She willed herself to concentrate. The form. She signed and pushed it back across the counter. This time a young man picked it up, looked it over, and waved her after him.

"You can come with me to the visitors' room. Someone will bring her in."

"Thanks."

More brown and beige hallways brought them to an empty area with a bunch of round tables and a few vending machines. Not very family friendly.

Nancy made her way to a table in the middle. Seemed as though they had it to themselves.

She didn't have to wait long before the metal doors swung open. Ryann walked in, a confused look on her face. A female officer, who appeared less than thrilled to be there, followed her closely. She always wondered what possessed anyone to take such a job. Though to be fair, she spent most of her career inside the same walls.

Nancy waved. Even that felt awkward.

Ryann reached her table. "What are you doing here? Our session isn't until this afternoon."

"I have a proposition. You say that there are gaps in your memory from the multiple blackouts during the time before and during the murders. I'd like to have a colleague of mine hypnotize you to see if we can uncover anything more. It may help you fill in the missing pieces." Her careful gaze studied every inch of Ryann, whose body noticeably stiffened, her eyes wide as saucers. She pulled herself back to a sitting position, wringing her hands in her lap.

"Hypnotize me?"

"Yes. It can be an important tool in therapy. It might be the final piece we're looking for. What do you say?"

Calmness settled around her eyes, replacing the fine lines of her frown. "Just tell me when and where. I'll be there."

Nancy wasted no time. Keith would meet them within the hour. He was on standby, and there was no way she was going to risk Ryann changing her mind. Her patient's instant agreement warmed her. Logic dictated that only someone with nothing to hide would risk being so vulnerable. Sure, some people were incapable of being hypnotized, but Ryann likely didn't know that. It was worth a chance. Nancy could only hope her motives for being so willing were honest. It was a way to prove she was rehabilitated.

The two of them made their way back to the office at the opposite end of the prison.

Taking their regular seats, Ryann asked, "Was this your idea?"

"Actually it was my colleague who will be performing the hypnosis on you. He's excellent. I've worked for him for over twenty years."

"So you've been talking to him about me? About my case?"

"Since he's my supervisor, I do discuss some general matters with him."

"So he'll know what to ask me about?"

Nancy pushed her smirk away. Sometimes she forgot how naïve Ryann could be despite her tumultuous past. It was almost refreshing. "You and your entire history have been in the media for over a decade. Most people know about you and the things you're responsible for."

Ryann slid down in her seat. "Right. Sometimes I forget how notorious I am."

"Isn't that what you were going for? You wanted to be infamous. You wanted everyone know your name. You have that now. Not what you thought it would be?"

She rolled her eyes. "Wow. Okay, I suppose I deserve that."

"It's not a jab. You need to consider how you're going to manage in the real world if you're released. A lot of people know who you are and what you did, especially around here. Your story made international headlines. Never before has there been a young female serial killer." She prayed Ryann wouldn't take her words as some sort of twisted praise. It was a purely factual assertion.

"I've dealt with it in here, but maybe it's different out there. I don't know what to expect from the outside anymore. So much has changed. I could be lynched, for all I know. Hey, do you think they'd put me into witness protection or something? I mean, I know I'm not a witness, but my life could be at risk . . . not that I'm safe in here."

This piqued Nancy's attention. "Has something else happened?"

"Since the cafeteria? No, but I feel the tension. I'm getting death glares, catty comments, 'accidental' shoves here and there. I never used to have problems when I was a lifer, but now it's different."

Nancy nodded. There wasn't much to say. She couldn't think of anyone other than Liz Wilkanson who would be happy about Ryann's release. But it was her job to deal with the facts, not personal emotion. "I don't know that the government will assist you if you're released. It doesn't really work that way."

"Really? Shitty. If only I was in Canada."

Nancy stifled a giggle. "Canada?"

"Did you ever hear the name Karla Homolka?"

"Sounds familiar, but I can't place it."

Ryann wiggled closer, like she was about to tell her best girl-friend some prime gossip. "She and her husband kidnapped, raped, and murdered three girls in Canada, and get this: one of the girls was her own sister. It was horrible. And the Canadian government paid for her to have plastic surgery and move away under a new identity so she'd be safe, because obviously people hated her after that."

"Well, I can't see that happening here. You're going to have to come up with a plan B."

"I could still change my name and maybe my look—"

The buzzing of the intercom sounded. "Excuse me, Dr. Clafin, but Dr. Burrows is here."

Nancy practically leapt from her seat to open the door and let Keith through. She had butterflies in her stomach, but instead of rhythmically lofting about, they seemed to be dive-bombing. "Hi," she managed. "Come in."

Dr. Clafin's 'colleague' or whatever is a silver fox. That I didn't expect. God, it's going be hard to concentrate with his Richard-Gere-circa-*Pretty-Woman* face staring at me. Why couldn't he look like Quasimodo instead?

He strides right up to me. I stand reflexively and stick out my hand. We shake.

"Nice to meet you, Ryann. May I call you Ryann, or would you prefer Ms. Wilkanson?"

He's even polite. I want to shrink into my scrubs. He's going to be inside my head soon. Is it too late to back out? "Ryann is fine." Dr. Nancy is really pulling out all the stops. First B, and now I'm going to be hypnotized. Well, bring it on.

"I'm Dr. Keith Burrows. I'm a forensic psychiatrist like Dr. Clafin, but I have another specialty. Hypnosis. Have you ever been hypnotized before?"

I shake my head. "No. But I've seen it done on TV." I flutter my eyelashes adorably at him.

"Don't be anxious. It's perfectly safe."

"Whatever you say. You're the expert, after all." I look at Dr. Clafin, who is standing next to him. If I didn't know any better, I'd say she looks a bit worse for wear. Are her jitters for me or does she have a thing for the boss? I log that into the back of my mind for later.

"Are you leaving for this, Dr. Clafin?" I ask.

"I planned on staying, unless you're uncomfortable with my attendance." Now she really looks panicked. It's just beneath the surface, but it's there nonetheless.

I enjoy her discomfort for a long ten seconds before I say, "I want you to stay. I think it's probably best, since you're the one assessing me."

Dr. Nancy brings her hands together with a small clap. "Well then, why don't we all make ourselves a bit more comfortable? Dr. Burrows can pull my chair up to you, Ryann. I'll sit on the sofa to observe." She pushes her fancy doctor chair toward me as the Richard Gere look-alike shuffles the coffee table over.

He must want to be very close to me, which makes my chest tight and my breathing shallow in a matter of seconds. It's one thing to pull this off, but it's another to do it with Dr. Hottie practically in my lap, watching and analyzing every micro-expression I make. The truth is, I have no idea if I'm hypnotizable. Regardless, I *won't* be today.

Dr. Clafin finally settles herself on the sofa to my right. She's got a great seat for the show.

Dr. Burrows, or Keith, as I'll think of him, sits in front of me. He's got woodsy cologne, and his charcoal suit and burgundy tie are expensive. Way nicer than anything my dad ever wore to court. But being a doctor pays far better than being a county cop. Presentation *is* everything. I imagine if he came waltzing in here in a tracksuit, I'd be out the door before he could shake my hand.

"How do we begin?"

He smiles. It soothes me a little. "First I'm going to put you at ease with a few relaxation visualizations. I'm also going to use a few keywords, which will help us control the experience. It's relatively painless."

"Relatively?" My heartbeat speeds up.

"Physically you'll be perfectly fine, but some patients may experience agitation or anxiety depending on what type of feelings and memories the hypnosis brings forth."

I nod, not sure what to say. My stomach churns with the anticipation. What if I say something that screws everything up?

What if I can't pull this off? My throat thickens, and it's difficult to swallow. My fists clench and unclench at my sides. I can't breathe.

"Are you all right, Ryann? You look a little distressed." A voice speaks to me, but I don't know if it's Dr. Clafin or Keith.

"Wh-what?" I can't focus. My breathing quickens until I'm wheezing and gasping. My hand flies to my chest as I struggle to get air into my lungs.

"She's hyperventilating." Another disembodied voice.

"Ryann, put your head between your knees and take slow breaths."

I do what I'm told and put my head down.

"That's it. Good."

A hand is on my back. Keith's? "That's it, slow and steady."

A minute or so later, I'm calming down. "I'm s-sorry. I don't know what's happen—"

"Don't try and talk, just breathe," he says, and I do. This has never happened to me before. Is it karma?

I take a few long, deep breaths. My muscles slowly unclench and my prickling hot skin begins to cool. The air fills my lungs. "What was that?" I laugh awkwardly to break the tension, but I know perfectly well what just happened. When we were kids, I witnessed it more than a dozen times with B.

"You had what appears to be an anxiety attack. But you're okay now." Keith's hand is on my knee. His warm smile and kind eyes soothe me further.

"I've never had one like *that* before. I'd remember something so awful."

"You're not in any danger. It's a perfectly normal response to immense stress, which you've been under a lot of lately." He says this like he knows me and all I've been through. Maybe Dr. Clafin talked a little bit more than she let on.

My gaze goes to her. I don't know what I'm looking for. Empathy? Understanding? The kindness I find in Keith?

All I see are her eyebrows knitted together over narrowed, suspicious eyes.

CHAPTER THIRTY-NINE

*N*ancy's gaze moved from Ryann to Keith. It did seem a bit too convenient that just as Keith was about to begin, Ryann was sidelined by a panic attack. Was that her way of stopping it? Was she hiding something after all?

It was possible, but then she had just spent the previous evening telling Keith how sure she was that Ryann had changed. The woman had fainted from the stress and shown genuine anguish at Bao-yu's feet. Her head swam with evidence for and against Ryann. The only thing she could do was proceed and see what came of it.

"Dr. Burrows, it seems Ryann has recovered. Perhaps we could begin." She watched Ryann's face. Her eyes. The way her small nose crinkled. *Show your hand, girl.*

Keith gave her a questioning look. "I'm not sure now is the best time considering her—"

"I'm fine. It's okay. I want to do this," Ryann said.

Nancy's clenched fists tightened, and her fingernails bit into the soft skin of her palms. Keith tilted his head, regarding Ryann. "Are you sure you don't want to reschedule?"

Ryann nodded vehemently. "I'm fine. Promise. This can help me. I need to do it."

"Can we continue, Dr. Burrows?" Nancy asked.

His gaze met hers. He looked worried, but seemed to read her silent communication. *Do it.*

"We can try." He turned away from her and faced Ryann.

Nancy settled back into the cushions. It was still going to happen. She needed this.

Keith had Ryann lay down on the sofa with her shoes off. His spiel of guided relaxation meditation was familiar, though she hadn't heard it in years.

When he was finished, he cleared his throat gently. "Okay, Ryann, I want you to lean back. Feel your shoulders sink into the softness of the cushions behind you. Let yourself melt. All your stresses and fears are disappearing, falling away. You are feeling refreshed, calm, in control, and safe. Your breathing is easy. Your mind is clear. You will remember everything of value, as much as your conscious mind can handle. When I count to twenty, you will return to the summer of 2005. You are safe and calm. Your mind is open and clear. One, two, three . . ." Keith let a beat go by before he asked, "How old are you, Ryann?"

"Fifteen years old."

"Where do you live?"

"One-five-three-six Harbour Lane, Dungrave, Colorado." Nancy was shocked by the change in her voice—small and childlike.

"Where are you in Dungrave right now, Ryann?"

"I'm at a house. I don't recognize it or know who lives inside."

"Can you explain what the house looks like?"

Her eyes were closed, her body limp, as she settled into the sofa. "It's a small bungalow with white or light gray siding. There's a large window in the front next to the door. Wait . . ."

"What is it, Ryann?" Dr. Burrows asked.

"I know this house." Her lip quivered. Her breathing hastened.

With a gentle, rhythmic voice, Dr. Burrows said, "Whose house is it?"

Nancy watched as Ryann's fists clenched and unclenched at her sides. Her eyes fluttered as she appeared to struggle to speak.

"It's okay, Ryann. You're okay. Just relax. Take a deep, soothing breath. Now who lives at the house?" Dr. Burrows asked again.

"M-Marvin." Her voice quivered along with her lips.

"Is Marvin there, at his home?"

"I don't see him."

"What are you doing now?"

"Walking up the front stairs. It's hot outside even though it's night. I'm sweating."

"Why are you going up his stairs?"

Ryann's breath hitched, and she coughed like she couldn't catch her wind. "Because I'm going to kill him."

"How did you choose him?"

"He was horrible to my mom at the diner. He is a lazy drunk who needs a lesson."

Nancy couldn't help but notice the soft, robotic, numbness to her voice—a far cry from her brazen confession videos.

"After you saw him at the diner, what did you do?"

"Followed him home on my bike. I think I looked around his house."

"Did you kill Marvin Dodson?"

She nodded swiftly. "Yes."

"How did you kill him?"

"I slit his throat."

"What are you feeling?"

The corners of her mouth turned up slightly. Her eyes remained closed. "Excited. Powerful. I love every second of it: the feeling, the view standing over him while he begs for mercy, the sounds of him crying."

"Do you want to keep killing?" Burrows asked, just as evenly as every other question.

The corners of her mouth turned up a little more. "Yes. And soon. I have my mission to get rid of all of them."

"Who are 'all of them'?"

"All the ungrateful, horrible people. The ones who don't care about anyone else. The ones who hurt others."

"How do you feel about killing Olivia McMann?" His voice remained soft.

Her eyes fluttered. "I've wanted to hurt her for a long time. I hate her. I can tell what kind of person she'll grow up to be. I can't let it happen."

"What kind of person is that?"

Ryan's smile faded. "Entitled and cruel. She'll expect everything handed to her on a silver platter. She's mean to other kids, manipulative and terrible," she said in a stressed voice.

"Do you regret what you did to her?"

Her breathing was slow and steady. "I don't want her to be dead anymore. I wish I didn't kill her, but I'm not sad that she's gone."

"Have you wanted to kill anyone since you've been in Dungrave Prison?"

The skin between her eyebrows furrowed intensely. "No. I don't want to hurt anyone else. Please don't let me." Her voice was suddenly frantic. "So many . . . are dead. Please, you have to stop me."

"It's okay, Ryann. You're not hurting anyone. You and everyone around you is safe."

"Everyone is safe from me? I don't want to kill anymore." She began to cry, shaking her head back and forth. "I can't hurt anybody else . . ."

"You're not hurting anyone. Listen to the sound of my voice, Ryann. You are feeling safe and relaxed. Any anxiety is dissipating and leaving down your arms and legs and out your hands, fingertips, feet, and toes. When I count down from five you will awake feeling refreshed and calm. Five, four, three, two, one."

Ryann's body almost immediately unclenched. Her forehead smoothed. Her hands relaxed at her sides and she opened her eyes.

"How do you feel?" Dr. Burrows asked.

"Good, actually. I wasn't . . . but now I'm better. How did you do that?"

"I'm glad. It's part of the practice. There are techniques I can show you to help reduce your anxiety, if you wish?"

Ryann nodded.

"If you'll excuse us for a quick minute, Ryann. I'd like to confer with Dr. Burrows alone," Nancy said. They both stood and walked toward the door, leaving her sitting on the sofa.

"Just through here." Nancy opened the door. When they were safely on the other side and out of earshot, she said, "So?"

"I think that gives you a good insight into Ryann's head. I see a very distraught and grief-stricken individual who can't associate the person she was then from who she is now. She's very confused, because on one hand I suspect she remembers very vividly the emotions she felt at the time—the thrill, the excitement, the seduction of the murders. But those feelings conflict drastically with who she is now. The sheer memory of the feelings associated with the murders is causing her prolonged guilt and trauma. She no longer identifies, and yet she can't separate herself from her acts."

"So do you think she's still dangerous?"

"That's difficult to say with certainty after only one session, but I'm inclined to think that she may indeed be rehabilitated. I wouldn't have believed it if I hadn't seen it myself. I'm not telling you what to recommend. You know far too much about her and her case for me to butt in."

She was hearing his words, but the gnawing pit in her stomach wouldn't subside. "Thank you for doing this, Keith. I really appreciate it. I'll call you."

"Anytime, Nancy. I'm available if you want to meet later. I know how overwhelming this must be."

———

"Welcome back, Wilks. Do anything super fun today? Did you

express your feelings with Play-Doh? Maybe recreate a death scene for your shrink? They have red Play-Doh, don't they?"

I'm not in the cafeteria more than two minutes and the heckling starts. Hell, there's not even time to revel in how convincing my hypnosis session was before I'm berated. I miss the time when everyone feared me. A few still do, after I choked out Georgina, and I'm sure Jodi told a few people about my outburst the week before. Rumor is Georgina's out of the hole, but I haven't had the pleasure of seeing her crater face yet. No time like the present.

It's as though I've willed it into fucking being.

I walk with my tray over to my usual table when I feel a sharp pang in my kidney, then another in the back of my head. I go down. Hard. Before I know it, I'm being kicked in the ribs. I try to get up, but it's impossible. The intensity of the pressure on my body keeps me trapped on the ground. I shrivel up in a ball and try to protect my head.

There are blasts to my sides. I think I feel a rib pop. I want to scream, but nothing is coming out.

It feels like an hour before it all stops. I hear yelling—the other inmates and the guards, I think. I'm not sure how much longer I lie there, the cold cement chilling me through my scrubs, before my body is picked up and put on a stretcher. I must be in bad shape. The stretchers don't come out for less than a six or seven out of ten. *Shit.* Judging by the throbbing and shooting pains through various parts of my body, I'd say I'm at a seven for sure.

I'm carried down a few hallways. I must be going to the infirmary.

I go through a few sets of double doors before they stop me in front of a counter.

I've been in here for the odd flu and occasional gyno exam, but not on this side. This is the side where the major injuries are treated. It's gray, like every other room in here except for Dr. Clafin's office.

I try and look around me, but my vision is blurred. I think there's blood in my eyes. I'm wheeled behind a small curtain.

"The doc will look at you in a minute, Wilks. How you holding up?"

I move my head the best I can to see who it is. "Officer Owens?"

"Don't try and talk."

I take her advice, mostly because I pass out.

When I wake up, I'm in a hospital bed. My head is pounding along with pretty much every other part of me. Whoever got me—and I suspect it was Georgina and her cronies—got me fucking good.

"You're awake."

I try to focus my gaze. "I assume you're a nurse and not someone sent to finish the job." I laugh, but it sends ripping pain through my ribs and I end up coughing, which hurts significantly more.

"Glad you still have a sense of humor."

"What's the damage?"

"Two cracked ribs and significant bruising to your back, sides, and left arm, along with a mild concussion. You're going to be in discomfort for a little while, but the doctor has prescribed you some pain meds to help."

"Do I go back to my cell now?" The thought of having to be around the other women makes my mouth water with sickness. I can't defend myself like this. And now I'm a huge target. Everyone knows I'm vulnerable. I've got to get out of here or I'm going to be killed.

"No, you still need time to recover. You have a few days in here, minimum. Try and get some rest. Press that button if you need me." She turns to leave but stops. "I'm Nurse Donovan, by the way."

"Nice to meet you."

She smiles. "Sleep."

I wave her down. "Wait. Can I talk to Officer Owens first, please? Do you know if she's still here?"

"I think she is. Can it wait? I really think you should take it easy."

"Please? It's important."

She gives a small huff and I know I've succeeded.

A minute later, a voice says, "Hey, Wilks. How you doing?"

"I've been better. You know why I asked you to come, don't you?"

Owens fiddles with her belt. Squared shoulders like always. Like there's always something to prove. "I can't give you any information."

"Please. I need to know who did this to me."

Her weight shifts from one foot to the other. I can see the wheels in her head spinning.

"How am I supposed to protect myself if I have no idea who attacked me? At this rate, I'll end up dead." Even I can hear the urgency in my voice. The fear.

In a loud voice she says, "I'm sorry, Wilkanson, but I can't." Owens moves closer to my hospital bed and bends down so her lips are at the side of my head. "I'll deny it if you tell anyone." She pauses for a long second before I hear the name I've been waiting for. "Roxanne Platts."

Roxie. That fucking bitch.

Stepping back again, Owens says, "Sorry I couldn't have been more help. Try and get some rest."

I nod calmly, though inside I'm about to boil.

She leaves, and I lie here silently raging. Roxie is God knows where—hopefully in the hole—and I'm stuck in here, battered and useless.

I should've expected it. Roxie hung around Georgina and her little crew. Georgina was rather nasty to her, and Roxie often looked the fool trying to find a way in with her. Maybe this finally did it.

The only thing I can do is relish the first peaceful sleep I've had since I came to Dungrave prison. At least in here I don't have to worry about being attacked. Unless somehow a nurse has been paid to knock me off, maybe take a page outta my own handbook with a needle full of air.

My mind reels, and I can barely swallow my spit, but I hunker down, pull the blanket to my chin, and close my eyes, begging for the blackness to take me.

CHAPTER FORTY

*I*t was nearly midnight and Nancy was still awake. Ryann's files were piled high on her coffee table. Half a bottle of white sat beside her. The bloody picture of Olivia was the reason for the first glass. The image of Yvonne's protruding eyeball was the reason for the second. She was now onto Omar, who looked quite peaceful. The fact that his family could have an open casket was the only, albeit small, mercy.

She had all the evidence, her session files, her notes from the hypnosis session earlier in the day, and a stack of letters for or against Ryann's release on top of a pile of printed court transcript testimony.

As soon as Nancy decided that Ryann was still dangerous, she changed her mind. She had endless evidence damning Ryann for all she'd done, but just as much new evidence that suggested she was no longer a threat.

But, God, what if she was wrong?

Her hand wriggled through the bottom pile. She yanked until a small stack was free. It was testimony from Ryann's sentencing hearing, more pleas to keep her locked away for the rest of her natural life. According to the documents and Estevez's firsthand account, Ryann didn't ask for leniency at first. There was talk of charging her as a juvenile, but the judge didn't agree. Not for six heinous murders, including the murder of a police officer. There would have been a riot.

After Columbine, the courts came down harder on juvenile offenders. There was almost zero tolerance. Forty years to life was a minimum in a lot of cases. No chance for parole.

But the tide was shifting. Science had evolved, with new theories on just how underdeveloped the teenage brain is. She was aware that Ryann's legal team was working on that angle as well as denouncing her initial trial as inexcusably flawed. Wagner and Roche were having a field day in the press, touting 'the mentally unstable kid who was failed by the system' defense. And it appeared that public opinion held a lot more weight than it probably should have.

Nancy had read reports that Ryann had been pushed to plead guilty by her own cop father—the father who permitted his daughter to be grilled by his seasoned partner without a lawyer or a parent to advise her. Her defense team had talked her into pleading not guilty by the time her trial came, but it didn't do much good.

Wagner and Roche told Nancy that Ryann had been railroaded. Sure, she'd admitted to it, but that was, apparently, beside the point. Maybe she hadn't been fit to stand trial. Her lawyers had seen her only three times in the lead-up. Everyone knew it was a lost cause, so apparently Ryann's legal team had done the bare minimum. Or so Nancy had been told.

Roche said that he and Wagner believed she was insane at the time of the murders and not properly counseled about her rights or plea options. The pre-trial competency evaluations done by the psychiatrists did nothing to help Ryann, deeming her fit to stand trial. After seeing the tapes—the psychiatrists likely hadn't— Nancy seriously questioned that.

Before she'd even been assigned Ryann's case, Nancy had been conflicted when advocacy groups in murder cases demanded that young offenders be re-examined. Some 'experts' suggested that brain development continued until the early twenties, and therefore teens weren't fully responsible for their actions. Teens lacked proper judgment, and impulse control, and they failed to wholly comprehend consequences. She'd been secretly appalled by the crutch some defense lawyers used.

A ringing interrupted her thoughts and had her rummaging around the table and sofa cushions for her cell. Who would be calling at this hour? Then she realized that Kim was staying over at Ray's.

Her heart practically beat through her ribs as she fumbled to answer it. "Hello?"

"Dr. Clafin?" A woman's voice said.

"Yes?"

"Sorry to call so late. This is Officer Owens at the Dungrave County prison. There's been an incident with one of your patients. Ryann Wilkanson was assaulted today. I thought you'd want to know. She's in the infirmary."

"Is she going to be okay?"

"Looks like it. She has a few bruises, a few cracked ribs, and a concussion, but she should recover in a few weeks."

"Did Georgina attack her again?"

"No, it was a different inmate, but one that has known affiliations with Georgina."

"Oh, okay. Thanks for calling," she said, still in a bit of a fog.

"You have a good night."

Nancy ended the call and placed her phone in her lap. Part of her wanted to rush over there and see how Ryann was doing. The other part of her was frozen, overwhelmed by a flood of mixed emotions. Her eyes found their way back to a hideous photo of Stanley Hastings's charred remains. Disgust fought against her newfound empathy.

There was no point in going there now. Ryann would be sleeping. Surely they'd given her pain meds to knock her out. Nancy would go first thing in the morning.

Wednesday, December 13

Nancy was awake before her alarm. She'd barely slept. A battered and bruised Ryann had played through her dreams, lying on the ground while inmates kicked her as she begged. Nancy had woken up drenched in sweat, screaming as the girl on the ground morphed from Ryann to Kim.

Kim was safe at Ray's. She'd called this morning, needing confirmation, yet she still had that gnawing in her gut—the kind that makes mothers protective and fierce. But if her children were fine, what was the dread she couldn't shake away?

She pulled her car in the underground parkade, bypassed her office, and made a beeline for the infirmary.

"Ryann Wilkanson's room, please," she said to the first person in medical scrubs she saw.

"The information desk is that way," the man said before running off. It was busy.

"Ryann Wilkanson's room, please," she said again to a young man behind the counter.

He typed a few things into the computer. "Room seventeen. Down the hall and straight on your left."

She wondered if she should knock. It wasn't a private room; she could see multiple beds through the window. Turning the handle, she opened the door and crept in, not wanting to wake the other patients.

At the foot of each bed was a wipe board with a name and prison ID number. She crept to last bed on the left.

Surprised to see Ryann's eyes open, she waved. The gnawing inside her intensified.

Ryann remained balled up under the covers like a frightened child.

"May I?" Nancy asked, pointing to the foot of the bed.

"Suit yourself." Her voice was soft and low, like it hurt even to speak.

Nancy perched herself at Ryann's feet, noting the shackles around her ankles. She took a deep breath. "What happened?"

"I'm not even sure. One minute I was walking to a table in the cafeteria, and the next I was hit from behind, knocked over, and kicked. Doc says I'll be all right." She smiled weakly. "Thank you for coming. How did you know I was in here?"

"I got a phone call last night around midnight. You're my patient. They thought I should know."

"I'll have to thank Officer Owens when I see her next."

Nancy smiled. "Are your parents coming too?" It was out of her mouth before she could stop herself. "Your mother?"

"I haven't called her. I might later, but she has enough stress. It's nothing that can't wait until Sunday when she visits."

"Are you in a lot of pain?"

"It doesn't tickle."

"I was told it wasn't Georgina. Any idea who was responsible?"

"I have a hunch. There are lots of women who want me hurt, but my guess is one of Georgina's affiliates. Georgina knows she can't personally come after me again—not if she doesn't want to triple her stay in solitary—so she had one of her thugs do the dirty work. It's probably a first-time infraction for them, so nothing much will happen."

"That's not right."

"No, but that's the way it works. I'll heal, go back, and pray it doesn't start happening on a regular basis. I'm tough, but I can only take so much, you know." She rolled her eyes. "God, what am I saying? I'm sorry. I realize how I sound. I'm probably the last person you want to hear whining."

Nancy put a hand on Ryann's covered leg. "Not at all. I'm sorry this is happening to you."

"Thanks. I guess I won't make our final session for a while."

"It's all right. I have everything I need from you."

She tried to pull herself up in the bed, wincing as she did. "Are you sure? If you need more, maybe we can do it here. I'm a captive audience." She feigned a laugh, but Nancy could see the weariness in her eyes.

"It's all right. We're good." She tapped her leg lightly and stood. "Recover quickly. Not sure the next time I'll see you."

As Nancy left the medical wing for her office, she couldn't stop analyzing her own feelings and instincts.

As much as she tried to ignore it, she'd developed feelings for Ryann. The gnawing in her stomach proved it. It was something akin to a motherly concern for Ryann's wellbeing.

That wasn't good. How could she be impartial if she cared about her? Transference happened. Patients confide in their doctors and often develop complicated emotional feelings, but countertransference was much less common. Nancy had never experienced it before—not to this degree and certainly not with a serial killer. She cared about the wellbeing of her patients, but this was more . . . protective, more nurturing. Her emotional entanglement with Ryann was unhealthy at best.

The walk to her office was frenetic, a weak attempt to burn off some of her anxiety. At her desk, she stewed some more. Phone in hand and Keith's number on the screen, she was ready to confess her unprofessional feelings and explain how wrong he'd been to trust her. She dreaded becoming an object of scrutiny and having her practice undermined. She was one precious year from retirement. This episode would forever damage her reputation and embarrass Keith and the practice.

But Keith's opinion and her hard-earned reputation caused only a fraction of her anxiety. Her hands quivered. The biggest reason was that she liked Ryann. Cared about her. Wanted to believe her. Maybe even did. Keith's session with her had been compelling, to say the least. The sessions were just as convincing. Ryann couldn't possibly have faked them all . . .

Keith should've listened to her when she told him she couldn't handle it.

CHAPTER FORTY-ONE

There was one more person Nancy needed to speak with. He'd rebuffed her twice already, but they say third times the charm for a reason.

Three hours after her visit with Ryann, she was in the one place David Wilkanson couldn't avoid her.

The Dungrave County police station was unimpressive. Dungrave was a small, sleepy town. The police were called for break-ins, domestics, and the odd drug deal, but not murder. Definitely not serial murder. When the homicides happened, naturally everyone was shocked and scared. After Ryann was caught, Dungrave became a tourist attraction for sickos who wanted to see where the youngest serial killer in the state lived. It caused absolute chaos for the first few years.

The hoopla calmed down over time save for the occasional car full of stupid teenage kids that came calling, asking for the locations of Ryann's childhood home, her school, and the victim's residences.

The police absolutely hated it, but none quite as much as Detective Dave Wilkanson, who had to relive the horrific shame each time. She understood his reluctance to discuss it. He wanted to distance himself from his daughter and everything she had done. You couldn't get a bigger conflict of interest. Why he didn't move baffled Nancy.

"Is Detective Wilkanson in?"

The woman at the counter looked older than her—her frosted blonde hair didn't hide her gray or soften the deep furrows around her eyes and mouth. "He is. Who may I say is asking?"

"I'm Dr. Nancy Clafin. I'm hoping to ask his opinion on a patient of mine."

The receptionist put her finger up to silence Nancy, who wasn't talking anymore. The woman picked up a receiver and dialed a three-digit number. "Can you send Wilkanson up front? He has a visitor. Yup, thanks." Her regard was once more on Nancy. "You can take a seat over there."

Over there was one round white table with four chairs that sat in front of a bay window. At least the sun was shining.

Ten grueling minutes later, a tall, salt-and-pepper-haired man in uniform strode in. She'd never actually seen him in person before. He looked older now than he did in the news clips and photos. Much older. The years hadn't been kind to him—no surprise with the stress he was under. Being a police officer was pressure enough. Add a serial killer daughter, and Nancy was shocked he was still on the job at all.

She didn't know if she should stand or remain seated. He approached her, hand on his belt. Near his gun. Maybe he knew who she was after all.

"You wanted to see me about a patient?" he said, towering in front of her.

With an outstretched hand she managed to say, "Please sit down."

She was relieved when he did. "I don't have a lot of time. How can I help you?"

Gruff but polite. Typical Dungrave sensibility. "I'm here to talk to you about Ryann. I'm the doctor in charge of evaluating your daughter's case, hired by her defense team. I was hoping we could discuss her for a few minutes. Your input will help me make my final recommendation." Could he hear her heart pounding from where he sat a mere three feet away? She could barely swallow.

His nostrils flared. "I thought I made it clear on the phone to you twice already that I have nothing to say on this matter or anything else pertaining to her."

He couldn't even say her name. "But you must have an opinion. A recommendation." He was already standing, his back to her. "Please. It would really help me. I'm not sure what to do, to be honest." The frailty in her voice had slipped out.

He turned around slowly and sat back in the chair. "All right, fine. I'm not one to mince words. She is as dangerous today as she ever was. I don't believe for one second that girl has repented, been redeemed, been rehabilitated, or anything else you want to call it. She's a manipulative predator who needs to stay locked up for the rest of her life, and God help us if she gets out, 'cause I assure you there will be more bodies. Can you live with that, *Doctor?*" His bite was sharp. A few of her suspicions about Ryann's character became crystal clear.

"With all due respect, how do you know what Ryann is like now? It's my understanding that you haven't seen or spoken to your daughter in eleven years."

His stare bore down on her. "With all due respect," he barked, mocking her, "I'd appreciate it if you didn't refer to her as my daughter. I have one daughter: Brianna. And yes, I haven't seen or spoken to Ryann, because I saw everything I needed to all those years ago. I went and visited her a few times before the conviction, but she never changed. She had people thinking she did. Did a number on a lot of folks. But she's the same cold-hearted, evil girl who was locked away years ago. I saw it in her eyes. She's the devil and no daughter of mine."

"Excuse me?"

"When I went to the prison I asked her a few things. Talked to her about all she'd done, and sure, she said all the right things, how sorry she was, how ashamed. But her eyes told me. I saw the same callous, cunning, crazy look in 'em as that day in the library when she killed Officer Knox and nearly slit her best friend's throat. She likes it. She liked it back then, and she still does now. I don't know where she got it from, because we sure didn't raise her like that, but she was always darker than was healthy."

"Darker?"

"When she was small, like six or seven, I caught her in my home study going through my books. She particularly liked the ones on serial killers. Was sitting criss-cross on the floor with the book in her lap, eyes wide, looking at a bloody murder scene. She had that look in her eyes then, I just didn't know it yet. I talked to her, told her not to entertain such filth, and never to go in my office again. I thought that was the end of it. Childhood curiosity." His fist met the tabletop with a low thud. "I was in denial."

Keeping her voice low, she said, "You can't know for certain that she was entertaining murderous thoughts back then. That's a book many children would look at, simply because it's forbidden. They are curious and want to see what all the fuss is about. It could've been pure coincidence."

Dave stood abruptly. "Sounds to me like you already got your mind made up. Don't know why you bothered to see me. Maybe you were hoping for some confirmation that letting her out is the right thing to do. It's not. Ask yourself: can you live with the responsibility of letting a calculated killer run free?"

"Detective Wilkanson, there is new evidence to indicate that Ryann may have suffered a type of psychosis that could have—"

His hand shot up. "Stop right there. That's what she'll want you to think—that she was crazy and it wasn't her fault." He shook his head.

"But there is a family history. You failed to disclose your father's mental illness in the pre-trial competency evaluations. You could've helped your daughter, but you—"

He rolled his eyes and snickered. "Seriously, is this your first year on the job? She's playing you. I told you, she's a master manipulator. She got over on a lot of people, and my old man ain't got anything to do with all that's wrong with her." He paused, swallowing hard. "Don't feel too bad. Even I couldn't tell, and it was *my* daughter, but I should've known. For months she practically paraded it under my nose. Even when my own partner came to me, I dismissed him. Don't be fooled, Dr. Clafin, or you'll live to regret it." He straightened up more, if that was possible. "Now if you'll excuse me."

He was gone before she could get out another word.

Nancy stood and turned to leave, opening the door for a young woman.

A flicker of recognition told Nancy she knew her.

"Thanks," the woman said. She was tall and thin with shoulder-length blonde hair.

Nancy's knees wanted to buckle as she registered the blonde. Brianna Wilkanson. Brianna Shrunk nowadays, but there was no doubt it was Ryann's older sister. Part of her wanted to keep moving and pretend they had nothing in common, especially with Brianna's angry letter still at the forefront of her mind: *I have no love left for her. She is nothing to me. People ask me if I'm afraid of her, and the truth is that I am afraid of what evil lives inside her . . .*

Nancy had to say something. Brianna had declined to meet with her and hadn't returned any of her messages. Swallowing hard, she stepped back inside and closed the door blocking out the frigid air. "Excuse me."

Brianna turned with a puzzled expression. "Yes."

"Are you Brianna Shrunk?"

Brianna's eyes scanned Nancy. "Do we know each other?"

Nancy cleared her throat, barely able to swallow. "Sort of. I'm Dr. Nancy Clafin. I'm not sure you..."

Brianna took a step back. The wide-eyed curiosity in her face was replaced with narrowed eyes and puckered lips. "I know who you are. What are you doing here?"

She hadn't yelled, but Nancy felt the harsh bite of her words nonetheless. "I was speaking with your father about your sister. I know in your email you stated that you didn't want to discuss Ryann, but since we're both here—"

She put her hand up between them. "Let me stop you right there. I have nothing to say to you other than I'm disgusted you are even entertaining the thought of letting her out. If she goes free and hurts anyone, you can consider it blood on your hands too." She pushed her designer handbag back up her arm and tossed her head back, causing a sweep of golden hair to fall behind her. "I'm here to see my father, so if you'll excuse me." But Brianna stopped a few feet away and turned back to Nancy. "Do you have any children, Dr. Clafin?"

"Yes, two."

"Would you trust Ryann around them?"

Nancy, stunned by the question, fought for a response.

"Maybe you need to think about that a little more before you unleash her."

Nancy's next stop would likely be no more pleasant, but it was a means to an end.

The court wasn't far from the station, and she arrived by one thirty that afternoon. This was no surprise visit, however. It was difficult to just pop in on a busy district attorney.

Gloria McLean evoked white knuckles in the toughest of the tough, and Nancy's body vibrated with nerves. She was a grown woman of fifty-four yet as intimidated as if it were her first day on the job. She despised that about herself. How was it that after all her education and experience in both life and work she was still insecure? She'd read about how some women in their forties and fifties finally had confidence they needed to take on the world. She was still waiting.

She was buzzed into the courthouse. Her bag was x-rayed, she walked through the metal detectors, and her ID was checked. Five minutes later she was put in a stuffy office to wait. It was bleak, taupe and brown, and smelled like it hadn't been aired out in years.

Nancy stood, so focused on trying to crack the window open that she didn't hear the door.

"It's a bit tricky. It actually opens like this." The DA was next to her, effectively shoving her aside. "That's better. Smells like dirty gym socks in here. I hate this room."

At least they agreed on something. Nancy was sure it would be the only thing. "Thanks. I know it's freezing outside, but it was a bit stale in here."

Gloria wore a black pantsuit and green blouse. She was a nice-looking woman in her early forties, with dark-framed glasses and highlighted hair that she wore in a low ponytail. She sat on one side of a conference room table that could easily accommodate a dozen people and seemed overwhelming for the two of them. "Please sit."

Gloria's judgment wasn't crucial. The case would still go to the clemency board, but the DA's opinion was a weighty one, and Nancy was curious to see what she'd say. Perhaps sitting would disguise her nerves, she thought, as her legs jittered under her. "Thank you for agreeing to meet with me. I know how busy you are."

"I'm always busy, but some things just need to be made a priority. You're here to discuss Ryann Wilkanson." One eyebrow rose as she leaned back in the brown leather swivel chair.

"Um, yes. As you know, Ryann's new legal team hired me to evaluate her mental state and get a feel for the risks of recidivism."

"And what did you find?"

"It has been quite challenging for me. I've gone over every piece of this case front to back, and to be honest, my professional opinion has been inconsistent until very recently."

"The way I see it, what that girl did was reprehensible, and there shouldn't even be a discussion around the possibility of releasing her."

"That's partly why I'm struggling. Her history and her present state of mind are not cohesive. Ms. Wilkanson appears to have changed. She has accomplished many things during her incarceration. You have the list, but more than that, I've spoken to many people who knew her before, during, and after the murders. The bulk of people known to her in prison, both peers and staff, seem to share the opinion that she is no longer a danger to others. Many of these people believe she is rehabilitated. And then there is the question of the fairness of her initial trial, the involvement and sway of her father, Detective David Wilkanson, and what I believe was a faulty competency evaluation that failed to diagnose her mental illness. Those are just to start."

"From my understanding, you have had therapy sessions with her extending over the past two weeks or so. What do you think?" Gloria's hands were crossed on the table in front of her as she gently rocked in the chair. Not a care in the world, it seemed.

It struck Nancy as odd that a woman with one of the most painstaking and stressful jobs in the world could seem so blithe. She envied that. "I tried to go in to this open-minded, but it was tough, with everything I knew from the cases. The media hasn't been kind to her over the years, understandably. I saw how cold and callous she was. How unfeeling and cruel. But the woman I have grown to know these few weeks isn't that girl anymore."

"So you think her conviction should be commuted?"

"I don't know. I'm afraid to say yes because of what she's admitted to doing, but that's just it. She's admitted everything—no cop-outs and no excuses. She seems genuinely sorry. She has tried to make amends to some of the victims, even had a recent meeting with Bao-yu Ng. The clincher for me was a hypnotherapy session. I was present the entire time. She was candid about the murders, but got really agitated and upset when asked if she'd ever hurt anyone again. My colleague, Dr. Burrows, believes that her true intentions and personality came out in that session—that she's truly remorseful."

"Yet you still doubt it?" Her tone was a step away from sarcastic.

"It seemed legitimate, but hypnosis isn't foolproof. I can only tack it onto the years of good behavior and altruism she's consistently demonstrated as an inmate. She's been physically attacked twice—that I know of—in the last month. I worry for her safety as well. She could end up dead if she remains inside."

"I can't agree with the release of a very dangerous inmate simply because of some in-house fighting. I'm sure you understand that. I need actual evidence, not assumptions and goodwill. As far as I'm concerned, Ryann Wilkanson should be in prison for life. As it stands now, it's unlikely that I won't fight her release, especially when the only argument in favour of her release is that her brain wasn't fully developed and she was— what? Temporarily insane?" Her eyebrows furrowed. "I apologize, I realize you're a psychiatrist. I'm not attempting to insult or downplay your life's work. I just have a difficult time believing that Wilkanson has done a one-eighty. I'll tell you now. I'm going to do my damnedest to keep her locked away." Her hands slapped the top of the table. "If there isn't anything else, I have another meeting."

The feeling of a sucker punch to the gut surprised Nancy. What had she expected from this meeting? For the DA of all people to give her blessing to the release of a serial killer?

"No, nothing else. Thanks for your time."

Nancy pulled herself from the office and back out to her car, her energy zapped.

She was nowhere closer to figuring out what the hell to do.

CHAPTER FORTY-TWO

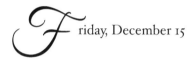riday, December 15

After three glorious days in the infirmary, it's over. The doctor has dropped the bomb.

"So I'm free to go back to general population. Great." My voice drips with sarcasm. I might as well wear a bulls-eye on my back during hunting season. It'd be a whole different story if I could defend myself the way I'm accustomed to.

Officer Owens is back to escort me. "Lead the way, I guess. Hopefully no one shanks me before my meeting with my lawyers tomorrow."

Owens smirks. "I'd say stop being dramatic, but you've had your fair share of shit lately."

We are in one of the adjoining hallways, out of earshot, when she leans in to whisper, "Are you nervous?"

"Uh-huh. I can't stay locked up. You and I both know I'll die in here, and not of natural causes."

"If we think you're in grave danger, you'll be moved to solitary."

"That might be worse. I'm young. Am I supposed to be locked up in a tiny room twenty-three hours a day, alone until I die? Just kill me now. I volunteer for lethal injection, hanging, stoning, firing squad, whatever."

"Okay, now you're being melodramatic." I hear the smile in her voice. "There's also the possibility of being moved to another prison. How do you feel, physically?"

"Still pretty sore, but better than I was."

"They have your ribs wrapped under there, right?"

I nod. "It helps me breathe a bit better, but it still sucks."

"I know the feeling. When I was away at training, we sparred, so if we were ever caught in a fight we'd be prepared. I took a few shots to the ribs."

We are in front of F Block now. All she has to do is unlock the door and I'm back amongst the animals. "Hopefully I heal before I get pounced on again."

She stops with her hand on the door handle. "You know what? I can get you put in solitary tonight. At least you know nothing else can happen to you before your meeting."

"You would do that?" I'm nearly speechless. I've never known compassion from anyone in here, besides a few pleasantries from my library supervisor.

"I can figure something out. Is that a yes?"

I nod my head vigorously. I'm no hero. Not with the shape I'm in. "That would be great, thanks."

"Come with me. You can wait in the temporary cells while I make the arrangements."

Ten minutes later Officer Owens is back with a frown on her face. "No go, Wilks. I've been instructed that there are no grounds to give you solitary. So you're shit out of luck unless you commit an offense."

"And that's counterproductive. I'll take my chances."

She walks me back to my cell. It might as well be the electric chair. It feels nearly as deadly. I wish I could trust my cellmates, but with all the backstabbing and jealousy that goes on in here, I'd be a complete idiot if I let my guard down. Though neither Stephanie nor Jodi have long sentences. I can't imagine either risking themselves for Georgina's dirty work. It's not like I ever did anything to them.

I never did anything to anyone in here.

"Sorry I couldn't come through for you," Owens says.

"You don't have to apologize. I appreciate you trying."

Our cells are kept locked during the day when we're out of them. It's a safety measure to prevent assaults, suicide attempts, and sexual encounters. Officer Owens opens the door to mine. "You want to grab your stuff and have a shower or something? I can wait inside the bathroom, just in case."

Truth is I'd be safer to do it now than tomorrow morning, surrounded by other, angry inmates. "Sure. And thanks again. You've been very kind. It's something I haven't experienced much. Rightfully so, but it's still a pleasant surprise." I grab my stuff and she locks the door behind us.

She smiles. "I don't mind hanging around. You can put your stuff back in your cell afterward, and by then it will be lunch."

My stomach knots. "I haven't had much luck in the cafeteria."

"I'll be watching, so try not to worry too much."

There are a few hours left before lights-out, so I sit in front of the television and attempt to watch *The Shawshank Redemption* over the rowdy noise and screaming. These women think they're in a fucking sorority.

If I wasn't crazy before, I'm definitely headed that way now. I can feel it.

I can't live like this anymore.

I could let Georgina have her way and finish me off, but I won't give her the satisfaction. No, I can think of a few more ways to go out. Like slaughtering as many people as I can before I'm finally taken out. I have a few weapons hidden if it comes down to it. I won't give this place the rest of my life.

Either way it'll all be over in a matter of days, so I'm going to enjoy watching Andy make it out in the movie.

It's beautiful and cosmically fitting that this is on TV now. Perhaps it's a good-luck sign from the universe. A nod to let me know this is all going to be all right.

I head to my cell. It's nearly lights-out anyway. I'm exhausted and hopeful, unsure if I'll even be able to sleep. Unsure if I even want to try.

Jodi is already reading a book in her bunk when I walk in.

Out of the corner of my eye, I see her put it down and stare at me. "Haven't seen you for a while."

"Miss me?" I don't smile. I'm not feeling particularly whimsical at the moment.

"Sure. It was weird to not have you in here the past few days. You okay?"

I get into my bunk and yank the blanket up to my neck. It's definitely a few steps down from the beds in the infirmary. "I'll live."

"We were worried about you."

Before I can respond, the cell opens again and Stephanie enters. "You're back!" She almost sounds excited.

"Yup," I say.

Before I know what's happening, her arms are around me. "I'm so glad you're all right. I was so freaked out."

"Really?"

"Well, yeah. I saw what happened. I asked about you, but the guards wouldn't tell me anything."

"I made it. Had a nice vacation in the infirmary and everything."

"Did you get your own TV in there?" Jodi asks, wide-eyed, like I'd been to a resort.

"Yeah." I try not to roll my eyes. I don't want to fight tonight. I want to calm myself down and sleep. Officer Owens said she was going to come get me personally tomorrow morning, and I want to be up and ready. "If you guys don't mind, I'm going to try and get some sleep."

"Big day tomorrow. Meeting with your fancy lawyers. It could really happen, huh?" Steph says. She sounds chirpy and animated. Is that jealousy or happiness for me?

"Yup, it could."

Jodi pulls herself up, seemingly more alert. "Are you excited? You could be free soon!"

"I am. And nervous." I don't want to say too much since I don't actually know if I can trust them. "It's nice that they moved the meeting to a Saturday."

Steph gapes at me. "Um, hello. It's not like you skipped the meeting. You almost died," she says with such dramatic flair that I have to hold back a laugh.

"I guess."

"Well, good luck, Ryann!" Steph says.

I smile then. "Thanks, guys." I hunker down a bit more and close my eyes. "Night."

"Good night," they say in unison.

CHAPTER FORTY-THREE

*S*aturday, December 16

I sit on the edge of my bunk, waiting. My legs are jittery so I keep moving them, tapping my feet on the ground. The vibrations run through me, which helps me fool my body into thinking it's not shaking the way it is. I try and take slow, deep breaths, but it makes me dizzy and does nothing to calm the mouse-like creatures that are running around inside of me.

Soon I'll find out from my lawyers if I'm free or if I'm going to die in here after all.

Steph and Jodi tried to convince me to eat breakfast with them, but I can't stomach food and coffee. I wish I had a dress or at least a pair of pants and sweater to wear in there, but it's not like I have a choice. It's never favorable for people to see you in prison garb. It screams guilt.

I put my hair back in a low pony and apply eyeliner and mascara.

Where is Officer Owens? If she doesn't make it soon, there

might be a hole in this floor from my endless pacing. I wasn't gifted with patience.

"Ready, Wilks?" I hear from behind me.

I jump.

"A little edgy, huh? Maybe you should've had decaf." She sounds jovial, and I would appreciate it if I wasn't on the verge of puking.

"No coffee. Too nervous."

"Apparently. Last time we spoke you managed full sentences."

I smile at that one. She's grown on me. "Are we ready?"

All the cell doors were unlocked an hour ago for the day, so Owens simply pulls the handle and waves me out. "You're shaking like a leaf."

"I just want to get this over with." I start walking. I know the way, having met with Mr. Wagner and Ms. Roche a few times before. Owens keeps up with me.

"I don't know what to think," I admit. "Today I'm going to learn my actual chances of being released. I've been in limbo for so long. At least I'll be closer to an answer, one way or another."

We're quiet the rest of the way. I'm not trying to be a bitch or anything, but my mind is racing too fast for me to do anything but walk. It doesn't take us long to get there. The hall is painted the same as the others: gray, with dark wooden doors that go from one end to the other.

Officer Owens stops us four doors down. "This is it. You ready?" Her hands are on her hips and she grins. I'm sure this is meant to be supportive, but I can't help but wonder why she would be. We're on different sides of the law. How can she give two shits about me? Perhaps her grin is really glee at the distinct possibility of my continued incarceration.

I manage to nod. "I'm ready."

Owens opens the door and leads me through. No handcuffs this time, which is a nice change. I suppose they don't worry about having armed guards posted within feet of me, since I'm only talking to my lawyers. People who are on my side. I wonder if Officer Owens could shoot me if she needed to? I doubt it. I'm a pretty good reader of people, and she's better suited to teaching first grade than corrections. It's only a matter of time before she either has a nervous breakdown or gets the fucking shit beaten out of her.

Mr. Wagner and Ms. Roche are sitting at a small rectangular table waiting for me. They smile and stand as Owens leads me in then quickly leaves. I'm allowed confidential meetings with my defense team. It's refreshing not to be monitored.

They look like they're ready for television in their expensive suits. Ms. Roche's engagement ring must be five carats. She wears matching diamond-stud earrings for good measure.

"It's nice to see you again, Ryann," she says, reaching out to shake my hand.

"Nice to see you too."

Wagner points to a seat across from them and I take it. "So, how are you feeling? We were sorry to hear of the assault. I know it must have been awful, but we can spin this to our advantage." Way to cut to the chase. I've always liked that about him.

"In what way?"

"That you're in danger in Dungrave prison. The victim of multiple targeted attacks. We can use it to sway public opinion and bolster the evidence that suggests you were mentally ill at the time of the incidents."

I appreciate that she replaced the term *murders*. *Incidents* has such a nice ring to it.

Wagner jumps in. "That, on top of all the blunders your first defense team made."

Ms. Roche looks like she's going to burst. "Your case is looking great. The fact that you've been repeatedly assaulted will only make your supporters more motivated to free you. Public opinion carries a lot of weight here, and I have someone on the inside who assures me that the governor's noticed. The advocacy group and celebrity support is growing by the day. There's so much pressure on the DA's office for your release. You have a real chance at getting your sentence commuted."

"And we need to act now. Build on the public's sympathy." Mr. Wagner steeples his fingers with a laser-focus expression.

"What do you have in mind?" I ask, nervous to hear his response.

"We put you on TV."

If I had been drinking water, I'm sure I would've spat it on both of them. "Excuse me?"

Roche leans forward. "It's perfect. Every reporter and news show has been chomping at the bit to get an interview with you. We simply pick one—very exclusive, of course—and let you tell the world how sorry you are and how much you've changed."

I can't even process this before he jumps in. "Nothing is more powerful than public opinion. It's what we need to clinch this."

"But . . . there are so many people that still hate me."

Roche smiles confidently. "And this is your opportunity to show them how wrong they are."

"It's one thing to go through every despicable thing I did with Dr. Clafin, but now you want me to talk about what I did to the entire world?" My head spins as I try and grasp the idea. I don't know what I was expecting, but it wasn't this.

"Look, I know this is scary and overwhelming, but we'll be with you every step of the way. You need this, Ryann. If you have a hope in hell of getting out of here, this is the way."

Every interview about me I've watched over the years flashes through my mind. The disgust, the anger, the hate. It will be my chance to speak out and change the way the rest of the public views me. How hard can it be? If I can con two forensic psychiatrists and seasoned COs, I can do this. Besides, it's been a while since I've been in the spotlight, and it's only right to give all my supporters what they want.

"I'll do it. Who are you thinking for the interview?"

They look at one another and smile.

"Aaron Robinson, of course," Wagner says.

Aaron Robinson is the biggest investigative journalist in America. Now I'm really dizzy. Giddy, even. "Have you asked him?"

Ms. Roche laughs. "You're one of the biggest news stories the world has ever seen. His office has harassed us for months to get the exclusive sit-down with you."

"Really?" The shock is not a put-on. I'm genuinely surprised. I didn't realize I was such a big deal. Not that I don't deserve it, but it's hard to gauge what goes on outside this prison.

Wagner clasps his hands on the tabletop. "Whether you like it or not, you're infamous. You've never granted an interview before. You're like the fucking white whale." He stops and leans closer, tilting his head slightly. "Sorry if I'm being insensitive, but facts are facts—people are voyeurs, and they want a look inside you, darling."

And there's that Wagner bluntness again. At least you never question where you stand.

"I trust you guys, so if you think I need this to get released, I'm all in." Something occurs to me. "Wait, how are you going to get permission from Warden Connelly for this interview?"

Roche grins, chest puffed. "Already done. Your interview is in an hour."

"What?" I scream. I feel a sudden surge of adrenaline, little pinpricks dancing just under my skin.

"We knew you'd trust our expert opinion, so we took the liberty of setting it up. The warden granted you two hours." Wagner takes out his cell and calls someone, telling them we'll be right over.

"Where are we going?"

"To a conference room, where your makeup and hair team is standing by. We don't have a lot of time, so let's move."

They usher me out of one room and into another one nearby. There's a small hair and makeup station set up. A pretty brunette stands waiting, looking a tad jumpy if you ask me. Just past her I see white panels, the kind used in photo shoots, and two chairs facing one another. There are two men scurrying around. One is probably the director, the other maybe the cameraman, since he is fidgeting with one.

My chest feels heavy. This is really happening.

Roche guides me by my arm and sits me in the makeup chair. "You have twenty minutes," she tells the brunette.

I've barely caught my breath when she says, "It's nice to meet you, Ryann. I'm Melanie."

I try not to wince. Unfortunate coincidence with the one who got away. Luckily no one knows about that except for Nancy. "You too."

"So. Any look you want in particular?" she asks me in a bubbly voice.

"I'm not used to wearing much makeup. Not really a reason to in here, you know?" She smiles and tilts her head like she has no idea what I'm saying. "Keep the makeup light, please. Maybe just get rid of the dark circles under my eyes and make me look as young as possible."

"Oh really? Cause I was thinking a smoky eye and maybe a pink lip."

Seriously? Is she trying to keep me locked up? "No thanks. Maybe next time." I smile.

"What about your hair?"

"I don't know." I look around for Roche. She's busy talking to the director, but I call her over anyway.

She hurries over as if I'm the most important person in the room. "What is it, Ryann?"

"Melanie wants to know how I want my hair."

She bites her lip and gives me a once-over. "Hmm. Keep it smoothed back in a low ponytail. If it's left down with volume it could look too sexy. We want conservative and apologetic. Nothing flashy."

"What about clothes?" I ask.

"We've discussed it, and we think it's more sympathetic to see you in your prison uniform. The poor girl who has been locked away for all these years. If they see you dressed up they might have less compassion for how rough you have it."

I'm slightly disappointed, but I understand.

Twenty-five minutes later I'm 'done' and being prepped. Wagner tells me what kinds of things to say and what to stay away from. Roche told Mr. Robinson what questions are not admissible and warned him that if he tries to sneak one in she'll end the interview. They won't be on camera with me, just watching off to the side. I breathe easier knowing they're here with me. Just in case.

I don't know if I was expecting an entourage of sorts, but I'm surprised when Aaron Robinson enters alone. Nice suit and tie, fresh haircut, flawless black skin. He makes a beeline for me with his hand extended. "Ryann, it's so nice to finally meet you. Thank you so much for agreeing to this interview."

I nod and pretend to 'find my voice' a second later. Truth is, I'm pumped to be center stage. I just have to make sure I come across as scared and intimidated, not 'I'm ready for my close-up.'

"Thank you. I-it's nice to meet you too."

"Don't worry, you're in good hands. No need to be anxious."

"Is it that obvious?" I say and laugh.

"Not at all, but most people are. It was a guess. We'll be ready to begin in just a few minutes." He pats me on the arm like we're old college chums who haven't seen each other for a while.

I sit in my chair while the camera guy attaches a small microphone to my shirt and adjusts the white panels and lighting around me. I feel like a movie star for a fleeting minute. All it takes is one glance at my beige scrubs and clunky brown work boots to remember who I am.

For now.

Mr. Robinson sits across from me. My palms are slick with nerves and anticipation. This is it.

"Shall we get started, then?" he asks in his smooth TV voice.

I manage a smile and hold my breath. A voice from beside me says, "And . . . rolling."

CHAPTER FORTY-FOUR

$\mathcal{M}$r. Robinson sits with one leg over the other, seemingly relaxed with a pen and notebook in his lap. It feels just like therapy. "Thank you for agreeing to sit down with me for this interview. I can imagine it was a difficult decision, considering the pressure you're under and the severity of your crimes. People have very strong opinions about you, and this interview could solidify those or change people's minds entirely."

Geez. No fucking pressure, Aaron.

"Yes, it was a difficult decision to make. I would never want my victims' families to think I was glorifying, or profiting from, what I did."

"Just for the record, CLK News has not offered you any compensation for this interview, correct?"

"That's correct. I'm talking today to try and explain what happened all those years ago."

"Let's recap, in case someone is watching who—for some reason—doesn't know the crimes we are referring to. You are presently incarcerated for the murders of six people, three of them children between the ages of twelve and sixteen, as well as a police officer, all when you were fifteen. Is that correct?"

I take in a jagged breath. This already looks atrocious for me. "Yes, sir."

"Since your incarceration, some issues regarding your mental health and stability at the time of the murders, as well as some issues with your original defense team, have been raised by your current legal team, and your case is being re-examined. In fact, your lawyers, Mr. Donald Wagner and Ms. Yvette Roche, have submitted a commutation application to the Executive Clemency Advisory Board in Colorado on your behalf. Correct?"

"Yes." I want to say more, but I can't stop focusing on the spot-lights and the camera. I have to grit my teeth so I don't grin with delight. *Get it together, Ryann.*

"Take me back to the summer of 2005. What happened to turn you—a young, bright girl with a promising future—into a killer?" He's so matter-of-fact that it's almost laughable.

I exhale slowly, place my palms flat on my thighs, and try to keep as calm as possible. I know that anything I say will infuriate and horrify the victims' families and countless other people watching.

"Take your time, Ms. Wilkanson," he says.

But the camera lens feels like it's getting closer. Like one big, judging eyeball. "This is very difficult for me. Sorry." I take a second and pretend to collect myself before continuing. "I've had a lot of time to help me come to terms with what I did. One of the things I did after I was incarcerated was study serial killers. I wanted to know if I was like them. If I had the same horrible and deranged things in common with them. I needed to see why I'd suddenly become that monster. And what I found was alarming."

"What alarmed you, Ryann?" he asks in a soothing voice.

"I had nothing in common with most of them. I was never abused, molested, or neglected. I had a wonderfully loving and supportive family. I wasn't bullied. I had lots of amazing friends. I had good grades, was a cheerleader, was even the teacher's pet in my English class. I was popular, pretty, and happy, and then slowly things started to change. I began feeling weird, very unlike myself.

I was moody, forgetful, anxious, and depressed—but not all the time. Sometimes it would change so quickly. Suddenly I'd be super hyper, bouncing up and down, laughing without a care in the world. I began to obsess over the smallest things and get angry. It wasn't like me. These dark and irrational thoughts and feelings starting popping up, and before long, they took over. I didn't feel like myself anymore. There were chunks of time that just . . . disappeared. I didn't understand what was happening to me."

"I understand from some reports released by your legal team that you had frequent blackouts. Can you elaborate on that?"

I nod and realize I'm not saying anything. "Uh, sure. I would wake up in the morning with no memory of the night before, or suddenly I'd be somewhere with no idea how or when I had gotten there. I don't have more specific details for most of the episodes, because I was too frightened to tell anyone. As I grew sicker, I hid more of my symptoms, and there came a point when I didn't believe anything was wrong with me at all. I thought I was invincible." I swallow hard. I don't want to say it, but it's the truth. "I felt God-like. I know that sounds awful . . ."

Mr. Robinson is a real professional because his face remains stone. "How did this personality change, as you describe it, lead you to kill six innocent people?"

"I honestly don't know. The only thing I can say is that I truly don't believe I was in my right mind at the time. I've been seeing a psychiatrist, and she has a theory that I may have suffered from a type of psychosis that could've made me do all those horrendous things. And I'm so sorry. I promise you I am." I do my best to bring on the waterworks. That's what people want to see. I still have the ability to cry on cue, and it's perfect. Tears trickle down my cheeks and I gently wipe them away with a touch of my fingertips.

Robinson lifts a piece of paper from his lap. "Yes, I have the diagnosis here. Schizophreniform disorder. A rare condition, yet one that can account for the drastic change in your personality and behavior, according to both Dr. Clafin and Dr. Keith Burrows, who evaluated you."

Wow, I didn't realize they'd had a chance to send anything to my lawyers yet, let alone have Wagner and Roche give it to Robinson. The world moves a lot faster on the outside.

Does this mean that Nancy and Keith vouched for me? I didn't have time to ask Roche in our meeting before being whisked over here.

I try not to show how utterly shocked I am. "It's the only thing that makes sense. I was normal before that summer, and then, after I was hospitalized and put on anti-psychotics, I was normal again. I went back to who I was before the murders. No more racing, obsessive thoughts. No more dark impulses. No more cloudiness and blackouts. I know none of this takes away what I've done, but that's just it. I don't believe it was the real me who did those things."

"So you believe you were a totally different person back then, and that who you are now is rehabilitated?"

"Yes. I have worked very hard to prove myself since my conviction. I tried to make amends by writing letters of apology to the victims' families. I didn't receive any response, but I don't blame them. I completely understand and respect their right to their feelings. I know I wouldn't forgive me." A few more tears. I reach for a tissue and blot my eyes. Good stuff. "After my medication kicked in and I realized what I'd done, I made the decision to own my actions and try to atone by becoming the best person I could be. There was a long while when I just wanted to give up. What was the point? I was going to die in prison, and I deserved it. But then I started to believe that I still had something left to give."

He straightens up in the chair—the first movement since we started. The guy's a statue. "I see here that you received your high school diploma and a bachelor's degree in English, with a minor in psychology."

"Yes, sir. I was intrigued to learn more about what happened to me. I also love novels. Escaping into them has been the only way I've survived in prison."

"There have been reports that you suffered two assaults recently. One quite severe. How are you holding up?"

"It's not easy. I'm scared all the time. I can't trust anyone. The only thing that the prison can do if it keeps happening is put me in solitary confinement for the rest of my life, which to me is worse than death. I'm only twenty-seven years old. I can't imagine living alone in a box for the next forty or fifty years. Assuming I live that long."

"There are many people out there who would say that you deserve far worse. At least you get to live. What do you say to those people?"

"That I understand their feelings and they have every right to them. I wish I could express how truly sorry I am. That's why I've tried to turn my life around."

"You've tutored other inmates, worked in the prison library, and volunteered for many prison programs. You attended therapy during the first few years of your sentence of your own volition. All in all, you've been a model inmate, but your crimes were horrendous. Ryann, do you expect people to forgive you now, in spite of what you've done?"

I meet his condescending, arrogant gaze. "I take full responsibility for what I did, mental illness or not. I hope the public and the clemency board find it in their hearts to give me a second chance. I'm no longer that sick and dangerous child. I'll spend the remainder of my life proving how much I've changed. Even if it's from inside my cell." Wow. Even I feel bad for me now.

"Why should you get a second chance when your victims will never get one?" he asks with the journalist's classic poker face.

I'm so beyond sick of this fucking question. "That's a fair question. I guess because I'm still here and I have an opportunity to make amends. I realize I can't fix what I did. I can't erase the agony and loss that I caused, but I can spend the rest of my days trying to heal myself and others if I'm given the chance."

"I have emails and posts of support here. Quite a few of them, and I don't want to diminish that. People haven written on your behalf, stating that they'd like to see you released to have a second chance. What does that feel like, to have support from strangers after everything you've done?"

"I'm humbled and touched. Truly. I had no idea. I'm segregated in here, and it's difficult to feel like I have any supporters—well, except for my mother, who's always been there for me."

"I have a letter here that I would like to read. Your attorneys gave it to me."

My eyebrows scrunch in genuine confusion. "A letter?"

"Yes. It's from one of your victims, the only one to have survived your attack. Bao-yu Ng has written a letter she wishes to share publicly."

My mouth waters with sickness. This could end me right now. I can't speak, so I nod.

He begins to read:

On the night of June 27, 2005, after I walked in on Ryann Wilkanson murdering Officer Eric Knox, she snatched me by the hair and held a knife to my throat. We'd been best friends all our lives, and I suddenly had no idea who this person was. The person I went to with all my celebrations and sorrows; the person who knew my whole life, knew me better than I knew myself; the person who gave me courage when I had none of my own was now my captor. It didn't make sense to me.

It was my friend . . . but it wasn't. The Ryann that was my best friend since we were little kids wasn't the same person in the library that night. That Ryann was sick. I know that now. I spent every waking moment since that day hating her, being confused and mourning her. I believed that I must have never known her at all—that I was a horrible judge of people because I couldn't see who my best friend really was.

After visiting her for the first time since that day in the library, I've had to face some very frightening truths, especially around my views of Ryann Wilkanson for the last twelve years. I now know that something happened to Ryann that summer, maybe in the months before. I'm not sure when the change happened, exactly, but my best friend faded and someone else took over. If I look back without anger and resentment, I can recognize the deviations in her personality. How she seemed 'off' on so many occasions, while I was too consumed with my own anxiety and problems to think about her.

I can't help but look back now and wonder if I could've done something had I only paid more attention. Maybe I could've helped her. Saved people. Saved her from herself. See, for the first time in all these years I don't blame Ryann. She was a victim like the rest of us. You couldn't have convinced me of this even two weeks ago. I wasn't prepared for who I met just a few weeks ago at the request of her therapist.

It was my friend. The one I remember from sleepovers and football games and late-night movie marathons. It was the friend who I laughed and cried with. The friend who loved me unconditionally. I wasn't prepared to ever see her again. I didn't believe she existed anymore. I'd considered that she may have never been real at all, but a few days ago in Dr. Clafin's office, I saw her. And that is why I am asking you today to grant Ryann Wilkanson clemency. I no longer hold her accountable for the awful things she did, because I believe it was the mental illness and not my friend. Allow her a second chance at life.

Thank you.

I am dumbstruck. My whole body is shaking uncontrollably. My throat is raw from holding back tears. Genuine tears. Ones I'm not prepared for and that truly astonish me. I believed I was impervious to being emotionally affected.

"That's quite the testament to you, Ryann. How does hearing that make you feel?"

"It's very unexpected." I wipe the moisture from my cheeks. "After all these years . . . I can't thank her enough. She'll never know how grateful I am for her forgiveness." I use my reaction to my advantage by attempting to 'compose myself' but 'breaking down' instead. Someone passes me a fresh tissue. Finally, I take a deep breath. "I'm sorry. I wasn't anticipating that. To hear forgiveness and support from strangers is amazing, but to hear it from her, of all people, is astonishing. I feel very lucky and humbled."

"Does it give you hope? If she can forgive you and support your release, do you feel confident that the board will agree?"

"I don't think I'll ever be confident. I'm terrified. I know what I've done is unforgivable, but I ask to be given a chance at restitution. Hopefully Governor Patrick will agree that I'm rehabilitated and allow me the opportunity."

"Anything else you'd like to say?"

"I'm deeply sorry for all the hurt and pain that my actions have caused, and I thank those of you who have stood by me. Your support and kindness is keeping me strong. Thank you so much."

"And thank you, Ryann, for sharing your story with us. Your case remains emotionally polarizing, but I appreciate your candidness. Good luck to you." He shakes my hand.

"Thank you."

And just like that, the main lights come back on, and Robinson is up and talking to the director.

I suppose I'm still sort of shell-shocked. I can't get B's words out of my head.

"You ready? We have to get you back to your cell now," Wagner says.

"Uh, yeah. Sure."

I make the walk back to F Block and don't remember a moment of it.

CHAPTER FORTY-FIVE

onday, January 3

"Wilkanson, you have a phone call!"

I'm in the middle of a heated poker game and up ten bucks in commissary when I hear my name. My body freezes. I drop my hand, showing my full house, and stare blankly ahead. I don't get phone calls.

This can only mean one thing.

The ruling is in.

I find my legs and see Officer Han. I follow him down the hallway to the phones.

"I've been following your case, Wilks. This call could finally be the verdict, huh?"

I nod. My mouth is dry and my vision is threatening to blur.

"Good luck, I guess," he says before backing up to give me some privacy. My fingers fumble as I try to grasp the receiver. "H-h-hello?"

"Hi honey, it's Mom."

The fluttering in my gut prevents my voice from sounding. I'm a bundle of emotions. My sweaty hand can barely hold the plastic. "Is everything okay?" I know there's a possibility she found out the board's decision before me. It's not unusual, since prisoners are still considered second-class citizens who don't matter.

"Yes . . ." I hear crying. Shit. She's sobbing so loudly it breaks my heart.

"Mom, it's okay. I can try again. It isn't over forever—"

"No, Ryann." She gasps a breath. "You did it. You're free, honey."

I nearly drop the receiver. Her words reverberate in my head. *Free?*

A burst of exhilaration hits me. "I'm going to be released?"

"Yes, sweetie! You're coming home! I love you so much."

I'm sobbing now, and jumping up and down. My body is on fire, tingling and flooded with excitement and adrenaline and happiness. "Oh my God, Mom. I can't believe it. I'm coming home!" I'm squeezing the plastic between my hands so tight I fear I might crush it. "What do I do? When can I go?"

"From what I gather you should be released today, maybe in a few hours. You did it, Ry. I knew you would."

"Because of you. You never stopped believing in me. Thank you, Mom. I love you."

"I love you too, honey. I'm on my way."

Nancy was on her third cup of coffee, poring over a new case, when she got the call.

"Thanks for letting me know, DA McLean. Okay, Gloria. You have a good day as well."

She wasn't sure how to feel. She wasn't sure what she would say when she finally had the chance. The only saving grace to her sanity was that her recommendation was only one of several others that weighed in on the verdict. She'd never know how the board voted. All she knew was that as soon as she'd recommended release, she wanted to crawl into a deep, dark hole.

It was partly about Ryann and her own self-doubt. But it was also about what she'd failed to do years ago.

Keith had always preached that she needed to give herself a break because it could have happened to anyone. But it didn't. It happened because of her.

In a way, *she* was a murderer. She'd never get over the suicide of the woman she'd condemned three years ago.

She couldn't make the same mistake again. What if Ryann had changed? Nancy believed she had. Keith believed it. Bao-yu believed it. Other board members believed it. All she could do was trust that she'd made the right decision.

Hours after Ryann's release, Nancy found Officer Owens. She'd waited until she knew Ryann was gone. It was a meeting she didn't want to have, yet she needed some sort of closure.

"I won't ask you how you feel today, since I know it's probably too sensitive."

"Thank you."

"So what can I do for you, Dr. Clafin?"

"I was wondering if you would escort me to Ryann's cell."

"Come again?" Owen squared her shoulders and stared down her nose at Nancy.

"I know it sounds preposterous, but I just need to see where she lived. We went through a lot together. Would you mind?"

"Follow me."

The cell was bigger than she'd thought, maybe because it housed three of them. "Which bunk was hers?"

"This one." Owens pointed to the bunk closest to the door.

"Since all the inmates are in the common areas, do you think I could have a second alone?"

"Suit yourself. I'll be back in five."

"Thank you."

She ran her fingertips along the bare mattress. There was

nothing left of her here. She wasn't sure what she'd anticipated. Posters on the walls? Books stacked on the shelf?

Maybe she took that kind of stuff with her.

She sat on the bunk, feet flat on the floor, and looked around. She wanted to see this place the way Ryann saw it. She wondered what Ryann had thought about at night in here. She inhaled deeply, aware that Ryann had been in the same spot hours earlier. Nancy could have come by then. Wished her luck. Said goodbye. But she couldn't bring herself to do it.

It was like sitting on a stone bench. Ryann was right. These beds really were awful.

Nancy shook her head and stood, but her foot kicked something that had been protruding from beneath the cot.

Bending down to take a better look, she noticed a small blue notebook. She picked it up, dusted it off with the sleeve of her coat, and opened the cover. It was Ryann's—some sort of journal. A rush of shivers ran under her skin. She held something very personal to Ryann in her hands. Something that could assure Nancy that she'd done the right thing.

Ryann must have been so excited to get out of there that she'd forgotten to grab it. Should she return it to her? No. Nancy couldn't see her again.

And she couldn't read it.

Could she?

It was unethical and immoral. An invasion of privacy.

Then a little voice in the back of her head spoke, telling her that inmates lose all rights to privacy after they break the law. The journal was the property of Ryann the inmate, not Ryann the free citizen.

Looking around and seeing no one, Nancy flipped hurriedly through the pages. Owens could be back at any moment. It didn't look like much. The typical daily coming and goings, some stream-of-consciousness entries, but Nancy's curiosity got the better of her and she searched for the most recent entries. Had Ryann written about *her*?

There was nothing. Not even a mention of Nancy's name, only how sorry she was, how much she'd changed, and how, if she was ever given the chance, she'd make it up to 'them,' whoever they were.

Her fingers flipped to the last written pages and stopped on a list of names. The bottom half of the page had been torn off, leaving behind only two names.

A wave of heat flooded her, and she sat back down on the bunk when she read the names of two lawyers from Ryann's initial defense team. What did that mean?

The sound of footsteps prodded her into action, and she quickly stuffed the journal into her purse.

"All good here?" Owens asked.

"All good." It took all her strength to muster a convincing voice. "Thanks for doing that, it was extremely helpful."

"I hope you got what you were looking for. You know, maybe I shouldn't say this but, I'm going to miss her."

Nancy managed, "Mmm," and smiled weakly before she sprinted out of there.

CHAPTER FORTY-SIX

*A*fter my mom picks me up we go to a drive-through. I haven't had a burger and fries like this in forever.

She talks a mile a minute, she's so excited. It's sweet, and still quieter than being in cells. I still can't believe I'm out. I wonder how long it will take to sink in.

We pull into the driveway and my heart beats loudly in my ears. It looks the same.

Except that only my mother lives here now. And me, I guess.

My father filed for divorce and moved out when it looked like I was going to get released. He couldn't deal with it. My mom refused to abandon me, so he abandoned her instead. Prick.

Despite the upheaval in her life, she is giddy, showing me around as though I never lived here before.

We get to my old room and she pushes open the door. "I didn't change a thing," she declares proudly.

My room is a big step up from my cell, even though it's outfitted for a teenager and I'm now twenty-seven. I have a real bed, a dresser, mirror, and carpet. I actually have four walls, a window, my own door, and most importantly, no snoring room-mates. It's remarkable.

I throw my tiny bag of worldly possessions on the bed. It can wait. I'm exhausted. It will be bliss to sleep on an actual mattress. I curl myself inside the soft cotton and fall fast asleep.

Tuesday, January 4

I wake up on my own time. No sirens, no bunkmates, no officer yelling in my ear. I can shower and eat whenever I want. No line-ups, and no fear of being stabbed from behind. This is near paradise.

The alarm clock next to my bed reads 6:00 a.m. Shit. I guess I'm too programmed to sleep in, which is fine by me, because this is my first day of freedom and I'm more than ready.

I bound out of bed, jump in the shower, and get dressed. My mom still has good taste in clothes, so I put on a pair of jeans and a blue cotton sweater. She even got me a pair of brown leather boots and a gray winter coat.

There is a cell phone and a wallet on the dresser. The wallet has a few hundred in cash, a debit card, and a note. *We'll get the phone hooked up whenever you are ready. Happy to have you back, honey. XO. Mom*

Thank you, Momma.

She was even nice enough to hook up a new computer in my room. I move the mouse and the Google screen appears. I don't need to think about what to search.

Dungrave prison blocked out half of the web, but not here. Here I can access anything I want.

My fingers glide over the keys and I hit *enter*. An entire page pops up. I click my cursor on the images tab, and my screen is filled with glorious colored photographs of none other than Dr. Nancy Clafin. She looks nice in them. Quite a bit younger in some. I scroll until I find the one I'm hoping is out there.

The family photograph. Nancy, James, Ray, and sweet Kimmy,

all carefree smiles for the camera. The picture has to be over fifteen years old.

I make a quick Facebook account and type in Nancy Clafin. Nothing.

Hmm. Thank God for my memory. One of the news articles I'd read about her listed her middle name. Geraldine. Only two Nancy Geraldines come up, so I count myself blessed.

A smiling Nancy with her hair down, wearing a purple silk scarf, stares back at me. Butterflies swarm my insides as I click.

Naughty, naughty, Nancy. You should have made your profile completely private, especially with all the whack jobs you deal with. Don't you know that using your middle name isn't enough? I snicker and scan through her pictures, delighted to see what Ray looks like now. My cursor freezes for a second as my heart speeds up. I click on the newest photo.

A young woman, not much older than me, with long dark hair and troubled eyes.

Kimmy.

I finish getting ready and rush downstairs, careful not to wake my mother. I'm not sure why I'm in a hurry, since nothing is open this early in the morning except for coffee shops. Maybe I can go and get actual, real coffee. Bliss.

Wrapped in my new coat and standing in my new boots, I feel ready.

I head into the kitchen and scan the room. It only takes a second to spot the butcher block, and I help myself to a long, sharp, silver blade.

It's been a long, long time since I've held a knife in my hands that wasn't plastic.

It feels heavy and firm. My fingers clutch the handle and I make a swiping motion. It cuts the air with a whoosh, and my skin floods with goose bumps.

I take a slow deep breath, inhaling the smell of my freedom and all its possibilities.

It's time to explore now. I start to place the knife back into the wooden block, but something stops me.

Unzipping the front pocket of my bag, I slip the blade in. Nice and safe.

For now.

CHAPTER FORTY-SEVEN

$\mathcal{M}$onday, January 10

"Are you here, Kim?" Nancy called out as she walked into the house. She had quickly grown used to coming home to someone again, and was grateful every day that Kim hadn't relapsed or run off. She knew the statistics were not on her side. Every day with her daughter was a gift.

A pounding sounded as Kim ran into the living room. "Hey, Mom."

"I'll never understand how you sound like a herd of buffalo when you're so petite." She smiled, content to have this exchange. Kim looked better each day. Her color had come back, she was less shaky, and she'd slept through the night three days in a row. "What were you up to today?"

"Not too much. Watched some TV. I walked to the store and got some ingredients to make dinner. I found this recipe online for pistachio-encrusted chicken. I know, fancy, huh?" Her gaze moved to the coffee table. "I almost forgot. Something came for you today." She practically bounded over to retrieve it. It was heart-warming to see Kim so energetic and, dare she say, happy.

Nancy removed her coat and boots. "That's odd. I didn't order anything."

"Don't look at me. Maybe Ray got you something."

Nancy took the box, surprised at its weight, and set it down on the mail center. There was no return address or store name. She retrieved the letter opener and slid the blade beneath the tape. The box sprung open, and beneath a thin layer of packing paper was a copy of *The Diagnostic and Statistical Manual of Mental Disorders*. Odd. Nancy not only hadn't ordered it, she already had a copy in her office.

"What is it?" Kim asked.

"It's a text used to diagnose mental illness."

"And you're sure you didn't order it? It seems like a book you'd buy."

Nancy flipped through the pages, her fingers catching on an invoice stuffed behind the back cover. Smoothing it out, she saw that it was from Amazon. She scanned the page, her eyes stopping on a name: Ryann Wilkanson, care of the Dungrave County Correctional Facility.

Her heartbeat sped in an instant, and the pulsating grew deafeningly in her ears.

The book had been sent to Ryann while she was still in prison. But how did it end up here? Had Ryann mailed this to Nancy herself? "Let me see the box again."

Kim handed it to her. Nancy inspected it, but there were no postal markings on it at all.

Her hands shook as she flipped through the pages looking for something, anything, to explain why Ryann had sent it. And then she saw a chunk of text highlighted in yellow. She gasped, nearly dropping the book.

"What's wrong, Mom?"

Nancy reeled to face Kim. "When did this come?"

"It was dropped off today—"

"By who? Who brought this here?" Her voice was loud and frantic. She didn't want to frighten Kim, but she couldn't help it.

"A woman. What is going on?"

Nancy let go of the tome and it hit the small tabletop of the mail center with a bang. Before she knew what she was doing, her hands were gripping Kim's shoulders. "What did she look like?"

"I don't know. Small, pretty, blonde hair—"

Nancy thought she would vomit. *Ryann*. She'd come to her home. Where her daughter had been all alone. "Did she hurt you? Are you okay?" Nancy's gaze traced the full length of Kim.

She pulled out of Nancy's grasp. "I'm fine, Mom. What are you freaking out about?"

Nancy went back to the book. Back to the page with the highlighted passage. Her eyes fixed on the words *schizophreniform disorder*.

Clasping the invoice again, Nancy looked for the date the text had been ordered.

Her blood turned to ice.

November twenty-seventh. Two days after their first session.

Weeks before Nancy had told Ryann her unofficial diagnosis.

The paper was thin, and Nancy could see that something had been written on the back. She quickly turned it over.

Dear Dr. Clafin,

Thank you so much for your help, and for believing in me when no one else did. There's no way to repay you for getting me my freedom back. I promise to use it well. I thought you might be able to use this helpful resource, since I won't be needing it anymore.

Your friend,

Ryann

ACKNOWLEDGMENTS

This book was possible because of the love and support of so many people who believed in me.

I'd like to thank my parents, Laurie and Chris, for their excitement and encouragement while I wrote and revised this book. No matter how many times I blabbered on about it to you, you acted thrilled and proud. You both mean the world to me. Thank you for being my biggest cheerleaders.

To my sister, Kristin, her husband Steve, and my beautiful niece and nephew Mckenna and Braeden for their love and support . . . and for forcing my books on your friends with genuine enthusiasm.

To Pam and Kevin for believing in me and being there with positive and sensible advice whenever I was in need.

To the fabulous and talented Eileen Cook for your support and for reading multiple drafts and giving me sage advice.

To Deana, and Tiana for reading early drafts and giving me invaluable and wise advice. I owe so much to you ladies. You inspire me. I shall pay you in wine—the currency of our people.

Many thanks and hugs to my other ladies: Bee, Cara, Helen, Debbie B., Lindsay, Ashley, and Kathy for being amazing, bad-ass writers who teach me so much about life and what makes a great story. You amaze me (regularly).

To my family and friends for showering me with unwavering support, encouragement, and love. You have helped me more than you know, and I'm so grateful and honored to have you all in my corner.

To my kick-ass editor, Amanda. I don't know what I would do without you. Thank you for answering all my strange questions, talking things through with me, and making my books so very shiny.

To my wonderful and generous friends, Gabe and Debbie B., for formatting this book and making it beautiful when I was not up to the task.

To Mary Ellen Reid and Linda Stanley for your legal counsel, insight, and professional expertise. Thank you for taking the time out of your busy careers to answer questions. You've given this story an accuracy that I could never have provided by simply Googling things. It made a world of difference.

And to my partner, Jason, for being my rock and putting up with the various stages of crazy that this book brought out in me. You continually listen and always make everything better. I couldn't have made my dream a reality without you.

ABOUT THE AUTHOR

Kelly Charron is the author of YA and adult horror, psychological thrillers and urban fantasy novels. All with gritty, murderous inclinations and some moderate amounts of humor. She spends far too much time consuming true crime television (and chocolate) while trying to decide if yes, it was the husband, with the wrench, in the library. She lives with her husband and cat, Moo Moo, in Vancouver, British Columbia.

Manufactured by Amazon.ca
Bolton, ON

11319621R00199